BLACK PULP

BLACK PULP

Introduction by

WALTER MOSLEY

Featuring Stories by

JOE R. LANSDALE
GARY PHILLIPS
CHARLES R. SAUNDERS
DERRICK FERGUSON
D. ALAN LEWIS
CHRISTOPHER CHAMBERS
MEL ODOM
KIMBERLY RICHARDSON
RON FORTIER
MICHAEL A. GONZALES
GAR ANTHONY HAYWOOD
TOMMY HANCOCK

Edited by

TOMMY HANCOCK, GARY PHILLIPS
and MORGAN MINOR

Editor in Chief, Pro Se Productions - Tommy Hancock
Submissions Editor - Barry Reese
Director of Corporate Operations- Morgan Minor
Publisher & Pro Se Productions, LLC - Chief Executive Officer - Fuller Bumpers

Pro Se Productions, LLC
133 1/2 Broad Street
Batesville, AR, 72501
870-834-4022

proseproductions@earthlink.net
www.prosepulp.com

Edited by - Tommy Hancock, Gary Phillips and Morgan Minor
Cover Art by Adam Shaw
Book & Cover Design, Logos, and Additional Graphics by Sean E. Ali
Formatting of E-Book by Russ Anderson

TABLE OF CONTENTS

THE NEW PULP FICTION

AN INTRODUCTION BY WALTER MOSLEY

IN A BYGONE DAY, before my time, there was an expansive era of fictional writing that existed in cheap pulp magazines. Every week a plethora of publications appeared on the newsstands providing crime stories, horror stories, science fiction, sword and sorcery, and more westerns than a rattlesnake could shake its tail at. These were short stories and novellas that filled the first few decades of the 20th Century giving the release of adventure to a broad population suffering under the weight of working class poverty that led, finally, to the Great Depression. This era spawned wonderful writers from Dashiell Hammett to Raymond Chandler, Robert E. Howard to H.P. Lovecraft; from Max Brand to Louis L'Amour and hundreds of others.

These stories got right to the point on the first page and kept your heart rate up until the final word. Some of our best writers graced the pages of these dime fortnightlies. Many a noire master did his apprenticeship in pulp.

People read these stories and novellas for fun. There was a hero, a chance for romance, possibly some magic, or maybe a world of science that we imagined and hoped for. Sometimes there was just a man or woman against nature in the wilderness of our recent or far flung past.

Whatever the genre the stories were exhilarating. This form was a transportative vehicle that could take us from the daily grind to a world where hard labor, the force of will, and physical strength could do more than provide a moldy loaf of bread and cold gravy.

Literature for the masses kindled the imagination and used our reading skills so that we could regale ourselves in the cold chambers of alienation and poverty. We could become Doc Savage or The Shadow, Conan the Barbarian or the brooding King Kull and make a difference in a world definitely gone wrong.

After World War Two fiction in magazines waned steadily until today there are few pulps, or really any other types of published magazine fiction. There was a time when there was a newsstand on every corner selling *Weird Tales* and *Magic Carpet Magazine*. So-called literary fiction has tried its best to banish the genres to the back rooms along with children's toys and pornography. The distribution systems have changed and magazine fiction (that spans from Charles Dickens to Robert A. Heinlein) has faltered.

This is a sad state of affairs not because of some sappy nostalgia but for the loss of the kind of stories that bring us out of the darkness of the common work-a-day world into the brilliance and true imagination that only fiction can provide. Movies and TV are okay but it is only reading and storytelling that allows our inner imagination to soar.

And so this collection speaks to us with great power. The beauty of reading is not a college course on existentialism or a psychology seminar on the disaffection brought about by suburban living. Reading can also allow us to imagine a different world, a different self. This vision is the first, or maybe the second, step in the liberation of the human spirit.

I am more than happy to read about the history and psychology of oppression, the disenfranchisement of our culture and the overwhelming power of capital – but these revelations are poor fare if I cannot also imagine a different world and a different life where the chains of the modern world can be shrugged.

Pulp fiction, in many cases, is the second movement in the dialectic of inner transition. It is the antithesis of what is expected and the stepping stone to true freedom.

SIX FINGER JACK

BY JOE R. LANSDALE

JACK HAD SIX FINGERS. That's how Big O, that big, fat, white, straw-hatted son-of-a-bitch, was supposed to know he was dead. Maybe, by some real weird luck a man could kill some other black man with six fingers, cut off his hand and bring it in and claim it belonged to Jack, but not likely. So he put the word out whoever killed Jack and cut off his paw and brought it back was gonna get one hundred thousand dollars and a lot of goodwill.

I went out there after Jack just like a lot of other fellas, and one woman I knew of, Lean Mama Tootin', who was known for shotgun shootin' and ice pick work. She went out there too.

But the thing I had on them was I was screwing Jack's old lady. Jack didn't know it of course. Jack was a bad dude, and it wouldn't have been smart to let him know my bucket was in his well. Nope. Wouldn't have been smart for me or for Jack's old lady. He'd known that before he had to make a run for it, might have been good to not sleep, cause he might show up and be most unpleasant. I can be unpleasant too, but I prefer when I'm on the stalk, not when I'm being stalked. It sets the dynamics all different.

You see, I'm a philosophical kind of guy.

Thing was, though, I'd been laying the pipe line to his lady for about six weeks, because Jack had been on the run ever since he'd tried to muscle in on Big O's whores and take over that business, found out he couldn't. That wasn't enough, he took up with Big O's old lady like it didn't matter none, but it did. Rumor was, Big O put the old lady under about three feet of concrete out by his lake boat stalls, put her in the hole while she was alive, hands tied behind her back, lookin' up at that concrete mixer truck dripping out the goo, right on top of her naked self.

Jack hears this little tid-bit of information, he quit foolin' around and made with the jack rabbit, took off lickity-split, so fast he almost left a vapor trail. It's one thing to fight one man, or two, but to fight a whole organization, not so easy. Especially if that organization belonged to Big O.

Loodie, Jack's personal woman, was a hot flash number who liked to have her ashes hauled, and me, I'm a tall, lean fellow with good smile and a willing attitude. Loodie was ready to lose Jack because he had a bad temper and a bit of a smell. He was short on baths and long on cologne. Smell good juice on top of his stinky smell, she said, made a kind of funk that would make a skunk roll over dead and cause a wild hyena to leave the body where it lay.

She, on the other hand, was like sweet, wet, sin dipped in coffee and sugar with a dash of cinnamon; god's own mistress with a surly attitude, which goes to show even god likes a little bit of the devil now and then.

She'd been asked about Jack by them who wanted to know. Bad folks with guns, and a need for dough. But she lied, said she didn't know where he was. Everyone believed her because she talked so bad about Jack. Said stuff about his habits, about how he beat her, how bad he was in bed, and how he stunk. It was convincin' stuff to everyone.

But me.

I knew that woman was a liar, because I knew her whole family, and they was the sort like my daddy used to say would rather climb a tree and lie than stand on the ground and tell the truth and be given free flowers. Lies flowed through their veins as surely as blood.

She told me about Jack one night while we were in bed, right after we had toted the water to the mountain. We're laying there lookin' at the ceilin', like there's gonna be manna from heaven, watchin' the defective light from the church across the way flash in and out and bounce along the wall, and she says in that burnt toast voice of hers, 'You split that money, I'll tell you where he is?"

"You wanna split it?"

"Naw, I'm thinkin' maybe you could keep half and I could give the other half to the cat."

"You don't got a cat."

"Well, I got another kind of cat, and that cat is one you like to pet."

"You're right there," I said. "Tellin' me where he is, that's okay, but I still got to do the ground work. Hasslin' with that dude ain't no easy matter, that's what I'm tryin' to tell you. So, me doin' what I'm gonna have to do, that's gonna be dangerous as trying to play with a daddy lion's balls. So, that makes me worth more than half, and you less than half."

"You're gonna shoot him when he ain't lookin', and you know it."

"I still got to take the chance."

She reached over to the nightstand, nabbed up a pack, shook out a cigarette, lit it with a cheap lighter, took a deep drag, coughed out a puff, said, "Split, or nothin'."

"Hell, honey, you know I'm funnin','" I said. "I'll split it right in half with you."

I was lyin' through my teeth. She may have figured such, but she figured with me she at least had a possibility, even if it was as thin as the edge of a playin' card.

She said, "He's done gone deep East Texas. He's over in Marvel Creek. Drove over there in his big black Cadillac that he had a chop shop turn blue."

"So he drove over in a blue Caddy, not a black," I said. "I mean, if it was black, and he had it painted blue, it ain't black no more. It's blue."

"Aren't you one for the details, and at a time like this," she said, and used her foot to rub my leg. "But, technically, baby, you are so correct."

—ɷ—

THAT NIGHT LOODIE LAID me out a map written in pencil on a brown paper sack, made me swear I was gonna split the money with her again. I told her what she wanted to hear. Next mornin', I started over to Marvel Creek.

Now, technically, Jack was in a place outside of the town, along the Sabine River, back in the bottom land where the woods was still thick, down a little trail that wound around and around, to a cabin Loodie said was about the size of a postage stamp, provided the stamp had been scissor trimmed.

I oiled my automatic, put on gloves, went to the store and bought a hatchet, cruised out early, made Marvel Creek in about an hour and fifteen, went glidin' over the Sabine River bridge. I took a gander at the water, which was dirty brown and up high on account of rain. I had grown up along that river, over near a place called Big Sandy. It was a place of hot sand and tall pines and no opportunity.

It wasn't a world I missed none.

I stopped at a little diner in Marvel Creek and had me a hamburger. There was a little white girl behind the counter with hair blonde as sunlight, and we made some goo-goo eyes at one another. Had I not been on a mission, I might have found out when she got off work, seen if me and her could get a drink and find a motel and try and make the beast with two backs.

Instead I finished up, got me a tall Styrofoam cup of coffee to go. I drove over to a food store and went in and bought a huge jar of pickles, a bag of cookies and a bottle of water. I put the pickles on the floor board between the back seat and the front. It was a huge jar and it fit snuggly. I laid the bag with the cookies and the water on the back seat.

The bottoms weren't far, about twenty minutes, but the roads were kind of tricky, some of them were little more than mud and a suggestion. Others were slick and shiny like snot on a water glass.

I drove carefully and sucked on my coffee. I went down a pretty wide road that became narrow, then took another road that wound off into the deeper woods. Drove until I found what I thought was the side road that led to the cabin. It was really a glorified path. Sun hardened, not very wide, bordered on one side by trees, and on the other side by marshy land that would suck the shoes off your feet, or bog up a car tire until you had to pull a gun and shoot the engine like a dying horse.

I stopped in the road and held Loodie's hand drawn map, checked it, looked up. There was a curve went around and between the trees and the marsh. There were tire tracks in it. Pretty fresh. At the bend in the curve was a little wooden bridge with no railings.

So far Loodie's map was on the money.

I finished off my coffee, got out and took a pee behind the car and watched some big white water birds flying over. When I was growing up over in Big Sandy I used to see that kind of thing all the time, not to mention all manner of wild life, and for a moment I felt nostalgic. That lasted about as long as it took me to stick my dick back in my pants and zipper up.

I got my hatchet out of the trunk and laid it on the front passenger seat as I got back in the car. I pulled out my automatic and checked it over, popped out the clip and slid it back in. I always liked the sound it made when it snapped into place. I looked at myself in the mirror, like maybe I was goin' on a date. Thought maybe if things fucked up, it might be the last time I got a good look at myself. I put the car in gear, wheeled around the curve and over the bridge, going at a slow pace, the map on the seat beside me, held in place by the hatchet.

I came to a wide patch, like on the map, and pulled off the road. Someone had dumped their garbage at the end of the spot where it ended close to the trees. There were broken up plastic bags spilling cans and paper, and there was an old bald tire leaning against a tree, as if taking a break before rolling on its way.

I got out and walked around the bend, looked down the road. There was a broad pond of water to the left, leaked there by the dirty Sabine. On the right, next to the woods, was a log cabin. Small, but well made and kind of cool lookin'. Loodie said it was on property Jack's parents had owned. Twenty acres or so. Cabin had a chimney chuggin' smoke. Out front was a big blue Cadillac El Dorado, the tires and sides splashed with mud. It was parked up close to the cabin. I could see through the Cadillac's windows, and they lined up with a window in the cabin. I moved to the side of the road, stepped in behind some trees, and studied the place carefully.

There weren't any wires runnin' to the cabin. There was a kind of lean-to shed off the back. Loodie told me that was where Jack kept the generator that gave the joint electricity. Mostly the cabin was heated by the fire wood piled against the shed, and lots of blankets come late at night. Had a gas stove with a nice sized tank. I could just imagine Jack in there with Loodie, his six fingers on her sweet chocolate skin. It made me want to kill him all the more, even though I knew Loodie was the kind of girl made a minx look virginal. You gave your heart to that woman, she'd eat it.

—⁂—

I WENT BACK TO the car and got my gun cleaning goods out of the glove box, and took out the clip, and cleaned my pistol and reloaded it. It was unnecessary, because the gun was a clean as a model's ass, but I liked to be sure.

I patted the hatchet on the seat like it was a dog.

I sat there and waited, thought about what I was gonna do with one hundred thousand dollars. You planned to kill someone and cut off their hand, you had to think about stuff like that, and a lot.

Considering on it, I decided I wasn't gonna get foolish and buy a car. One I had got me around and it looked all right enough. I wasn't gonna spend it on Loodie or some other split tail in a big time way. I was gonna use it carefully. I might get some new clothes and put some money down on a place instead of rentin'. Fact was, I might move to Houston.

If I lived closed to the bone and picked up the odd bounty job now and again, just stuff I wanted to do, like bits that didn't involve me having to deal with some goon big enough to pull off one of my legs and beat me with it, I could live safer, and better. Could have some stretches where I didn't have to do a damn thing but take it easy, all on account of that one hundred thousand dollar nest egg.

Course, Jack wasn't gonna bend over and grease up for me. He wasn't like that. He could be a problem.

I got a paperback out of the glove box and read for awhile. I couldn't get my mind to stick to it. The sky turned gray. My light was goin'. I put the paperback in the glove box with the gun cleaning kit. It started to rain. I watched it splat on the windshield. Thunder knocked at the sky. Lighting licked a crooked path against the clouds and passed away.

I thought about all manner of different ways of pullin' this off, and finally came up with somethin', decided it was good enough, because all I needed was a little edge.

The rain was hard and wild. It made me think Jack wasn't gonna be comin' outside. I felt safe enough for the moment. I tilted the seat back and lay there with the gun in my hand, my arm folded across my chest, and dozed for awhile with the rain pounding the roof.

—m—

IT WAS FRESH NIGHT when I awoke. I waited about an hour, picked up the hatchet, and got out of the car. It was still raining, and the rain was cold. I pulled my coat tight around me, stuck the hatchet through my belt and went to the back of the car and unlocked the trunk. I got the jack handle out of there, stuck it in my belt opposite the hatchet, started walking around the curve.

The cabin had a faint light shining through the window that in turn shone through the lined up windows of the car. As I walked, I saw a shape, like a huge bullet with arms, move in front of the glass. That size made me lose a step briefly, but I gathered up my courage, kept going.

When I got to the back of the cabin, I carefully climbed on the pile of firewood, made my way to the top of the lean-to. It sloped down off the main roof of the cabin, so it didn't take too much work to get up there, except that hatchet and tire iron gave me a bit of trouble in my belt and my gloves made my grip a little slippery.

On top of the cabin, I didn't stand up and walk, but instead carefully made my way on hands and knees toward the front of the place.

When I got there, I leaned over the edge and took a look. The cabin door was about three feet below me. I made my way to the edge so I was overlooking the Cadillac. A knock on the door wouldn't bring Jack out. Even he was too smart for that, but that Cadillac, he loved it. Bought a new one every year. I pulled out the tire iron, laid down on the roof, looking over the edge, cocked my arm back and threw the iron at the windshield. It made a hell of a crash, cracking the glass so that it looked like a spider web, setting off the car alarm.

I pulled my gun and waited. I heard the cabin door open, heard the thumping of Jack's big feet. He came around there mad as a hornet. He was wearing a long sleeve white shirt with the sleeves rolled up. He hadn't had time to notice the cold. But the best thing was it didn't look like he had a gun on him.

I aimed and shot him. I think I hit him somewhere on top of the shoulder, but I wasn't sure. But I hit him. He did a kind of bend at the knees, twisted his body, then snapped back into shape and looked up.

"You," he said.

I shot him again, and it had about the same impact. Jack was on the hood of his car and then on the roof, and then he jumped. That big bastard could jump, could probably dunk a basket ball and grab the rim. He hit with both hands on the edge of the roof, started pulling himself up. I was up now, and I stuck the gun in his face, and pulled the trigger.

And, let me tell you how the gas went out me. I had cleaned that gun and cleaned that gun, and now...It jammed. First time ever. But it was a time that mattered.

Jack lifted himself onto the roof, and then he was on me, snatching the gun away and flinging it into the dark. I couldn't believe it. What the hell was he made of? Even in the wet night, I could see that much of his white shirt had turned dark with blood.

We circled each other for a moment. I tried to decide what to do next, and then he was on me. I remembered the hatchet, but it was too late. We were going back off the roof and onto the lean-to, rolling down that. We hit the stacked firewood and it went in all directions and we splattered to the ground.

I lost my breath. Jack kept his. He grabbed me by my coat collars and lifted me and flung me around and against the side of the lean-to. I hit on my back and came down on my butt.

Jack grabbed up a piece of firewood. It looked to me that that piece of wood had a lot of heft. He came at me. I made myself stand. I pulled the hatchet free. As he came and struck down with the wood, I sidestepped and swung the hatchet.

The sound the hatchet made as it caught the top of his head was a little like what you might expect if a strong man took hold of a piece of cardboard and ripped it.

I hit him so hard his knees bent and hot blood jumped out of his head and hit my face. The hatchet came loose of my hands, stayed in his skull. His knees straightened. I thought: What is this motherfucker, Rasputin?

He grabbed me and started to lift me again. His mouth was partially open and his teeth looked like machinery cogs to me. The rain was washing the blood on his head down his face in murky rivers. He stunk like road kill.

And then his expression changed. It seemed as if he had just realized he had a hatchet in his head. He let go, turned, started walking off, taking hold of the hatchet with both hands, trying to pull it loose. I picked up a piece of fire wood and followed after him. I went up behind him and hit him in the back of the head as hard as I could. It was like hitting an elephant in the ass with a twig. He turned and looked at me. The look on his face was so strange, I almost felt sorry for him.

He went down on one knee, and I hauled back and hit him with the firewood, hitting the top of the hatchet. He vibrated, and his neck twisted to one side, and then his head snapped back in line.

He said, "Gonna need some new pigs," and then fell out.

Pigs?

He was laying face forward with the stock of the hatchet holding his head slightly off the ground. I dropped the fire wood and rolled him over on his back, which only took about as much work as trying to roll his

Cadillac. I pulled the hatchet out of his head. I had to put my food on his neck to do it.

I picked up the firewood I had dropped, put it on the ground beside him, and stretched his arm out until I had the hand with the six fingers positioned across it. I got down on my knees and lifted the hatchet, hit as hard as I could. It took me three whacks, but I cut his hand loose.

—∾—

I PUT THE BLOODY hand in my coat pocket and dug through his pants for his car keys, didn't come across them. I went inside the cabin and found them on the table. I drove the Cadillac to the back where Jack lay, pulled him into the backseat, almost having a hernia in the process. I put the hatchet in there with him.

I drove the El Dorado over close to the pond and rolled all the windows down and put it in neutral. I got out of the car, went to the back of it and started shoving. My feet slipped in the mud, but finally I gained traction. The car went forward and slipped into the water, but the back end of it hung on the bank.

Damn.

I pushed and I pushed, and finally I got it moving, and it went in, and with the windows down, it sunk pretty fast.

I went back to the cabin and looked around. I found some candles. I turned off the light, and I went and turned off the generator. I went back inside and lit about three of the big fat candles and stuck them in drinking glasses and watched them burn for a moment. I went over to the stove and turned on the gas. I let it run a few seconds, looked around the cabin. Nothing there I needed.

I left, closed the door behind me. When the gas filled the room enough, those candles would set the air on fire, the whole place would blow. I don't know exactly why I did it, except maybe I just didn't like Jack. Didn't like that he had a Cadillac and a cabin and some land, and for a while there, he had Loodie. Because of all that, I had done all I could do that could be done to him. I even had his six-fingered hand in my pocket.

By the time I got back to the car, I was feeling weak. Jack had worked me over pretty good, and now that the adrenaline had started to ease out of me, I was feeling it. I took off my jacket and opened the jar of pickles in the floor board, pulled out a few of them and threw them away. I ate one, and had my bottle of water with it and some cookies.

I took Jack's hand and put it in the big pickle jar. I sat in the front seat, and was overcome with a feeling of nausea. I didn't know if it was the pickle or what I had done, or both. I opened the car door and threw up. I felt cold and damp from the rain. I started the car and turned on the heater. I cranked back my seat and closed my eyes. I had to rest before I left, had to. All of me seemed to be running out through the soles of my feet.

I slept until the cabin blew. The sound of the gas generator and stove going up with a one, two boom, snapped me awake.

I got out of the car and walked around the curve. The cabin was nothing more than a square dark shape inside an envelope of fire. The fire wavered up high and grew narrow at the top like a cone. The fire crackled like someone wadding up cellophane.

I doubted, out here, anyone heard the explosion, and no one could see the flames. Wet as it was, I figured the fire wouldn't go any farther than the cabin. By morning, even with the rain still coming down, that place would be smoked down to the mineral rights.

I drove out of there, and pretty soon the heater was too hot, and I turned it off. It was as if my body was as on fire as the cabin. I rolled down the window and let in some cool air. I felt strange. Not good, not bad. I had bounty hunted for years, and I had done a bit of head whopping before, but this was my first murder.

I had really hated Jack and I had hardly known him.

It was the woman that made me hate him. The woman I was gonna cheat out of some money. But a hundred thousand dollars is a whole lot of money, honey.

—⚒—

WHEN I GOT HOME, the automatic garage opener lifted the door and I wheeled in and closed the place up. I went inside and took off my clothes and showered carefully and looked in the mirror. There was knot on my head that looked as if you might need mountaineering equipment to scale it. I got some ice and put it in a sock and pressed it to my head while I sat on the toilet lid and thought about things. If any thoughts actually came to me, I don't remember them well.

I dressed, bunched up my murder clothes, and put them in a black plastic garbage bag.

In the garage, I removed the pickle jar and cleaned the car. I opened the jar and looked at the hand. It looked like a black crab in there amongst the pickles. I studied it for a long time until it started to look like one hundred thousand dollars.

I couldn't wait until morning, and after awhile I drove toward Big O's place. Now, you would think a man with the money he's got would live in a mansion, but he didn't. He lived in three double wide mobile homes that had been lined together by screened in porches. I had been inside once, when I had done Big O a very small favor, and had never been inside since. But one of those homes was nothing but one big space, no room, and it was Big O's lounge. He hung in there with some ladies and some body guards. He had two main guys. Be Bop Lewis, who was a skinny white guy who always acted as if someone was sneaking up on him, and a black guy named Lou Boo (keep in mind, I didn't name them) who thought he was way cool and smooth as velvet.

The rain had followed me from the bottom land, on into Tyler, to the outskirts, and on the far side. It was way early morning, and I figured on waking Big O up and dragging his ass out of bed and showing him them six fingers and getting me one hundred thousand dollars, a pat on the head, and hell, he might ask Be Bop to give me a hand job, on account of I had done so well.

More I thought about it, more I thought he might not be as happy to see me as I thought. A man like Big O liked his sleep, so I pulled into a motel not too far from where I had to go to see Big O, the big jar of pickles and one black six fingered hand beside my bed, the automatic under my pillow.

I dreamed Jack was driving the Cadillac out of that pond. I saw the lights first and then the car. Jack was steering with his nub laid against the wheel, and his face behind the glass was a black mass without eyes or smile or features of any kind.

It was a bad dream and it woke me up. I washed my face, went back to bed, slept this time until late morning. I got up and put back on my same clothes, loaded up my pickle jar and left out of there. I thought about the axe in Jack's head, his hand chopped off and in the pickle jar, and regret moved through me like shit through a goose and was gone.

I drove out to Big O's place.

—⚋—

BY THE TIME I arrived at the property, which was surrounded by a barb wire fence, and had driven over a cattle guard, I could see there were men in a white pickup coming my way. Two in the front and three in the bed in the back, and they had some heavy duty fire power. Parked behind them, up by the doublewides, were the cement trucks and dump trucks and back hoes and graders that were part of the business Big O claimed to operate. Construction. But his real business was a bit of this, and a little of that, construction being little more than the surface paint.

I stopped and rolled down my window and waited. Outside the rain had burned off and it was an unseasonably hot day, sticky as honey on the fingers.

When they drove up beside my window, the three guys in the bed pointed their weapons at me. The driver was none other than one of the two men I recognized from before. Be Bop. His skin was so pale and thin, I could almost see the skull beneath it.

"Well, now," he said. "I know you."

I agreed he did. I smiled like me and him was best friends. I said, "I got some good news for Big O about Six Finger Jack."

"Six Finger Jack, huh," Be Bop said. "Get out of the car."

I got out. Be Bop got out and frisked me. I had nothing sharp or anything full of bullets. He asked if there was anything in the car. I told him no. He had one of the men in the back of the pickup search it anyway. The man came back, said, "Ain't got no gun, just a big jar of pickles."

"Pickles," Be Bop said. "You a man loves pickles?"

"Not exactly," I said.

"Follow us on up," Be Bop said.

We drove on up to the trio of doublewides. There had been some work done since I had last been here, and there was a frame of boards laid out for a foundation, and out to the side there was a big hole that looked as if it was going to be a swimming pool.

I got out of the car and leaned on it and looked things over. Be Bop and his men got out of the truck. Be Bop came over.

"He buildin' a house on that foundation?" I asked.

"Naw, he's gonna put an extension on one of the trailers. I think he's gonna put in a pool room and maybe some gamin' stuff. Swimmin' pool over there. Come on."

I got my jar of pickles out of the backseat, and Be Bop said, "Now wait a minute. Your pickles got to go with you?"

I sat the jar down and screwed off the lid and stepped back. Be Bop looked inside. When he lifted his head, he said, "Well, now."

—m—

NEXT THING I KNOW I'm in the big trailer, the one that's got nothin' but the couch, some chairs and stands for drinks, a TV set about the size of a down town theater. It's on, and there's sports goin'. I glance at it and see it's an old basketball game that was played a year back, but they're watchin' it, Big O and a few of his boys, includin' Lou Boo, the black guy I've seen before. This time, there aren't any women there.

Be Bop came inside with me, but the rest of the pickup posse didn't. They were still protecting the perimeter. It seemed silly, but truth was, there was lots of people wanted to kill Big O.

No one said a thing to me for a full five minutes. They were waitin' for a big score in the game, somethin' they had seen before. When the shot came they all cheered. I thought only Big O sounded sincere.

I didn't look at the game. I couldn't take my eyes off Big O. He wasn't wearin' his cowboy hat. His head had only a few hairs left on it, like worms working their way over the face of the moon. His skin was white and lumpy like cold oatmeal. He was wearin' a brown pair of stretch overalls. When the fat moved, the material moved with him, which was a good idea, cause it looked as if Big O had packed on about one hundred extra pounds since I saw him last.

He was sitting in a motorized scooter, had his tree trunk legs stretched out in front of him on a leg lift. His stomach flowed up and fell forward and over his sides, like four hundred pounds of bagged mercury. I could hear him wheezing across the room. His right foot was missing. There was a nub there and his stretch pants had been sewn up at the end. On the stand, near his right elbow was a tall bottle of malt liquor and a greasy box of fried chicken.

His men sat on the couch to his left. The couch was unusually long and there were six men on it, like pigeons in a row. They all had guns in shoulder holsters. The scene made Big O look like a whale on vacation with a male harem of sucker fish to attend him.

Big O spoke to me, his voice sounded small coming from that big body. "Been a long time since I seen you last."

I nodded.

"I had a foot then."

I nodded again.

"The diabetes. Had to cut it off. Doctor Jacobs says I need more exercise, but, hey, glandular problems, so what you gonna do? Packs the weight on. But still, I got to go there ever Thursday mornin'. Next time, he might tell me the other foot's got to go. But you know, that's not so bad. This chair, it can really get you around. Motorized you know."

Be Bop, who was still by me, said, "He's got somethin' for you, Big O."

"Chucky," Big O said, "cut off the game."

Chucky was one of the men on the couch, a white guy. He got up and found a remote control and cut off the game. He took it with him back to the couch, sat down.

"Come on up," Big O said.

I carried my jar of pickles up there, got a whiff of him that made my memory of Jack's stink seem mild. Big O smelled like dried urine, sweat, and death. I had to fight my gag reflex.

I sat the jar down and twisted off the lid and reached inside the blood stained pickle juice, and brought out Jack's dripping hand. Big O said, "Give me that."

I gave it to him. He turned it around and around in front of him. Pickle juice dripped off of the hand and into his lap. He started to laugh. His fat vibrated, and then he coughed. "That there is somethin'."

He held the hand up above his head. Well, he lifted it to about shoulder height. Probably the most he had moved in a while. He said, "Boys, do you see this? Do you see the humanity in this?"

I thought: Humanity?

"This hand tried to take my money and stuck its finger up my old lady's ass...Maybe all six. Look at it now."

His boys all laughed. It was like the best goddamn joke ever told, way they yucked it up.

"Well now," Big O said, "that motherfucker won't be touchin' nothin', won't be handlin' nobody's money, not even his own, and we got this dude to thank."

Way Big O looked at me then made me a little choked up. I thought there might even be a tear in his eye. "Oh," he said. "I loved that woman. God, I did. But, I had to cut her loose. She hadn't fucked around, me and her might have gotten married, and all this—" he waved Jack's hand around, "would have been hers to share. But no. She couldn't keep her pants on. It's a sad situation. And though I can't bring her back, this here hand, it gives me some kind of happiness. I want you to know that."

"I'm glad I could have been of assistance," I said.

"That's good. That's good. Put this back in the pickle jar, will you?"

I took the hand and dropped it in the pickle jar.

Big O looked at me, and I looked at him. After a long moment, he said, "Well, thanks."

I said, "You're welcome."

We kept looking at one another. I cleared my throat. Big O shifted a little in his chair. Not much, but a little.

"Seems to me," I said, "there was a bounty on Jack. Some money."

"Oh," Big O said. "That's right, there was."

"He was quite a problem."

"Was he now...Yeah, well, I can see the knot on your head. You ought to buy that thing its own cap. Somethin' nice."

Everyone on the couch laughed. I laughed too. I said, "Yeah, it's big. And, I had some money, like say, one hundred thousand dollars, I'd maybe put out ten or twenty for a nice designer cap."

I was smilin', waiting for my laugh, but nothin' came. I glanced at Be Bop. He was lookin' off like maybe he heard his mother callin' somewhere in the distance.

Big O said, "Now that Jack's dead, I got to tell you, I've sort of lost the fever."

"Lost the fever?" I said.

"He was alive, I was all worked up. Now that he's dead, I got to consider, is he really worth one hundred thousand dollars?"

"Wait a minute, that was the deal. That's the deal you spread all over."

"I've heard those rumors," Big O said.

"Rumors?"

"Oh, you can't believe everything you hear. You just can't."

I stood there stunned.

Big O said, "But I want you to know, I'm grateful. You want a Coke, a beer before you go?"

"No. I want the goddamn money you promised."

That had come out of my mouth like vomit. It surprised even me.

Everyone in the room was silent.

Big O breathed heavy, said, "Here's the deal, friend. You take your jar of pickles, and Jack's six fingers, and you carry them away. Cause if you don't, if you want to keep askin' me for money I don't want to pay, you're head is gonna be in that jar, but not before I have it shoved up your ass. You savvy?'

It took me a moment, but I said, "Yeah. I savvy."

—◊—

LYING IN BED WITH Loodie, not being able to do the deed, I said, "I'm gonna get that fat sonofabitch. He promised me money. I fought Jack with a piece of firewood and a hatchet. I fell off a roof. I slept in my car in the cold. I was nearly killed."

"That's sucks," Loodie said.

"Sucks? You got snookered too. You was gonna get fifty thousand, now you're gonna get dick."

"Actually, tonight, I'm not even gettin' that."

"Sorry, baby. I'm just so mad...Ever Thursday mornin', Big O, he goes to a doctor's appointment at Dr. Jacobs. I can get him there."

"He has his men, you know."

"Yeah. But when he goes in the office, maybe he don't. And maybe I check it out this Thursday, find out when he goes in, and next Thursday, I maybe go inside and wait on him."

"How would you do that?"

"I'm thinkin' on it, baby."

"I don't think it's such a good idea."

"You lost fifty grand, and so did I, so blowin' a hole in his head is as close as we'll get to satisfaction."

—⟋⟍—

S O THURSDAY MORNIN', I'M goin' in the garage, to go and
check things out, and when I get in the car, before I can open up the
garage and back out, a head raises up in the back seat, and a gun barrel,
like a wet kiss, pushes against the side of my neck.

I can see him in the mirror. It's Lou Boo. He says: "You got to go
where I tell you, else I shoot a hole in you."

I said, "Loodie."

"Yeah, she come to us right away."

"Come on, man. I was just mad. I wasn't gonna do nothin'."

"So here it is Thursday mornin', and now you're tellin' me you wasn't
goin' nowhere."

"I was gonna go out and get some breakfast. Really."

"Don't believe you."

"Shit," I said.

"Yeah, shit," Lou Boo said.

"How'd you get in here without me knowin'?"

"I'm like a fuckin' ninja...And the door slides up you pull it from the
bottom."

"Really?"

"Yeah, really."

"Come on, Lou Boo, give a brother a break. You know how it is?"

Lou Boo laughed a little. "Ah, man. Don't play the brother card. I'm
what you might call one of them social progressives. I don't see color,
even if it's the same as mine. Let's go, my man."

—⟋⟍—

I T WAS HIGH MORNING and cool when we arrived. I drove my
car right up to where the pool was dug out, way Lou Boo told me.
There was a cement mixer truck parked nearby for cementing the pool.
We stopped and Lou Boo told me to leave it in neutral. I did. I got out
and walked with him to where Big O was sitting in his motorized scooter
with Loodie on his lap. His boys were all around him. Be Bop pointed his
finger at me and dropped his thumb.

"My man," Be Bop said.

When I was standing in front of Big O, he said, "Now, I want you to understand, you wouldn't be here had you not decided to kill me. I can't have that, now can I?"

I didn't say anything.

I looked at Loodie, she shrugged.

"I figured you owed me money," I said.

"Yeah," Big O said. "I know. You see, Loodie, she comes and tells me she's gonna make a deal with you to kill Jack and make you think you made a deal with her. That way, the deal I made was with her, not you. You followin' me on this, swivel dick? Then, you come up with this idea to kill me at the doctor's office. Loodie, she came right to me."

"So," I said, "you're gettin' Loodie out of the deal, and she's gettin' one hundred thousand."

"That sounds about right, yeah," Big O said.

I thought about that. Her straddin' that fat bastard in his scooter. I shook my head, glared at her, said, "Damn, girl."

She didn't look right at me.

Big O said, "Loodie, you go on in the house there, and amuse yourself. Get a beer, or somethin'. Watch a little TV. Do your nails. Whatever."

Loodie started walking toward the trailers. When she was inside, Big O said,

"Hell, boy. I know how she is, and I know what she is. It's gonna be white gravy on sweet chocolate bread for me. And when I get tired of it, she gonna find a hole out here next to you. I got me all kind of room here. I ain't usin' the lake boat stalls no more. That's risky. Here is good. Though I'm gonna have to dig another spot for a pool, but that's how it is. Ain't no big thing, really."

"She used me," I said. "She's the one led me to this."

"No doubt, boy. But, you got to understand. She come to me and made the deal before you did anything. I got to honor that."

"I could just go on," I said. "I could forget all about it. I was just mad. I wouldn't never bother you. Hell, I can move. I can go out of state."

"I know that," he said, "but, I got this rule, and it's simple. You threaten to kill me, I got to have you taken care of. Ain't that my rule boys?"

There was a lot of agreement.

Lou Boo was last. He said, "Yep, that's the way you do it, boss."

Big O said. "Lou Boo, put him in the car, will you?"

Lou Boo put the gun to the back of my head, said, "Get on your knees."

"Fuck you," I said, but he hit me hard behind the head. Next thing I know I'm on my knees, and he's got my hands behind my back, and has fastened a plastic tie over my wrists.

"Get in the car," Lou Boo said.

I fought him all the way, but Be Bop came out and kicked me in the nuts a couple of times, hard enough I threw up, and then they dragged me to the car and shoved me inside behind the wheel and rolled down the windows and closed the door.

They went behind the car then and pushed. The car wobbled, then fell, straight down, hit so hard the air bag blew out and knocked the shit out of me. I couldn't move with it the way it was, my hands bound behind my back, the car on its nose, its back wheels against the side of the hole. It looked like I was tryin' to drive to hell. I was stunned and bleeding. The bag had knocked a tooth out. I heard the sound of a motor above me, a little motor. The scooter.

I could hear Big O up there. "If you hear me, want you to know I'm having one of the boys bring the cement truck around. We're gonna fill this hole with cement, and put, I don't know, a tennis court or somethin' on top of it. But the thing I want you to know is this is what happens when someone fucks with Big O."

"You stink," I said. "And you're fat. And you're ugly."

He couldn't hear me. I was mostly talking into the air bag.

I heard the scooter go away, followed by the sound of a truck and a beeping as it backed up. Next I heard the churning of the cement in the big mixer that was on the back of it. Then the cement slid down and pounded on the roof and started to slide over the windshield. I closed my eyes and held my breath, and then I felt the cold wet cement touch my elbow as it came through the open window. I thought about some way out, but there was nothing there, and I knew that within moments there wouldn't be anything left for me to think about at all.

DECIMATOR SMITH AND THE FANGS OF THE FIRE SERPENT

BY GARY PHILLIPS

"**U**H, OH, FOLKS, MCCALL has Smith on the ropes and is working his breadbasket. Suddenly an uppercut catches Smith on the side of his jaw but looks like he slipped most of that blow. Okay, okay, Smith counters with a combination hard right to McCall's chest and a left he ducked. But this gives Smith an opening and he moves sideways and now he's back on his bicycle, dancing and bobbing backwards, and this again flusters McCall.

"He's saying something to Smith but I dare not repeat such to you, our dear radio audience here on KNX. Ha, ha. Oh, wait, Smith abruptly stopped and pivoting more like a toreador than a pugilist sunk a straight hard right past McCall's guard and caught him flush under the left eye. I tell you folks, the speed at which Smith is able to deliver his shots, often off-balance, is truly amazing. It's no wonder this is a sold out crowd here at the Olympic Auditorium given McCall's Irish following and Smith's allure among our colored citizenry and the entertainers and musicians he hobnobs with.

"Referee Arthur Leibling breaks the contenders apart from a clench. Rocco Kaufman is yelling at his fighter to lower his shoulders and keep his head tucked in like he's supposed to. The fighters are back in the center of the ring, ladies and gentlemen, trading blows but nothing decisive. Oh, wait, McCall thought he had an opening as Smith has gone flat-footed, dropping his arms. He seemed to be running out of gas here in the eleventh round but I think it was a ploy. McCall looped in what looked to be a devastating left, I could feel the wind draft I tell you, folks. But Smith easily took the blow on his forearm and in rapid succession, his hands a veritable blur, peppered McCall's face and head with a series of fisticuffs. As my sweet, corn cob pipe smoking granny is want to say, he combed his hair back. McCall is woozy I tell you and the crowd, you can hear the men and women on their feet and demanding a knock out, boxing fans.

"McCall, his mouth guard red from blood, looks to rally with a jab, trying to open up that cut he put over Smith's brow early in the fifth. The punch lands solid but seemingly has no effect. Unfazed Smith moves in, crosses and overhands patterned in a dizzying display of ring generalship putting McCall on his back.

"Jimmy, Jimmy, turn up the volume so they can hear me over the roar. Referee Leibling is standing over McCall who is down on a knee, sweat and hope dripping off him like a wrung out wet sheet on the clothesline… six, seven, eight…McCall rises, he's back up I tell you, he's back up. Smith circles. McCall lashes out but his punches are weak, off-target. Smith gets in under a left and hammers McCall downstairs and upstairs and oh, mama, the punishment being meted out to Bruiser McCall. He stumbles and drops over on his side. The ref is giving him the count… and that's it, brother, the fight is over. Leibling raises Smith's arm as the crowd explodes. He gave them their knockout and then some. And let me tell you, if I hadn't just witnessed him going eleven grueling rounds of championship level boxing, you'd say he was just some fella who'd come in for n egg cream he looks so refreshed.

"And speaking of refreshing, this swell-looking colored dame in a silk get up with brocade stitching and a feathered hat has come into the ring and is all over the winner like a second skin much to the consternation of Rocco Kaufman. Ha, ha. Well, folks, I'm getting in there too so I can get a few words with the man who is more than likely to face Solly Krieger, the middleweight title holder. The man who for good reason demonstrated tonight why pound for pound, he's the best around. Why they call him Decimator."

—⁂—

IT FINALLY GOT QUIET in the dressing room. Achilles Smith had showered and was buttoning his shirt. Millard "Rocco" Kaufman returned from using the phone in the Olympic Auditorium's back office.

"How's it looking?" Smith asked, tucking in his shirt tail and zipping up and buckling his tweed slacks.

Absently Kaufman, an older man in baggy pants with a tangle of white hair, loosened then retightened the cap on a bottle of liniment as he talked. "Krieger's guy Shep is playing coy."

"Meaning they want to play me cheap for a match."

"Yeah, but I'm going to let him stew for a few days. He's not going to pin us as hungry. I was talking with Hildy from the Herald-Ex and what with his article that runs in the morning edition and figure some other noise that'll come from the boxing bunch, it'll seem like Krieger is ducking you if they don't make the fight."

"Sounds good to me, Rocco." Smith had been sitting with a haunch on the examination table and now stood up. "I gotta get going over to the Dunbar."

Kaufman rolled his tongue inside his mouth. "Seeing Rose?" She was the woman in silk who'd climbed into the ring to congratulate the fighter.

The middleweight smiled. "I'm'a find you a girlfriend to occupy your time other than that John Reed and Spinoza you're always reading, Rocco." He clapped his large hands together once, enthusiastically. "I know, what about Pig Iron Lil who hawks the news over on Broadway next to the Orpheum?"

"You're a regular Fred Allen, you know that?" Kaufman said. He shook a mashed up towel at Smith. "Just you don't go running off with that wild broad to Tijuana or parts unknown. The Krieger fight is going to be made and I want you on a regime now as we lead in to it. One that does not include chasing skirts."

Laughing, Smith was going to make another crack but there was a knock on the door and without pausing for an answer, in stepped a lanky black man in a checked light gray box coat and dark slacks. He wore a hat and removed it while he identified himself.

"My name is Percy Kimbrough, I'm with the police."

Smith and Kaufman exchanged a look. "Ha, they let us spades work plainclothes, gate?" Smith chided. "I guess you get to chase colored robbers all over town."

Kimbrough, a light-skinned man with square good-natured features and a mustache like singer Billy Eckstein's, smiled wanly. "I'm afraid this is not good news, Mr. Smith."

"What is it?"

"It's about your sister, Helena. She's dead. Murdered."

Smith sagged against the padded examination table like being sucker punched. Kaufman put a hand on his boxer's shoulder. "When did this happen, Detective?"

"Her body washed up under the Lido pier earlier tonight. A couple of kids down there necking found her." He halted, watching the two.

"What else?" Smith asked. "Tell me all of it."

"She'd had relations recently is what I understand from the medical examiner but there was no tearing if you know what I mean. But there were bruises and her neck was broken."

Smith lowered his head and folded his arms as if to contain himself. "I'll make arrangements of course." He seemed to be saying it for the benefit of others not in the room.

"How long had she been in the water?" Kaufman asked.

"We figure no more than a day or two. Say, she was a nurse over at Queen of Angels, wasn't she?"

"Yeah," Smith answered.

"I need to ask, when was the last time you saw her? And she was a looker, she having any boyfriend troubles? Some mug you might have told to lay off and he took it out on her?"

Smith regarded the cop evenly. "I talked to her, must have been Wednesday afternoon. She told me she couldn't make it tonight 'cause she was going to be on duty. So, you know, I just figured I'd see her later like always. But I won't be seeing her again I guess." He was tearing up but got himself under control. "I know a couple of the guys Helena used to date. I doubt if any one of them could have done this, but I'll give you their names and where they stay."

"You know where they live, huh?" Kimbrough observed, taking a steno pad out of his inner breast pocket.

"I damn sure better know," Smith replied chillingly, already missing his big sister.

After giving the detective the information and his particulars like his address and phone number to his apartment on Maple, the plainclothesman left saying he'd be back in touch.

"Achilles, I don't know what to say," Kaufman began. "I'm sure sorry about this, it's a goddamn shame is what it is. She was awfully nice."

"She sure was." Smith put on his leather jacket. "That's why I'm going to find out who killed her and make that son of a bitch pay."

"You better leave this to the cops, son."

"Don't blow no gaskets, Rocco, you ain't an officer of the court anymore." In the Roaring '20s, a young Rocco Kaufman had been a criminal attorney until he was disbarred.

"Go over to the Dunbar and tell Rose, will you, Rocco? She'll be downstairs in the Zanzibar Room." The boxer headed for the door.

"Where you going?"

"Over to the hospital, see a friend who worked with Helena." Smith nodded curtly at his manager and left.

Kaufman was inclined to argue but hoped the younger man would cool down after tonight. Let him get this out of his system, this futile attempt, then he figured he'd get him out of town for a week or so to keep him away from the newshounds.

Descending the stairs to his car parked in back, Achilles "Decimator" Smith was glad what little talking he'd had to do to the papers had been done. Tomorrow the news of his sister's death and his win would be on the same pages and it made him ill inside just imagining that. The only cure was to set this right for Helena he vowed. It would also be tomorrow when he'd make the call to their father Augustus in Galveston -- at least to some cousins there. He would telephone in an effort to find his father, a professional gambler, sometimes vending machine mechanic and full-time womanizer.

Putting his Ford Cabriolet into gear, Decimator Smith hoped Detective Kimbrough would be busy with the names he'd given him for a day. Just maybe enough time to make a little headway. He wanted whoever did this to die by his hands. It wouldn't be the first time Smith had killed – though it would be the first time in California he noted grimly. He got out to Queen of Angels Hospital in Echo Park and at this time of night, found a place to park almost in front on Bellevue.

Inside the main building he went to the unofficial colored ward. Segregation in Los Angeles was official in housing covenants and resulting neighborhood patterns, and unofficial in public accommodations like the hospital. It simply was that black patients were on certain floors and in certain rooms. A Japanese-American doctor, Mark Kagawa, who knew Smith, was walking along a hallway he'd just turned onto. He'd been skimming through papers attached to a clip board.

"Heard the last rounds of your fight tonight on the radio, Achilles, congratulations." The two shook hands.

"Thanks, Doc. Is Zora around?"

He hooked a thumb behind him. "I passed her at the nurses' station on the corridor to the right."

" 'Preciate that." Smith began walking briskly.

"I got my money on you if you fight Krieger," the doctor said, heading in the opposite direction.

He found Zora Montclair leaving a room with three patients in it. One was under a translucent oxygen tent, its sides moving in and out slightly like the membrane of a large sea creature.

"Des, hey," she said. "Helena didn't come in tonight. That girl must be staying out late these days gaycatting." She was a pretty copper-skinned woman of mixed heritage but considered herself, as society did, as black. She had a captivating smile to go with a figure her plain nurse's uniform couldn't hide. She and Smith had been an item once until she fell for an insurance man with more money and future than him.

Smith gently took her by the elbow and guided her to a spot along a wall. "There's no easy way to say this so here it is. Helena was killed. Murdered."

"Oh God, Des," she said, gripping his arm, a hand to her mouth. She looked up at him with teary eyes. "Who could have done this?"

Decimator Smith was in ring attack mode, the only way he could function and not be frozen by the terrible fact of his sister's violent death. "Was she seeing some new boyfriend, Zora?"

Montclair wiped at her tears and looked into the middle distance, frowning. "No, not anybody you wouldn't have known about, Des."

"I need anything you can give me, Zora. This is very important to me, understand?" Not meaning to, he gripped her arm and tightened.

"Des," she said, referring to the pressure.

He released her. "I'm sorry. I'm just, you know…"

"Hey, wait," she said, snapping her fingers and lowering her voice as an orderly walked past. "Helena was making some extra money, off the books, see?"

"Yeah?"

She elevated her shoulders. "That's all I've got, Des. This has been going on for about a month. She mentioned to me last week the grown son of this woman she's been caring for had words with her about his mother's care." She looked at him hopefully.

"This son got a name?"

"I don't know his, but the elderly patient is named Harcourt."

"As in Harcourt Tire and Rubber? The ones outfitting the buses up and down the West Coast?"

"I don't know. But Helena said she had a big house in Los Feliz. Maids and the whole bit."

"Thanks for this, Zora." He started to leave.

"I gotta tell the girls," she murmured. "When's the funeral, Des?"

"Not sure yet," he called back, already at the end of the hallway. He didn't want to picture himself at his sister's coffin, looking down into it. He next drove to her place, two rented rooms and a bath all to herself in a good-sized two-story Craftsman on 68th Street near Hoover.

The widow Mrs. Gasparento greeted him at the door, the porch light on. "Oh my, Achilles, this is so awful," she commiserated.

"You know?"

"That policeman, Kimbrough called. Said for me to not let anyone in her rooms until he came here tomorrow morning." She put her muscular arms around him and squeezed his shoulders as he stood in the open doorway.

He squeezed her back then pulled away, his eyes steady on hers. "But I'm family, Mrs. Gasparento, and I need to see about some of her things tonight."

"I don't know, I can't have any trouble with the law," she said.

Her round face was framed by a full length of curly black hair, the grey in it hidden by hair dye. She was forty or so pounds too heavy but even in her early sixties, there were reminders of the beauty she'd been back when – back when she and the late Mr. Gasparento ran a truck stop and bootleg whiskey operation in California's Central Valley.

"Won't be none," Smith said, "I'll be just like a little mouse."

"Sure you will, carrisima, because I just got here off the squid boat."

Smith was already heading to the stairs. "You're tops, Mrs. Gasparento."

In his sister's main room Smith pulled down the Murphy bed and looked through her possessions, smiling at a picture of the two of them as kids in Galveston, Texas. There was their mother and father on either side of them, his sister squinting into the camera. She'd grown up to favor their deceased mother quite a bit he reminded himself. Momentarily he sat, gripped by melancholy. The picture had been taken in front of their father's boat repair business on the water. About a year before he gave that up to give his full attention to the cards and little attention to his family.

He shook the past off and pressed on. He found Helena's address book and copied the address she'd written down of a Juliet Harcourt. He left the book, figuring if he was unsuccessful in finding his sister's killer, maybe Kimbrough would be. Though he doubted the cop's white bosses cared that much about a colored girl's murder, so how long would it be a priority? He continued searching and found a gold chain necklace in a dresser drawer . There was a small pendant on the chain and he assumed given its sparkle, it was the real McCoy. Now who gave her a diamond? None of the ones he knew she'd dated could afford that kind of ice. They were doing good to afford drinks and dinner for two at one of the jazz joints like the Club Alabam on Central. He briefly debated taking the item then pocketed the jewelry. He turned up nothing else of interest and left.

Descending the stairs, Smith saw entering the house a tall, reedy man dressed in a black suit and a white collarless shirt buttoned all the way up underneath. This was Elijah Morbilus, or so he called himself. He was of undetermined ethnicity and age. A dime store spiritualist hustler is what Smith had said to Helena about him. He rented a large room in the rear of the house off the service porch. Morbilus looked up, absently adjusting his rimless round spectacles on his shallow face.

"Brother Smith. The avenues are abuzz with your victory." He clasped his hands together as if in prayer, and bowed slightly.

"Thanks," he said, stepping past the dusky-colored man who smelled of incense and oils. Probably out giving a 'reading' as he called them to some gullible old dame Smith figured.

"Is there…something amiss?" Morbilus said. He'd stopped on his way to his room in the half-light of the hallway. Mrs. Gasparento came though the kitchen's swing door, worrying a dish towel in both of her hands.

A cold snake went across Smith's spine. He looked back at Morbilus. "Why do you ask?"

Slowly he waved a hand about as if sifting through vapor. "I, I don't know, but seems there is a disturbance around you, Achilles Smith. A great disturbance."

The boxer considered then dismissed any notions this hokum peddler could have harmed his sister. "I gotta get gone." With that he quit the rooming house.

Morbilus addressed the widow in a calm, reassuring tone. "Please Missus, tell me what's happened."

Mrs. Gasparento sighed audibly and told him what she knew.

—*m*—

DECIMATOR SMITH WENT TO the Golden Bough Funeral Home on San Pedro, driving past the construction site of the new Coca-Cola bottling plant on Central Avenue. It was a Streamline Modern structure designed like a landlocked boat. Diagonally across the street was Engine Company Number 30, an all-black fire fighting unit, one of two in the city. At the funeral home he talked with the night man on duty there, the semi-retired Reverend Milton Harshaw. The one thing Negroes had in common with white folks, the preacher was wont to say, was dying at peculiar hours.

Smith had interrupted his late night snack of a hogshead cheese sandwich with a side of brandy. After his condolences and a brief prayer the holy man insisted on doing for her soul, the middleweight made the various burial arrangements, including the pick-up of his sister's body at the coroner's lab. He paid with his winning from that night's fight.

"I would be honored if you would let me speak at her send off, Decimator."

"That would be fine, Reverend." They shook hands. Arriving at his apartment, Smith found Rocco Kaufman waiting for him on the street in his battered Plymouth coupe. His trainer joined him on the sidewalk. He carried a bottle wrapped in a paper bag.

"You didn't have to come here, Rocco."

"Sure I did," the older man said, clapping the younger man on the shoulder. He held aloft the bottle. "Let's have a few belts. Your trainer's orders."

They went inside and Kaufman poured whiskey in two water glasses the boxer retrieved from the cupboard. They clinked them together sitting angled to each other in two secondhand club chairs in the living room. There was a Zenith radio in a walnut cabinet in the corner, and a range of books from W.E.B. DuBois to Roman history to the controversial *Nigger Heaven* novel by the white Carl Van Vechten on a built-in bookcase.

"You're not going to let this go, are you?" His trainer asked, after taking a sip.

"I can't, Rocco. I couldn't abide myself if I just sat around. You the one taught me to always take the fight to my opponent."

The older man nodded, looking off then back at the young pugilist.

"Remind me to call Abe later, okay?"

Smith frowned. "Your brother? The kind of...out there one I met that time?"

Kaufman smiled thinly. "The one and only."

They drank and talked some more and wound up sleeping in their clothes in the chairs. The following morning Smith, bathed, hatted, shaven and in the one suit he owned, wearing black wool socks with dark blue clocks on them, went up the drive of a tree shaded two-story castle-like mansion of stained glass windows and two turrets in Los Feliz. He parked in the roundabout and thumped the door with the lion headed knocker on the large front door.

"Yes?" said a black maid in her uniform who opened the door. She eyed him suspiciously.

In a voice cold and flat he said, "I'm the brother of Helena Smith. I'd like to talk to Mrs. Harcourt about her. You see she was killed and I'm looking into her murder."

The maid gaped at him and stammered, "Hold on." She pushed the door to but not to catch and went to tell her employer. Momentarily she returned. "This way, please."

Smith took his hat off and followed her into a tiled hallway through a dark wood paneled dining room the size of his apartment and into a back yard, garden really, of various colorful flowers and plants. He expected to find a frail old woman possibly in a wheelchair, wrapped in layers of shawls. Instead he did find an elderly thin woman but she stood with the aid of a cane, while another maid, this one Mexican-American, stood close by. She too eyed Smith with wariness.

"Thank you, Garacella," Mrs. Harcourt said. "Please sit, young man. I believe you're a boxer. Helena was quite proud of you, said you were also taking classes over at the city college too."

"She made me, Ma'am. She knew I couldn't box forever." Regret came and went behind his eyes. The maid drifted off but Smith had the impression she remained in earshot.

The old woman indicated a set of wicker chairs and each sat in one at a matching table. On it was an open pack of Home Run cigarettes, a crystal ashtray and a fancy silver lighter. "Would you care for anything to drink?"

"No, I'm fine. I just wanted to ask you a few questions about my sister."

"And you say she was murdered?"

"Yes, Mrs. Harcourt." For the second time in less that twenty-four hours he retold what he knew of the details of her death.

"Oh, my, that's simply ghastly," the elderly woman said. "Poor girl. I would like to help you, really, but, I can't see how. Surely what happened to her has something to do with, well," she cast her gaze sideways momentarily, "with well, where you people live," she breathed. "One hears these stories on the radio I'm afraid." She looked at him for confirmation.

Decimator Smith almost snorted but kept a straight face. "I'm not ignoring that angle, Ma'am. But did any man come around here bothering her or did she get a call maybe one of your maids overheard?"

She made a dismissive wave. "Oh, nothing like that, no. Helena came, attended to me and that was that."

He gestured with his hat in his hand. "Maybe I could ask them, the maids I mean."

"I already said that didn't happen." She looked toward her cigarettes.

"How was it you hired my sister?"

Her solicitous faced slipped back into place. "Why that was because of my son, Van...Dr. Van Harcourt. He's a physicist at Cal Tech you see. He does very important work. He'd mentioned given my recent operation it might be a good idea to have a nurse on duty at certain times until I fully recovered."

"How did he find her?"

"Oh, I wouldn't know about such things. I'm sure through some registry or whatever it is nurses have." She jutted a chin in the direction of some gloves and pruning shears laying on the ground. "Now, I'm sorry, but I must get back to my flowers. They need me."

Smith was on his feet. "I'd like to talk to your son, Mrs. Harcourt."

She smiled. "He's quite busy. But leave your number with Olphelia and we'll see. Good day and again, I mourn your loss."

Suddenly both maids were there and he followed the black one back to the front door. "I want to leave my number," he said.

The maid snickered. "Mr. Van ain't got no time to call regular white folks let alone a spook."

"Your missus said I could."

The woman all but rolled her eyes but went away, then returned with a fountain pen and folded envelope. He wrote his name and phone number on the envelope, then added a 'regarding' and his sister's name. He blew on his handwriting to dry the ink, and handed it back to the maid. She pocketed the information and waved toward the door. Smith let himself out and drove away. The base of the driveway was blocked by a DeSoto parked sideways across it. Two white men stood near the car. The larger of the two had his foot on the bumper of the DeSoto. Shutting off the engine, Smith got out of his Ford.

"You lost, boy?" The larger one said, taking his foot off the bumper.

"I know where I'm going," the boxer said.

"You say Mister when you're talking to a white man," the second one said. He wore a black shirt under a dark brown jacket and grey tie.

Smith moved so as not to get pinned between the two.

The larger man advanced, jabbing a finger at him. "Whatchu doing around here bothering Mrs. Harcourt, snowflake? Huh? Get on back to your side of town, Smith."

The man outweighed him by at least thirty pounds and he wasn't flabby. There was no sense wasting time talking. Decimator Smith stepped right into him and unleashed two rapid punches at the man's mid-section, doubling him over.

"You black bastard," he wheezed, scrambling forward, getting his arms around Smith's legs. The two fell back against his Ford and untangled. The other man charged forward, reaching into his inner coat pocket for his gun.

"I'll put my gat on him, Paul."

The big one, Paul, glared at his companion. "You telling me I can't take this dinge?"

"It ain't that, Paul, it's just we're supposed to, you know..."

"Nix, I said, nix. I got this bo." Paul came around swinging but Smith was too fast and easily ducked his first heavy blows. His assailant had assumed the pugilist would resort to ring tactics and therefore he'd have the advantage with street brawling techniques. But where Achilles Smith grew up in Galveston, running errands for his dad and Quill Lacouix's casino and sporting house at twelve, he'd learned to be a scrapper.

Paul grazed him with a right but Smith wasn't about to get into a boxing match. Particularly not with the other man itching to use his gun. He kicked out with his heel and clipped the one called Paul in the center of his knee.

The big man yelled, stumbling forward. Smith brought an overhand right down on the side of his face and just as quickly, followed with a right uppercut. Paul reeled as the gunman drew his .38.

Smith got his arms around the larger man and drove him toward his partner. The other man tried to move aside but got tangled up and all three went down.

"This goddamn jig," the gunman swore. He was on the bottom of the pile, pushing at his buddy Paul on top of him.

Smith clapped the larger man's ears and he cried out, gritting his teeth, grabbing at the middleweight. But Smith rolled and up on his feet, punched at the gunman's face with a rain of blows, making him woozy. He grabbed the gun from his loosened grip and got to his feet.

"You better give me that roscoe," Paul demanded, also rising.

Calmly Smith clubbed the large man on the head twice with the body of the revolver, sending him to the ground bleeding and senseless. He then grabbed the other man and threw him into the side of the DeSoto. He put fearful unfocused eyes on the contender.

"What are you going to do?"

"Who had you staking out the old lady?" Smith came closer, the gun leveled on the man. "Her son? How come?"

"I can't tell you that."

Smith slugged him and he wilted.

"Keep away from me."

"Who?"

He tried to run and Smith yanked him back by the yoke of his jacket, twirling him around against the front of the DeSoto and onto the ground. Nearby Paul groaned but didn't get up.

"I'm going to ask it one more time and you better give me some answers."

The man began to stammer and Smith jammed the hood's right arm in between the DeSoto's extended bumper and its grill. Smith put his foot on the elbow. "You want them to start calling you Lefty?" He put pressure on the arm.

The hood talked. He didn't know much, but he knew enough.

Smith then drove over to the *Eagle* on Central Avenue. Along with the *Sentinel*, it was one of two black weeklies in town. He'd come to see a boxing fan and reporter he knew named Loren Miller. Miller was a graduate of Howard University. He was attending law school at night and traveled in various circles.

"He's an egghead," Miller told him in his closet of an office after Smith laid out what had happened during the last twenty-four hours. "Van Harcourt teaches physics at Cal Tech in Pasadena. Brilliant, he's big on Buck Rogers stuff, figuring out how to build space ships to the Moon and Mars."

His friend paused, worrying the stem of his lit pipe against his teeth. "But he's supposed to be some kind of witchdoctor too. I've been sitting on a story for a year now from a colored gal, a maid who had to clean up after one of his occult sessions or some such at his house. But if we ran the story, given his family's rich, he'd sue and shut us down lickety-split."

"You talking about devil worship?" Smith asked.

His friend raised his eyebrows. "I don't rightly know, man, but I do know you better keep your country ass away from him."

Smith rose and put his hat back on. "I'll see you, Loren."

"I ain't foolin' Des."

"Neither am I."

Feeling edgy, Smith needed a tune up. He next went to the Broadway Gym where he trained between bouts. He greeted several of the fighters inside as he headed to his locker. There was a pay phone near the lockers and he used it to check in with Rocco Kaufman, telling him of his progress.

Kaufman said on the other end of the line when he told him about the thugs working for Van Harcourt, "Oh brother, like it or not, I guess you're in deep now, Des."

"Yep," the boxer opined.

He was an hour into his routine, sweating, skipping rope vigorously for coordination purposes, when Rocco Kaufman entered. With him was a lean balding man with owlish glasses hefting a large Gladstone luggage bag. Smith recognized his trainer's brother, Abe.

"Sorry about your sister, Decimator," the older Kaufman said, sticking out his hand. It was stained with various chemicals and burned in two spots.

" 'Preciate that," Smith said, shaking the other man's hand.

"Let's go in the back," Kaufman said, jerking his head in that direction.

The three did so. There they gathered in an office that technically didn't belong to Kaufman, but due to his boxer's rising status, he was allowed to use unmolested. Rocco Kaufman closed the door as Abe Kaufman put the suitcase on a scarred wooden table and undid the latches.

Rocco Kaufman said, "As you know, Des, my brother is something of an inventor."

"Rocco figures you could use a few of my items."

Smith was fascinated by the odd-looking contents of the case, which included several handguns as well. "This is your hobby?"

"Not exactly," the older brother said. "When I was back east, I did some work for a few vigilante types you might say. I belonged to a kind of a loose association of scientists who helped out the best way we could."

"You heard of that bloodthirsty joker with the weird laugh and slouch hat in New York?" Rocco Kaufman said. "Abe designed a few gadgets for him through his operatives."

"I'll be," Smith said. He'd picked up a .45 in the case and began expertly disassembling it.

"Where'd you learn that?' his trainer said.

"In between carousing, Daddy managed to teach me a few things," Smith uttered offhandedly as he reassembled the gun.

Abe Kaufman rubbed his hands together. "Then let me show you a few other things, Mr. Smith."

—◆—

THE NEXT DAY, DIGGING around for as much information as he could glean about Van Harcourt, Decimator Smith stopped for a sandwich to go at a café he frequented on Gage near Figueroa after a trip to the library. The counterman nicknamed Toolie handed him a folded slip of paper as he sat on a stool.

"Loren Miller's been looking for you, Champ."

"Thanks Toolie."

Smith read the note and whistled. Later, he went to the mortuary to view his sister's body in its coffin. Fresh gardenias and orchids scented the room.

"I don't have the right words, Helena," he said, standing over her. "I never would have made it out of Galveston but for you. Pushing me to not be like Dad, to imagine what life could bring for us." He teared up and wiped at his eyes with a handkerchief. He sat in a folding chair and remained still for some time. He wasn't sure what was ahead, but he was determined to see it through.

The smartly designed split-level house was partially built into the hill it crested. The house was of angular lines, plate glass windows and chrome flourishes. There were various cars parked about as there was a large irregularly shaped gravel area for this purpose adjacent to the home. There were also at least four men on guard duty Decimator Smith counted. But he hadn't driven up the path to the house like the other visitors. He was crashing the party and had scouted the location by ascending on foot through the greenery decorating a side of the hill.

Smith wondered if Loren Miller, who'd done some recent legwork of his own looking into Harcourt's shenanigans, had been misinformed -- that he'd come upon a house party the physicist was throwing. But he heard no laughter, no tinkling of glasses from within. Then he spotted four men in purple robes, two each carrying a nude woman, tied and gagged, down a less steep rise than the hill to a wooded area. The women, one blonde the other dark-haired, were terrified and the men smiling. He also saw a robed and masked figure handing a hip flask to a stocky man who drank from it. A light breeze flapped his coat open revealing a shoulder holster underneath. Smith concluded he was one among several guards.

Smith circled around. At this time of year fortunately there were not too many dry leaves on the ground so he could proceed noiselessly. Through a gap in some brush, he could also see the drivers of the cars, some in similar purple robes and some in their regular clothes, entering a cave. He recognized an L.A. city council member, a couple of movie actors and an actress among the gathered.

Scanning, he spotted a Japanese face and another colored man in the bunch, so he took the chance that even though these integrated idolaters, as his grandmother would've called them, probably knew each other, maybe some came and went in the group. In the center of the cave were two raised slabs carved from rock. There was also boxy equipment with gauges and dials about, including two large conical-shaped electrical coil towers, which struck Smith like something out of a Flash Gordon serial.

Smith had simply come in with the last of the thirty some odd people traipsing into the cavern. Several were chanting and not paying him any attention anyway, as all eyes were on Harcourt in his black robe. Smith kept his hat low, watching.

"We are gathered because we believe," Harcourt was saying, "we will do what others have attempted but with no success for they were not given the light from the ancient one. For it is marrying science and the arcane that we will open the gateway and the lord above all lords will walk among us again. But first we must mark his way by the serpent of fire," he intoned.

Around Smith people began chanting, "Ze-uhl-co-tal, Zi-uhl-co-tal," along with other phrasings he didn't get, but he pretended to chant them too.

The women had been secured spread eagle with rope tied to iron rings in the raised slabs, the stone altars. A middle-aged man in a gray robe turned on the machinery and bolts of electricity surged between the coil towers. In between the towers was a row of tall oval beakers with various chemicals in them along a metal table. Copper tubing dipped in and out of these chemical baths and in turn, wire led from the tubing to the machinery. In the center was a large loop antenna some eight feet in diameter.

Van Harcourt produced a stone blade with an emerald handle. "And so it is wrought."

The people around Smith began to sway and act like they were possessed. He went along with this, working his way forward. The altars were each constructed with a channel next to the women's throats that let out on its side down below to wooden bowls.

Electricity crackled between the two towers. The crowd chanted and gesticulated and the two sacrifices tried vainly to get free. Close now, Smith could see the sweat on Harcourt and the possessed look on his face as he cried out, "Oh, Master, oh Moyocoya, with blood as the catalyst, I will open the celestial gate for the arrival of your familiar and our supplication." Inside the loop of the antenna a blue haze materialized. Behind this was an indistinct shape.

He bent forward to cut the first throat and Smith shot off two rounds in the air from the .45 he'd brought under his leather jacket. Some of the people fled, others remained, unsure of what to do.

"Smith," Harcourt rasped.

The gray robed figure jumped the boxer from behind, knocking the gun out of his hand. But he broke free of his grasp and a combination sent the older man to the ground, down and out.

Harcourt dove for the gun as did Smith. They grappled, Harcourt stronger than Smith had anticipated. The knife flashed toward his body and he got a hold of the other man's wrist to stop it.

"We must kill this defiler," Harcourt yelled. Several of the followers, one of them in a mask, rushed forward but Smith got a jab in, disorienting Harcourt. One of the others pulled on Smith, inadvertently helping him up. The prizefighter easily blocked a punch from this man and hit him very hard in his solar plexus. As he gasped for breath, Smith shoved another man, an actor he'd seen in horse operas, who'd picked up the automatic.

"Let me show you what to do with that, Tex," Smith cracked. He punched him and snatched the gun loose and fired it into the machinery. There was a spewing cascade of sparks and bolts, and the chemicals in the beakers caught fire as the electricity short-circuited. The blue haze evaporated inside the antenna's loop. For the briefest of moments, it seemed a reptilian face poked through but then that too was gone. A trick of the flickering light Smith told himself.

He had several large capsules on him and he threw these all around. Abe Kaufman called them his electro grenades. They exploded in tight puffs of smoke and sparks. But the floating dark clouds the devices left behind gave off electrical charges of tiny lightning bolts that surged into and knocked out several participants.

"Interloper," Harcourt said, charging with the knife raised.

Smith shot him, dead center in the chest. He thudded onto the ground. What was left of the conscious demonists ran, except the robed figure in the mask. Smith shook his head in disbelief. Eccentric white physicist dead at the hands of crazed Negro was how the headlines would read, he foresaw.

"Good work, Des,"

Open-mouthed he stared at the masked figure who revealed herself.

"Zora," he whispered.

"He killed Helena. He was quite taken with her after she came to work for his mother. They started dating." Zora Montclair came closer. "But because of the race mixing they both agreed to keep it quiet for awhile. Of course that was before I told her who he really was…who we all are."

Smith was trying to comprehend. "Just what the hell –"

Her knife had been in her sleeve. He hadn't seen it until she stabbed him. Fortunately it wasn't a long blade, but it was effective. She took it out slowly as he staggered back. He had enough strength left to squeeze the trigger but she was on him and a slice to his wrist sent the weapon skittering.

"Bye bye, Achilles. I always was fond of you."

She kissed him briefly and, with a hand to his torso, pushed him into the table of beakers and electrical wiring. He crashed into the chemicals and as he fell over, wires crackled in the solution that washed over him as he lay on his side. He was jolted with voltage and his body shook and smoked. Zora Montcalir departed, whistling a tune.

Smoke and flame consumed the cavern. The two women remained bound to the altars. One of the towers had fallen on part of the slab holding the dark-haired one, discharging electrical current that threatened to strike her. Smith willed himself upright. Bleeding, unsteady on his feet, he nonetheless was able to pick up the stone blade, and used it to push the leaning tower away, snapping the upper portion of the blade.

But there was enough of its rough edge left for him to saw at the rope and get one hand free of the dark-haired captive. She looked worried but kept her head. The blonde screamed hysterically. He sagged against the altar, weakened and then he fell over, blacking out.

—⁂—

"YOU SEE, NO CAUSE for alarm," he heard a familiar voice say. Decimator Smith opened his eyes.

"How do you feel?" It was the smiling face of the dark haired woman he'd last seen tied to Harcourt's sacrificial altar. Next to her was Elijah Morbilus. He held an empty cylindrical glass bottle, smiling oddly.

Smith sat up. He was in pajamas in his bed. "I feel okay." He could tell his lower torso was wound with gauze over a bandage where the knife wound was. "Not that I'm complaining, but how did I get here?"

Rocco Kaufman said, "You can thank Anna for that."

Smith looked at the dark haired woman.

She said, "You got my hand free and I was able to use the stone knife to get me and the other woman fully loose."

'"Who was she?"

She made a face. "Couldn't say really. She ran out of there in her birthday suit as soon as I cut her loose. She's probably still running."

"Only Miss Borsage didn't quit on you, Achilles," Kaufman said. "You were out on your feet but she got you out of there and hid you in the bushes, doing her best to stop the bleeding."

Smith looked at the pretty woman, each holding their gaze on the other a beat or two longer than proper. "So what happened?"

For an answer, Morbilus showed him a copy of the morning's *Herald Examiner*. There was a front page picture of Van Harcourt's house with a picture of him and the burned out cave as inset shots. There was also an article about war news from Europe.

The faith healer said, "In the article, Councilman Mayfair, Judge Gainer and a couple of others were rumored to be at the ceremony."

Smith asked, "Hey, what about those guards I saw? I wondered why they never rushed into the cave when the commotion started."

"They were doped," Borsage said.

"Right, I saw Zora in her mask giving a guard a drink." Smith got out of bed and put on his boxing robe, his ring name stenciled in an arc in big letters on his back.

"So Zora hips me to Harcourt because she wanted him out of the way to take over, right?"

"More like getting both of you out of the way at the same time we figure," Kaufman said.

Smith turned to Anna Borsage. "So you're one of those demon lovers?"

"Not hardly. I made the mistake of being sweet on Rex Stampton and he put a mickey in my coffee. Next thing I knew I was in my all-together about to be skewered."

Smith nodded. Stampton was the movie cowboy he'd slugged.

"Good thing you had a membership card in your wallet from the Broadway Gym," Anna Borsage said. "I called over there and they got a hold of Mr. Kaufman."

Rocco Kaufman said, "I was scared to death last night by the time me and the young lady managed to sneak you back here and not get nabbed by the cops." He had his hands in his back pockets, the way he talked when matters weighed on his mind. "I couldn't take a chance on taking you to a hospital, what with the fire, all that Boris Karloff business that went on up in the hills, not to mention a dead rich white man you might have to answer for."

The boxer and his trainer exchanged wan smiles. Kaufman continued, "So I sewed you up."

"And I administered certain medicines learned in the East," Morbilus said, bowing slightly.

Smith had to admit he didn't feel too bad, considering. "So what was all that hooey in the cave?" He remembered the reptile face but again dismissed it as a trick of the mind.

"Blackmail essentially," Borsage said, indicating the newspaper folded over on the bed. "The machinery were fancy props. Harcourt had cameras hidden around the cave to photograph the councilman, the judge and a few others at the supposed summoning of the fire serpent. They'd be willing accomplices in murder."

"Why?" Smith said.

"Harcourt invested in various projects like housing developments and factories. He wanted strings pulled and favors met," Borsage illuminated.

Smith noted, "You sound like you know what you're talking about."

"Anna's something of a philanthropist," Kaufman offered.

She added, "Every once in awhile, I'd run into Harcourt at this or that dinner party. He was quite witty and charismatic when talking about the occult. Those in the cave had fallen under his sway."

Smith folded his arms. "But Zora got away and I bet that means there's more of these occult types she's going to use for what she wants."

There was silent agreement of his assessment.

—॰॰—

AFTER HIS SISTER'S FUNERAL, the mourners gathered for a repast in the dining hall in the Mount Olive Methodist Church on Avalon. Plainclothes detective Percy Kimbrough talked to Smith.

"So this missing Zora Montclair twist was tied up in all this black magic mumbo-jumbo?"

"Seems so." Smith sipped his punch. "Heard this Harcourt had a nest egg of his dead daddy's money socked away and now it's gone too."

Kimbrough regarded him. "Stampton, that movie cowboy facing the chair for kidnapping, he swears he recognized you as shooting Van Harcourt."

"Only the woman he drugged swears it wasn't me," Smith mentioned.

It helped too the .45 he used burned in the fire, destroying fingerprints.

Kimbrough added, "We also found that other dame who was trussed up and she says that you, or some colored fella, got stabbed."

Smith hunched a shoulder, "You know them ofays get us spades all mixed up, Detective. "If I was there and got knifed, I'd be all sown up and sore wouldn't I?" He unbuttoned the lower part of his shirt to show there weren't wrappings around his abdomen. Whatever it was that Morbilus had given him had healed him fast.

Kimbrough pursed his lips. "Had to check, you know."

"No sweat. See you around, man." Smith buttoned his shirt as he walked off to compliment Reverend Harshaw on his eulogy. As Kimbrough left, passing him as he entered was Achilles' father, Gus Smith. He wore a black suit with wide pin-stripes and two-tone, black and white shoes. He carried a battered suitcase strapped closed and was unshaven. Father and son spotted each other.

"Sorry, I meant to get here sooner." He dropped the bag and put his arms around his son's shoulders. "I can't believe this happened to my baby girl."

The younger man returned the gesture. "It's been handled, Dad."

There were creases in the corners of Gus Smith's eyes but otherwise his handsome face remained unblemished. "Yeah?"

"He's thinking about getting out of the fight game and taking up a different line of work," Kaufman said.

"Hey, Rocco," the elder Smith said, shaking the trainer's hand.

"Could be," Decimator Smith said.

"What are you two going on about?"

"Come on," Decimator Smith said to his father. "Let's get something to eat and I'll tell you about it."

"Okay, son."

Walking to the table laid out with food, they passed Elijah Morbilus who nodded to the two men. "Father and son back together, excellent."

"Who's the junior grade Lugosi?" his father asked in a low voice as they went on.

"My spiritual advisor."

"Huh?"

Decimator Smith laughed for the first time in a week.

MTIMU

BY CHARLES R. SAUNDERS

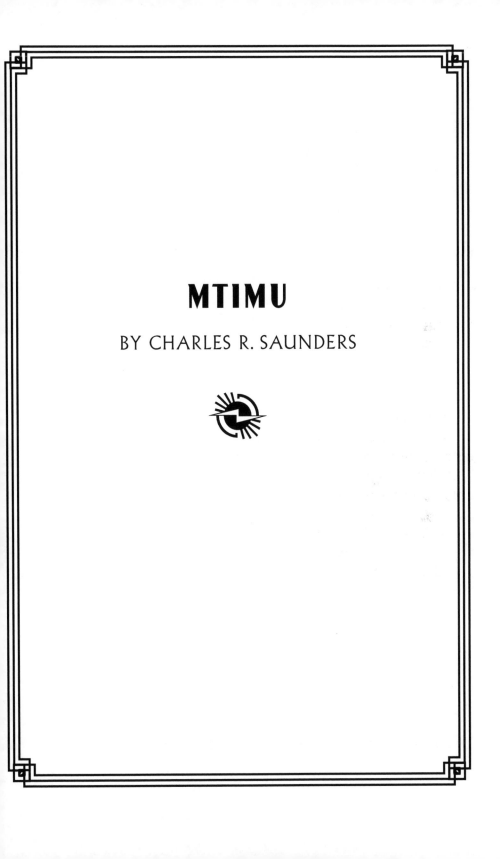

A GROWL WAS COMING from the sky. It was a sound unlike any other that had ever before reached the ears of the man in the trees – not in the sky, or in the trees, or on the ground. He stood, balancing carefully amid the uppermost branches, his hand holding a half-eaten piece of one of the fruits that hung abundantly around him. Peering upward through a thin lattice of leaves, he quickly discerned the source of the strange sound.

His keen vision revealed that the growling thing was no bird. Not only did birds not growl; they did not leave long trails of smoke behind them like the wake of a crocodile in a river. The not-bird would have appeared as little more than a speck to ordinary eyes. The watcher's eyes, however, were far from ordinary.

As the growl grew louder, the other sounds of the jungle diminished. The chattering of the pack of monkeys with whom the watcher had been sharing his feast of fruit ceased. Birds paused in their singing and fluttered down to perches beneath the leaves to conceal themselves from whatever this *thing* was that had suddenly usurped their domain. Only the insects continued their chorus – a sound that reminded the watcher of the noise made by the unthinkable object that was descending from the sky.

Abruptly, the growling broke into a series of sputtering coughs, like the sounds that might have been made by a choking elephant. Moments later, the coughs stopped, and the not-bird continued to descend in eerie silence.

The watcher could see the creature – if it could be called that – more clearly now, even though it was still far higher in the air than he could shoot an arrow. He was aware that it was larger than any bird could be. Its wings were widespread, like those of a soaring eagle. But they were rigid in a way that was unnatural. Its tail looked like a second smaller pair of wings. There was no head that the watcher could discern … only a flat front against which something – *a beak?* – twirled slowly. Its feet were round, with no discernable claws.

Still descending, smoke still trailing, the not-bird drifted into the distance. The watcher followed its flight. Then he made a decision – an instant one, as all choices in the jungle had to be.

Tossing aside his fragment of fruit, the watcher dropped to a lower tier of branches. Then he began to traverse the spaces between the trees, heading in the direction in which the incomprehensible object was gliding. Curiosity winning out over instinctive caution, the monkeys followed.

So did other watchers, coming from a different direction …

—ᘉ—

"**D**AMMIT, DAMMIT, DAMMIT!" ENID Brown swore as she suppressed an overwhelming urge to repeatedly bang her fists against the instrument panel of her aircraft.

The ship was a brand new Fairchild single engine monoplane. And it was falling out of the sky over an unknown part of Africa, the continent over which she was attempting a non-stop solo flight from Cairo, Egypt, to Cape Town, South Africa. If successful, she would be the first woman pilot to have accomplished that feat – and the first colored woman in the bargain.

Now, she was about to become a dead colored woman, lost forever in a godforsaken jungle that had never been explored.

But Enid Brown had no intention of going out easily, even as the treetops that had rolled beneath her like a vast green carpet at a higher altitude swiftly turned into an array of spikes waiting to rip the Fairchild – and her – into pieces.

Only moments before, Enid's thoughts had risen along with her aircraft. Ever since she was a child, she had dreamed of continuing the trail blazed by Bessie Coleman, the first black woman pilot of note, who had passed away nearly ten years before. She also longed to match the achievements of Amelia Earhart, the white darling of the aviation world.

The Cape-to-Cairo flight would be the first step …

Then the engine sputtered, spewed smoke … and failed. Now Enid was struggling to maintain a controlled glide downward. The good news was her speed had diminished. The bad news was that wouldn't mean anything if she didn't soon find a space on which she could land.

So far, the barrier of treetops remained unbroken. Then she saw it – an immense giant of the forest, with top branches that spread outward like the fingers of a huge, open hand.

Hope flared in Enid's heart at the sight of the anomaly. If she could slow her glide … if she could find an angle that would lessen the impact … she just might survive this crash landing. She could not afford to spare a thought about what would happen afterward.

"Lord help me," she muttered as she fought the controls. The tree's fingers waited to catch her.

—⚏—

CONSCIOUSNESS RETURNED ABRUPTLY. ENID blinked as bright sunlight streamed into her eyes. Her head ached, and her arms and legs felt as though they had been twisted by a professional wrestler. Still, she was alive.

Cautiously, she climbed out of the broken cockpit. The branches of the huge tree swayed dangerously under her feet, causing her to cling to the wreckage until the movement stopped. She looked at the Fairchild. Its wings and tail were gone, and the front of its fuselage was crumpled like a tin can that had been shoved against a brick wall. That she had emerged intact from such a horrific wreck was, indeed, a miracle.

"Thank you, Lord," she said softly.

Now, she needed at least two more miracles: one to get her down from the tree; the other to get her out of the jungle.

Before Enid could begin to contemplate the precariousness of her plight, she heard a low growl coming from behind her.

Dread knotted Enid's stomach as she turned to face the maker of that ominous sound. A scream caught in her throat as she stared wide-eyed at the nightmare image of a huge black leopard poised at the juncture between the trunk of the tree and the branches that had snared her and her aircraft. The beast's claws dug into the wood. Its eyes blazed like baleful amber lamps, and white fangs glistened in the red, snarling maw of its mouth.

Then the leopard sprang, and the scream Enid had throttled burst loudly from her throat. Without thinking, she let go of the wreckage and dropped downward a split second before the leopard's claws raked across the space she had occupied.

Still screaming, Enid plummeted, bouncing painfully from the lower branches while scrabbling to find some sort of handhold. From the periphery of her vision, she could see the shadowy shape of the leopard bounding downward as fast as she was falling.

One of Enid's hands finally caught something … and held, nearly wrenching her shoulder out of its socket. Her fall halted, she reached up with her other hand to secure her grasp on a branch that was, thankfully, thick enough to bear her weight without breaking.

She looked down, and realized she was still too high above the ground. If she fell again, she was certain she would end up with more than just broken bones. The irony that she could survive the crash of an airplane into a tree, only to die in a fall from that same tree, was not lost on her.

Then she again heard the chilling growl of the leopard. She turned her head toward the sound. The great cat was creeping toward her. Its movements were slow and deliberate, as though the beast derived pleasure from prolonging the terror it induced in its prey.

An overwhelming wave of despair washed through Enid then. Two pathways to death confronted her: falling to serious injury or death, or being eaten alive by the approaching leopard. The latter fate was unthinkable. Gathering what remained of her willpower, Enid prepared herself to let go of the branch …

Suddenly, a huge, dark shape plunged onto the leopard and swept the yowling beast off the tree limb. Reflexively, Enid's fingers tightened the grip she'd been about to release. Dazed by the latest in an unrelenting series of shocks, she looked down just as the two falling figures hit the ground with a thump that was softer than she would have expected.

She could see that the interloper had landed on top of the leopard. Yet the impact appeared to have had little effect on either. Immediately, they began to roll across the jungle floor in deadly combat. The leopard's angry snarls reached Enid's ears – as did those of the interloper, which were different in timbre.

From the height at which she dangled, the airwoman could barely discern the form of the interloper. It seemed manlike and almost as dark as the leopard's pelt. But as far as she knew, men did not growl … yet at the same time, beasts did not wield shining objects like the one that plunged again and again into the body of the great cat.

Soon the leopard's snarls ceased, and its struggles ended. The shape of the interloper detached itself from that of its victim. Then the interloper – Enid's rescuer – stood erect.

A man, Enid observed. *A black man ...*

The man raised his head, but he did not look at Enid. A strange outcry burst from his throat. At first, it seemed to be the call of some sort of animal – perhaps an ape. Listening more closely, however, Enid could discern distinct syllables, as though the sound were some kind of chant or song.

As the echoes of the outcry died down, Enid abruptly realized that the strain of hanging on to the limb by her fingertips had become unbearable. Distracted by the battle below, she had – if only briefly – remained oblivious to the downward pull of her weight. Though she was a reasonably fit and athletic woman, she was neither an acrobat nor a gymnast. Inexorably, her fingers were losing their hold.

As she felt her grasp slipping, Enid cursed at the unfairness of her predicament. There was no way her mysterious rescuer could scale the tree quickly enough to prevent her from falling. Despite all her desperate efforts, she was still going to die ...

Enid could not hold on any longer. She screamed all the way down – until a pair of powerful arms caught her and broke her fall.

Only for a moment did she remain in the embrace of her rescuer. Then she squirmed out of his arms and stepped back to look at him. At a subtle, unconscious level, she comprehended that he had allowed her to pull away from his grasp. He could have held her as easily as though she were a child, had he so desired.

He was, indeed, a black man. At first, Enid thought he was naked. Then she realized that he was clad in a garment of black leopard hide that covered his loins. Although at ten inches over five feet Enid was uncommonly tall for a woman, the man stood a good half foot taller.

His leanly muscled frame was devoid of the ornamentation and scarification that prevailed among the natives of Central Africa. His face was quintessentially Negroid: broad nose, fully everted lips, wooly black hair forming a shot cap on his head. Black irised eyes gazed at her intently ... curiously.

Enid wondered what the mind behind those eyes was thinking. Although the crash had left her thoroughly disheveled, her looks had often been favorably compared to those of Lena Horne, the popular colored singer and actress. But Enid's skin was several shades darker than that of the entertainer, and she harbored no desire to try her luck in show business, which was to her mind far riskier than aviation.

Chattering noises suddenly claimed her attention, and she remembered the bestial growls her rescuer had uttered while battling the leopard. Looking down, she saw that several monkeys had gathered at the tall man's feet. Their pelts were long and black, save for a white fringe around their faces and strips of white that descended from their shoulders to the tips of their tails. They stared up at her, curiosity wrinkling their small faces.

A white-toothed smile flashed against the ebony background of the man's face. Annoyance at his apparent amusement flashed in Enid's mind, and she was about to put it in words. But before she could say anything, the man suddenly tensed, crouched, turned away from her, and seemed ready to spring into action.

A faint, zipping noise reached Enid's ears a moment before the man clutched at his throat and staggered. After a second, similar sound, she felt a sharp jab on her neck. Immediately, the jungle scene whirled before her eyes, and her legs folded as though their bones had turned into rubber.

The last sound she heard before consciousness fled was the screeching of the black-and-white monkeys as they scattered back into the trees.

—ᴥ—

FOR THE SECOND TIME in a momentous day, Enid's eyelids fluttered open. This time, though, the pain behind her eyes had subsided to a dull ache, and her cuts and abrasions carried less sting.

The illumination that greeted her awakening was not steady sunshine. Instead, it flickered like the light shed by candles or lanterns. As she looked up, she saw that she was inside the walls of a large tent. The softness beneath her indicated that she was lying on bedding rather than the ground.

As Enid gazed around to try to ascertain where she was, her breath suddenly caught, and her body jerked in surprise. She saw a stool carved from a single block of wood to her right – the side that faced away from the flap of canvas that hung over the entrance to the tent. The stool was occupied by a black woman wearing a white uniform.

A nurse's uniform, Enid thought as she looked more closely at the woman. *Complete with cap ...*

The woman's face, as well as the skin the notched collar of her uniform revealed, was etched with an array of tribal scars. The hair beneath the cap spiraled outward in numerous thin, short braids. Her eyes were expressionless as they regarded Enid.

"Who are you?" the airwoman asked. "Where am I?"

The white clad woman stared at her for a moment. Then she pointed to a rough hewn block of wood closer to Enid's bedside. Its flat surface held a platter laden with slices of exotic looking fruit and a carved wooden cup filled with water.

"*Kunya,*" the woman said. "*Isaku.*"

Enid did not understand those words. But she suddenly became aware of how ravenous she was and of an overwhelming thirst as well. Swinging her legs over the side of what she now saw to be a low cot, she drained the contents of the cup and stuffed the fruit slices into her mouth without regard for the niceties of table manners. The white clad woman watched impassively.

More than half the platter's contents had reached Enid's stomach before the entrance flap opened and a man walked into the tent.

—m—

THE SIZE OF THE man who seated himself in a camp chair between Enid's cot and the entrance to the tent approximated that of her rescuer. But that was all the two men had in common. The man in the chair was white and he was clad in a bush outfit that was immaculate, though far from new. A handgun hung in a holster attached to his belt. His pith helmet, which he had removed as soon as he entered the tent, rested in his lap. His close cropped hair was a pale shade of blond that was almost white.

Ice blue eyes dominated his features, which were handsome in a rugged way. Faint seams scored his sunburned skin – a sign that he was beginning to cross the threshold from young manhood to middle age. The faint smile on his lips did not match the evaluative glint in his eyes.

He looked somehow familiar to Enid. As though he were reading her thoughts, the man answered some yet to be spoken questions.

"Welcome back to the waking world," he said in a deep baritone. "I'm Clive Bailey, at your service."

Of course! Enid thought. Clive 'Take 'Em Alive' Bailey, the world's most eminent animal catcher, procurer of specimens ranging from elephants to aardvarks for zoos and circuses in a dozen countries.

"And I'm – " Enid began. But Bailey cut her off.

"Enid Brown, the Blackbird," he said. "The 'Black Amelia Earhart.' The Negress who takes to the skies for the betterment of her race. I read about your planned flight before I came here."

A frown creased Enid's brow. "Negress" was not as offensive to her as another word that began with the letter "n." But she had never liked it. Nor did she particularly care for being called "Blackbird" or "The Black Amelia Earhart," though she respected her fellow airwoman's accomplishments. And she thought she could detect a subtly sardonic undertone in Bailey's polite manner. But she could not be certain. So she let it pass.

"Thank you for … bringing me here," Enid murmured. She'd been about to say "rescuing me." But hadn't the mysterious black man already done that? The moment she thought of him, a swarm of questions sprang into her mind. She voiced the ones that were foremost.

"Why did you shoot me with … whatever it was?" she demanded. "And what happened to the man who saved me from the leopard?"

Bailey's smile broadened as he leaned forward. Unconsciously, Enid leaned a bit backward before catching herself and sitting erect.

"That was for your own safety, Miss Brown," Bailey said. "As for the man … I must thank you for inadvertently leading me to him."

Enid shook her head in confusion.

"I'm not following," she said.

"Tell me, Miss Brown … have you ever heard the name 'Mtimu'?"

"No," Enid replied.

"Few outside this part of Africa ever have," Bailey said. "I heard that name, and the tale behind it, from a wandering native who had fled from a tribal war. It was the story of a black man who lives among the animals in the deepest part of the jungle … a man who avoids contact with other people … a man who speaks in growls rather than words. The natives of the area call him 'Mtimu,' which means 'Wild Man' in the local native dialects.

"From the moment I first heard of this 'Mtimu,' I was determined to capture him alive and put him on display myself, rather than merely allow others to profit from my discovery of a black who – close to the beasts though his kind are – has actually become one."

Enid's frown deepened. She did not like the direction in which Bailey's narrative appeared to be heading. Oblivious to her concern, the animal-catcher continued.

"Recently, I obtained information that indicated Mtimu could be found in this region, which is unknown to white men. I came here – but could not find him, no matter how hard I tried.

"Then I saw your airplane coming down. I went to the site of the crash to provide whatever aid I could to the survivors – if any. And in the back of my mind, I guessed that the crash would arouse the curiosity of the Wild Man, if he were near.

"And I was right! I found you – and Mtimu. I brought both of you down with pellets coated in *onaye*, an African equivalent to curare, fired from an air rifle. *Onaye* is the secret to my success. It's the reason I always 'take 'em alive.'

"I hit you with a pellet because I had no way of knowing what Mtimu might do. He could have killed you the way he did that leopard. Now, thanks to you, Miss Blackbird, I have captured the greatest prize of all!"

Enid's mind reeled as Bailey's words, which were spoken in a shout at the end of his oration, reverberated in the confines of the tent. Of one thing she was sure, though. She did not for a moment believe that the jungle man, 'Mtimu,' could possibly have killed her.

She was also certain that Clive Bailey was out of his mind...

"Stand up, Miss Brown," the animal catcher ordered, all pretense of civility now gone from his demeanor.

"I'm feeling ... faint," Enid said, pressing the back of one hand against her forehead.

A scowl crossed Bailey's features.

"Lulama!" he barked. "*Yakuna-yuo!*"

The woman in the nurse's uniform – Lulama – had been so silent that Enid had momentarily forgotten she was in the tent. Now, strong hands clamped onto the airwoman's shoulders and hauled her to her feet. Before Enid could cry out in protest, Lulama forced her to the flap of the tent's entrance, which Bailey held open with mock courtesy.

"I have something to show you, Miss Brown," he said triumphantly as he and Lulama both pushed her forward.

For a moment, Enid blinked as her eyes adjusted to the wavering light cast by standing torches that fought to hold back the night that pressed against Bailey's encampment. The jungle chorus of animal cries made scant impact on Enid's senses. Nor did the sight of the other tents that made up the encampment, nor the black men and women who went about their duties with sullen expressions on their faces – natives clad in the uniforms of soldiers, cooks, and laborers, scar patterns visible wherever skin showed.

Instead, the airwoman's attention was transfixed by a pair of metal cages in the middle of the clearing that accommodated the encampment. Each of them was large enough to hold a lion. One cage stood empty. The other was occupied.

Enid saw a shadowy form in the occupied cage: a man, squatting and silent, the firelight failing to reveal even a glimmer of eyes or teeth. The man – Mtimu – remained motionless, though Enid could see no signs of chains or any other form of binding.

This man should not be confined like an animal, she thought angrily. Then she looked toward the cage that was empty. Bailey followed her gaze. A mirthless smile curved his thin lips.

"The second cage, little Blackbird, is for you," he said.

—⚓—

MTIMU'S EYES NARROWED AS he saw the woman he had saved from the claws of Ekan the leopard suddenly begin to struggle against her captors. Ever since he had awakened inside this strange nest of sticks that were harder than any wood he had ever encountered among structures unlike any he had seen before, inhabited by people like him who were wearing outlandish garments and one whose skin was paler than any person's should have been, Mtimu had waited with the grim patience of the wild. He'd wanted to know what had happened to the woman who had fallen from the sky in the growling winged beast. She had not been in the nest next to the one that held him. Until she appeared, he remained as still as Ekan would have been, waiting for its quarry to come into view.

Now he saw her. The black woman and the white man holding her tightly, despite her attempts to get away from them. The tone of the man's voice was angry. The woman from the sky's voice betrayed fear. That fear was all Mtimu needed to decide what to do next.

He rose to his feet smoothly, effortlessly, showing no sign of having squatted in one position for the past several hours. He opened his mouth wide, and a series of outcries boomed from his throat, each one different, as though a menagerie were trapped in his body. The cries carried above the noises of the encampment and the jungle.

Sudden silence fell over the encampment as all eyes focused on Mtimu. Even the cacophony of the jungle subsided as Mtimu continued his call, which had changed from animal sounds to vocalizations that were not words, but nonetheless adhered to a discernable pattern.

Abruptly, Mtimu's outcries ceased. For a brief beat, no sound from any source could be heard. Then the encampment erupted in baffled consternation. And the noises from the jungle redoubled in intensity as Mtimu strode to the front of the nest that confined him and grasped two of its sticks in his huge hands.

—⚉—

IT ONLY TOOK A MOMENT – a blink of an eye – for Clive Bailey's rigid control of his encampment to unravel. In that brief passage of time, the jungle erupted, spilling animals like streams of lava from a volcano. Elephants squeezed through gaps between the trees that seemed too small to accommodate the great beasts' bulk. Leopards, both spotted and black, wreaked havoc with their fangs and claws. Monkeys of many breeds swarmed amid the tents, their numbers and sharp teeth compensating for their small size. Simians of a different kind – larger than a chimpanzee but smaller than a gorilla – had also joined the snarling, screeching, trumpeting horde of wildlife.

There was even a lion amid the swarm. Although it was a fully grown male, its mane was thin and the spots of cubhood speckled its legs.

Lions do not belong among trees, Bailey thought oddly.

Yet at least one did, and it was tearing one of Bailey's retainers apart limb from limb.

The strict discipline the animal catcher had instilled among his native staff had disappeared, evaporating like dew on a hot morning. The retainers who were armed tried to defend themselves, but the beasts were too swift, too strong, too numerous. The other natives either died or fled into the jungle, their screams of terror punctuating the chorus of growls and roars.

Only Lulama remained calm. Standing at Bailey's side, the black woman continued to hold Enid in a firm grasp.

Some of the standing torches had been knocked over in the melee. Inevitably, flames from one of them caught the canvas of a nearby tent and quickly engulfed the structure. The resulting fire brightened the illumination in the clearing.

In that lurid orange glare, the attention of Bailey, Enid, and Lulama was fixed on the cage that held Mtimu. Slowly but inexorably, two of its bars were bending outward to create a gap through which a large man could extricate himself.

Finally, Mtimu stepped out of the cage. And he began to make his way through the swirling, howling pandemonium of humans and beasts. He was headed toward the three people who stood at the entrance of the tent across from the cage that had held him. He paused only to pick up a dagger from a fallen native, to replace the one that was gone when he awakened in the cage.

Two of the apes accompanied him. Unlike others of their kind, these anthropoids walked upright. Each of them was nearly as tall as Mtimu, but their legs were shorter than his and they walked with a waddling gait. Still, they kept up with the black man.

It was then that Enid saw her opportunity.

—〰—

THE PROSPECT OF BEING locked in a cage like an animal had unnerved the airwoman. And the attack from the jungle had overwhelmed her senses to the point where she could barely think coherently. Mtimu's escape from his cage, however, had snapped her mind back into clear focus.

At the sight of the nearly naked giant and the two apes approaching, Lulama's grip loosened and she took an involuntary step backward, creating a small space between herself and her captive.

That opening was all Enid needed. She jerked her head backward, and her leather flight helmet smacked hard against Lulama's face. The native woman stumbled for a step, then went down even as Enid wrenched free from her captor's slackened grasp.

Then the airwoman began to run toward Mtimu and his companions. But she didn't manage more than a single stride before Bailey grabbed her by the arm and pulled her to him. The barrel of the gun he had drawn from its holster pressed against the side of her head. She could feel it even through the leather of her helmet.

"Not so fast, little Blackbird," he hissed. "Not so fast …"

Then Bailey turned his attention to Mtimu and the apes, who were now only a few paces away.

"Stay back, or I'll kill her," the animal catcher warned.

He did not know whether or not Mtimu understood his words. He was certain, however, that his actions would convey a plain enough message. But he never knew whether his assumption was right or wrong. For a black-and-white blur suddenly dropped onto his head from the top of the tent. Another fell on Lulama, who had regained her footing.

Crying out in agony, Bailey dropped his gun and released his hold on Enid. Desperately, he tried to tear the biting, clawing, screeching simian away from his head. So did Lulama. Enid immediately rushed toward Mtimu and the apes. For all their fearsome appearance the anthropoids posed, she believed, less of a threat to her than Bailey and Lulama had proved to be. And she did not think Mtimu was a threat to her in any way.

A moment later, she almost rethought that assessment as Mtimu scooped her off her feet, slung her across his shoulder, and sprinted toward the trees. He carried her easily, as though she were made of straw. The pair of apes followed. Then the jungle swallowed them.

The monkeys that had attacked Bailey and Lulama departed as well. So did the rest of the bestial invaders. Only the corpses of the native retainers who had not gotten away and the few animals they had managed to bring down remained as the white man and black woman crouched on the ground, hands clutched to their faces, blood rilling between their fingers.

—⚉—

ISHOULD HAVE PUT my damned helmet back on," Bailey muttered as he blinked in the dim light the remaining torches provided.

At least his eyes had not been damaged by the monkeys' attack. Nor had those of Lulama. The blood on both their faces had dried. As he looked at the wounds on the black woman's visage, the paths of their crusted blood intersecting with the scar patterns on her skin, he wondered how bad his own face looked.

Lulama's nurse's cap was torn and it hung halfway down the side of her head. Blood spattered her white uniform. She stood stolid and silent, waiting for Bailey to tell her what to do. She gave no indication as to what she was thinking.

Do these people even "think" at all? Bailey asked himself as he surveyed the smoking remains of the tents that had caught fire and the strewn body parts of the retainers the beast horde had slain.

He winced and shook his head as he thought about his lost captives. Putting the Wild Man on exhibit would have more than recouped the financial losses he was incurring during a Depression that was getting worse each year, despite the efforts of the new American President. The fortuitous addition of another captive would have redoubled his windfall. He was certain that curiosity to see the Missing Link and his mate would open even the thinnest of wallets.

Of course Enid Brown's appearance would have required a certain amount of … alteration. Her face and body needed to be scarified beyond recognition. Her tongue would have needed reshaping as well, to take away her ability to speak. He would teach Lulama the skills necessary to perform those grisly tasks, which he considered beneath him, but suitable for a savage.

"And you'd enjoy every minute of it, wouldn't you?" the animal catcher whispered to the native woman.

Lulama remained silent.

Bailey's thoughts turned to the unusual beasts that were apparently part of Mtimu's retinue. *Those upright apes … that forest lion …* Neither of those species was known to science. Capturing either or both would add even more to the bounty of wealth and fame he had envisioned when he set out on his hunt for the black Wild Man.

Now, his ambitions lay in ashes. But he was not finished. Not as long as he possessed his uncanny skill for tracking … an inborn ability that impressed even the most proficient native trailers in Africa, Asia, and South America; an ability that had lifted him from obscurity to renown;

an ability that, combined with his blind determination, had pushed him past the edge of sanity ...

"We'll follow them ... and find them," Bailey said. "Gather the guns, Lulama. We'll need rifles – including the air gun and its pellets. We'll need water and food. Get to it."

"*Ndi*," Lulama said with a single nod of her head. "Yes."

She understood English – Bailey had taught the rudiments of the language to all his retainers. But Lulama alone refused to utter a word in the white man's tongue. Bailey could have forced her to do so. However, Lulama had become so useful to him that her intransigence over this one matter was not all that important. He watched while she collected the items he had specified, along with one other for herself: a spear.

"I'm coming for you, Wild Man," Bailey murmured. "And you as well, Little Blackbird."

He went back into his tent to retrieve his pith helmet. Lulama adjusted her torn nurse's cap.

—m—

ENID LOOKED ACROSS THE few feet of space that separated her from Mtimu. It was morning, and sunlight streamed through the canopy of leaves above the bough in which she and the Wild Man were sitting. One of his ape companions remained with him; the other had departed as soon as Mtimu had found this spot the previous night.

Physically and mentally exhausted from her ordeal the day before, she had immediately fallen into a deep slumber, giving less than a moment's thought to the propriety of spending the night with a man who was not her husband – not that she had one.

Now, she observed Mtimu more closely. He peered back at her, his dark eyes gazing calmly. So did the ape. But the creature's eyes were shadowed beneath prominent brow ridges, and Enid could read nothing there. At least neither of the two seemed menacing ...

Then Enid chastised herself for harboring such a thought in connection to the man who had rescued her not once, but twice. Intuitively, she was more certain than ever that Mtimu would never harm her. Still, she needed to find a way to communicate with him, so that she could ask him to get her out of this buzzing, booming chaos of a jungle.

No better time to start than now, she told herself.

Pointing a finger toward herself, she said: "Enid."

Mtimu did not respond.

This is not going to be easy, she thought.

"Enid," she said again, repeating her gesture as well. Then she pointed to the Wild Man.

"Mtimu?" she asked.

"That is one of the names I am known by," the Wild Man replied. "There are others."

Enid had to grab a nearby branch to prevent herself from falling out of the tree.

"You... speak... English!" she sputtered. Not only that, but in the midst of her astonishment, she detected a Southern Negro intonation.

"Why? How?" was all she could add.

Mtimu smiled. The smile was guileless, not mocking. He gestured toward the ape that sat at his side.

"This is Gu-Kor," he said.

The ape opened its mouth in a wide grin that would have been reassuring were it not for the long canine teeth that were thus revealed.

"Gu-Kor does not speak English," Mtimu continued. "He speaks … differently. As to your questions, if you will come with me, I will show you the answers."

Enid looked at him and at the ape called Gu-Kor. The closer she looked at Gu-Kor, the less he resembled the gorillas, chimpanzees, and orangutans she had seen in pictures and zoos. His arms were not as long in relation to his body as those of known anthropoid species, though they were longer than those of a human. His forehead sloped backward, but it was twice as high as that of any known ape. His feet lacked the jutting, thumb like big toe characteristic of apekind. Even so, all his toes were longer and more prehensile than those of a human.

"Have you decided?" Mtimu asked, breaking Enid's concentration on Gu-Kor's anomalies.

There was not much to consider. She felt safer with Mtimu than she had with Clive Bailey even before the mask of sanity had slipped from the animal catcher's mien. And her curiosity in regard to Mtimu's ability to so fluently speak her language was overwhelming.

"So show me, Mr. Mtimu," she said.

He turned and gestured for Enid to climb onto his back. It was the same way he had carried her the night before. She wrapped her arms around his shoulders and hooked her legs about his waist, piggyback style. As soon as her grasp was secure, he leaped from the bough and began swinging with his arms from tree to tree, carrying her as though she were weightless. Gu-Kor preceded them.

Well aware of the way Mtimu's muscles moved beneath his smooth skin, Enid marveled at the sheer strength of the man, and his ability to keep up with Gu-Kor, who was naturally adapted to a life amid the trees. She remembered how he had bent the metal bars of his cage in Bailey's encampment and seemingly summoned the animals to aid him.

What's he going to show me? Enid wondered as the trees flew past her in a green blur. She had heard that line more than once from other men: "I got somethin' to show you, baby." She hadn't fallen for it then. She hoped she wasn't falling for it now.

She would know soon enough.

—⚡—

WHEN MTIMU REACHED HIS destination, Enid self consciously disengaged her hold on him. The thoughts that had surfaced in her mind as she had clung to him during their passage through the trees were embarrassing … but also far from unpleasant. To distract herself from entertaining further ruminations along those lines, she gazed at her latest surroundings.

They were still high in the trees, but the branches grew so thickly they were almost like a floor. Mtimu, Enid, and Gu-Kor stood in front of a structure made of twigs and leaves woven so closely together that no opening could be seen other than a single aperture that was large enough for a person to go through.

Gu-Kor stood at one side of the opening. He had an expectant look on his face. A moment later, the inhabitant of the structure emerged.

It was a man … an elderly, coffee-colored Negro, bald-headed save for a wooly white fringe that circled the bottom part of his pate. His face sported a handlebar style mustache that would have been fashionable at the turn of the century. Despite his years, he stood ramrod straight, without a hint of a stoop to his shoulders. Still, he was an inch or two shorter than

Enid.

He wore a vest and knee length shorts made from antelope hide. The arms and legs the outfit revealed were thin, but also sinewy. In each of his hands, he held a gourd filled with clear liquid. A broad smile revealed teeth a young man would have envied.

Gu-Kor grunted something to the man, who responded in kind. Then the man turned back to Enid.

"Alpheus Wilson, at your service," he said in the same Southern intonation that marked Mtimu's speech.

"Enid Brown," the airwoman responded.

She turned to Mtimu.

"Is he your ... father?" she asked.

"In a way," Mtimu replied. "He will have much to say to you. There is something I must do. I will return soon."

Then he spoke to Gu-Kor in the short, breathy syllables that Enid now realized were a rudimentary form of speech. Gu-Kor uttered a single bark in response. Then man and ape took to the upper levels of the trees.

"Sit, my dear, and have some refreshment," Wilson said, holding out one of the gourds. "It is only fruit flavored water, but I'm sure it will fulfill your current requirements."

"Thank you," Enid said. She took the proffered gourd and sat down on the thick branches. Wilson did the same. She took a sip of the liquid. Its taste was different, yet pleasing.

"Delicious," Enid said.

Wilson nodded agreement.

"Your name sounds familiar," Enid said. "But I can't place it."

"That's not surprising," the old man said. "I've been ... away ... for thirty years. Longer than you've been alive, I daresay."

That time span jogged Enid's memory, and her eyes widened in recognition of the man's name, if not his face.

"Of course ... 'The Lost Professor,'" she murmured. "The colored newspapers run stories about you every year or so."

"So that's what they call me now," Wilson said with a wry chuckle. "That, I suppose, is more flattering than some of the things I've been called in my day. Let me tell you about it ..."

—〰—

MTIMU AND GU-KOR SWUNG silently through the trees. A vague, nonspecific sense guided them. They knew intruders had entered the most secret part of their domain. Mtimu was certain that the interlopers were the pitiless white man and whatever followers remained alive and loyal to him.

But how did they know to come here? Mtimu wondered, his thoughts streaming in a mixture of ape and English words. *Does the white one have the ability to follow a scent trail through the trees?*

He dismissed that surmise. Only someone who was bred in the ways of the wild would have that capacity.

But how, then? The question persisted.

Shrugging off the riddle, Mtimu turned his thoughts to the other stranger in his country: Enid, the woman from the sky. When he heard her speak the language of the man he considered to be his father, Mtimu's mind swirled like a whirlpool. Alpheus had always been reluctant to talk about the place from which he came – a place far beyond the environs of the jungle. He had said only that it was a very dangerous place – in its own way, even more perilous than the bush country.

Mtimu slowed his pace, for he believed he and Gu-Kor were closing in on the intruders. The slight noises the pursuers made were camouflaged by the screeches of birds and monkeys. Man and ape dropped closer to the ground. Branches and leaves shielded them from sight.

Then Mtimu saw them … not far below. The cruel man and the woman in the white clothing …

—⚒—

I"WAS A PROFESSOR in the biology department at Tugalusa College in Georgia," Wilson said. "That's right – the great rival of Tuskegee next door in Alabama. My specialty was botany. That made me a rival of Tuskegee's George Washington Carver. Not that there was any bad blood between us. I just wanted to find a plant that would do for me what the peanut did for Carver.

"My research suggested that I could find such a plant here – in 'Darkest Africa.' It took a great deal of time and talk to gather the funds necessary to mount my expedition. It was 1905 – a new century. But the notion of a

Negro leading a scientific journey of any kind was unthinkable to most – including, sad to say, more than a few Negroes.

"However, I persisted, and I prevailed. After long months and many privations, I was certain that I was close to my goal. I had come to a village in a remote part of the Congo Free State – a misnomer if ever there was one. There were no rubber trees in the area, so the natives were left alone.

"I tested many of the plants the native sorcerers and healers brought to me. One – which they called *papinya* – showed promise as a healing agent.

"During my time in the village – which was called Mkuta – a little boy who was barely old enough to walk became attached to me. His name was Yeke. He was an orphan whose parents had died of a disease the healers couldn't cure. Relatives were taking care of him, but for some reason he found me fascinating. He followed me everywhere. We 'took to' one another, as they say down home.

"Then everything went to hell – pardon the expression. Even though there were no rubber trees near Mkuta, the plantations elsewhere still needed workers. A gang of slavers attacked the village. Everything turned into a screaming chaos. Without thinking, I snatched up Yeke and ran blindly into the jungle, with no plan other than to get as far away from Mkuta as possible.

"Somehow, we survived. Fortunately, Yeke was old enough to be weaned and could eat what I found for us. My only plan then was to get myself, Yeke, and the *papinya* samples I had salvaged back to what is loosely described as 'civilization.' But I had no idea of where we were, so I blundered on, not knowing that I was going deeper into the jungle rather than making my way out of it.

"Then the Soko found us. The Soko are the ape people, like the one who came here with you and Yeke. At first, they were terrifying. But we soon learned that is only in their appearance. Yes, they are fierce when attacked. But otherwise, they are gentle. They allowed Yeke and I to live among them. As Yeke grew up, the Soko taught him the ways of the wild. His senses became keener and he grew stronger than ordinary men. And I taught him my language – for the sake of sentiment, I suppose. I guess I am as close to a father as he has ever known.

"Only a few tribes dwell in this part of the jungle. They fear the Soko.

Having caught glimpses of Yeke, the natives called him 'Mtimu' – the Wild Man - and I began to call him that myself. The natives fear him as much as they do the Soko, even though he returns to safety anyone who wanders too deeply into the wild.

"And now you know the answer to the mystery of the 'Lost Professor,' Miss Brown. It is time for you to tell me a tale in return. How did you get here? And what has happened in the world – and for our people – during the time I've been gone?"

Enid looked at him. And she wasn't certain whether she should tell this man the entire truth about the outside world that had gone on without him for the past three decades.

—ᴍ—

BAILEY CURSED AS HE turned in a slow circle, attempting to regain his bearings. For the first time in his life, he was lost. He had been confident that he was closing in on the Wild Man and the Blackbird. Now, he was not so certain.

He watched and listened carefully. His eyes and ears told him nothing. The jungle, which he had prided himself in knowing better than the natives who dwelt in it ever could, seemed to be closed against him ... and closing in on him as well.

He cursed again as he looked at Lulama. The native woman returned his glare imperturbably ... insolently? She had borne the burden of guns and supplies without question, as always. Even so, Bailey thought he could detect something in her eyes beyond the usual flat indifference. For a moment, he thought he saw a glimmer of something close to contempt.

Then the moment passed, and the glimmer was gone.

"They're not going to get away," Bailey muttered. His eyes shimmered like beacons of madness. One of his hands reached up and touched the scars from the monkeys' attack that marred his tanned skin. His other hand held a rifle.

Visions of wealth and glory danced before Bailey's febrile eyes. Displaying the Wild Man and the Blackbird would bring him more money than he could ever have imagined. He would be king of the entertainment world. And he could take his pick of movie stars to be his queen ...

Too late, he heard a slight rustle above him. Then a pair of powerful arms encircled him and lifted him off the ground. And he saw other arms – long and covered with hair – seize Lulama.

—ɯ—

"SO, THOSE WRIGHT BROTHERS weren't so crazy after all," Wilson commented after Enid told him about the airplane in which she had crashed in the jungle and of the amazing progress the new field of aviation had made since the first flight at Kitty Hawk – only a few years before the beginning of Wilson's ill fated expedition.

"Tell me more," the professor urged, his eyes bright with inquisitiveness.

Although she was no historian, Enid did her best to serve as a window through which Wilson could view the past he had missed. He shook his head sadly when she spoke of the Great War, which had consumed so many lives and devastated Europe.

"Did our people join the fight?" Wilson asked.

"Yes, but in segregated units."

He shook his head in sadness.

"I'm not surprised," he said.

He smiled, however, when Enid told him about Jack Johnson becoming the first black heavyweight boxing champion of the world a few years after Wilson went to Africa. But Wilson frowned when she described the race riots that followed Johnson's victories and the champion's eventual exile and imprisonment.

"That man was just too doggone full of himself for his own good," Wilson lamented.

He wiped a tear from his eye when she told him that Booker T. Washington, president of Tuskegee, had long since passed away. But he brightened when she said George Washington Carver was still alive.

She told him about Prohibition, jazz, and talking motion pictures. She told him about the Roaring Twenties and the Great Depression. She told him that segregation continued: subtle in the North, savage in the South. She told him about the fights and the firsts – fights against the barriers of race and first inroads into many fields, such as aviation.

"Would you like to come back to America, Professor, and share what you have discovered here?" Enid asked after her narrative wound down.

"Never!" Wilson replied emphatically.

Before Enid could say anything in response, the sound of a distant gunshot startled both her and the professor. With an alacrity that belied his years, Wilson leaped to his feet and issued a loud summons in the Sokos' speech. A moment later, a pair of Soko descended from the upper branches. Wilson spoke to the man-apes in an urgent tone. They bent, and Enid and Wilson climbed onto the animals' backs. Then the Soko carried the humans toward the source of the sound.

—∿—

THE SCENE THE SOKO reached was gruesome. Mtimu and Lulama were bent over Gu-Kor, who was bleeding from a wound in his chest. Clive Bailey's body lay sprawled like a piece of refuse. His neck was bent at an unnatural angle, and his blue eyes were glazed and lifeless as they stared at eternity. His broken rifle lay in two pieces near his side.

Enid and Wilson released their holds on the Soko and ran over to the others. Gu-Kor's eyes were open, like Bailey's. But the Soko's eyes were not lifeless. They were clouded with pain. Yet the man-ape neither groaned nor cried out.

The other two Soko hovered anxiously over Gu-Kor. One of them bared his teeth in menace at Lulama, who simply stared back at the man-ape without blinking or flinching. In one hand, she held a clump of leaves. Her other hand was clenched into a fist.

"We found them here," Mtimu said. "We meant only to capture them. The white man struggled. His thunder-stick spoke. Its metal stone hit Gu-Kor. I killed the man. The woman saved Gu-Kor."

He nodded toward Lulama. When the native woman opened her closed fist, a blood covered bullet dropped to the ground. Then Lulama bent and pressed the leaves in her other hand against Gu-Kor's wound.

"You did what you had to do, Mtimu," Wilson said.

"'What he *had* to do?'" cried Enid. "He *murdered* a man!"

"How different is this from killing the leopard that was about to kill you?" Mtimu asked.

Enid stared speechlessly. She could not bring herself to agree with Mtimu's grim logic. But still …

Then Lulama claimed everyone's attention as she stood up and walked over to Bailey's corpse. She pulled the nurse's cap from her head and threw it on the body. Then she tore off her stained, ripped uniform and hurled it onto the remains as well. Naked now, save for a patch of cloth that covered her crotch, she glared down at her erstwhile master. Sunlight picked out the patterns of scars that covered almost every inch of her skin.

"Bad man," Lulama said, speaking Bailey's tongue for the first time. "He come to my village. Save my father, who was healer, from lion. Spirits say we owe him. He make my people, the Uthama, his dogs. Make us do things … learn things … wear strange clothes … all for him. We could not kill him … because of debt. Spirits angry … if we not pay."

Then she looked at Mtimu.

"You kill Bai-ley. I … Lulama … free now. I … Lulama … owe you."

Mtimu nodded, as did Wilson. Noticing the byplay among the others, Enid spoke.

"I cannot stay here," she said.

Looking at Wilson, she continued: "I can understand why you would want to stay, Professor. And, perhaps, you can understand why I must go."

Wilson was about to interject, but she held up her hand to forestall interruption.

"I will tell no one about the existence of you, Mtimu, or the Soko. I will say that I don't remember much of what happened after my plane went down."

Again Mtimu nodded. A look passed between him and Enid, similar to the one they had shared before Bailey's pellets had rendered them unconscious. This time, regret tinged their gazes. Finally, they looked away from each other.

"Lulama," Mtimu said. "Your debt will be paid if you take Miss Brown safely to a place where she can return to her own land."

"I can," Lulama said.

Enid looked at the native woman who had been a captor back at Bailey's encampment. The sullen resentment that had marked Lulama's demeanor then was gone now, replaced by an air of quiet confidence. Lulama stripped the pistol and ammunition belt from Bailey's corpse and handed the ordnance to Enid.

"Know how to use?" Lulama demanded.

"Yes," said Enid. *I can always say I was rescued by friendly natives,* she thought.

Lulama retrieved a rifle, her spear, and what was left of the supplies. "We go now," she said.

She turned and began to retrace the trail by which she and Bailey had come to this place. Enid was about to follow. Then she turned back to Mtimu and Wilson.

"Farewell, Professor," she said. "Farewell, Mtimu."

"Farewell, my dear," Wilson said.

Mtimu nodded.

Without a backward glance, Enid hurried to catch up with Lulama.

"Will we ever see her again, Alpheus?" Mtimu wondered.

A shrug was the only reply Wilson could give. Then the two men and the Soko began the bleak task of burying the remains of Clive 'Take 'Em Alive' Bailey.

DILLON AND THE
ALCHEMIST'S MORNING COFFEE

BY DERRICK FERGUSON

1.

The Sun Palace of Prince Adaren, in the province of Carikir, located in the North African country of Gudjara

"THERE YOU ARE. YOU want to stop hitting on every woman in the place and maybe do the job I hired you for?"

"I am. I'm checking them out and making sure that they aren't possible threats."

"There's only one thing about them you're checking out and-"

Dillon casually took the elbow of the furious Captain Edna Hartless and steered her away from the beautiful young Badri woman he had been talking with before Edna said something impolite. "Hartless, my operating procedures are somewhat different from yours and that includes my methods of scoping out potential threats. Trust me, I know what I'm doing."

They weaved in and out of the mass of men and women attired in formal evening wear, as they were, even though it was the middle of the afternoon. But one simply did not attend any affair at Prince Adaren's fabled Sun Palace in jeans and a hoodie. Any invitation to The Sun Palace meant that you came in formal wear or you didn't bother to come at all.

At the age of fourteen Prince Adaren swore that he was going to build the largest and most beautiful palace in the world and fifty years later it was still being built. In that part of the world the endless construction of The Sun Palace had become legend. It had been a renowned tourist attraction for the past twenty five years as people came from all over the world to marvel at the sheer size of the structure.

Because in all those years, Prince Adaren had simply never called a halt to the building of his Sun Palace. The Sun Palace contained nearly three thousand rooms, one hundred galleries, seven hundred suites, two hundred kitchens, indoor and outdoor gardens, ten Olympic sized swimming pools, four hundred bathrooms, its own reservoirs, courtyards, chapels, theaters…it just simply went on and on. Indeed, a small town had been constructed near the immense palace to provide housing for the army of staff needed to maintain the place and for the construction engineers and their families, all of whom worked for Prince Adaren. In fact, many of the workmen who now labored on the construction of The Sun Palace were second and third generation descendants of the laborers who had begun construction of the palace. When would The Sun Palace be finished? Who knew? Some said that work would not cease until Prince Adaren died and that didn't look to happen anytime soon as the Prince kept himself in excellent health and, though in his sixties, now looked barely forty.

Captain Edna Hartless refused to be mollified. Statuesque, solidly built with a lion's mane of thick wavy platinum gray hair that fell to her shoulders done up in a style that immediately made one think of popular depictions of Greek goddesses, she hadn't gotten to be the Chief of Field Operations for the Advanced Counter Espionage Syndicate by letting the smooth talk and the winning smiles of men get the best of her. Not even Dillon's. *Especially* not Dillon's. Even though privately she had to admit he looked absolutely smashing in his Franzese tuxedo. Four inches over six feet, Dillon's two hundred and twenty pounds fit well in formal wear. His dark skin and copper colored eyes, which shone like freshly minted pennies, helped as well.

"What you're supposed to be doing," Edna said, "is watching my back. Not watching the backsides of every sweet young thing that catches your roving eye."

Dillon cocked his head at a slender Danish beauty standing near the entrance. "She's with the Danish Defense Intelligence Service." He turned Edna so that she could clearly see a dark-haired woman standing by the entrance, her hard suspicious eyes looking at everybody in the huge room as if they all owed her money. "She's with the Turkish National Intelligence Organization. You want me to go on?"

Edna eyed him, not knowing if she should be impressed or embarrassed. "How do you know for sure?"

"I'm sure. You've got at least two dozen people here from different intelligence agencies, government scientific bureaus and criminal organizations. What kind of snake pit have you put me in?"

As they made their way to the buffet table, Edna replied, "Just what I told you over the phone. A.C.E.S. has been assigned to acquire the object Prince Adaren is putting up for auction. I've been told to bid as high as possible to purchase the object."

"Who's the money coming from?"

"I don't know."

"Who assigned you?"

"My superiors."

"What's the object?"

"I don't know."

Dillon sucked his teeth in disgust. "See, that's why I could never work for you or Velvet or Tipp on a permanent basis. You guys just go ahead and do what you're told and never even think to ask what you're risking your lives for or why."

"You couldn't work for us because you don't believe in following orders and doing what you're told or playing by the rules. Face it, Dillon… you don't have the discipline to do what we do."

"If I'm such a undisciplined wild card, then why did you hire me?" Dillon snagged two flutes of champagne from a passing silver tray held aloft by a slow moving waiter. He handed one to Edna. "I figured that after the Sunjoy debacle, A.C.E.S. wouldn't hire me to clean toilets."

"They wouldn't. And if my superiors knew you were involved, they'd have me up on so many charges so quickly it would turn my hair from gray to white. I hired you out of my own pocket."

"Really? I wish I'd known that from the start. I'd have given you the friend discount." Dillon sipped his champagne. "So why did you hire me?"

"Because my superiors didn't tell me where the money is coming from or what the object is. Yes, I follow orders. Yes, I play by the rules. But I'm not stupid." Edna gestured. "Come on, let's start drifting to the auction area."

The auction area actually was a long, open arcade of Moroccan marble with the best Ichiarnessu diamond design on the flooring that Dillon had ever seen. The arcade faced the Mediterranean Sea, which glittered and sparkled in the intense sunlight, dazzling the eye with the almost supernatural blueness of the water.

"And may I say how lovely you look in that dress?"

And Edna Hartless most certainly did look lovely. She wore the merlot colored pleated silk chiffon strapless gown as if she did so every day. "I didn't think you'd noticed," she sniffed.

Dillon most certainly had noticed. Edna was somewhere in her late fifties, but easily gave chicks half her age a run for their money when she stepped into a roomful of men. She had turned way more than her share of male heads in the thirty minutes they had been here.

"Well, this is the first time I've ever seen you in a dress, Hartless. It's quite overwhelming. Stunning, even. Took me some time to find the words. I mean, you only called me this morning for this job. Lucky for you I was in this part of the world."

Edna sniffed again. "Luck had nothing to do with it. I knew you were in Spain."

"What if I hadn't been? What would you have done then?"

"Thankfully I don't have to figure that out now." They passed a huge crab-shaped fountain and Edna motioned at a couple of seats. "Let's sit here." Elegant antique looking chairs had been set up in painfully neat rows facing a podium. Another beautiful marble fountain tinkled merrily behind the podium and the air was filled with the delightful odor of the scented fountain water.

"So you knew I was in Spain. Sounds like you've been keeping an eye on me, Hartless."

"Tell you something for free if you keep it to yourself."

"Like the jackass said when he looked in the mirror: I'm all ears."

"There's a number of us, including your good friend John Velvet, who take turns assigning people to stay on your trail. Just in case we need you in an emergency. When we hear of where you are, we send people to pick up your trail and keep an eye on you. We tell our people not to interfere with you. Just let us know where you are."

Dillon crossed his long legs, sighed. "Gone are the days when I could bounce around the world in relative obscurity."

"You've nobody to blame but yourself. You're way too high profile now. You've put yourself on too many radar screens. What were you doing in Spain anyway?"

"The usual. Joining the peasants in their revelry. Going to church. Writing my memoirs."

Edna cocked a dubious eye at him, but said nothing.

Dillon figured it was high time they got back to business. "How many of your people you got here?"

"Just two. Cleaver is over there by the staircase and Hitchcock is hanging back at the entrance."

"Just two?"

"Well, there's not supposed to be any trouble, remember. Prince Adaren has his own private army here so there was no point in me bringing my own. And you went through the security searches same as we all did. Nobody has any weapons of any sort here."

Dillon indicated the many seats that were filled with people who looked as if money was something they worried about the least. "You've got an awful lot of competition here, Hartless. Think you'll be able to outbid them?"

Edna Hartless shrugged. "I've been authorized to go as high as necessary. Just make sure I win the auction. Once I do that, I'll be given a code to access a Bahamian bank account to make the payment and that's it."

Dillon gestured to a slim, elegant praying mantis of a man walking to the podium. "Looks like the show is about to start."

Edna nodded. "That's his nibs himself, Prince Adaren."

Prince Adaren boasted a full head of thick silver hair on top of a long, puritanical face with a wide chin. But he smiled readily enough when he got to the podium. The way he moved told Dillon that the man worked out often. His body language further told him that Prince Adaren would be dangerous in a fight. Dillon didn't know much about him. He'd heard the name in his past visits to this part of the world and quite naturally he'd heard of The Sun Palace. Gudjara as a country was well known to him as well as to the world intelligence communities for giving safe haven to members of various terrorist organizations. But as for Prince Adaren himself, Dillon had never heard of him being mixed up in anything of that nature. Matter of fact, Prince Adaren appeared to go to great lengths to stay clear of political matters altogether, satisfied to let his father and two brothers run the country while he built his palace.

Prince Adaren lifted his right hand, indicating that he wished to speak. The slight murmuring of the seated assemblage drifted away as he spoke. "Welcome, all of you, to my Sun Palace. Consider yourselves the masters of my humble home while you are here. Once this auction is over, those of you who wish to stay the night are of course more than welcome. Your every comfort will be assured and whatever you desire will be made available.

"I would like to make a few things clear before we start. The item that is to be auctioned today is one that I myself have no interest in. I am merely the go between, the facilitator, if you will. Once I have sold the item to whomever purchases it, I have nothing further to do with this matter. Therefore I do not expect any sort of retaliatory action made against me by disgruntled losers. If so-" Prince Adaren indicated the many black suited, sunglass wearing men standing in strategic locations about the arcade.

Two young women, also dressed in black and wearing sunglasses, pushed a small metal cart over to the left side of the podium. The object on the cart was covered by a white silk cloth which Prince Adaren whipped off with a flourish. The two foot high steel cylinder appeared to glow slightly, the surface encrusted with circuitry that looked to Dillon's eyes like electronic glyphs. Technological hieroglyphics, representing something more than just electronic seals to keep whatever was within the cylinder safe from exterior harm.

"Ladies and gentlemen. I give you what you have come to bid on. Some of you know what it is, but most of you I wager have no idea. That is because many of you work for various intelligence agencies that did not see fit to clarify the nature of what is in the cylinder. And it is not my job to provide that clarity. But it must have a name and so in a moment of whimsy I have provided one. Ladies and gentleman, the bidding for The Alchemist's Morning Coffee begins now. Shall we start the bidding at five million dollars?"

Hands began going up, eyebrows started raising, subtle stroking of the jaw or ear commenced and within two minutes the bid was up to eight million.

Dillon slipped out of the inside pocket of his jacket the brand new smartphone that had been made for him by the man he was calling, his technical expert, the marvelously brilliant Wyatt Hyatt. "Wyatt," Dillon said to the phone and it dialed the number and within four seconds, Dillon saw Wyatt's bearded, bespectacled face grinning back at him on the screen.

A hand dropped on Dillon's shoulder. He looked around and up into the black sunglasses of one of Prince Adaren's guards. "Beg your pardon, sir. But if you wish to make a phone call you will have to leave the auction floor."

"Of course. My bad." To the phone, Dillon said, "Hold on for a few, Wyatt." Dillon stood up, slipped past an annoyed Edna Hartless who was trying to raise her hand to up the bid to twelve million. He strode rapidly out of the auction area and lifted the phone to look at Wyatt. "Hey there, big boy."

Wyatt grinned back. "What's shakin' baby? You still in Spain?"

"I was until a few hours ago. Flew over to Gudjara on a job. Watching Edna Hartless' back while she works."

"I just think you got a thing for older women, myself."

"I got a thing for women, period. Look, I need a favor."

"You got it. Whatcha need?"

"She's here at some high tech auction buying something and she doesn't know what it is. Most of the people bidding on it don't know what it is. I need you to find out for me just what this gehooka is."

"So what is it? Send me a picture if you can."

"Hold up." Dillon looked around without appearing to look around. Adaren's people were not paying attention to him as their attention focused on the auction floor. He manipulated his phone camera's zoom to get a close-up, took a quick picture.

"Oooooo," Wyatt said with interest. "Nifty looking gehooka, indeed."

"Adaren said he calls it 'The Alchemist's Morning Coffee'." Dillon saw the expression on Wyatt's face change from one of acute interest to that of startled alarm. "What's wrong, Wyatt?"

"Where'd he get that name from? Did he say?"

"Naw. Said he made it up in a moment of whimsy. His words."

"No he didn't. I gotta make some calls. Be right back." And Wyatt was gone, just that quick. As Dillon put his phone away and returned to his seat, his thoughts troubling indeed. Wyatt Hyatt was one of the most easy going people he knew. Always smiling, always pleasant. There was little that upset him. But The Alchemist's Morning Coffee upset him. And that upset Dillon.

Back in his seat he asked Edna, "How it's going?"

"Up to fifty million and-" she stopped to raise her hand to up the bid. "-looks like it isn't going to stop anytime soon. What *is* that thing?"

"I'm working on it. Called my tech guy. He acted really strange. I told him Adaren called it 'The Alchemist's Morning Coffee' and he reacted like I pissed on his favorite keyboard."

Edna, not taking her eyes off the prince, said, "He give you any indication at all of what it could be?"

"He'll call me back. How's it going?"

"Who knows how high this thing is going to go for. What the hell *is* it?'

"Be worth buying the dingus just to find out. Now you got me curious." Dillon fell silent as the auction continued, the price going up and up. When it reached sixty million his phone vibrated in his pocket for attention. Once again he got up and left the auction area and slipped the phone out of his pocket. "That was quick. What's the news?"

"Leave it alone, Dillon. Walk away." Wyatt's normally smiling face was now as miserably serious as if he'd just accidentally drank drain cleaner. "Serious, man. Leave this job alone."

"You have to give me more than that, Wyatt. What's wrong? What is that thing?"

"It's something extraordinarily dangerous. I actually was called in four years ago to consult on it but I never heard anything else about it and so-" Wyatt shrugged. "-outta sight, outta mind. And in any case, I figured it was at least twenty years away from being fully developed. I should have known-"

"Wyatt, you're not making sense."

"The Alchemist is a nickname the scientific community has for Professor Alejandro Candu. He's the world's leading geneticist who has devoted himself to synthetic biology and cellular reprogramming research. The Morning Coffee is the project he's spent the past twenty years of his life working on and-"

But Dillon wasn't listening. His acute hearing, which had saved his life on more occasions that he could count, had picked up something. A very familiar sound. He broke into a run, heading right for Edna. For a man his size, six foot four carrying two hundred and twenty pounds of solid muscle, Dillon could move like a track star when he had to. The last few feet he leaped into the air, hollering "Incoming!" even as he wrapped Edna in his muscular arms and threw them both to the ground.

The end of the arcade vanished in a fireball of orange flame that gushed outwards in all directions, the force of the explosion shattering the delicate fountains, knocking everybody off their feet or out of their seats as hot air covered them like a thick smothering blanket, making it difficult to breathe for a few seconds. Rubble splashed into the water or landed back on what was left of the arcade in a shower of pebbles and pulverized marble dust.

Dillon rolled off of Edna and looked at his phone. "Stay handy, Wyatt. I'm gonna want to talk to you after I get out of this." He stowed the phone away and helped Edna to her feet.

"What the hell is happening-" she began and yowled as Dillon once again yanked her down into a tight ball, throwing his arms over her as another explosion tore into the arcade, throwing debris everywhere.

Armed men in full combat gear with helmets obscuring their faces charged down the stairs, engaging Prince Adaren's men, their automatic weapons filling the air with the sounds of death as they ruthlessly slew the black suited guards. Since nobody at the auction had weapons they wisely decided it was best to simply scatter and get out of the line of fire and they did so. Some simply curled up and stayed put, their eyes big as dinner plates as they watched the cruel butchery.

"Somebody's shelling the arcade," Dillon said from his defensive crouch, wishing he had a gun. "Probably from a boat. Hartless, c'mon, we have to-" Dillon turned. Edna was gone. With her dress hiked up, she was busy giving chase to three of the attackers who had seized the canister and were beating it back into The Sun Palace.

Dillon muttered something unkind as he pursued. He stopped just long enough to scoop up a handgun dropped by one of Adaren's security people. Then he continued to follow Edna who followed the three men, one of them thrusting The Alchemist's Morning Coffee into a rucksack. Edna had stopped to pick up a gun herself and she fired a couple of shots at the three who didn't even turn around, so intent were they on making their escape.

They ran up a wide staircase, meeting no opposition. Yet another shell slammed into the arcade, this time obliterating it completely. Dillon was thrown to his feet as the once beautiful structure simply disappeared in a massive explosion that shook the entire palace. Delicate stained glass windows burst into powder and alarms went off all over the place, adding to the general chaos.

Dillon got to his feet and caught up to Edna who stood in a firm firing stance, shooting at the three men who leaped into a Jeep Hurricane that they obviously had waiting for them. They still did not turn around. "Dammit!" Edna snarled. "I know I hit at least two of them!"

"Body armor, Hartless. You're just wasting ammo." Dillon looked around. "What we need is a way to follow them and quick. Come on!"

2.

DILLON LED EDNA BACK through the entrance hall that led to the now smoking ruin of the arcade and up a flight of marble stairs to a landing. The entire palace was in a panic. Adaren's security force rushed to and fro, rounding up everybody and anybody they could. Dillon elbowed one man in the throat who ordered him to drop his gun and stop. The man fell heavily, gasping for air. "Get his machine gun," Dillon ordered. Edna immediately complied, picked up the dropped Beretta ARX-160 assault rifle and slung the strap around her her shoulder, letting the weapon hang like a shoulder bag. "Now what?" she demanded.

"Now *that*." Dillon said, pointing at the security station, one of many he had noticed as they had come through the palace. "We were brought from the airfield in golf carts but I noticed that every security station also has *those*."

Edna saw a pair of gleaming Segway personal transport vehicles. "We're never going to catch up to them on those!"

Dillon grinned. "I know, but they'll get us to where we can get something that we can catch up to them with. Come on! If we hurry, we can cut them off in time."

"How do you know which way to go?"

"On the flight over I pulled up the floor plan of of this monstrosity and studied it."

"And you expect me to believe you memorized the floor plan of this entire castle?"

"Didn't you?"

—◊◊◊—

THE JEEP HURRICANE ROARED through the hallways of The Sun Palace. It was no problem because the halls were easily thirty feet wide. The members of the palace staff dove out of the way of the speeding vehicle, cursing and shrieking. The Jeep Hurricane took a corner on smoking, screaming tires, leaving black skid marks on the hideously expensive marble floor.

The driver expertly handled the wheel as the Jeep Hurricane barreled past The Sun Palace's reservoir. So huge was the palace and so great its need for fresh water that the reservoir had been built fifteen years ago. The Jeep Hurricane screeched along the curving path that encircled the huge reservoir, bright sunshine sparkling off the water. The domed roof could be opened to take advantage when there was a rainstorm. And then the Jeep Hurricane was out and past the reservoir and into an access tunnel. The tunnel would take the three men to the palace's main boulevard that stretched from one end of the palace to the other. And at the end would be the airfield and they would be in a helicopter and out of there with their prize.

A new roar joined with that of the Jeep Hurricane's engine. This one of a Yamaha motorcycle that burst from a side corridor. Dillon drove the motorcycle while Edna sat behind him, holding on fiercely, both arms wrapped around Dillon's torso so hard his ribs creaked. Dillon gunned the engine and zoomed in pursuit of the rapidly accelerating Jeep Hurricane.

"How did you know where they would be?" Edna yelled.

"I didn't!" Dillon yelled back. "But this is the quickest route through the palace so I just took a best guesstimate!"

"How'd you know where a whole roomful of motorcycles would be?"

"Same way I knew how to catch up to those guys!"

They both stopped yelling at each other as one of the men unloosed his machine gun and started throwing lead at them. Dillon swerved the bike into a S-pattern as bullets chewed up the walls and floors.

The Jeep Hurricane hung a sudden left, taking it on two wheels. Dillon continued the pursuit. They were now in a vast, arch-roofed rectangular hall where they passed barrel-vaulted transepts every forty feet or so.

"You want to shoot back, maybe?" Dillon suggested.

Edna twisted her body, slung the assault rifle into her waiting hands, and locked her knees against Dillon's hips. "This is going to sting your ears!" she warned.

"Long as you sting them!"

Edna fired in short, controlled bursts. Bullets ricocheted as they struck the rear of the Jeep Hurricane.

"Go for the tires!" Dillon threw over his shoulder.

"I will if you hold this thing still!" Edna threw back as Dillon still weaved the motorcycle in a S-pattern to avoid the fire of the two thieves who were now both shooting at them.

"We don't have body armor, Hartless!"

It had to be nothing less than divine intervention that prevented them from getting hit so far. But the driver of the Jeep Hurricane had his own problems driving at such a high speed on a surface that was meant for walking, not driving. The two shooters reloaded their weapons and Edna took advantage to pop off a couple of shots. One of the thieves caught a lucky round right in the throat and he tumbled off of the Jeep Hurricane, thrown into a wall. He bounced off and Dillon swerved to avoid the body flying right at them. It sailed over their heads, legs and arms bent into grisly angles.

The Jeep Hurricane made a right turn, rumbled up a flight of stairs and Dillon went right up after it. The Jeep Hurricane hit an intermediate landing and took the next flight of stairs in a tight turn that smashed into the marble baluster, sending chunks flying. One bounced off the front wheel of the motorcycle, making it wobble. Dillon snarled as he fought to keep the machine under control and continue the pursuit.

The Jeep Hurricane gained the final landing and burst through a pair of double glass doors and continued on through in a blizzard of glass shards. Dillon and Edna both ducked their heads to avoid being blinded by the razor sharp bits that flew like shrapnel. They roared through the huge salon decorated with Oriental landscape paintings and the Jeep Hurricane crashed through the glass double doors at the opposite end of the salon.

Once past that, Edna fired another couple of shots, trying again to hit the tires but to no avail.

Another right turn and then they were in the main boulevard of The Sun Palace, which looked as if it had been lifted from the Champs-Elysees. The shooter in the Jeep Hurricane ran out of ammo and threw his weapon at Dillon in frustration. Dillon ducked to the right while Edna leaned to the left and fired. The bullets smashed into the body armor, knocking him down.

The Jeep Hurricane made a left, speeded through a reception area, and smashed out through double doors into the outside and there was the airfield. The Jeep Hurricane headed toward a helicopter that waiting for the two thieves, the main and tail rotors already spinning, becoming a blur as it prepared for take-off.

"Any ideas on how to stop that helicopter from taking off? I'm out of bullets!" Edna threw the useless weapon aside.

"Working on it," Dillon muttered even though he had no idea at all how he was going to pull it off. He still had the handgun. Maybe he could-

That was when a rocket fired by a contingent of Prince Adaren's security people slammed into the helicopter and it erupted in a fireball of annihilation. Dillon and Edna were knocked off the motorcycle, which continued on, flipping over and over several times before crashing to the tarmac.

Dillon sat up, coughing. The helicopter was now a smoking, flaming pile of melted machinery. Edna propped herself up on her elbows. They both looked at each other. "Good thing I didn't give you the friend discount after all," Dillon said.

"Never mind that. Where'd that Jeep go?"

Dillon looked around. The Jeep Hurricane was nowhere to be seen. "My guess is they just kept going once they saw their ride was toasted. What we have to do is-"

"Get to your feet! Hands on top of your heads! And no sudden moves!"

Fully a dozen of Adaren's security people surrounded them, assault rifles pointed at Dillon and Edna. Dillon stood up slowly, helped Edna to her feet. They both interlaced their fingers on top of their heads and, prodded by the muzzles of the weapons, started marching back toward The Sun Palace.

"Let me do the talking!" Edna hissed.

"Oh, most certainly. I'm just the hired help."

—

PRINCE ADAREN WAS NOT a happy man. He quickly scanned the identification cards that his security staff had issued to Edna and Dillon upon their arrival. Adaren looked up from the cards at them. "Captain Edna Hartless of the Advanced Counter Espionage Syndicate.

And this is your agent Mr. James West."

"I think I should clarify something right away, Your Highness, hopefully to show our good faith." Edna said quickly. "This gentleman's name isn't West. It's Dillon."

Adaren's eyes first went wide with surprise and then narrowed in open suspicion. "So. The well-known global instigator himself." Adaren looked back at Edna. "The term 'good faith' is a meaningless one now, Captain Hartless, in view of what has just happened and your involvement in it. Why did you feel it necessary to sneak this man in here? To give my security people false information about his identity?"

"Because of what just happened, Your Highness! Apparently this item is extraordinarily valuable and somebody didn't want to bid on it."

"My home has been violated! I have people dead and injured!" Adaren shouted. "And I have you two who were trying to escape with the thieves!"

"Uh-" Dillon raised his hand like a timid schoolboy. "-that's not quite right. Captain Hartless and I were trying to stop them."

"You must not have been trying very hard. You chased them right through my palace." Adaren gave Dillon a cancerous look. "And I am not convinced of the truth of your words. You came into my home using false credentials. You fired weapons in my home. You drove a motorcycle through my home!"

"Hey, hey," When Dillon felt the need to, he could throw a pretty intimidating look himself and he did so now. "I appreciate you're upset. And I apologize for the deception. But Captain Hartless felt the need for some extra backup and obviously she was right to do so. How is it that your security people couldn't stop the attackers before they got to the auction area?"

Adaren breathed heavily. "It would seem I have traitors on my staff who allowed them access. I will deal with them."

"And in the meantime we'll go find The Alchemist's Morning Coffee if that's alright with you?" Edna said. "The last two men in the Jeep must be holed up somewhere around here."

Adaren looked highly doubtful. "The auction was a total failure and the item is gone. Why should you continue to look for it?"

"A better question," Dillon put in, "is why you're not. Surely the people you represent will hold you responsible for losing their property?"

Prince Adaren looked at Dillon for a long time. Dillon merely looked back, a smile on his face. Prince Adaren was a powerful man in that part of the world, but Edna Hartless wielded a pretty big stick herself. A.C.E.S. was not an organization to treat lightly and as one of their top field operatives she had a very high profile. And Prince Adaren obviously knew who Dillon was which meant he knew that Dillon's friends undoubtedly knew where he was and he didn't want that kind of heat down on him either.

Prince Adaren gestured to his security people. "Get them out of my palace."

—∭—

EDNA'S PLANE AS WELL as Dillon's were parked on the same apron, side by side. Upon arriving there, Edna went into her plane to change while Dillon went into his plane, nicknamed 'Archie' by its designer and builder, Dillon's semi-retired partner and best friend Elias Patrick Creed. He ruefully looked down at his dirty, torn tuxedo. "This is the third one this year," he sighed as he stripped it off, heading for the rear of the plane for a shower.

Twenty minutes later, Edna jogged up the steps leading into Archie. She stood just inside the hatchway in the main cabin and shouted; "Where are you?" Edna was now dressed in a desert camouflage uniform with her thick platinum gray hair tied out of the way into a sensible ponytail.

"Just getting my phone to finish a conversation I started before everything went to hell." Dillon joined Edna, now dressed in what he called his 'working clothes.' Ankle-high lug soled custom made all-purpose boots that secured with straps and latches. Tough black jeans, a pullover, collarless short sleeve sand-colored shirt. His Steranko belt with its many pouches that held all sorts of useful tools and devices. He shrugged into his well-worn bronze colored leather jacket with the braided passants.

Dillon walked into the cockpit, motioning for Edna to follow him. He sat in the pilot's chair, motioning for Edna to take the co-pilot's seat. Both of the chairs looked more like the executive chairs found in corporate boardrooms. Sensors in the co-pilot's chair automatically adjusted the seat to accommodate Edna's height. The curving control panel wasn't metal. Eli had used a polymer that resembled oak. Dillon took his phone, plugged it into a socket on the control panel and tapped a button. A ten-inch monitor unfolded with silent smoothness and activated, showing Wyatt's anxious face.

Dillon made the introductions. "Dr. Wyatt Hyatt, Captain Edna Hartless."

Edna smiled. "Your reputation precedes you, Dr. Hyatt. A pleasure to meet you."

"Same here. And please, call me Wyatt."

"Then I insist you call me Edna."

Dillon said, "Wyatt, tell Hartless what you were telling me. Start at the beginning."

"Sure. Edna, what you're dealing with is a technological Pandora's Box that if opened could have catastrophic consequences for whoever fools around with it. The Alchemist's Morning Coffee is highly dangerous. I told Dillon to leave it alone but he says that if it's that dangerous then it needs to be recovered or destroyed."

"So can you to explain to me exactly what it is?"

Wyatt nodded, sipped from a large can of Red Bull before continuing. "Dr. Alejandro Candu was nicknamed 'The Alchemist" years ago because of his undisputed brilliance in genetics. The man is simply dazzling when it comes to biological transmutation which led to his current work in synthetic biology and cellular reprogramming."

Edna nodded. "So far, so good. What has that go to do with our situation?"

"Dr. Candu has been working on a project for the past twenty years that will utterly and totally change humanity as we know it. I myself was called into consult on his project and I had to sign so many confidentiality agreements it wasn't funny. He works for The Henderson Institute of Alternative Technologies."

Edna looked at Dillon in surprise. "This is getting interesting."

"Don't worry, Wyatt. Whatever you tells us stays with us." Dillon looked significantly at Edna who nodded in agreement. Dillon turned back to the screen. "Go ahead, Wyatt."

Wyatt continued. "Dr. Candu works for The Henderson Institute of Alternative Technologies. Has worked for them for most of his professional career. The actual name for Dr. Candu's project is so long it would take me an hour to pronounce it so I guess calling it his Morning Coffee is just as good as anything else. But what it is is this: it's a stable method of using genetic sequencing to encode digital information and archive it in human DNA." Wyatt's voice became more excited as he continued. "The world's information is being produced at a rate so quickly that we can barely keep up with it now. Soon we won't have any place to store it. But human DNA...it has virtually unlimited storage space. Theoretically a single strand of DNA can contain a billion terabytes of information. Can you imagine the possibilities?"

"Wait a minute...wait a minute..." Edna held up her hands while she digested that. "So what you're telling me is that this Dr. Candu came up with a way to turn human beings into living hard drives?"

Dillon quirked his lips in approval. "That's not bad, Hartless. I think you got it. Right, Wyatt?"

"Well, it's rather more complicated than that. But if you want to bottom line it, then yeah. That's pretty much what we're talking about here." Wyatt seemed a little disappointed that Edna had simplified it to such a degree but he went on ahead. "I think I don't have to tell you the practical applications this can have. Corporations could hire people to act as living hard drives, as you put it. Give them a shot of Morning Coffee and databases spread out among a dozen different Cray supercomputers can be stored in the DNA of one person."

"Criminals organizations wouldn't have to keep a single thing on paper," Dillon said. "Sensitive government information, national security information...there's not a single criminal intelligence agency or corporation on Earth who wouldn't kill their own mothers to get a hold of The Alchemist's Morning Coffee. It's the means to utilize the ultimate information storage unit: the human DNA." He shook his head. "Dammit, Hartless, why did you have to get me involved in this mess?"

"What's your problem?"

"We have to get that thing before it gets out of Gudjara. Once it gets out into the world it's game over. It's way too dangerous. Would you trust some of the people you work with to use Morning Coffee responsibly?"

"We can't be the only one looking for those two. What makes you think we can find them before everybody else?"

Dillon gestured at the screen. "My brother has already got that covered."

Wyatt grinned for the first time since this thing had started and Dillon was glad to see that wonderful wide grin back on his friend's face. "The American Intelligence Machine has a dedicated satellite keeping an eye on Gudjara and its neighboring countries Khusra and Harak due to Harak and Gudjara being sympathetic to terrorist organizations. Khusra is a friend to the United States and she's right in between the two. So the satellite has a dual purpose."

"But the main thing that concerns us is that it's there," Dillon said. "Go on, Wyatt."

"When Dillon told me what had happened, I hacked the satellite, repositioned it to point at your location and found your guys for you."

Edna looked highly dubious. "It hasn't even been two hours since that happened. You certainly couldn't have hacked into one of The Machine's satellites that fast!"

Dillon grinned. "Hartless, you're looking at a guy who's been hacking into government agency computers since he was a kid. Get him to tell you about when he hacked into CTU's computer core. What were you, Wyatt? Fourteen? Fifteen?"

"Thirteen. Damn near gave my poor mom a heart attack when they busted in the house. But they paid for the damage and gave me a really nice fee for plugging up the holes in their firewall. But that's not important. This is."

The picture on the screen changed from Wyatt's face to show what appeared to be a ruined fort just outside of the town. "It's about two or three miles from your present location," Wyatt's voice said. "Check this out." The picture zoomed in to show the Jeep Hurricane parked in the fort.

"They must be waiting for a pickup." Edna looked at Dillon. "You still working for me?"

"I take a contract, I honor it. What's the plan?"

"Simple. We go there and get back the Morning Coffee."

"And then?"

Dillon's face and voice were now both serious as he said, "Hartless, that thing is far too dangerous. It should be destroyed."

"I disagree. It's far too valuable and useful. We're going to recover it."

"For your people."

Edna sighed in annoyance. "Look, we haven't got it yet. What say we get it back first and then we argue about what to do with it. Deal?" She stuck out her hand.

Dillon nodded and took her hand in a firm shake. "Deal. Wyatt?"

"Hiyo!"

"You stay right where you are in case we need tech support. And call Allie Pierri, apprise her of the situation and ask her to be on standby."

"Done."

Dillon gestured at Edna. "Let's go get us some firepower and go hunting."

3.

THEY HAD NO PROBLEM getting inside the fort itself. The walls had plenty of gaping holes in them big enough for Dillon and Edna to slip inside. Dillon went first, a H&K MP5 in his gloved hands and his favorite handgun, a Jericho 941 in a cross draw holster. Edna also had one as well as a Beretta 92. Dillon visually scanned the interior of the ruined structure. The place hadn't been used in a long time, maybe about fifty years he judged.

Edna nudged him to get his attention. Dillon turned to see what she wanted him to look at: a number of skeletons leaning up against what was left of the wall. Thoroughly rusted weapons were still in their bony fingers. "They died like soldiers," Edna said. "At their posts."

"Say a quick prayer if you like," Dillon said.

Edna gestured with her weapon. "I can do that later. Let's take care of business first. There's the jeep."

It was parked next to the main building. No signs of life at all in any of the buildings or the Jeep Hurricane itself. Dillon and Edna walked over to the vehicle and stopped in surprise. "Now that's something you don't see every day," Edna said.

A large square pit about thirty or forty feet deep had been dug in the middle of the fort. But it was a pit with walkways, ladders providing access from one level to another. Edna frowned. "What the hell is that for?"

"It looks like archaeological digs I've seen."

"How would you know what an archaeological dig looks like?"

"Been on a couple with a friend of mine, Elisa Hill."

"She's an archaeologist?"

"Sort of." Dillon didn't elaborate as they approached the pit. Edna whirled about. Dillon stopped and looked over his shoulder. "What's wrong with you?"

"Thought I saw something out of the corner of my eye. Maybe it was a rat."

"Or maybe it was something else. I don't like this, Hartless. Where did these guys go?"

"Maybe down there? It looks like tunnels have been dug down there."

Dillon slung his H&K over a shoulder and started down a ladder even as he said, "But there's no reason for them to go down here. All they had to do was wait by the jeep for their pickup. Why go exploring?"

Edna joined him and shortly they stood half way down the pit. Edna jumped again.

"I really wish you'd stop doing that," Dillon said.

"I keep seeing something out of the corner of my eye, I tell you!"

Dillon said nothing, just crouched down to look around the pit. On the different levels of the excavation it looked as if side tunnels had been dug. "Where do you think those tunnels go? Why were they dug in the first place? Who dug this pit?"

"Lot of questions, Hartless. And no answers." Dillon stroked his chin. "I guess the only thing to do is-"

Edna yowled as a slender, long-limbed man swaddled in dirty clothing that was little more than strips and rags of cloth wrapped around his lanky body landed on her back. Where he had come from, Dillon had no idea. He leaped to his feet, trying to bring his H&K around, and caught a bare foot in his chest for his pains. It knocked him off the level they stood on and he fell five feet to a lower level, landing hard.

Edna yanked herself free, swung a fist that missed as her attacker ducked under the blow. He swept her legs out from under her and she landed with such force that black blobs danced in front of her eyes. Her attacker gibbered with delight as he bent over her, a wickedly curved knife in his right hand.

Dillon's fingers tangled in the man's hair and he yanked him away from Edna. Dillon viciously chopped at the man's neck, kicked him off the level. But another knife wielder leaped to the attack, yelling wildly. He caught the butt of Dillon's H&K on the side of his head for his trouble. The two attackers, still gibbering like lunatics, scrambled into the nearest tunnel on all fours.

"Stay here!" Dillon ordered. He tossed his H&K to Edna. He scrambled after their attackers, the entrance barely big enough to accommodate his large body.

"Hey! Don't leave me here!" Edna yelled. She ran over to the tunnel and bent down to look in. She saw nothing but dusty blackness. "Dillon! DILLON! Get back here!" Nothing but silence answered her back. She stepped away from the tunnel, whirled about, looking for more attackers, her weapon at the ready. She swore under her breath. Damn the man! He had no idea what was in those tunnels, where they went. Why would he take such a stupid chance? She heard nothing but the wind whistling through the gaps in the fort's walls.

"Hartless."

Edna spun around in a one eighty to see Dillon standing on a level above her, pointing his Jericho right at her.

"What the hell-"

The weapon boomed. Hearing a strangled yelp from behind her, Hartless turned to see that yet another man had been creeping up on her, a long knife in his right hand. His left hand was at his throat, trying to hold back the blood spurting madly between the fingers. The knife wielder toppled over backwards.

Dillon climbed down to where she was. "You okay?"

"You scared the ever-lovin' shit outta of me with that stunt! Why would you take such a crazy chance?"

"Whenever you turn to the right or left, you take a step in that direction. I needed you to move out of the way so I could shoot that guy. That's why I called your name. Your taking that step got you clear of my shot."

Edna blinked. "Are you making that up?"

"No. I'm not."

"You really noticed that about me? And when did you notice it?"

"About two hours after we first met during the Sunjoy job."

"Have you ever thought about getting a real job?"

Dillon holstered his gun, copper eyes sparkling. He held out his hands for his H&K. "This is my real job." He motioned for Edna to follow him. "C'mon."

"In there? Are you nuts?"

"There's a whole network of these tunnels. I've seen similar in

Cambodia and India. These tunnels provide different routes of access to underground chambers. I think if we want to find our two missing thieves as well as The Alchemist's Morning Coffee, we're gonna have to go in."

"Go in? Go in *where?*"

"Well, that's what we're gonna find out. Where's your spirit of adventure, Hartless?" Dillon plunged into the tunnel. Edna gave a last look around and sighed. Her hand drifted to her belt for a second before following Dillon.

The tunnel went on for about twenty feet and soon Dillon and Edna found themselves in a larger underground chamber big enough for them to stand up in. It also was well lit, thanks to a bright light hanging from a beam supporting the ceiling. Dillon pointed at the other tunnels, an even dozen and all of them large enough for a tall man such as Dillon to walk with another three or four feet to spare and wide enough for four or five people to easily walk side by side.

"Which way do you suppose we go?" Edna asked.

The solution was taken out of their hands by the emergence of a horde of men and women from several of the side tunnels, some fully clothed in burnooses, others in loincloths, and some were totally naked. They swarmed over Dillon and Edna, pouring from the side tunnels in such numbers and so quickly that both of them didn't even have time to get off a shot. It wouldn't have helped in any case. Their weapons were ripped from their holsters and yanked from around their necks. Gibbering and hooting, the mob dragged Dillon and Edna into a tunnel.

"You got a contingency plan for this?" Edna yelled.

"Yeah! Just haven't thought of it yet!" Dillon yelled back.

They were hauled into a surprisingly huge and well-lit chamber apparently hewn out of solid rock. Huge braziers crackled with roaring fires but the chamber had to be well ventilated because there was no smoke in the room as one would have expected. In the center of the chamber a rectangular step pool contained muddy water. A wooden platform extended a few feet out over the pool. Surrounding it were more of these underground dwellers, hooting and hollering like wildcats.

And sitting on a rude throne hewn from black stone, his immaculate tuxedoed appearance quite incongruous with the surroundings, Prince Adaren smiled at Dillon and Edna. "Welcome," he said with jovial grimness.

"Son of a bitch!" Edna snarled. She struggled in the grip of a dozen hands that held her as solidly as if she were weighed down with iron chains. "You gotta be kidding me! *You* were behind this whole thing?"

"You mean you didn't figure it out?" Dillon asked her. "Didn't you hear me say back in his palace that I thought it odd he wasn't trying to catch the men who stole the Morning Coffee? You see the security he has. There was no way in hell thieves were going to get that far into The Sun Palace without being stopped. Even if they had help from the inside. Only way they could steal the Morning Coffee is if they had help from the top."

"I thought you were just being snarky like you usually are," Edna replied. "Dammit, Adaren, you went through a whole lot of trouble just to steal the thing! Why didn't you bid on it like everybody else?"

"Because I was forbidden to. The organization I work for is a hard one and the man who controls and runs that organization is an unforgiving one. His slightest wish is to be obeyed without question. He has gone to an enormous amount of trouble and expense to steal the Morning Coffee and he expects a hefty profit." Adaren reached down to the side of the throne and brought the container into sight. It hummed softly as Adaren stroked it as he might a beloved pet. "One does not lightly offend S.P.E.A.R. and its master."

Dillon and Edna swapped surprised looks. Both of them had heard of S.P.E.A.R. but the organization was so secretive that very little information was known. The same idea was in both their minds: if they could get out of this, recover the Morning Coffee and capture Adaren it would be an unprecedented opportunity to learn more about S.P.E.A.R.

"Look here, Adaren-" Dillon began.

"*Prince* Adaren, dog!"

Dillon's eyes burned golden hot but his voice was civil enough as he replied, "My apologies, Your Highness. Surely we can come to some kind of agreement here? We're not looking to make enemies."

"Neither am I. You have quite the extensive network of friends who will certainly take revenge if it is ever found out that I killed you. The woman is an important executive high up in the command structure of A.C.E.S. and her death would also be avenged. And I am not fool enough to think that the both of you would forget this with a handshake."

"What if we gave you our word that we would?" Edna said.

"The word of a woman is worthless and the word of a black dog even more so. You are not even on the level of these-" and here Adaren indicated the throng that crowded into the chamber, "-the dregs of those who are honored to serve me. Occasionally there are those who are born of feeble mind or physical weakness. I will not have such serve me and so they are sent here."

"But what do they do here?" Dillon asked.

"Do?" Adaren seemed honestly baffled by the thought. "Why, they do nothing. At least not anything I care about. Oh, I visit them from time to time as they have the most fascinating rituals they have created and they seem to think that I am a visitor worth worshipping as they carved this throne for me long ago."

"So what do you intend doing with us?" Edna demanded.

"These creatures found an interesting denizen living in an underground lake not far from here and they brought it to this pool where they apparently worship it. And like any good god, it demands sacrifices. It's had two already but I'm positive it wouldn't mind two more." Adaren lifted a hand. The people holding Dillon lifted him up bodily and chucked him up and out. He flew through the air, giving voice to a weird yodeling yell, and landed in the muddy water with a tremendous splash.

The ragged underground dwellers cheered and howled, stamped their feet, and clapped with insane glee.

Dillon burst from the water, sputtering and wiping his face clean of the slimy muck. Amazingly, the pool wasn't as deep as he thought. Standing up, his head and shoulders were clear of the water.

"Dillon!" Edna shouted.

"I'm okay! I'm okay!" he shouted back. Feeling something ripple in the water near him, he turned around, trying to see what it was. "There's something in here with me!"

"No shit! Look to your right, your right!"

Dillon did so and saw huge air bubbles rising and popping, splattering him with more of the nasty brown water. "Holy-" that was all the time he had before something underneath the water yanked him by the leg. Dillon disappeared under the surface of the brackish water.

Adaren smiled. "Disappointing. From everything I heard about him I had hoped he would at least put on an entertaining show before he was eaten." He looked at Edna. "I do so hope you'll put on a better performance, my darling."

"I'm going to kill you, you son of a bitch!" Edna's attention was drawn back to the pool as it now churned and convulsed, throwing great sprays of water into the air. Dillon emerged out of the pool, blowing and stumbling backwards. They'd taken his survival knife along with his guns but they hadn't thought to search for any other weapons. Dillon reached up and around and pulled out the four inch tanto he kept in a sheath sewn into his jacket at the back of his neck. He got hold of the knife just in time as he was again pulled under the water, which again began to agitate and froth as Dillon and the creature resumed their titanic underwater struggle.

Gunfire cut across the bloodthirsty yells and savage yowling of the underground dwellers as a number of armed men in desert fatigues burst into the chamber, wearing A.C.E.S. patches on their shoulders. Edna whooped with delight as her men poured into the chamber, quickly routing the rabble who, despite their greater numbers, clearly had much respect for automatic weapons. Hooting and howling they fled in all directions, scrambling into side tunnels.

Prince Adaren wasted valuable seconds when he could have been getting away in gaping at the A.C.E.S. assault team in shocked surprise. By the time it occurred to him to get up and run for it, it was too late.

Edna leaped on him like the hungriest leopard on the slowest zebra. "Wait! Wait!" Adaren screamed. "We can talk!"

"We already did," Edna said with dark humor as she yanked the canister from his grip while giving him a firm shove. Adaren fell backwards into the still churning waters of the pool.

Adaren thrashed about, got his footing and began climbing out, grabbing onto the steps to help pull himself out of the pool. Then a strong hand clamped on his ankle. Adaren turned to see Dillon climbing out of the pool. His face was covered with greenish ichor and slimy water but his hot, molten gold eyes burned with a terrible anger and his Cheshire Cat grin promised death. "Hey there, Your Highness."

"I'll give you anything you want if you let me go! Anything!"

"This black dog has only two words for you, Your Highness."

"What? What?"

Dillon's grin widened. "Arf, arf."

Dillon yanked Adaren completely into the air, swinging him over his head and throwing him into the pool backwards where he hit with an astoundingly large splash.

Dillon climbed up and out of the step pool where Edna squatted waiting for him, the canister containing The Alchemist's Morning Coffee cradled in her arms. "Greetings," she said.

"Howdy."

"Looked like you were in a spot of trouble a few minutes ago."

Dillon slowly got to his feet. "It's been one helluva day, I'll tell you that."

Edna gestured to the pool. They both looked as a dot of crimson on the brown surface of the foul water grew larger and larger, expanding to the size of a dinner plate, then a manhole cover, then a truck tire. "Dillon... exactly what is down there?"

"You don't want to know, trust me. I've never seen anything like it and I hope never to see it again."

Edna leaned over the pool, still curious. And her curiosity was satisfied. The creature's head emerged from the water, the shredded body of Prince Adaren in its mouth.

"HOLY GOD-" Edna staggered backwards, dropping the canister and shoving her fist into her mouth to keep from screaming. Dillon scooped up the canister, threw an arm around her shoulders to turn her away from the pool.

"Told you that you didn't want to know. When are you going to learn to listen to me, Hartless?"

—⚉—

"SO YOU HAD A standby team all the time, then?" Dillon and Edna sat in the cockpit of his plane. He'd showered and changed into fresh clothing and now listened as Edna explained where their timely rescue had come from.

"Well...I thought it would be prudent to have a few spare guns in the neighborhood just in case I needed them." Edna shrugged. "I'm a cautious woman, what can I say?"

"Hey, you don't hear me arguing, do you? How'd they know where to find us, though?"

Edna reached down to her belt, unclipped a small tube the size of her thumb and held it up for Dillon to see. "Homing beacon. You think you're the only one walking around with a belt full of gadgets?" Edna gestured at the canister sitting on the control panel. "Time to address the elephant in the room."

Dillon looked at the steel cylinder containing The Alchemist's Morning Coffee. "There's nothing to address, Hartless. You hired me for a job. I did the job. You recovered the Morning Coffee so that gives you the say over what you do with it."

"You're not going to lecture me?"

Dillon shook his head. "You're free, white, and over twenty one. *Way* over twenty one in fact-"

"Watch it, now."

"-the point being that you're a professional and I respect you as such. I would never have taken the job if I didn't. The gehooka is yours to do with what you wish."

Edna smiled warmly. "I'm glad you said that. How'd you like another job?"

"Which is…?"

"Making sure I get this safely to South Carolina. That's where the research and corporate headquarters of Alternative Technologies is located." She gestured at the canister. "I've decided to return it to its rightful owner. It was stolen and the right thing to do is to give it back."

"What about your superiors?"

"They have dealt with disappointment in the past. They'll learn to live with this one."

"This is a new job so we're going to have to renegotiate a new contract, Hartless."

"But of course. This thing does have an autopilot, doesn't it?"

"But of course."

"Then let's get underway. Once we're in the air and on autopilot we can…begin renegotiations. Fair enough?"

Dillon grinned. "Are you as good at renegotiation as you are at planning last minute rescues?"

"Even better."

"Y'know, Hartless…I like working for you."

BLACK WOLFE'S DEBT

BY D. ALAN LEWIS

SURROUNDED BY THE SCENTS of roses and jasmine, the goddess graced me with her presence; at least, that's how I wanted to see this. Unfortunately, the sweet fragrance of her perfume did little to soften her bitter disposition.

"So you're the infamous Black Wolfe."

Abigail Murray glared from the doorway between my office and the outer room where my secretary sat and acted busy. She made a quick glance to Roxie then back to me, and gave a knowing look that spoke volumes of her mental prowess. My 'special' or should I say, 'taboo' relationship with my young white secretary had been immediately sensed.

"Come in," I said and waved to an empty chair.

She'd called earlier and arranged this discreet, after hours meeting. Despite her discomfort, she strolled in as if making an entrance at a formal ball. Her hips and ample breasts, barely contained in the thin cotton dress, swayed with each step. She reminded me of a cat in heat; seductive and enticing.

"Would you mind not looking at me that way?" she asked and slid into the chair.

"What way is that?"

"The same one I get from every man. I'm here on business, not to be your fantasy." She glanced to the side and huffed. Several family pictures hung on my office wall, but she focused on my pride and joy, an autographed photo which hung in the center. A younger version of herself smiled from behind a mask and cape. A disappointed groan showed her displeasure at the signed publicity shot. "I don't like having a nig…"

She stopped before saying it. As the wife of Port Victoria's mayor, she'd become accustomed to life in high society. But even before their wedding, she'd lived a whites only kind of lifestyle.

She wrung her hands and started over. "Sorry. I'm not used to coming into…"

"The slums of Port Vic and hiring a black man?" I said and watched her nod. "It's 8pm, a little late but I usually don't take calls from the mayor's wife."

"You'll understand that I require discretion." As she drew an oversized envelope from her handbag, her gaze flashed back to Roxie. "This isn't a matter I can take to the police. My husband has enemies and some are on their payroll."

"Hey, Rox," I shouted. "Run over to Joe's and grab some sandwiches and coffee. It's gonna be a late night."

Half a minute later, Roxie rushed out the door, purse in hand. Abigail relaxed a little and handed me the envelope.

"These came to the mansion this afternoon. An officer trailed the delivery boy to the Waterford district, but lost him in an alleyway near Main." She said.

"You had an officer at the mansion? Why?"

She shifted uncomfortably and I noticed her hands shook very slightly. "We don't want the press to know that our daughter, Stephanie, disappeared three days ago."

The envelope held several photos and a letter. I flipped through them and ignored her discomfort. A young woman with looks and curves like her mother graced the images. Stephanie's nude form was the focus of the pictures, along with the thin black man who rode her.

"Sickening." Her whisper pulled my eyes up to hers, but the words that followed took on a sharper tone. "I want the man raping my daughter found and killed."

"She's not being raped." I laid the photos down and glanced over the letter. "You saw them. She looks too happy. Drunk is my guess, or drugged."

The ransom note asked for ten grand in exchange for the photos and negatives. Otherwise, the press and the city would get an eye full of Stephanie. Another note would be delivered within a couple of days with instructions on delivering the cash.

"Good news is she's in the area. Those alleys are a maze; keeps the cops from being able to catch anyone ducking into 'em. Their courier knew he was being followed."

"That's why I'm here," she snapped. "You know the cops stay away from this slum. Not a one of them are willing to crawl around in this jungle."

As I pulled my last cigarette and lit it, she withdrew another envelope and plopped it on the desk. Fingers with heavily painted nails pushed it toward me.

"I want her found." She said and noted my reaction to the thickness of her offer. "There's ten thousand in cash. Find her and bring her home. But I want the man that defiled her killed. I don't care how, just make it painful."

"Did you see what was painted on the door? I'm a private investigator, not an assassin."

Her eyes narrowed. "Ignore the paint and do what the money says."

After a long draw, I dropped the money in the top drawer. "You have anything else that I can use? Where was she last seen?"

"Stephanie attends Woodwards." She referred to the private high school favored by the city's elite. "She attended her morning classes but disappeared after lunch." Her eyes glazed over as if old memories flooded her thoughts. "She's a senior."

"Is that all?"

"That's all I know," she said.

"Seems a little light. Back in the day, you'd have gone after her yourself. So why not now? Why ask me?" I said and watched the blood drain from her face. She didn't answer. "I know you used to be Lady Victoria, the queen of justice. Come on, that information is the worst guarded secret in town."

She nodded. Twenty five years ago, three college kids volunteered for some government testing, or so the story went. An experimental formula gave each one superhuman strength, agility, and reflexes. Hiding behind masks and capes, they struggled for six years against the organized mobs that kept Port Victoria crime ridden. The police had proven to be powerless and corrupt, but a savvy district attorney began working with the would-be heroes. Eventually, the mob's back broke. The superheroes' heavy handed tactics made the streets safe again. But the cost of winning had claimed two of the heroes. Only Lady Victoria survived.

The D.A. eventually married a young beauty named Abigail, just before winning his first term as Mayor. But that was decades ago and the ravages of time showed. As sensuous as she may be, she was still a woman in her late forties. Superpowers hadn't kept the lines from appearing on her face, albeit the thick makeup did its best to hide them.

She looked down at her hands and clenched her fists. "There was a time when I could have thrown you through the wall. But… my strength is gone. I'm too old for this kind of thing." She looked up and her expression transformed into one of desperation. Like any mother, she worried about her daughter's well being. "I've heard stories about the Black Wolfe. They say you're as fast and strong as I used to be. You know this part of town. Port Victoria is a big place, but I know she's in the Waterford district. Please… please, bring my daughter home."

The change in her demeanor was unsettling. Growing up around here, I remembered her exploits. I didn't enjoy seeing the former goddess beg.

"I'll find her. In the meanwhile, I'll need to keep these photographs. I need you to stay in touch. If you get any news from the kidnappers, I need to know immediately. Roxie will be by the phone around the clock."

I saw her glance at the photos and realized she didn't fully trust me. I knew she worried about who'd see them. I grabbed a bottle of ink. Dabbing my finger in it, I lightly smeared the black liquid over the young girl's face on each photo. I looked up and saw the relief wash over her. Her eyes caught mine and she gave a nod.

"I need you to stay in touch as much as you can." I said and saw that the request wasn't well received.

As she rose from her chair, something on the wall grabbed her attention. "You have a college degree? In psychology? From Fisk University?"

"I do. Guess you're wondering why I'm a P.I. instead of making a better living." She gave me a suspicious look. "Knowing how people think is an advantage in my line of work. But after growing up in the streets of this town, being a part of this gang and that, I needed to prove that I was more than a common thug." I considered telling her more, but refrained.

"Good night, Mr. Wolfe. I'll be expecting your call soon."

—⚹—

IWALKED AND OPENED the window as I considered my next move. The cool night breeze felt good as my sweat soaked shirt caught it. Three floors below, Abigail stepped from my building and into a waiting car. I watched as the vehicle pulled away and headed east for a few blocks before turning toward the 'better' parts of town.

"I saw her leave. Figured it'd be safe to come back." Roxie appeared in the doorway and cocked her head to the side. "You really hungry, cause I gotchya a roast beef on rye."

A thought hit me. "Yeah, I could use it. Come here and look at these."

I stepped behind the desk and spread the photos out for her. Her face showed no emotions as she looked at the naked figures. A twinge of guilt gnawed at me for exposing her to this again.

Last year, she'd been a working girl who came into Joe's Diner with a set of bruises. Her pimp, a brute named Fat Eddie, got his kicks beating the women in his stable. She and I struck up a friendship. After a chat with Eddie in which his jaw was broken, I offered her a job where her clothes would stay on. That working relationship lasted about twelve hours before we were in my bed. She's slept there ever since.

"Is that her daughter, the mayor's daughter?"

"What makes you think that?" I asked.

"She's got the same figure as her mom. Nice apple bottom and watermelons on her chest." She remarked without looking away from the photos. When I didn't respond, she looked up at me with those doe eyes. "Oh, you like those big ole things, eh?"

"I like yours better. Hers are overkill."

She laughed, "Sure ya do."

"What can you tell me about the guy? He look familiar?"

Her head tilted and she bit her lip in that sexy way that I loved.

"Yeah. I remember him. Slimey… no, Slick Willy Jones. Worked over on Bellview Avenue. Had a couple of girls but wanted to take over the block. Wanted me, pretty bad." Her voice faded and I realized that some unpleasant memories had come to mind.

"Bellview? Think he's still in the area?" I asked and she nodded.

With a tug, the top drawer of my filing cabinet opened with a squeal of protest. I grabbed my gear. With practiced skill, the collection of throwing knives and pistols was concealed within my clothing.

"I take it you're going out tonight." She said and laughed, "By the way, you should be extra careful around him."

"Oh yeah," I said, "Why? Afraid Willy will get me?"

"He likes both girls and boys, from what I heard. Just don't let him buy you any drinks."

—✵—

ILEFT ROXIE BEHIND and walked the six blocks to Bellview. The streets crawled with lonely and depraved men. All sought the companionship of a woman and most carried enough cash to get some sort of attention from both the girls and the thieves alike.

A low voice behind me caught my attention. I turned my head slightly to get a better angle. Since my childhood, certain senses and abilities had become vastly more acute than normal folks'. My strength and reflexes could outdo anyone's; maybe even equal Lady Victoria's when she was in her prime.

A man's voice echoed off the shuttered storefronts. "Don't lose 'im or da boss will have our balls."

One shop owner had his door propped open as I passed. A glance at the reflection in its glass confirmed my suspicions; I'd picked up a tail. Three men, half a block back, eyed me like dinner. White men in clean clothes never came into the Waterford district unless they worked for the DeCarlos. The first two appeared to be the usual thugs, but the third stood a couple of feet taller and had more muscles than I thought possible.

Don DeCarlos had forced his way into the local numbers rackets a few months back. The sight of his boys didn't bother me, but I felt itchy about it. Their presence wasn't unusual, but I didn't understand why they would follow me. Had someone seen my recent visitor?

I kept my pace, but had a plan. At the next alley, I stepped in and disappeared from their sight. Pressing myself against the wall, I waited. It didn't take long to hear them running. The footfalls of the first two sounded loud and close together. My mind raced as I calculated their speed. The third moved about half as fast. I only hoped his IQ matched his running ability, slow and sluggish.

When the first rounded the corner, I stuck out my foot and tripped him. His momentum sent him careening into the opposite wall. My right fist was cocked back and I stepped away from the hiding spot as the second man rounded the corner. The sound of cracking bone echoed down the alley as my punch shattered his face. He left the ground and fell back to the asphalt.

Pain shot through my arm. I'd cracked a knuckle on my right hand some weeks ago. Every time I thought it'd healed up, I had to throw a punch and irritate it again. I shook off the pain and looked up as the hulk rounded the corner.

I'm six two and I found myself looking up. I cleared my throat, nodded politely and said, "A challenge."

He lunged forward and grabbed for me, but I anticipated the move and ducked quickly to the side. Another man would've been caught, but my reflexes are better then the average Joe's. Frustrated, he threw a punch, which I deflected and then jumped in close and landed an uppercut that staggered him. The look on his face told me enough. He wasn't used to that level of pain and wasn't used to someone as agile as me.

With a deafening roar, he drew a knife and slashed at the air where I'd stood. Back and forth the blade whooshed, but I managed to dodge. The first man laughed and rose to stand. The second man stirred, crawled to the wall, and pulled himself upright. From the look of his bloody face, he wasn't going to jump into the fray.

The blade flashed again but this time, I ducked and spun. I seized the opportunity and kicked. My boot connected with his groin. The giant growled and I snatched the knife from his hand. Before he realized what had happened, I'd spun around him and pushed the blade into his back. He jerked upright as it tore through his left kidney.

"Here's the way it's going to be, boys," I said. When their attention was mine, I jerked the blade out and jumped back. "The big guy has a punctured kidney. He'll bleed out in 'bout fifteen minutes. Mercy hospital is 'bout ten minutes away. You can leave and save him. Or, stay and let me poke holes in you too."

The giant pushed his hand hard against the wound. The blood glistened under the streetlamps as it oozed between his fingers. His pain could be heard in his sharp, noisy breathing but he refused to go quietly.

In a harsh tone, he grunted, "Kill dat spook."

The first guy's hand moved for a gun, but the knife left my hand before he touched his steel. The blade sank into his chest and stopped his heart permanently. The second man took a few steps back then sprinted away.

"Wanna tell me who's paying you to tail me?" I asked. "I'll be nice, if you're a good boy."

"You gonna die, boy," he said. I nodded but as more blood escaped his fingers, his lips loosened. "DeCarlos had us tailing da mayor's wife. Saw her leaving your place so we're supposed ta follow and stop you from stickin' your nose where it don't belong."

"Why is DeCarlos messing with her?"

He grunted and stepped back toward the street. He straightened up and said, "You think he tells me anything important?"

I saw his point and decided to make a quick escape. He turned and limped away while I continued toward my date with Slick Willy.

—w—

LISTEN HUN, HOW BAD you needin' to know bouts Slick?" I'd asked a few of the local girls about Willy's whereabouts, but only this one had stepped up. The hooker was somewhere in her late twenties. The glow from the streetlamp made her caramel skin glow. She glanced to the side a couple of times and in the corner of my vision, I spotted a man in a doorway. Her pimp, I guessed. She acted composed but I could see the desperation in her expression. She needed a score.

"They call me Sugar," she leaned close and wrapped her arms around me. "I got a room in the same building as Slick," she nodded slightly toward the pimp. "Take me back there for a good time and I'll show ya his room."

I quickly glanced over the woman. Sugar had looks, in that plain Jane sort of way; the kind of girl that you'd take to the bedroom, but that's about all. I waved my hand for her to lead the way. I nodded to the pimp to let him know his girl would be gone for a while. Hints of gold sparkled off his teeth as he smiled.

We walked to a nearby tenement building. It reeked of urine and filth. The stairs were littered with bodies, some conscious and some engaged in various carnal acts. We stepped lightly and cautiously. After three flights, she pointed to a room at the end of the hall.

"Willy's room is down there," she said and looked me up and down. Her hands snaked their way across my chest and pulled me closer. "I'm hoping you want more than just that. Been a while since I had a real man like you, someone worth looking at while we have some fun. "

With a light touch, I moved her away. The look of disappointment was evident and understandable. The men who frequented the area were the men that women didn't want; old, worn out, or violent. I extracted a couple of bills from my pocket and slipped them into her hand.

"Thanks, Sugar. But I've got business down the hall."

She glared until I tapped the bills in her hand.

"I…" Stunned at her new fortune, she stuttered, "I… Thank you."

I nodded, "Tell your pimp I gave you the twenty. Split it with him and keep the C note for yourself. And, if I'm ever down this way again, just keep in mind that I pay well for information."

The money disappeared into her cleavage and we parted ways.

I tried the knob, but the door was locked. Grunts and groans filtered through from the other side. Willy wasn't expecting guests, other than the one in there with him. I silently prayed that it was a woman who shared his bed tonight.

The door splintered as I kicked it from its hinges. The surprised couple jumped. Willy snatched up the sheet and wrapped it around him. I almost laughed at the look on the girl's face when she found herself completely bare for my viewing pleasure. Willy was a real gentleman.

"Slick Willy?" I asked. He grabbed for his pants but stopped when I pulled my jacket open to reveal a pistol on my hip. "Just stay where you are for now."

"What the hell you want? And who are yous anyway?"

"The photos of you and Stephanie Murray, I want to know all about them."

I jerked the folded photos from my jacket pocket and tossed them on the bed. He glanced at them but only smirked. Frustrated, I stepped a little closer. The smell of sex and sweat sickened me. I glanced at the girl on the bed. She gave a half hearted try to cover her breasts but her attention was focused on the photos. I didn't need her knowing about Stephanie's romp.

"You," I said to her, "Get dressed and get out."

She didn't waste time and was back in her dress as fast as Willy had gotten her out of it. When the door closed behind her, an eerie silence fell on the room. The pimp and I stared at one another. When I saw him blink, I knew I had him.

"You can tell me what I wanna know," I said and pulled a switchblade from my pocket. The button made a soft click and the blade appeared. Willy jumped and I smiled, "or…"

"What, you gonna cut me?" Willy's voice shook.

"Cut?" I pointed the knife at his shrinking manhood. "Cut off is more like it."

His eyes widened and I motioned to the bed with the blade. Like a scared dog, he sat, head down and looked at the photos again.

"Whatchya wanna know?"

"Everything. Who took them? Not you cause I don't think you're that smart." I said.

"A white guy brought her here. Told me to have some fun. He wanted pictures of the white princess getting balled by a big black…" He stopped when my eyes narrowed.

"This white guy got a name?"

"Bryant something." He said, then shook his head, "But something weren't right with that girl. She was drugged or something. All glassy eyed and everything. Acted like a slave girl. You know, like she were under his control. He told her what to do and damn, if the white bitch didn't up and do it."

My eyes narrowed at the revelation, mind control and Bryant. A big piece of the puzzle just fell into place

—∞—

"**D**EX, HONEY," ROXIE'S VOICE pulled me from my slumber and the dream. It'd haunted me for years. Abigail or Lady Victoria as I called her in the dream always showed up in the nick of time to save me. I never knew the danger, only the blood that poured from my broken body. And just as the cold breath of death touched my face, she came to me.

I sat up and rubbed my burning eyes. Roxie stood in the bathroom with a towel and a thin cloud of steam wrapped around her.

"It's eight thirty. I thought you'd wanna get your ass out of bed and back on your case." She said.

"What makes you think I wanna get back on this case?" I said through a yawn.

"Because you were calling out her name in your sleep." I could see the hurt in her eyes. "Look Dex, I don't care if you like thinking about other dames, but you don't have to rub it in."

"It's not what you think." I mumbled as I stood. "She did something for me, years ago."

"Like what?"

I refused to let myself get mad at her harsh tone. "We'll talk about it later. I need you to do some running for me this morning. I got a good lead last night."

Roxie strolled to her writing table and allowed the towel to fall. She bent at the waist and stuck her assets toward me as she snatched up a pen.

"Okay, whatchya need?"

The view caught me off guard, but I shook off my desires and said, "Get in touch with Mrs. Murray and see if she's heard anything from the kidnappers. And ask our usual sources at City Hall about any enemies of the mayor inside the police department. I'll be gone most of the morning, but I'll touch base with ya before lunch."

"Where you going?" she asked.

"I'm going to jail."

—𝕨—

ASHTON PRISON ROSE OUT of the coastal swampland like a crypt. Moss covered trees stood around the bleak walls of the former Confederate fortress turned home to several hundred of the worst offenders that the Carolinas had to offer. The morning fog hadn't burnt off yet and it blurred the prison's stonework and swamp beyond it. The foul stench of death and decay seemed appropriate here.

I parked my Ford a short ways from the gate and stepped out. I loved driving but living in the city gave me few chances to get out on the road. After one last draw, I flipped my finished cigarette into the wet grass as I walked. Something bothered me, tugged at the back of my mind, but I couldn't see it yet. My intuition never told me what I really needed to know, but it usually gave me a clue.

Inside the prison lay a labyrinth of corridors. I knew the way though, and walked until I found the office I needed.

"I'm here to see Basil Bryant," I said and watched the old man behind the counter scrunch up his face in disgust.

"Why would anyone wanna see that old perv?" he coughed out and then stepped to a filing cabinet. "Sign in on the clip..." he paused in mid sentence and looked back at me with a confused expression. "Wait, we released him last week."

"Did you say released or escaped?"

"Released," he stepped to the counter and eyed me with suspicion. "I did the paperwork. He got an appeal, think it was his fifth or sixth try. This time the court overturned his life sentence. Gave him time served."

Someone with connections had helped him out. He'd been a menace decades ago. As a hypnotist and mind control expert, he'd been at the head of several gangs. But each time, Lady Vic or the other heroes had stopped him. His last crime spree had been twenty years ago and in the end, he'd been sentenced to life without parole.

"Why did you call him an old perv?"

He gave me a soured expression and cleared his throat. "Cause he's always had pictures of Lady Victoria stuck all over the walls of his cell. Still, he wasn't that bad of a guy, inside here."

"Do you know anything about him? I mean from the old days?"

He looked me over. "Why is a spook like you asking so many questions about him?"

I placed a twenty on the counter and slid it to him. "I have a client and I'm on a case. Is that a problem?"

He looked at me through bigoted eyes, but the money loosened his lips. "I was a guard back when they brought him in for good. He tried using that hocus pocus on some of us, but without that ring of his, he weren't no good at it."

The words brought back some memories from my childhood. "That's right; he had some sort of ring that he used to work his magic. Hypnotize people or whatever it was. Do you know what happened to it?"

"Well that was the thing, ya see. When he was caught, they say he didn't have it. I don't know if the police took it or he lost it. Seems to me that after he came in here, there were a lot of folks asking him about it. But he never said nothing."

"Any idea where he'd be heading?" I asked.

"Shit, don't tell me the ol' boy got himself in trouble. Thought for sure he was gonna go legit."

"Did he ever have any visitors?" I asked.

He snorted and took his time going through a filing cabinet until a folder was drawn out. He studied it and looked at me.

"He had one guy, came in a bunch of times over the summer. Named G. Banton."

"I've heard of him. One of DeCarlos' couriers." I said.

"If Bryant wanted a fresh start, even at his age, why go after revenge now? He'd be the most likely suspect." I thought. It didn't make sense.

I thanked the clerk and left.

My mind raced while I drove back to town. Basil had to be in his sixties but his former adversaries weren't much younger. Surely Basil hadn't held a grudge for all these years. But from the sound of things, maybe it wasn't a grudge, but something more personal for him.

As soon as I hit the city limits, I pulled over to the closest phone booth and called Roxie.

"Hey babe, tell me some good news."

"Dex? Glad you called. Boy have I got some news for you. No one at City Hall could help out. It wasn't like they didn't know, but like they were afraid to say anything. I called Dietrich over at the Westside police precinct and asked him. He got real quiet and said for you to meet him at Joe's for lunch at one."

I looked at my watch. There was plenty of time. "Anything from Abigail?"

"No. No word from Mrs. High and Mighty."

I ignored the quip about Abigail. "Alright babe, do me another favor. Head back to the courthouse and see if you can dig up any dirt on Basil Bryant's appeal. See if anyone pulled some strings to help him."

"Should I know that name?"

I couldn't help but laugh. Bryant had gone to prison the same year she was born. "No, kitten. Just see what you can find out. And keep on trying to reach Mrs. High and Mighty."

———※———

"**D**IETRICH," I NODDED AS I slid into the chair opposite the police detective.

Lunch hour at Joe's never failed to be an adventure. As the best food joint in Waterford, if not all of Port Vic, the joint stayed busy. But I knew the crowd and noise offered us a certain amount of anonymity, which is why Detective John Dietrich offered to meet there. Plus, it sat across the street from my office.

"Is there a reason why your bimbo is doing all your leg work?" he said through a mouth full of hamburger.

"Leg work? Would you rather see my legs or hers?" He gave me a half-hearted smile and shrugged.

"Know anything 'bout some boys on the force who might have it in for the mayor?"

He stared as he chewed another bite and shook his head. "Lots of new folks rising up in the ranks, a little too fast, if you know what I mean. But no one I know of is that upset."

"Any reason for the promotions?"

"Rumor is that they are adding new folks for a big push. Beefing up the place." When he saw my questioning look, he whispered, "I think they plan on invading Waterford and shutting down the gangs."

I slapped a couple of bills down to cover his lunch, "Thanks. That's good to know."

As I stood to leave, he motioned me closer, "Roxie is looking good."

I turned and saw her in front of my building. She crossed the street and headed toward the door. She gave me an odd smile that told me something was very wrong.

"Thanks, Dietrich." I said and then headed out.

We met outside and I took her arm.

"Babe?"

"Not here. Come on." She said and led me across the street. As we got into our building, she turned. "Hun, what are you into with all this? Nobody at the courthouse would talk. They all got scared when I mentioned Bryant's name. When I left, one of the clerks followed me out for a ciggy. She said that some bigwigs made sure that Bryant got released."

"And it'd take big wigs to make the high level changes in the police department." I added. "What about Abigail?"

"I've been calling all morning. They keep saying she isn't available. And I tried again a little while ago and our phone line is dead. I looked and someone cut the wire outside our building." Roxie said and glanced around nervously. "Someone is trying to keep you out of the loop."

She slipped her hand behind my head and pulled my lips to hers. Her mouth was warm and I needed it. But I jerked back. Even though most folks in the neighborhood knew about us, it wasn't something we needed to show off in public.

"Go find her," she said.

—m—

MY CAR SLID TO a stop in front of the Mayor's mansion half an hour later. A single cop outside the front doors watched my approach. He seemed content until I started up the walkway. I knew the look. He didn't like my color.

"Hey Bo-bo, servant's entrance is 'round back." He smarted off with a grin. I kept walking to the door but he stepped in front of me with one hand up and the other on the butt of his pistol. "Stop right there, ashy. This ain't no place for you."

"I'm here to see Abigail Murray," I said nicely and tried to ignore his bigoted arrogance. But when his hand touched my chest to stop me, I started to show a little anger. "Officer, move your hand or lose it. Mrs. Murray is my client and she is in…"

"Yeah, like she'd be needin' a gorilla." He laughed and when I tried to push past him, he pointed the pistol at my forehead. "Just back away, Bo-bo. Da boys at lockup been itching for someone to play with and you're making me think it's gonna be you."

I didn't have time for this. In a blur, I spun. My right hand grabbed the pistol away from him before he knew what had happened. Then I jerked back around, grabbed his throat with my free hand, and lifted him from the ground. He jerked violently and I considered crushing his throat. I squeezed and listened to the choking sounds.

I placed the pistol back into its holster. With that done, I stepped to the door and rang the bell. He dangled as I waited patiently until the door opened.

"May I help…" was all the butler got out before he saw the cop at the end of my outstretched arm. His eyes widened for a moment before his thin lips twitched upward into a smile. Obviously, he was not a fan of the officer's bigotry either. "You must be Mr. Wolfe. Madame Murray said you'd come by and left a note for you."

He disappeared back into the mansion before I could get a word out. I looked back to the cop. He struggled less now, but still fought for breath. When the butler returned, he held out a crème colored envelope with my name scribbled on the front.

"She left about an hour and a half ago after receiving a phone call. Mentioned driving to the bank but insisted that she take the car herself."

He said in a worried tone. "I fear she may be in danger. She's always been too headstrong to ask for help, well, until she called on you."

"You knew she came to me?"

He smiled. "You helped out a member of the staff last year. So, I recommended you."

"Thank you."

I put the cop down. When his hand moved back to the gun, I narrowed my eyes and growled.

"I was nice and shoved your gun back in its holster. You ever draw it on me again and I'll shove it someplace where surgeons can't get to it."

He backed down.

As I left the driveway, I fumbled with the card and drew it from the envelope. Hints of her perfume filled the car as I lifted it up to read.

Mr. Wolfe,
The blackmailer called and gave me the instructions for the ransom. I tried to call but was unable to reach you. I am to meet a contact at the corner of Market and 1ˢᵗ Street at 2pm. With luck, I'll see you there.
Abigail

I floored the accelerator. The hands on my watch showed 1:50. The traffic lights were ignored as I careened through town and managed to get to the meeting spot, albeit fifteen minutes late. The tires squealed in protest as the car slid to an abrupt halt. Looking around, I saw no sign of her.

A pair of drunks sat propped against the building. They gave me the evil eye so I approached.

"Did you see a woman? Pretty blond with big tits?" I shouted.

One nodded but the other, a bearded man, shushed him. He held up an empty bottle and shook it. I took his meaning. A five dollar bill, drawn from my pocket, made their eyes pop open. I held it out but snapped it back when their hands approached.

In a harsh tone, I said, "Spill!"

"Yeah, saw her. She was a looker. Car pulled up, three men got out and they took her with 'em."

"Did she have anything with her? What kind of car were they in?" I asked.

The other man spoke up, "Had a big hand bag."

"Yea, and they were in a blue car…"

"Baby blue," interjected the second man. "One of them Model A's. Headed towards the bay."

"Thanks. How long ago?" I asked.

"Just before you got here."

If they were still close enough, I might spot them. The engine roared and tires spun as I shot off down the street toward the harbor. Luckily, traffic was light. My head turned back and forth as I passed through each intersection. A block from the harbor, I spotted blue in the distance. Their slow moving Ford was far enough out that I'd be hard pressed to catch it. I jerked the wheel hard to the right. My car fishtailed but straightened out. As I got a little closer, they turned off the road into an abandoned warehouse, a DeCarlos owned warehouse.

With my car hidden out of sight, I carefully made my way closer. A solitary guard stood at the rear entrance. He didn't stand a chance. In fact, he never saw my run. At top speed, I moved in a blur. My fist connected with his jaw and shattered it. He tumbled several feet. I don't bother to check if he was unconscious or dead. Either way, he wasn't making any noise. I downed two more guards in the same manner at the front of the building.

An open window gave me stealthy access into the building. A small office stood empty and I slid through the window without a sound. With care, I lightly stepped to the door, cracked it open, and listened.

Unfamiliar voices echoed off of the stacks of crates piled high throughout the warehouse. One voice dominated the conversation. The man sounded old and tired, but pushed his words out with emotion.

"There's no deals. You surrender your mind to me and I let your daughter go. Otherwise…"

The poor lighting created a vast number of shadows that I used to my advantage. I slipped out from the office and moved through the darkness. An idea struck me and I spotted a good place to get a bird's eye view of things. I climbed up the backside of a stack of crates and surveyed the scene.

Abigail stood defiant in front of Bryant. With her hands on her hips, she looked every bit the part of her former superheroine self. Three goons with Tommy guns trained on her back kept her from choking the life out of him. She glanced to her left a few times. With a careful lean, I saw Stephanie, entranced and on her knees with a fourth goon beside her.

In a corner behind them, Slick Willy stood. His glazed over eyes seemed unaware of everything around him. I guessed Bryant had used the ring on him just as he had used it on Stephanie.

Abigail's voice conveyed her fury, but I could sense the fear that she tried to cover. Age and the comforts of the mayoral mansion had dulled her strengths and reflexes. She could take down one, maybe two of the goons, but those Tommys would cut her in half if she tried.

"You're an idiot if you think I'm surrendering to you. Let her go now!" She barked.

Bryant stepped closer, but stayed out of arm's reach. I noticed his right thumb twitched back and forth over a shiny gold ring.

"I don't want to hurt her or you." Bryant's voice trailed off as he lost himself in her eyes. His love or obsession for her was his weakness, at least for the moment. "Please, just give yourself up and let me inside your head and I promise … I swear the girl can go free. I'll even erase her memories of everything that's happened. Stephanie will never know what she was made to do."

She shook her head. His voice rose with frustration. "You don't understand the big picture here. You're going to die if you don't. And Stephanie? She's already a whore; you saw the pictures. I may not have a choice and she'll remain a toy for the black boys in Waterford."

"And what do you want with me?" Her voice cracked. The maternal instinct to protect her child took over. I had to do something before she surrendered.

He chuckled, "Abby, you won't be hurt and your girl will be set free. The choice is yours, but you know that despite all the exploits, I've always been a man of my word."

She had no choice. Whether his word could be trusted was beyond me. But she knew him better. Maybe that was his angle. I started to move but stopped in surprise when she spoke up.

"If you swear…."

I stopped and watched the events. He raised his hand and motioned for her to kneel. She dropped to her knees, eyes lowered to the floor. An eerie silence fell over the room, but I saw a tear on her cheek as it fell. The ring glowed as it moved closer to her face. He mumbled some words and her body relaxed. Her shoulders lost their defiance and slumped. Her head fell to the side somewhat. It only took seconds for her to fall under his spell.

Bryant's face lit up but his moment of triumph didn't last long. A voice, deep and familiar, rang out as someone walked into view.

"Impressive, Bryant. I didn't think she'd give up to you that easily."

Mayor Charles Murray wore a smug grin as he stepped up and looked down on his enslaved wife. The sight of him stunned me enough that I didn't catch the goon who'd stepped back and spotted me.

"Hey! You, hands up." He shouted with the business end of a machine gun pointed at my head.

'Damn it," I whispered to myself.

My hands went up and I hopped from the crates. He grabbed me by the arm and, instead of resisting, I let him push me toward the men. No reason, I thought, to let them know what I'm capable of doing. Not yet, anyway.

"Who are you?" Bryant asked, but the Mayor spoke up.

"He's the private dick that I asked that bitch not to hire. Let's get this over with, I have a dinner reservation and I want everything to look convincing."

Murray extracted a chrome plated pistol from a pocket as he casually strolled to Willy. Without hesitation, the weapon came up and fired almost pointblank into the pimp's forehead.

"Hmm. I'd say killing the man that defiled your daughter is—justifiable." As he turned and walked closer to me, a blue silk handkerchief was plucked from his jacket and wiped the weapon clean of his prints. But he hesitated and looked me over. In a condescending voice, he added, "What to do with you? I didn't expect the Black Wolfe to be here."

My eyes moved from him to the leaking head of Willy and then to Abby. He smiled and nodded.

"You got it figured out yet, boy?"

The remark struck a nerve. That word, *boy*, infuriated me. It always had. But I tried to pull the last pieces of the puzzle together.

"This is all about gaining control over the Waterford district's crime syndicates." I said. He nodded and waved a hand to imply he wanted to hear more. "I guess the job as mayor wasn't paying enough so you…"

"Went bad? No, no, my boy. Think bigger." His voice echoed off the walls.

"Lady Vic and the others destroyed the gangs decades ago and they did it with your—help. This goes back that far?" He nodded. "You helped them eradicate the syndicates with the plan of restarting them. You've been the new puppet master over all the crime families in town and slowly rebuilt their little empires. Your only weakness is that you're white and Waterford isn't. So you stacked the police department with people on your payroll and kept the white gangs on a leash, but let the black gangs thrive."

"Excellent! I can see why my wife wanted to hire you. So while the black gangs are growing out of control, I keep pushing the City Council to add additional manpower to the police force. Add more of MY people."

I looked at Bryant. His eyes were on his kneeling victim but he must have felt my stare because he looked over at me. For a moment, there was sadness in his eyes.

"What are you getting out of this?" I asked and watched him nod toward Abby.

"As a reward for his services, he gets to have her again before she dies from several nasty gunshot wounds." Murray almost laughed as he finished the sentence.

"You'd kill her? Why not have Bryant use his power to turn her into a docile housewife for you?" Then it struck me. "Because you need a reason to convince the City Council and the public to wage war against the Waterford district."

"Very good! The press will learn that my daughter was kidnapped, raped and molested by that…" he waved back to Willy. "black trash. My wife comes to deliver the ransom but as a former superhero, she fights back. She kills Willy but his men kill her. The press will eat this up. The city's great heroine, gunned down in her retirement while trying to save her daughter from the spooks that infest these streets. The citizens and politicians alike will rally behind my cause. I'll get all the manpower I need to steamroll over Waterford—clean out every gang hideout and then let my people take over."

"You are one sick bastard. You'd arrange to have your own daughter raped? Your wife murdered?"

The overweight man in the expensive suit just laughed, "Yes. I would."

I couldn't help but look over at Abby. Her eyes stared blankly and her jaw hung open. Despite her defeat, her beauty remained. He saw something in my expression because his next words made my blood freeze.

"She is a beauty, a wildcat in bed, but she's past her prime. Women with her looks are a dime a dozen to a man with power. You made the mistake of showing up here. Bryant here will turn you into one of my puppets. I think I'll have you pull the trigger on her."

Something said earlier struck me. "Wait, you said Bryant would have her again?"

"Think about it." he said but saw that I wasn't in the mood for more guessing games. "Twenty years ago, she was the only super left alive. The gangs were finished. Only Bryant remained, terrorizing the city. Abigail disappeared for a few weeks. When the police found her, she'd been turned into Bryant's sex toy. I could've given him the death sentence, but we worked out a deal. He'd use the ring on her, make her forget about what had happened and fill her with an undying love for me." Murray gestured to Stephanie. "What I didn't plan on was him knocking her up."

"It didn't happen that way," Bryant growled but a harsh look from Murray silenced him.

"Stephanie is your daughter?" I looked at Bryant. "And you did that to her?"

"After I'm done with her, she'll never remember," Bryant remarked in a panicked tone.

"Yes, after you've had your thrill with Abby." Murray replied and pointed a twitching finger at me.

Bryant stepped closer and I could see something in his expression. For a once great villain, he didn't have the look of a man excited about victory. He appeared conflicted and hesitant.

He brought the ring up at my face. I mentally noted the positions of the three goons behind me and the one beside Stephanie. Before he knew what had happened, I lurched forward, grabbed Bryant's hand, and pushed it into the face of the closest goon. His frail arm snapped and he screamed. I didn't mean to break the bone, but in all honesty, I didn't care. I kept my eyes away from his hand and glared into Bryant's eyes. The ring glowed briefly. Its green light illuminated his pale face and gave him the look of a specter. I shoved Bryant away and turned with lightning speed.

Grabbing the barrel of the tommy gun from of one the men, I tore it from his grasp. Then I spun in place and used the weapon as a club.

It splintered the skull of the man beside him. The first man reacted defensively as blood and brains splattered over him. He never saw the butt of the tommy gun as it impacted his face, sending him to the floor. Neither of the men would last long enough to make it to a hospital.

Two shots rang out from the goon beside Stephanie but a pair of quick knife throws ended him. I glanced over my shoulder and saw that the goon who'd looked at the ring just stood. His eyes were as lifeless as Abby's.

I felt something punch me in the arm. It took a split second for me to connect the gunshot to the punch. The pain and burning could be ignored for now, but not the gun that Murray held. When the second shot rang out, I'd already moved clear and lashed out with a third throwing knife. It caught him in the forearm and knocked the weapon from his hand.

Murray turned to run, but my last knife found the back of his right thigh and put him down. He cried out in pain, but there wasn't anyone left to help him. I stepped over and knelt beside him.

"You're a dead man, ya know it?" He spit the words at me. My smirk only infuriated him more. When his hand grabbed for his pistol, my fist slammed down. He was out for the night.

Sobbing mixed with laughter grabbed my attention. Bryant just sat on the floor and cradled his broken arm while tears streaked his cheeks. His head tilted this way and that as he looked at Abby. Finally his gaze turned to me as I strolled to him.

"All I wanted to do was move to Florida and start over," he whispered then nodded toward Murray. "Did ya kill him?"

I shook my head. "If you wanted to start over, then why help him? Was she worth it?"

"Why? He offered me freedom. I loved her, ya know? The last twenty years have all been lies. All those years ago, he had a gun to my head and to hers. Made me fix things so she'd be in love with him and think that he was the girl's daddy." The words were whispered but anger began seeping in as he continued. "The bastard had my ring. Spent years trying to figure out how to use it himself. When he couldn't, he came back to me. Thing is, I'd never used the ring on her back then. We were bitter enemies turned lovers. He made me erase her feelings for me, erase her memories. He threatened to kill me and her both. He was gonna kill her tonight but I just wanted her to remember the truth before she died."

We sat together as he sobbed. I looked at her and wondered where to go from here. She'd be ruined when news of the mayor's crimes were exposed. Heartbroken if she knew the truth about the forbidden relationship between herself, and Bryant and about their child.

"The ring, can it be used by someone else?"

He laughed, " 'Course. I'd found it in a museum and learned its secret." He turned his attention back to Murray. "You gonna kill him? Can't turn him into the police, he owns them."

I looked at my arm. Murray's bullet had grazed it. The bleeding hadn't lasted long, but it stung. But I wasn't the only one injured.

Gently, I took Bryant's arm and lifted it. "This will hurt for a minute." I said, then gave a jerk. The bones snapped back into place. As I released his arm, I slipped the ring from his finger. He didn't resist and in fact, straightened the digit to make it easier.

The gold circle and its solitary green stone shimmered in the light.

"Can I make you a deal?" I asked.

—◊◊—

I DON'T UNDERSTAND EVERYTHING that happened." Abby said.

She sat in my office, confused and lightheaded. The clock read midnight. Jazz from the bar down the street drifted in the open window. She didn't notice the ring as I slipped it off my finger and dropped it into the top desk drawer.

"Where is Stephanie now?"

"I had the police take her home." She listened as I explained most of what'd happened. The crimes of her husband, his betrayal and plans for her and Stephanie, and how he'd used Bryant's powers. I saw the confusion at the mention of his name.

"Bryant? I don't know who that is. Should I?"

I kept a serious expression, but inwardly smiled. Bryant had been right. I'd been able to use the ring, just like he'd shown me.

"No, you shouldn't know him. He's a hypnotist. He'd enslaved Stephanie and…" She nodded in understanding. "But in the end, I had him erase all memories of that. She'll wake up in the morning, thinking that she's been sick with the flu."

"And my husband?" her voice rumbled. "After what he's done to us?"

"Bryant's ability made him see the error of his ways. In the morning, he'll call the FBI and make a full confession about his involvement with the local crime families."

I saw her anger give way to hurt. For so long, her husband had concealed the truth. She sat, broken and humiliated. This wasn't how things should've ended. I snatched an envelope from the drawer and tossed it on the desk.

"That's the money you gave me, minus my normal fee. With your husband turning himself in tomorrow, I think you and your daughter will need it more than me."

She reluctantly picked it up and looked at me. "What about Bryant?"

"He's been dealt with." I said.

A car horn brought both of us to our feet. She straightened out her skirt as I stepped around the desk.

"I… I should go." She stepped back and gave me a knowing look. "Thank you. But one last thing." She held up the cash-filled envelope. "Why give this back?"

"Because I owed you. I owed you my life." She looked confused, so I confessed. "When I was ten, I got stabbed by a gang of older kids. I was bleeding bad. My mom got me to the closest hospital, but Spencer Hospital is whites only. A nurse there broke the rules and plugged a bottle of blood into me. It kept me going until we got to the next place. Mom found out later that you'd given blood at the hospital earlier that day. The nurse was jailed because she gave your blood to a black boy."

"I remember giving blood back then," she stuttered.

"I think, because I was a kid and still growing, your super powers rubbed off on me. That was the day I gained my strength and speed. That was the day that I decided to be more than just another kid in a gang. So, I owed you something. I'd like to think my debt is paid."

As her taxi pulled away, I turned to see Roxie propped against the doorway.

"So you wanna tell me what really happened at the warehouse? Why would that old man help you?"

I pulled the ring from the top desk drawer and looked at it. "I gave him what he wanted. He showed me what to do and I used it to clean up things. The mayor will turn himself in, the daughter will never remember her romp with Willy, and Bryant got what he wanted."

She gave me a funny look. "What did he want? Her?"

"He wanted Abby to know the truth. I couldn't do that. But I gave him something better. Abby and the mayor have a cottage on the Gulf Shore. She's going to divorce the mayor since he tried to have her killed and move down there. She'll meet a man there, who she'll fall madly in love with. It'll be him."

"Bryant? You erased her memories of him."

"Yep. They were in love once and now they will be again. Just that she'll never know about what happened all those years ago."

As I plopped down into my chair, she strutted toward me.

"How do I know you're not going to use that thing on me?" she asked. "That's some powerful shit and ya know, they say power corrupts."

"I'd never use it on you. You're perfect as is." I said but added a little something extra, "Now, dance, kitten, dance."

She suddenly took on a whole new demeanor as her body began to sway to some unheard music. The ring had, in fact, been used on her thirty minutes earlier when Abby and I had returned. Her hips rocked back and forth as she turned. The fires ignited by Abby hadn't left and now were fanned by my girl's seductive moves. Her fingers move to unbutton the thin cotton blouse, which quickly fell away.

If I'd asked, Roxie would have done a striptease for me. But the idea of her doing it because she was under the ring's power added a certain thrill. I watched her skirt fall to reveal her smooth bare legs.

Guilt smacked at me. I bit my lip and tried to ignore it, but she was right. Power corrupts and her impromptu dance was ample proof of that. The weight of the ring in my fingers made me wonder how many before me had used its powers for evil. The green crystal caught the light and invited my eyes to look deeper.

Damn, I thought and shook my head. I knew that it had to be destroyed. If given an opportunity, its power would corrupt me. I pulled the drawer open and dropped the ring inside. When my eyes returned to her, she gave me a pouty face.

"Sorry babe, you have my full attention now."

She smiled and continued her dance. A hand snaked across her back and unhooked her bra. As the warm flesh of her breasts was exposed to me, I knew that its corrupting power already had taken root within me. I may have used it for good tonight by righting the wrongs that Murray and Bryant had created, but given time, all power destroys.

She turned her back and playfully tugged at her pink panties. As she slowly bent and drew them down, I decided that it had to be destroyed.

But, I could wait until Roxie's next show was over.

ROCKET CROCKETT AND THE JADE DRAGON

BY CHRISTOPHER CHAMBERS

WINTER STORM CLOUDS DISSIPATED over the North Korean coast at Chongjin. Just low overcast -- occasionally punctured by tracer rounds looking like evil fireflies and the fierce blossoms of bursting flak shells. Such was the usual welcome the Chinese offered when Lt. Rufus "Rocket" Crockett, U.S. Navy, arrived to jump and jive from the frigid sky.

"Flight Control, this the Typewriter Four Six Four Tango, come in *Bonhomme Richard.*"

"Typewriter Four Six Four Tango, Control copies. Your Intelligence boys want to know if you got some pretty pinup pictures in your nose camera."

"Aye aye, Control. Buxom and thick-thighed. First had to do a little tapping on the typewriter while they was eatin' their chop suey. No bandits, though."

There was a pause and static, then suddenly. "Typewriter Four Six Four Tango you got three-strike-four, four bandits closing on your four o'clock, range two miles!"

"Shit. MiGs?" MiGs would make Rocket spit his cigar into his mask. He was in a "banjo" -- an F2H Banshee, the Navy's first jet fighter. Banjos were straight-winged, like the P-51s Sammy jockeyed in the 332nd during the war. No match for MiGs unless Rocket did the 'Harlem Hop' Sammy's Tuskegee cohorts danced with the Kraut Me 262 jets: climb then dive, cut then shoot. He'd done it before, and frightened two MiG pilots so much they ran for base. But the gooks and ChiComs were getting better at handling the hardware. Rocket's draws felt a bit looser when, thankfully, Control told him the bandits were too slow to be MiGs. Prop fighters, likely Yak-9s.

"Outrun 'em, Typewriter!" Control warned. "We need those recon photos!"

Rocket broke the banjo right to meet the swarm, already firing their 20mm tracers to scare him. "Nah unh, ain't comin' home if I don't dance with this gang, 'cause they sure wanna dance with me…" Rocket chomped on his unlit cigar. *So let's dance…*

Yet rather than overfly the banjo as it banked into their formation, the Yaks scattered. Two looped to get on Rocket's six o'clock, two climbed to gain speed and gun him from the above. *You ain't no rookie eggrolls or gooks. Y'all are honchos.* Rocket broke their frequency for a second. Indeed, the pilots called to each other in Russian. Likely trainees, cutting their teeth on the Yaks before they climbed into a MiG cockpit. *That's okay, I'm gonna school ya.*

Rocket pushed the banjo into a screaming dive with two Yaks still on his tail. Playing chicken with the ocean wasn't in their repertoire, clearly. One Yak broke off, unable to pull the Gs even in a slow piston fighter. The second became a submarine. Scratch one honcho, now fish food. The banjo parted the surf with its jetstream then climbed like a hawk, cannon blazing, toward the next two bandits. The Yaks broke left in unison to protect each other; Rocket, grunting through the Gs like he was giving birth, looped and stapled himself on their six o'clock. He fired. One bandit exploded before the honcho could bail. That's war. Rocket let the other go. And what a story this ofay could tell over vodka, about the spade pilot who kicked his ass.

"*Bonhomme Richard*, this the Typewriter. Comin' home baby…"

It may have been clearing over the coast, but the Sea of Japan was a roiling mess. The signalman, a hayseed chief petty officer named Buckley, was flashing and flapping the red paddles. That cracker would wave Rocket off even in a flat calm and sunshine, all just to mess with a colored aviator because there weren't supposed to be any colored aviators. Not in the white man's Navy, no matter what Harry Truman decreed about Jim Crow. Nor did Captain Connor do Rocket any favors that angry, gray afternoon by keeping the ole Goodtime Dickie—what the crew called the *Bonhomme Richard* –turned into the howling wind. Indeed, the flattop's flight deck was pitching in twenty foot swells and whitecaps sprayed like Joe Louis uncorking New Year's Eve champagne geysers at Small's Paradise back in Harlem.

Sleet pelted the bubble canopy. The air in the cockpit wasn't much better: freezing after the acrid smell from Rocket's spent stogie melded with Gentleman Jim aftershave and Smoov Mallard pomade -- congealed under Rocket's flight helmet. Rocket didn't need Smoov Mallard to stay smooth, after the conk he gave himself a week past. But in case the Chinese nailed the Typewriter, his hair had to shine and lay down, even in a POW camp!

Rocket was cold, exhausted. Enough of this bull. He eased the throttle, pulled the stick to bleed speed, gain altitude. The banjo climbed, banked, then leveled. White knuckle time for most pilots, but as Rocket boasted, his knuckles were born brown. Still, even a second's distraction meant ditching in the savage, freezing ocean, or slamming on the deck like a bomb.

And then that one second's distraction hit like the stroke that hobbled his proud daddy, like a hot poker to the brain. Tearing into his eyes and ears at the worst possible moment were the images that usually seized him at night, alone. Always more terrifying than flak fire or the sloppy orange-peel textured thighs of *Mama-san* Michiko at the Teahouse of the Sublime Slippery Grip. All Rocket saw in the cockpit was Sammy, swinging by a lynching rope from that old gaslight post by the railroad siding, his body glowing green with freakish pallor. No sound but the Number Five Chicago Central hitting its whistle in the distant night. And the buzz: flies, invisible in the dark. Gas, in the bulb. Those crackers in Memphis hated seeing him in his Air Corps dress uniform and white gloves, escorting Redbone Tina to Nellie's Ribshack & Beer Garden on Beale Street, and yes, they all thought Tina was a white girl. Captain Sammy Crockett of the 332nd, eleven Kraut Me-109's shot down. Home three days after V-E Day, showing off his medals…now tangled in the air, three feet off the Tennessee dirt. And in that dirt, at his feet, was a smashed-up model of his own P-51 Mustang. His gift to his younger brother…

"*They hung him, Daddy, they killed your boy, Mamma! I got to cut Sammy down!*"

In Rocket's ears came the sting of reality. "Typewriter…Four Six Four Tango…Banshee Four Six Four Tango! Crockett what the hell're you doing?"

"Oh *shit!*" Rocket broke from the searing phantom images.

In one second he'd hit one hundred seventy knots… just a mile from a World War Two vintage flattop bobbing in the Sea of Japan…in a banjo—already obsolete compared to the Air Force's shiny new Sabres—but a jet nonetheless. Buckley was flapping red like a crazy seagull; flight control counseled abort. *Nah Sammy, I got this*! Flaps down, gear down, tailhook down. "Hope you cats de-iced the deck," Rocket called into his mic, " 'cause this spook's on final approach…"

With roar of reverse thrust and the jerk of the hook on the cables, he was down. "Rocket Crockett's home till the next blast off, baby…"

Fifteen minutes later, the dark gray wings of the banjo were folded like a huge roosting bat's. Rocket rode the massive deck elevator down to the service bay with his jet steed, along with his squire "Bonelip" Broussard. Bonelip, still wearing his steward's apron, handed Rocket a fresh cigar, then tugged at Rocket's G-1 bomber jacket.

"Y'all gotta let me oil this here leather, man," Bonelip said, breathless from the cold, bandy legs unsteady in the heavy seas. He was light-skinned and squat as a pond toad, thus the other stewards compared him to actor Edward G. Robinson, whom most were convinced was passing anyway.

Bonelip himself was part of the white man's *old* Navy. He'd been a mess boy on a battlewagon during the war, serving ice cream to officers while Marines got cut to pieces in the tarry sands of Peleliu and Iwo Jima. Deactivated in '45, he returned to New Orleans, where he played trombone in a Faubourg-Treme whorehouse band until the Commies ran the ROK all the way down to Pusan in 1950. In 1950 Rocket was scoring touchdowns and chasing high yella chippies at Howard U. in D.C., and Pusan was something that almost rhymed with…well...

The Goodtime Dickie was scheduled to revictual at the Yokosuka Navy Base in Tokyo Bay. "We be docked fo' two weeks wid no mo' than two days sho' leave," Bonelip advised. "Even in two days you gonna need me to have yo' back case them peckerwoods don't like seeing you flossied up in your dress blues wid them geisha broads. And don't forget, Mae Tanaka be looking for you."

"My faithful Sancho Panza," Rocket said, biting on the sweet new stogie as mechanics inspected the Typewriter, "there's a bottle of *saki* in it for you if you can line up some action with Mae's boss."

"Rocket, come on wid dat mess. You done took dat pimp fo' whut— *three large* two monffs ago? Mae tole me he wanna take $3,000 out yo' *ass.*"

"He wants more than that. So does *she*. Now listen, go to Ito's in the Ginza, tell him—"

"*Shush,* the Man come," Bonelip cut off his dusky knight of the skies, for blocking the hatch to the warmth of the ship's innards was Lt. Commander Leiffer, the squadron C.O. Leiffer's nose was so far up Captain Connor's butt he could smell what the old man had on his choppers before he brushed his teeth.

"Lieutenant Crockett!" Leiffer hollered. Rocket give an anemic salute in return. "You muff an approach and landing, and men die. Didn't they teach you that at colored 'pilot' training? You were waved off *twice*. What were you dreaming about up there—Jackie Robinson and Roy Campanella double-screwing your sister?" He spied Rocket's silk scarf, white and fluffed as a cloud. "And the hell do think you are, god-damned Cab Calloway?"

"No sir. Jumpin' Jimmy Johnson at the Lafayette Ballroom, Lennox Ave, *sir*."

"Listen, Smart ass. The nose camera of that banjo better have the shots of the Sui-jong Bridges, not the crotches of darkie chorus girls, or I will have you keel hauled. "

Rocket knew he could easily Sugar Ray Robinson this wolf-ticket selling *ofay*, yet nothing would delight the Dixiecrats back home more than seeing a unicorn-rare Negro officer in the brig. But just as Leiffer was about to snarl another *ofay* voice intoned from the hatch. Rather than Leiffer's prosaic Ohio drone, it had a Texas twang.

"Rufus, that was circus flying, you young rascal, you!" It was the old man himself, Conner, flanked by the X.O. and a slack jawed acne faced ensign.

"Captain, sir," Leiffer began, sprouting a smile of glowing obsequiousness. "I was just debriefing Crockett, here on his—"

"Stow it, Leiffer. Yep, my little brown rapscallion, if anyone can land a jet in this weather after a four hour solo recon patrol, getting shot at like you was some goose on fire…hot dog, it was you, Rufus. And two kills, I hear?"

"Kills?" Leiffer said, craning his neck.

"Son, didn't you monitor Rufus' incoming? Our boy here got two Yak-9s flown by Soviet bastards, no less! Well done, boy."

"Aye aye, sir." Rocket replied, grinning under his thin mustache, cigar still clenched.

"Piston engine fighters," Leiffer huffed. "No match for an F2H."

"Nah unh sir," Bonelip inserted, forgetting his place. "Yaks ain't joke.

Las' month they jumped them Marines and shot 'em up bad—that Red Socks slugger Ted Williams, an' that John Glenn fella on the *Essex*…and they flyin' Panthers sir, not no broke-dick Banshee."

Conner looked down to Bonelip, "Boy, fix my rascal here up with a T-bone, French Fries and that bodacious chess pie of yours before he hits his rack." The skipper then turned to Rocket. "Rufus, you are a credit to your race. Ralph Dunce with wings."

"It's Bunche, sir, not Dunce."

"Uh-huh. Full *week's* liberty when we dock at Yokosuka. See to it, Leiffer."

As Conner hobbled away with his retainers and Leiffer in tow, Rocket could hear him whisper, "See, the Air Force might have its nigger aces but we got ours. Send a cable to *Life* magazine…"

Later that night, Rocket dined in the mess, alone as usual, after the white officers had eaten.

"Tell me again, man," Bonelip said, lifting a big slice of chess pie onto a dessert plate. "I knows why you 'Rocket,' *heh*. But you never say why y'all call yo' banjo 'Typewriter?' Them Air Force niggas like Chappie, they git ta paint Lena Horne on they planes."

Rocket gave his sidekick a dead stare. " 'Cause I tap-tap-tap a story of killing with my twenny millimeters, Bonelip. Now fetch me some bourbon for my Hershey's coco…"

Yet not even a full pint of bourbon, or a drag of reefer copped at Subic Bay, could knock Rocket out in his rack. The lurid nightmare came back. Twice. Sammy, swinging. The toy P-51, smashed. Whenever the dream hit, it was portends. Not even a week's liberty in Tokyo could salve Rocket's trepidation. There was only one cure for that…

The Ginza had been firebombed during the war. It was the Japanese Fifth Avenue and Times Square—or 125th Street, depending. Now it was lit by neon, not napalm. Ito's Bar & Steakhouse was always dim and dingy, however, tucked there in Tsukiji Alley where the Ginza turned bad.

Bonelip, in his winter blues, elbowed through the shady patrons to the grill where Ito tended the meat. Ito had been a cavalry officer in Manchuria before the surrender, so the rumor was his beef whinnied rather than mooed. He was less a hash-slinger and more a dependable fence and arranger of floating high stakes poker.

"*Konbanwa, Ito-san*," Bonelip said with a Louisiana accent as he pulled an envelope from his USN peacoat. " $200 American. Rocket sez he wants *in* Boss Hama's game, ya dig?"

Ito winced at Boss Hama's name. "*Dozo.*" He motioned Bonelip to the back to where he kept the Ichiban lager iced and the mystery meat frozen in bamboo lockers.

"Man whut's the jive?"

The walls were literally paper-thin, so Ito whispered, shoulders hunched, "Hokay, Bone-rip. No jive. Me in big mess trouble Boss Hama. No games now anyprace."

"Bullshit, man—he out here runnin' madness on every nigga in Asia whut need a payday loan to cover bets. Fifty percent vig."

After a hurried look over his shoulder, Ito explained, "Him take brack G.I.'s dorrars, him take white G.I.'s dorrars. Him need money to pay off judges, cops…him scared Koreans come after him. And now, him mad at *me*. Me need Locket's help big time. No jive."

"'Locket' don't do nuthin' wid out me checkin' first, so why you scared, cuz?"

Ito leaned in so close Bonelip could smell the cabbage on his breath. "*Jade Dragon.*"

Rocket told Bonelip that white folks were oblivious to the differences among Japanese, Chinese, and Koreans. They all looked alike, jabbered alike, supposedly. That was until you actually understood and observed all three. And by now, every swinging dick in Asia had heard about the "Comfort Girls"—young women brought from Korea by the thousands to become prostitutes for the Imperial Army, wet nurse big shots' children, or otherwise be worked to death in armaments factories. To Negroes, it all sounded familiar. Uncle Sam didn't seem to care about that mess, or Japanese war crimes in China, because he now needed a rebuilt Japan as a fortress against Mao, Joe Stalin and their little henchmen in North Korea. Same jive in Germany, allowing Nazis to remain loose. The story went that before Pearl Harbor, as insurance against a Korean revolt to retrieve their hostage women, Japanese soldiers stole a sacred relic. ROK soldiers said that the relic was stored in Hiroshima because Korean slave laborers were working in the factories there. The relic, unlike the people, survived, because it was supposedly so magical that even now, in 1951, seeing it might make Commies and the ROK reunite.

It was a thousand year-old dragon, carved in the rarest pink jade. The same one Bonelip now beheld in Ito's meat locker, on ice.

"Mutha-fu—"

Suddenly the flimsy paper and pine sliding door blew open in splinters and shreds. Four huge men, blubber and muscle bursting their zoot suits, lumbered in. Boss Hama employed *sumo* wrestlers. One grinned, nodded to another, while Ito pleaded, bowed, wept. The other two grabbed Bonelip, drove him to his knees.

"Hey, *gaijin*. We no kirr you so you tell Locket, bling photos, or die in cottonfierred. "

Before he passed out, Bonelip watched the glint of a *katana*'s blade in the bare bulb light, heard Ito's guttural scream, felt a splash of hot blood on his face…

—ᗰ—

ROCKET ROSE FROM THE mosaic tub, bronze skin glistening. Hariko-san wrapped him in a silk yakuta. She cooed because the other rocket, like a German V-2 without the fins, ignored the robe's cover.

"You no ronger constricted, *maesutoro*?"

"Loose as a goose, baby. Real as steel. Now pour me some tea, then shimmy over to that bed and get ready for blast off."

"*Hi,*" Hariko-san acknowledged, covering her mouth to stifle a giggle. She remembered that Rocket, unlike the typical customer of the Teahouse of the Sublime Slippery Grip, didn't go in for those childlike squeaks and thrills men forced from *geisha*. He wanted a woman, not a girl, and Hariko would be the temple priestess who would artfully control his sexual immolation.

The din of the cold, snowy street—honking horns and scooters, radios blaring American swing, cursing rickshaw pullers—beyond the garden's stone wall seldom penetrated the teahouse when bliss was about to be achieved. This time Rocket heard something odd yet familiar. A siren getting closer, then piercing the room. Gruff shouts in English followed, and a tell whistle tweet . The thumping of mama-san Michiko's fat feet preceded her slinging back the door to Hariko's chamber.

"*Locket!*" Her plump face was flushed red. "Trou-buuuuuurrrr!"

Trouble, all right, as two beefy white SPs heaved the fleshy kiminoed mound that was Michiko aside. One tweeted the earsplitting whistle, the other brandished his baton grunting, "You the spade flyer, huh?" The little rocket didn't even wilt, and the sight made the SP swallow hard. "Look, um…we got orders to bring you to Yokosuka. Jeep's outside."

The scum who hung Sammy were in uniform, too, and drove a Jeep. Many a colored soldier, sailor or airman had to gauge whether a trip would end in a stockade or brig, or at the end of a rope. Tonight, with the images of Sammy still raw in his brain, Rocket figured he'd make a third alternative.

Like a panther he leapt on the SP, yanking away the baton. With a fluid metronome motion he cracked the white helmets of both men. The whistle popped out of one SP's mouth as the other went cross-eyed. Michiko, doing her best Night Train Lane, charged and bulldozed the men into the bath. Rocket scooped up his shoes and socks; Hariko tossed him his uniform, coat and his white cap— which he placed at a cocked angle on his smooth, laid down hair.

"*Sayonara*, baby!"

But there were two more SPs outside. Colored ones, and Rocket stopped barefoot in the slush.

"Sorry, Lieutenant," one said. "We told them fools not to mess with you, but whiteboys're hardheaded. We'll call an ambulance for 'em."

Panting, half naked but for his yakuta and cap, Rocket said, "Don't mean to be biggity, fellas, but what the hell?"

"Seaman-Steward Rene Broussard from the *Bonhomme Richard*? Well he's half dead in the sick bay at Yokosuka, cracked skull, broken ribs. When he could talk he said you're in danger. Then the corpsman says he said something about a 'pink dragon' and Koreans, and he went straight into a coma."

"Get outta my way."

"Nah, hold up, Sir—he was at a murder scene. Cat named Ito got his head cut straight off. Looks like with one of those samurai swords. So ONI wants to speak to you first."

Rocket wriggled into his skivvies and uniform. "Fellas, I'm not going to ask you for your sidearms, but I will trouble you for the keys to the Jeep."

"All due respect, Lieutenant," the second SP said, sighing, "we ain't gonna get busted for you."

Rocket took out two ten dollar bills from his trouser pockets, shoved one in the left white spat of each SP. "Hold out your chins; I can give both a nice bruise and no one's the wiser. So how about those keys?"

The SPs exchanged nods, then one said, "Deal...but you gotta give up that tin of Smoov Mallard pomade I see in your kit. All they got in the commissary is that damn Brylcream."

"Here's an extra ten spot. I don't give up my Smoov Mallard to no one but my daddy Reverend Crockett back in Tennessee, and Ray Robinson and Joe Louis in Harlem."

—∞—

THE SNOW HAD STOPPED and the sky gave way to moonlight by the time Rocket ditched the conspicuous gray USN Jeep in Akasaka. Akasaka was like Brooklyn perhaps, and U.S. servicemen looking for gambling and contraband knew Akasaka was Boss Hama's turf. Rocket figured the sight of a *gaijin* in a Naval aviator's uniform was enough to send the locals scurrying to their feudal lord.

Rocket didn't mind using himself as bait, just as he didn't mind strafing a Chinese convoy at 300 feet then screaming skyward to duel with nimble, faster MiG-15's. Sammy faced worse in life and in death. Besides, he'd studied the lure power of myth, as symbolized by dragons, in Professor Alain Locke's class at Howard. Of course he signed up because most of the students in the course were cheerleaders who admired him on the field. At least he learned that myth and symbols could move souls surer than words and thought. And sure enough, as Rocket lit a cigar, a dark blue Datsun sedan, looking like a cheap imitation of a '47 Packard, pulled up. The door opened. The scent of jasmine perfume wafted out.

"Get in, flyboy," crooned the female voice, in perfect English. The grim fat faces of the *sumo* driver and his pal up front made it clear he had no choice. The Datsun rumbled off into the night, toward the silhouette of Mt. Fuji, miles distant.

"How you doin', Mae?" Rocket said, tracing his thin mustache.

Mae Tanaka was *Nisei*: an American, born and raised in Los Angeles. Her rich grocer daddy lost everything when the government rounded up the family and shipped them to Arizona in 1942. Unable to find work despite her newly minted business degree from USC, she moved to Japan in 1950 as an interpreter. Somehow she ended up as Hama's moll. And she was good with a knife -- learned helping her pop slice fruit and fillet fish.

"Got a light, handsome?" Mae purred, crossing and uncrossing her legs. In the garter to her Nylons was a short blade hilt.

"I don't trust you with my Zippo."

"Rufus Crockett, you're afraid of lil' ole *moi*?" She moved her big eyes and wet red lips into the light of the passing street lamps.

"Y'all are pirates. You beheaded my most lucrative contact in Tokyo, and your apes, here, almost killed the only man I trust and love in this part of the world. *Afraid* ain't the word, baby. *Seething* is more apropos. Look it up in the dictionary. It's between seesaw and see-through."

"See-through, like my blouse under my Hermes cashmere coat?"

"Seesaw, as in how I'm going to bounce some heads up and down."

"Well, Dark Gable, you might not have the chance to see or do either very soon. Boss Hama's very cross with you. He thinks you knew that Ito had been trying to unload a valuable piece of property without his knowledge. This piece of property could only get Hama hot water, and I don't mean the stuff in one of your delectable baths at the Tea of the Sublime Slippery Grip. And I know how much is there to grip, eh lover?"

Convinced the dizzying jasmine perfume was some sort of Mickey Finn, Rocket asked permission to crack a window.

"Oh but baby its soooo cold outside, like the song," Mae said, smiling. The *sumo* in the front passenger seat turned his bulk around, aimed a revolver. "Just stay away from the doors and windows, please. Now, where were we? Ah yes, this item. Ito was supposed to sell it back to 'private representatives' of President Rhee of the Republic of Korea. A gesture from one gangster to another, let's say? But Ito decided to grow a conscience and contact the Japanese government. Make it an official public donation and apology, rather than a sale."

"If it's the Jade Dragon, then it's called *restitution*. Look that up in the dictionary, too."

Mae lit her own smoke, took a drag then said, "Quick study aren't we, flyboy? You know, Hama's convinced you beat him and his cronies at poker because all the while he was worried you had those photographs. The ones you stole from British MI-5."

"I didn't steal them. A Jamaican gal just happened to be impressed with me. Was thinking about maybe being the wife of an American naval aviator, and I suppose she was trying to impress me in return. Though I was more impressed by her perfect brown watermelon sized tits. Nothing like those yellow skeeter bites under your 'see-through' blouse, huh, Mae?"

Rankled, Mae blew smoke in Rocket's face. "I'm listening."

"She was a maid for some Limey intelligence officer…I told her I was shipping out to Japan, compliments of Harry Truman and Doug McArthur. During some pillow talk she told me about the only known pictures of Colonel Akira Matsumoto, 'Butcher of Rangoon.' Killed hundreds of British and Australian POWs, thousands of Burmese and Thais. Before that posting, I believe the good colonel was a colonial magistrate in, uh— Korea, right?"

"So you did unnerve him at poker. Hama…I mean, *Matsumoto*, hates losing."

"I beat him straight up. He just underestimated me because ofays and yellow folk alike think Negroes are chimpanzees. So, nah, I didn't use the photos to bluff him. I used the photos to make sure he didn't stiff me for the three grand." Rocket then placed his hand on Mae's knee; the *sumo* in the front seat growled. "Now, let's talk about the Jade Dragon."

"Remove your mitt, flyboy. And if you put it there again, *unsolicited*, you might end up with minus three fingers." When Rocket complied Mae continued. "Do you know any normal women, Rocket? Women you *respect*?"

"Uh huh. Two. One in Memphis, Viola Jean Smithers Crockett. One in Harlem, whom I loved all through college, but who hated me 'cause I acted a fool. Her husband was killed last month near Kaesong."

"No one else?"

"No one in this car."

In twenty minutes the Datsun rolled up to the gate of a Shinto temple. The shrine itself was occluded by tall, dark poplars, but Rocket could see lights glowing. The sumo shoved Rocket ahead on the cobblestone path to the shrine, while Mae floated behind on her three inch ankle-tied heels. The lights got brighter, and there was music -- a Japanese blowing saxophone, another plucking a bass, one more in a porkpie hat strumming a boogie woogie beat on a snare drum. That's when Rocket saw two girls hoofing to the tune. Giggling, snorting from a shared bottle of champagne. From their features he could tell they were Koreans. They were barefoot in the winter cold and nude underneath black sable coats. From their height and body shape, they couldn't have been more than sixteen. A sputtering generator appeared to supply the juice for the lights, and to power a top-lid Coca-Cola cooler dispensing more bottles of champagne.

Boss Hama lay on a divan in the middle of the old shrine, cackling and exhorting the dancing. He wore a smoking jacket, ascot and spats. Perfect for a hustler on 135th and Broadway twenty years ago. To Rocket, he looked like a bald clown.

"Ain't your little jook joint here a tad sacrilegious, *Hama-sama*?

"Ha! I am priest, too, Lieutenant!" Hama called, grinning broadly. "You want cigar, Caviar from Russia? I smuggle through Vladivostok. Like I get sable coats you see my girrs wear, eh? Or maybe you want what *under* the coats, like all brack boys want, eh? I give them you free, *Samurai*…"

"Fuck you, man."

Hama's jovial mood evaporated. He smashed a champagne glass, cursed in Japanese, and had to wave off his thugs from swarming Rocket.

You think I not kirr you because you Navy? You *gaijin. Niggeru*! No one care."

"*You* should care, because even though the American government lets you cakewalk, the British and Aussies want your ass, and they'll have it, if they find out who you really are. I think I'll have some champagne now, *Colonel*. But no caviar. Gives me farts something awful." Rocket took off his cap, smoothed back his perpetually smooth black mane.

That brought Hama's smile back. He shouted for one of his men to bring Rocket a glass, then said to Mae in English, "Come, sit. We have pic-nic, eh?"

Mae obliged; the *sumo* seated Rocket and flanked him so he couldn't move.

"Locket, zoom zoom in the sky?" Hama mused. "We had locket, too. *Ohka*. Guided by *kamikaze*. German V-1 copy of *ohka*! Ah so… you not new, Locket Clockett. You just annoying, A bedbug. Korea is bedbug. Nippon, eternal giant. You tell me where photos, you go free. You keep money from cards. I even give you alibi—'patsy,' you say—so you, you retainer in hospital no get court-martial over incidents tonight, eh?"

He gestured to one of his goons. Like a loyal *samurai*, the goon would sacrifice himself by taking the blame for killing Ito, assaulting Bonelip, even stalking Rocket to the teahouse.

"I'll trade you," Rocket replied.

"*Kare ni kiite wa ikenai, Hama-sama.*" Mae intoned, crushing out her cigarette with her peep-toed shoe. "He's a born liar. Reckless, too, as you see by the ease in which we found him. Nothing like his *brother*."

"That's cold, Mae. Nah, I'm nothing like Sammy. I'm alive. Now listen, Colonel, I got the pictures hid. We both know you ain't gonna torture it out of me. You hand over the Jade Dragon, I give you the pictures."

"*Ish*…why you want Dragon?" Hama prodded.

"Maybe I want my own photo in *Stars & Stripes*. Maybe I want to end this war. North Koreans might even kick out the Chinese when they see that thing. The CIA might even take it away from me for that reason… oh, and so the folks back home, south of the Mason-Dixon, don't have to endure a smiling spade aviator on the front page."

Hama cocked his head. "CIA? You mean O.S.S.—American spies?"

"You been underground too long, man," Rocket chuckled. "O.S.S. changed its name to CIA 'bout three, four years ago. Guess Mae here's been holding back basic intel from you, Boss."

Mae shot up from her chair, hissing. "*Rocket*, so help me…"

"I know those cats. I flew a recon mission a week ago over Chongjin for them. They love me, and Mae thinks they might just punt you, if they get something more valuable. Like a pink jade dragon made in 900 A.D. that'll make every Korean from the Yalu to Pusan do the Lindy Hop. I mean, Mae was wondering how that would work, in the car. She also worked for the U.S. Embassy for a bit, and we know who's in the embassy. But hey, she's a woman. You can't take what women say as gospel, right Colonel? No matter how smart they think they are…"

Rocket felt the sting of Mae's glove across his face. "Shut up!"

Hama stepped off his altar and moved to his moll. "You used work for American Army. But you say it just supply talk…food, fuel oil. Things you help me steal." His pale forehead knitted. "You meet American spies, too?"

"State Department interpreter. It's how I got here. I answered an ad in the *LA Times*, for christsakes. Then I worked for Allied Command and the quartermaster. You knew all of this."

"*No tell me what I know! I know what I know!*" Hama's eyes were wide as hen's eggs. Spittle flew, for Mae was staring at him as an American chick would. All she needed was a colored woman's neck roll and Hama would have exploded. *"You look at me? You keep eye down! You bow!"* A goon shoved her back in her seat.

"No honor among pirates, huh, baby?"

Hama now hovered over Rocket. "You hide photos in teahouse. Only prace could be."

"And the SPs are swarming it. Check, but not mate. You show me the jade dragon?"

Hama mugged, puffed out his chest. "Hokay." He ordered the band to stop playing and barked for the girls to be taken away. "You stay, Mae," he hissed. "No want you out of sight."

A *sumo* heaved an entire bamboo ice locker from a flatbed Ford parked beside the shrine. Hama opened it. There, in straw and meltwater, was a blush pink bearded dragon, tail coiled around the body, three feet long, eyes and teeth made of inlaid red rubies.

"Beautiful," Rocket said, impressed. "Its not radioactive, is it?"

"Maybe," Hama smiled. "How 'bout *we* keep. You work for me, eh?"

Rocket stood. "Go AWOL? And have the NAACP disgraced...I don't think so. Best to have me on the inside. After all, I told you about Mae. And I can teach you how to play better poker hands."

"*Ish*...you teach me? Ha! What you teach?"

"First, always find the cat with the heater...the gun...at the game. Take him out."

Rocket spun Hama into one of his goons, cracked the nose of the other above Mae. Before the other henchmen could react he plunged his hand between Mae's silky thighs, lifted her knife and flung it at the *sumo* now reaching for his revolver. Only the blade handle was visible in the man's forehead.

Mae jumped up, threw off her high heels and roundhouse kicked two more of Hama's men into unconsciousness. One *sumo* pulled Hama to safety, but another, apparently relishing the thought of slicing up little Mae Tanaka, drew a *katana* from his oversized trenchcoat, screamed and charged. Mae dodged the bull, flipped to his back, and in a flurry that impressed even Rocket, hit the beast with an elbow to the base of the neck, then a *karate* chop. The *sumo* dropped his sword. Bad move. Mae flicked it up off the cold stone with her stockinged toes, gripped the handle and cut the man quickly in one figure eight sweep.

"*My* girl," Rocket laughed as he lunged for the revolver still in the other dead *sumo*'s paw. He grabbed it, rolled to his feet, and winged Hama as he tried to escape to the Datsun. The remaining *sumo* dropped his master. Turned, motioned to Rocket, *mano-a-mano*.

Rocket put a round in his eye.

Colonel Akira Matsumoto was writhing in the melting snow, mumbling in Japanese. Rocket stood above him, tucked the revolver into his waistband. Mae came up, still brandishing the sword.

"You only winged him," she panted.

"I meant to." Rocket turned his quarry over. "He's got too many high placed friends who'd just as soon see him dead than alive, wounded, and talking."

"How'd you know I was a double agent? The C.I.A. wouldn't have shared that with…*you*."

"I didn't, I bluffed."

"You said you never bluff."

"Don't believe everything, baby." Rocket brushed back her unpinned hair from her face. "You're coiff's messed up."

Mae laughed. "Yours still looks perfect."

"Smoov Mallard pomade."

Suddenly the two crusaders were hit by the glare of Jeep-mounted searchlights. Mae angled the sword, Rocket fingered the gun.

"Stand down!" called the voice in the bullhorn. "This is the United States Navy Shore Patrol!"

Bonelip was insistent on more morphine; Rocket only offered a sip of orange juice.

"Awww, man," Bonelip groaned, his head bandaged like half a mummy's, "they got some fine colored nurses in here, man. Only thing whut keep me goin'. Sorry I let y'all down, daddy."

"Ain't no thing, Sancho Panza. You gonna be all right. Ship you home soon. I'll come visit you down the Treme. You can make me some gumbo, then you can play that new instrument of yours."

"Whut dat?"

"The new metal plate in your crown, man!"

"Lawd don't make me laugh, Rocket, it hurt to laugh. Say, where the dragon at?"

"Can't say, man. C.I.A. cats came and bailed me and Mae out. They took the locker, holding the dragon. Hauled away all the bodies. Told Leiffer not to mess with me."

"Hama?"

"I winged that fool, Bonelip. Now they say he did seppuku in the jail's hospital ward. Yeah, like cops say niggas hang themselves in a cell with their own bedsheet. And this war goes on." Rocket stood, swiped his coat and cap off the rack in the hospital room. "I gotta hoof it. Reporting to the Goodtime Dickie by fourteen hundred hours. I'll send you a cable from sea."

"Aye aye," Bonelip said, trying to salute with IV tubes tangling his arm. "*Mah* man."

Rocket read his own telegram while riding in the cab toward Yokosuka.

Stay safe-Will meet again-Better still-Go see that woman whose husband died-Show her you are no fool. Mae.

With a roar of thrust the banjo was airborne off the carrier deck. In an hour, the port town of Chongjin and the Sui-jong bridges were visible. Flak lit the dawn sky, the air above the reach of the exploding shells thick with jet MiGs and propeller Yaks. They were like the flies, buzzing around Sammy's corpse. But Sammy's ghost was exorcized from the cockpit. For now.

"This is the Typewriter, Four Six Four Tango, about to begin my run. Watch this spade aviator, boys. Then follow my lead! Tap-Tap-Tap!"

Back home in the black weeklies, the refrain of 'Rocket Crockett, he's *the* man. If he can't do it, no one can,' accompanied the articles about him.

DRUMS OF THE OGBANJE
A CAPTAIN NGOLA STORY

BY MEL ODOM

1. Moonlit Steel

Bay of Luanda
West Africa
1825

WITH A HEAVY FIGHTING knife clamped between his teeth, Ngola Kilunaji climbed the thick anchor rope up the ship's hull to deliver death to Portuguese slavers.

The vessel tugged against its anchor, riding restlessly atop the white-topped waves. Dark clouds obscured the full moon as they scudded across the sky, promising a squall by morning or shortly thereafter if the thick air was any indication.

Ngola felt the coming change of weather in the old whip scars that striped his back. The sour stench of human misery clung to the vessel, hammered into the ship's timbers, made part of the ship by blood and death. More than that, though, Ngola's nostrils took in the sick scent of hopelessness.

At the gunwale, he paused and listened. Voices drifted on the breeze, snatches that were ripped apart on the wind. He understood Portuguese well enough, though he spoke English and French much better. Instead of being bored, the sailors sounded ill at ease.

"I do not trust that old man, Luis. I think he is going to bring down some heathen curse on us with everything he is doing."

"Captain Salazar will not allow that to happen. He will kill Lukamba first. Just be glad that that old demon worshipper is gone from the ship."

The names stirred a memory within Ngola. Though their paths had never before crossed, Ngola had heard the whispered stories of the old witch doctor and of the greedy Portuguese captain who hunted lost treasures as well as slaves. The dead were supposed to walk at Lukamba's command, and demons were allowed entrance to the world through his knowledge of the dark magic that was Africa.

"Salazar is hypnotized by Lukamba's tales of treasure. The captain dreams of riches. Instead of chasing myths and lies, he should be thinking of the money this cargo of slaves will bring us. After we deliver these wretches to the Caribbean, we will have wealth enough to keep us in rum and women for days. Then we can return here for more slaves and begin again." The man cursed. "Instead we are here while that old man leads the captain after ghost ships and searches for more of his evil vodun spirits."

"Pray that those spirits take Lukamba to hell and drive the captain back to us. Or maybe take the captain as well and that Carneiro becomes the ship's master. I would follow him."

"Careful, you fool! There are many here who like Salazar and dream of the same riches he does. If they hear you, they may tell Salazar, and then you'll end up at the bottom of the sea."

"Faugh! Were he to find those riches, you know that precious little will trickle down to the ship's crew."

Glancing back down the anchor rope, Ngola spotted Colin Drury only a few feet beneath him. The Irishman held steady, his face grim and determined as his pale blue eyes blazed in the light from the lanterns hanging at the stern. Below Drury, three more men, two Africans and an Englishman, held onto the rope as well. Seven more men bobbed in the water, waiting their turn at the rope. Ngola's ship lay a quarter-mile away to the north, black against the backdrop of the tree-covered coastline.

All of the men were proven warriors, used to boarding ships and fighting with edged steel. They'd been handpicked by Ngola and blooded again and again against the Portuguese and the tribes who took slaves.

Ngola swarmed up the rope and heaved himself over the side, landing on callused bare feet. He had to protect his men as they came on board and he knew their presence would not long be secret. On the deck, the wind whipped over him, cooling the wet pants against his skin.

He fisted one of the cutlasses hanging at his hip and drew it from its leather sheath with a thin whisper. He put the knife in the sheath at his back and took up the mambele from his other hip, unhooking it from his second cutlass.

The mambele throwing dagger looked like a falcon's claw, providing a total of three blades and an excellent chance of sinking deeply into its target. The heavy weapon looked unwieldy, but in Ngola's hands it was lethal and swift as a diving hawk.

Colin Drury stood beside Ngola on the stern deck. Although the Irishman was only a couple inches short of six feet, Ngola loomed over him. Where Drury was compact and lean and pale, Ngola was broad and thickly thewed with ebony skin. Drury wore his hair pulled back in a queue and went clean-faced. Ngola's bare head gleamed in the lantern light. Water droplets clung to his short, curly beard.

Footsteps padded over the wooden deck, heading for the stern. Ngola flowed into motion, shifting from stillness to action in a single lithe stride. Behind him, Drury stood watch over the anchor rope as their men kept boarding.

Three Portuguese sailors crossed the main deck below and headed toward the stern castle where Ngola was. Knowing there was no way his men would escape notice and that a cry of alarm would be short in coming, Ngola decided to take advantage of their brief edge of surprise. Weapons in hand, he launched himself at the three men while they were still engaged in their argument about the ship's captain and the certainty of *vodun* curses.

Ngola smashed into the men, knocking them all sprawling across the deck. Heaving himself up on one knuckled fist, Ngola set himself and swung the cutlass at his nearest enemy. There was no mercy in his heart. The men were slavers and Ngola had sworn to kill as many of them as he was able.

The heavy blade of the cutlass smashed through the slaver's skull as much as it sliced. The dead man spilled away when Ngola yanked the blade free. One of the other men came up quickly, lashing out with a long fighting knife rather than trying for his sword.

The move almost caught Ngola off-guard. Reflexes honed by years of fighting for his life in Haiti during the slave uprisings against the French, then more years on a ship in Lord Nelson's Navy battling still more French spurred Ngola to lift the mambele to intercept his opponent's knife.

Razor edged metal screamed as the blades met, but the knife stopped inches short of Ngola's throat. The Portuguese slaver's eyes widened in fear, then emptied of life when Ngola split the man's skull with his cutlass.

With an oath, the dead man's blood spattered across his bare chest,

Ngola kicked the corpse from his blade and shook the trapped blade from the mambele. The other two slavers recovered quickly and shouted in alarm as they drew their weapons.

Colin Drury fell in beside Ngola, adding his blade to his captain's as they battled the two slavers. Swords clashed and the clangor of metal swelled over the ship and the nearby waves. More Portuguese slavers poured from the ship's hold with weapons in their hands, crying out for their brothers to rouse and follow them into battle.

The slave ships usually kept a crew of thirty to forty sailors. Once chained in the hold belowdecks, the slaves didn't offer much resistance. And every man over what was needed was another mouth to feed and less space for cargo. But Salazar was an aggressive captain and kept extra men to crew a British ship if he had the chance to take one as a prize in battle. The Portuguese vessel had already taken two ships from captains in the West Africa Squadron, the small fleet the British Empire had sent to combat the slave trade.

Ngola blocked an overhand blow that streaked for his head, catching his opponent's cutlass with the mambele. The blades clanked as they clashed. Holding the blade trapped, Ngola went chest-to-chest with the man. The Portuguese slaver's fetid breath reeked of decay as it sprayed over Ngola's face.

Then Ngola smashed his forehead into the man's nose, shattering the vulpine beak and sending the slaver stumbling back. A quick slash of the cutlass spilled the man's guts across the deck, drenching the dry wood in blood.

Ngola's crew spread out behind him, taking up fighting positions, but they were being pressed hard by the thirty Portuguese slavers filling the deck in front of them. Lantern light danced along the naked blades.

"Joao!" Ngola roared.

"Aye, Cap'n!" Slight and wiry, the young man fought at the fringes of the crowd. He was of mixed blood, his mother a slave and his father a Portuguese rapist he'd never met and had sworn to kill. The young sailor was handsome and had hazel eyes that belonged on a large cat.

"Charge that blunderbuss!" Ngola commanded. "Let's cull these dogs."

"Aye, Cap'n." Joao swung his cutlass in a savage slash that cleaved into the side of a slaver's head and dropped him mewling to the deck.

Instantly, Joao spun and retreated to the stern castle while Mamadou and Kayode shifted to cover his back.

On the stern castle, Joao unlimbered the short muzzleloader he'd carried in a watertight sleeve over his shoulder. He readied the weapon in short order and dropped to one knee, bringing the blunderbuss to his shoulder. Less than two feet in length and near big around as Joao's wrist, the thick barrel gleamed like it was covered in dark oil.

"Ready, Cap'n!"

Parrying two blades at once with his cutlass, slashing the throat of the third man with the mambele, Ngola raised his voice. "Give ground!" He disengaged from the slavers he swapped parries with and took two steps back.

Instantly, his crew did the same, displaying the discipline he had trained into them.

For a moment the Portuguese slavers held back. Bloodied and caught unprepared, they hesitated at stepping over the bodies of their own dead to attack.

"Fire!" Ngola shouted.

The blunderbuss's frizzen struck sparks that ignited the black powder on the flash pan. An instant later, the weapon detonated with a sonorous *BOOM!* and belched forth bronze balls and a cloud of swirling gray smoke.

The projectiles smashed into the front line of the Portuguese and cut them down, sending the luckless men stumbling back into their fellows with their faces shattered in and their hands missing fingers, their arms broken and bloody.

"Reload!" Ngola yelled.

"Reloading, Cap'n!"

Ngola stepped forward, giving his hated enemy no quarter as he swung his heavy blade, removing a man's weapon along with his hand. "Advance!" His crew moved with him, slashing out at the stunned Portuguese.

Though the slavers were shell-shocked and bloodied, they fought for their lives. At Ngola's side, Ikenna dropped with a ball in his brain, and at the end of the line Corporal Horace Dinwiddy, lately of the West Africa Squadron, went down from too much blood loss from his wounds.

Losing both of the men saddened Ngola because he knew them well, as he did all of the men that sailed under his command, but he pushed the emotion away. There would be time to grieve later. Now was the time to fight. He slid the mambele into the sheath at his back.

Reaching down as he blocked the swing of a cutlass with his own, he fisted a pistol in his left hand, drawing it from the dead man at his feet. He eared the hammer back, shoved the muzzle into the mouth of the slaver in front of him, breaking the slaver's teeth, and pulled the trigger.

The ball exploded through the back of the slaver's head and into the face of the man behind him. Squalling in pain, not dead but maybe dying, the second slaver fell backward, taking one of his mates with him.

Ngola used the pistol to block another blade, then dodged to the left, bumping into Colin Drury for an instant as another slaver fired his weapon. The ball whipped by Ngola, leaving a trail of heat that kissed his cheek lightly. Blocking another man's blade with his cutlass, Ngola used the pistol like a hammer, swinging it with all his strength into his opponent's face.

The man's forehead cracked open under the impact and blood ran into his eyes as he dropped. Dead, dying, or unconscious, the man would not soon return to the fight if at all.

"Ready, Cap'n!" Joao called.

Quelling the blood lust for battle that filled him, Ngola forced himself to order the brief retreat. "Give ground!"

Again, his men stepped back. Another of the men had fallen, but Ngola couldn't tell who it was yet. At the command, the Portuguese slavers knew what was coming this time and most of them tried to flee. Two of them, however, lifted firearms.

Ngola plucked the mambele from its sheath, set himself, and whipped the dagger forward. The multi-bladed weapon spun through the air, splintering the unsteady lantern light as the ship rocked at its anchors, then buried in the chest of one of the men holding a leveled pistol. Instead of firing his weapon, the man stood transfixed and stared down at the knife that had split his heart.

"Fire!" Ngola ordered.

The blunderbuss exploded again. Caught by the fringe of the blast, the second slaver with a pistol went down. The bronze balls chewed through the retreating pack of men.

"Reloading!" Joao sang out.

"Advance!" Ngola strode forward and grabbed the dead man's fallen pistol.

The Portuguese hadn't stopped running toward the ship's prow. The slaver took brief aim with the pistol and fired, not waiting to see the effects of his shot. Ngola fired his pistol and the ball caught the fleeing man in the back of the neck, pitching him forward in a heap.

Placing a foot on the dead man with the mambele in his heart, Ngola yanked free the blade and led the charge after their foes. Overwhelmed, the Portuguese fell in short order. A few dove over the side into the sea.

"Get the lanterns!" Drury ordered, seizing one from the railing himself, then grabbing a pistol from a dead Portuguese.

The Irishman held the lantern up and out over the ship's side. He steadied the pistol, his face lean and hard and merciless. He, too, bore scars from the slavers, and not all of them showed on his body. He had lost good men and several friends when the ship he'd served on had gone down to the Portuguese.

The pistol cracked in Drury's fist and the ball sped true, punching through the head of the slaver swimming for the coastline. The man stopped swimming and went slack as oily blood slicked the ocean's surface. The corpse floated in the water till a triangular fin cut toward him. The dead man disappeared a moment later, then a severed arm floated to the top.

Gray smoke plumed Drury's head, and his grim satisfaction made Ngola think he must resemble a demon from the Christian Hell. Drury turned with a grin to face Ngola. "Fancy that. We were swimming all that way with sharks in the water."

"Would you have stayed back if you had known?"

"Of course not." Drury knelt and found powder and shot on the dead man. "But I might not have been so carefree in doing it."

More sharks fed on the hapless Portuguese, yanking them down into the dark water. The sailors who knew how to swim didn't know which direction to head. Ngola's men fired at them as soon as they could find or reload weapons. The sharks steadily seized their prey, the living and the dead.

"Later, when we tell this story over grog, you and I will swear that the sharks swam with us," Drury said.

Ngola grinned, then scoured the ship's deck. He sheathed his mambele and lifted powder and shot from the nearest dead man, then reloaded the pistol he'd picked up. He nodded at Drury. "Bring your lantern. Let's go see what awaits us belowdecks."

Seeing men, women, and children shackled in the bowels of a slave ship was something Ngola had never gotten used to. He wasn't looking forward to repeating the experience. He took a fresh grip on his cutlass and headed for the nearest hatch, stopping only for a moment to take a ring of keys from one of the dead Portuguese.

As he neared the opening, Ngola opened his mouth and breathed through it instead of his nose. The stench wasn't so bad that way. Nothing would ever make it bearable. Despite the hard way many of the Portuguese sailors had died under the blades of his men, Ngola had no mercy in his heart for his enemies. If any yet lived, he would slit their throats.

He stepped down into the hold.

2. THE SCORPION

THE FOUL, FETID AIR that closed in on Ngola below the ship's deck felt heavy and oppressive. He resisted the urge to cut through it with his cutlass as Drury lifted the lantern to shine down into the hold.

Murmurs and whispers echoed in the confined space. Frightened eyes stared back at the lantern.

No matter the number of horrors and degradations he'd seen in Africa, on Haiti, and while serving in Lord Nelson's Navy, Ngola knew that he would never get used to seeing people stripped of their humanity as they were in that hold. Scores of men, women, and children lay bound by chains and dressed in filthy rags. Their helplessness tore at Ngola. He forced himself to be strong, knowing that most of them would be saved through his crew's efforts tonight.

And they would be given back their freedom.

"My God," Drury said hoarsely.

Slowly, Ngola sheathed his cutlass, then spread his hands out before him, showing their emptiness. He spoke in Portuguese, which most of the coastal people had some experience with, though most of that was unpleasant.

"We mean you no harm. We are here to free you." He repeated the words in English and French, then as best as he could in the half-dozen dialects he knew from the areas he had traveled through.

Many of the men and women wept with relief and gave thanks to their gods and ancestors.

Standing in front of them, Ngola's memories of masters and whips and chains rolled through his thoughts. Sold into slavery as a child, impressed by the British Navy as a young man, he had been free for the last seven years, and he knew he would never serve a day as a slave again. He would die first, with an enemy's blood in his teeth.

Kneeling, Ngola used the keys he'd taken from the dead Portuguese slaver to open the locks holding the nearest, strongest man. He offered the man his hand and pulled him to his feet, then began on the next lock.

Hanging his lantern on a nearby crossbeam, Drury called for more of the sailors above, then fell to opening the locks on chains as well. The heavy links smacked against the deck again and again as they worked.

A small girl only nine or ten years old wept and shivered and drew away from Ngola as he approached. Bloody sores at her wrists and ankles showed where the iron cuffs had worn at her tender flesh.

"Easy, child." Ngola's voice rumbled softly as he reached for her chains. "I will not harm you." He hated the fear that he saw in her dark eyes, but he twisted his lips into a reassuring smile.

She trembled as he released her, then got up and ran to the back of the ship, screaming for her mother. A woman reached for the girl and took her into her arms. Both of them cried and wept as they clung each to the other.

For a moment, Ngola thought of his wife and of their son. At times on *Mambele*, he considered putting down his sword and living with Kangela in her village, and of giving up his battle against the slavers. He hated being away from his family. But just as the scars on his back and his wrists and ankles would never fade, nor would his desire to fight those who subjugated others. As long as the Portuguese and others took slaves, he knew he would seek them out and kill them.

He focused on the task at hand and reached for another lock.

"Ngola!"

The man's voice was dry and thin, only brushing against Ngola's ears. Ngola rose from his crouch and stared into the darkness at the end of the ship. His hand rested on the hilt of his cutlass. "Who calls my name?"

"I do." A thin arm rose from near the stern.

Ngola took the lantern Joao handed him, then gave the younger man the key ring. Holding up the lantern, Ngola walked toward the stern till he reached the man who had called for him.

The man was old and withered, gray with sickness. He looked up at Ngola and spoke in a croaking voice. "Do you know me?"

The man's features were familiar, but it took Ngola a moment to summon a name. "You are Olufemi. You are of my wife's tribe."

Though Ngola had lived sporadically among his wife's people for six years, and her people didn't feel comfortable around him, he had gotten to know a few of them. Eight years ago, he'd almost been killed in an attack on a Portuguese fort and escaped into the jungle, more dead than alive. Since his recovery and his marriage to Kangela, he had not mixed with the tribal people on a regular basis. Their ways were not his, and he had never quite been accepted among them. Ngola would always be known as an outsider among them. He had not made many friends even though they knew he fought the Portuguese. His wife's people also hated him for taking their young sons to crew his ship. Many of those young men did not return, either because they were dead or because they wanted to see the world.

"I am Olufemi. My wife is aunt to your wife's father."

Ngola thought he might have known that, but the familial relationships among the tribe were too many and too complicated to keep track of.

"What are you doing here?"

"The slavers attacked our village."

A chill passed through Ngola and he held the lantern up high so he could survey the nearby faces. His heart sped up as he realized he recognized at least a dozen more people from Kangela's tribe. He didn't see her there, nor did he see Emeka, their son. But his relief was washed away by the old man's next words.

"The slavers took Kangela, Ngola, and they have your son too. Lukamba ordered that they be brought along with the shore party to look for the captain's treasure. And the demons Lukamba seeks."

—⚹—

OLUFEMI SAT ON A stool on the ship's deck. The fresh air seemed to do the old man some good, as did the bread and wine Ngola had one of his men bring from the ship's galley.

Ngola struggled to keep himself calm, forcing himself to think when every fiber of his being demanded that he set sail to the coast to begin looking for his lost family. He clung to the belief that Kangela and Emeka were still alive, but knowing they lived to become prey for Lukamba almost unhinged Ngola.

"The slavers came to our village four or five days ago." Olufemi shook his head. "I think I have kept track, but I cannot say for certain how much time has passed." He sipped wine from a bottle. "Captain Salazar came among us looking for you."

"Me?" That surprised Ngola. He was careful to leave no trail back to the village, which was farther inland than many of the Portuguese traveled. Normally they depended on the African tribes that dealt in slavery to sell prisoners into chains.

"Yes." The old man nodded. Pain showed in his rheumy eyes, but it wasn't from his current physical distresses. "Someone in the village told the Portuguese captain that you lived among us."

"Who did such a thing?"

"I do not know. I have heard that whoever gave the slaver captain the information did so for gold, or revenge over a son that was lost to your crew and never returned."

Ngola said nothing. He had the blood of several of the tribe's young men on his hands, and there was no way he could dispute that.

"The slavers came in the dead of night. We had no chance for escape. Your wife fought bravely, but they captured your son. Once the Portuguese had Emeka, Kangela surrendered."

Ngola breathed in, forcing himself to listen.

"You should have seen her, Ngola. She killed two of the men before she surrendered, and she would have killed more." The old man looked proud, but the fearful sadness quickly shone again in his eyes. "There were men among the slavers that would have murdered her for those that she killed, but Captain Salazar stayed their hands."

"Where are they now?"

The old man waved at the darkened coastline to the east over the prow. "There. While the slavers took prisoners from the village, Lukamba killed Uzochi and raided his house."

Uzochi was the tribe's *houngan*, versed in the ways of the *vodun* spirits and the art of healing.

"Lukamba searched among Uzochi's belongings and took from them the medicinal roots and fetishes the *houngan* had made. Among those things, Lukamba found a map."

"What kind of map?"

"I do not know. I only heard this, and saw that Captain Salazar was at once interested. I heard a Portuguese ship's name mentioned. *Escorpiao*."

Drury glanced at Ngola. "*The Scorpion*?" He shook his head. "That ship is a myth, Ngola, a tale that is told by men with wine to drink and time on their hands."

The Scorpion had supposedly sailed West Africa over a hundred years ago. Captain Antonio de Cardoso had gotten rich from the slave trade, then he had vanished. Some said that he had sunk at sea, weighed down by his riches, or that a tentacled water demon dragged him below the waves.

Others insisted that de Cardoso had sailed up a West African river to hide his treasure.

"Perhaps the tale of *The Scorpion* is only a legend." Ngola stared at the shadow-filled coastline. "But there is where Captain Salazar has gone, so I will follow."

—◊—

C LAD IN BOOTS AND a thick cotton shirt to blunt the wind's cruel teeth, a brace of pistols slung across his chest, Ngola clambered down the side of the ship to the waiting longboat. His pulse beat at his temples even though he was certain his heart must have stopped in his chest.

Eight of his men sat ready at the oars, all of them armed to the teeth. Joao crouched in the stern to man the tiller. The wind came out of the west and blew toward the dark coast a quarter mile to the east.

Before Ngola could take his place at one of the oars, Drury dropped down into the longboat beside him. Ngola looked at his friend with displeasure. "You're not coming."

Drury's eyes narrowed and he shook his head. "I'm not staying, mate."

"Someone has to remain with *Mambele*." Ngola's ship had sailed nearer, only a stone's throw from the slave vessel.

"I put Olamilekan in charge of the ship."

"Olamilekan is not a captain."

"He is till we get back." Drury sat on the bench on the other side of Ngola.

Anger and uncertainty rolled in Ngola's belly like coals. "I do not want to lose my ship."

Drury returned Ngola's gaze full measure. "You don't want to lose your wife and son, mate." He put a hand on Ngola's shoulder. "You need me. And if you don't, then Kangela and Emeka do. I'm not going to hang about and hope for the best." He took a breath and picked up his oar. "Now…are you going to argue some more? Or are we going to go save your family?"

—ᴍ—

FEELING THE POWER OF the sea as he braced himself and flexed, Ngola pulled the oar with even strokes. All of the longboat's crew did. At one time or another, they had all been sailors or slaves. Most of them had been both.

The longboat rose and fell with the waves that rolled in to the coast. The prow cleaved the white caps.

Ngola shook his head and concentrated on his rowing. Each pull took him closer to the coast, closer to his family…and closer to the men he would kill.

"Do you think Lukamba knows he has your wife and child?" Drury asked.

Ngola pulled again. Stories were often told of the things Lukamba knew, and the bloodthirsty way he learned of those things. "Perhaps I will ask Lukamba when I see him. Perhaps I'll just cut his throat and listen to him drown in his own blood. Why he has done what he has done will not matter because he will be dead."

—ᴍ—

WADING THROUGH THE KNEE-HIGH rolling tide, Ngola helped pull the longboat up onto the beach only a few feet from the four longboats that had been left on the sand by the Portuguese and Lukamba. Captain Salazar had taken a large number of men with him.

In the pale moonlight, Ngola spotted the imprints of boots as well as the smaller footprints of women and children.

"Wait here." Ngola held up a hand to hold his men back. Slowly, like a hunting cat, he walked across the beach, senses alert to the jungle twenty feet away.

Making himself remain patient, telling himself that the time he spent now would increase his chances of getting Kangela and Emeka back alive, Ngola studied the impressions of boots and footprints by torchlight. He noted the differences among them, thrusting sticks into the ground as he distinguished the tracks, trailing them for a ways till he was certain of his deductions.

He looked back at the sticks standing up in the sand and quickly counted them. The torch whipped in the wind and burned warmly across his cheek. "There are five or six children, four women, and twenty-seven or twenty-nine slavers." He looked at his warriors. "We will be outnumbered, but I do not want to send for more men. That would take too long and a larger group will be harder to hide as we pursue them."

Joao smiled coldly. "Then it would be best if we killed Lukamba and the Portuguese quickly when we find them."

"Douse the torches." Ngola thrust his own torch into the wet sand. The flames hissed as they drowned. Then he turned and followed the tracks into the dark expanse of the jungle, thankful the moonlight was finally bright enough to allow that.

Now that the scudding clouds had cleared, the full moon beamed down on the coast, but its attention filled Ngola with dread. Many evil things, legends often said, were possible under the light of a full moon.

3. THE RISEN DEAD

CARRYING A BAKER RIFLE in one hand, Ngola tracked the trail of the slavers easily through the brush. The Portuguese crew followed an old game trail and their boots had scored the ground, marking their path.

Ngola moved at a near-run, eating up the distance quickly, and he knew he was gaining on his quarry. The earth turned up by the boot marks was fresher, still damp to the touch. He felt certain he was only minutes behind them now. The way led uphill and he wondered what had made Lukamba and the Portuguese certain that *The Scorpion* was nearby.

He also wondered why they had come at night.

Unless what they have to do can only be done in the darkness.

The thought jangled uncomfortably in Ngola's mind and he glanced spitefully at the huge moon. *Vodun* magic was fierce and strong, and Lukamba was reputed to be a master of the dark arts. On Haiti, *houngans, mambos,* and *bokors* had wielded the spirits to work their magic. The *houngans* and *mambos* sought to cure and use their powers for good, but the *bokors* brought the *loa* into the world to kill their enemies. The French landowners hadn't been able to stand against them, and even their fallen dead had risen once more as zombies to fight against them.

Ngola had seen such supernatural entities and had sometimes fought with them. The zombies were hard to kill.

—⁂—

LESS THAN A HALF-HOUR later, torchlight gleamed higher up in the mountain where the Portuguese had traveled. The weak golden glow pooled against low-hanging trees that barely held the heavy darkness at bay. Faint wisps of an old man's voice lifted in song pealed in the distance.

Ngola held up a hand to halt his warriors and studied the land. Drury stood tensely at Ngola's side. The Irishman didn't care for *vodun* magic either, and his people had their own brand of mysticism and fey spirits that wished only ill for men, so Drury knew firsthand what dark forces could do before he'd come to West Africa.

"Colin and I will go take a look to see what the Portuguese are doing," Ngola told his crew. "The rest of you wait here."

Without a word, his men melted into the jungle so cleanly it was like they'd folded up their shadows to carry with them.

Taking a fresh grip on the Baker rifle, Ngola started up the mountain, avoiding the game trail he'd been following and staying within the trees. Drury followed only a few steps behind, moving as sure-footed as Ngola.

—⁂—

CAUTIOUSLY, NGOLA CREPT ALONG the final few feet to a ridge that overlooked the hollow filled with torchlight and chanting. He lay on his stomach, Drury only a short distance away, and surveyed the events taking place.

A hundred feet distant, Lukamba danced slowly over a barren area where no trees or grass grew. The *bokor* was thin, stripped down to skin over bones. He shook a feathered staff in his right hand. Strings of human teeth clacked against the wooden walking stick. A half skull from a great ape or gorilla covered the top of his head and down his face to his mouth. Long fangs framed his hollow cheeks. The yellowed bone gleamed dully in the moonlight.

The old man's voice was surprisingly strong, but his words were unintelligible. They sounded ancient and hurtful, blunt weapons that had been designed to maim and destroy. Back in Haiti and in other parts of Africa, Ngola had seen the power such words could call up.

Despite the distance that lay between them, Ngola shuddered just a little, and the hair on his forearms lifted slightly. He watched intently, scouring the clearing for his wife and son.

The Portuguese sailors stood to one side. Light from the blazing torches they'd driven into the ground played over the slavers and glinted from their heavy brass buttons, helmets, swords, rifles, and pistol butts. They stood close together, not talking, and many of them gazed fearfully at Lukamba.

At their feet, the four women and six children crouched or lay on the ground. Ropes bound their hands behind their backs.

Kangela knelt in the back of the group. Despite her situation, she looked proud and regal, her head high and her eyes watchful. Athletic and womanly, her hair cut short and neat, dressed in a colorful blouse and skirt, the sight of her made Ngola's heart swell.

The first time he'd seen Kangela, he'd thought she had the face of an angel, though he was not so convinced of the Christian heaven. He'd been wounded near unto death and had felt the life slipping from him, certain he would never wake from the black void. Then Kangela had been there, beautiful and tender and giving. She had nursed him back to health though the rest of her people had told her she should surrender Ngola to the jungle predators.

He had loved her at once because she'd been like no other woman he'd ever been with. She was strong and tender, compassionate, yet – under the right circumstances – without mercy. No one in her village was a better hunter, and she had taught Ngola much about moving stealthily in the jungle.

Emeka, their son, lay halfway draped across his mother's knees. He was four years old, still small and innocent, his hair wild and his body so thin as he grew. Seeing him bound as he was hardened Ngola's heart against those who had taken him. Emeka only wore a loincloth and he looked vulnerable among the armed men. Fear filled and widened his eyes.

Unconsciously, Ngola edged the Baker rifle forward as he shifted his gaze to Lukamba.

The *bokor* ended his litany in a high-pitched shriek and struck his staff against the barren ground as if demanding an answer or response.

Drury laid his hand upon Ngola's shoulder and whispered almost inaudibly. "Wait, my friend, I beg you. We need to plan this, not simply leap into it if we are to save them."

Restraining his homicidal impulses, but only just, Ngola nodded and drew the rifle back. He scanned the jungle, looking for other ways to close in on the Portuguese slavers. If he and his crew succeeded in driving them away from the captives, then the women and children would have a chance of surviving the encounter.

Lukamba gave a screeching command and threw his open hand down to hover only inches above the ground. He tugged again and again, as if he had hold of something. Even a hundred feet away, Ngola felt the sudden chill as the warmth was sucked from the air.

Glowing, malignant purple embers dropped from Lukamba's palm and fell to the earth like rain. The embers winked out of existence as soon as they touched the ground.

At first, nothing seemed to come of the *bokor's* effort. Then cracks tore through the earth and something pushed up, like a seed breaking free of its tomb to reach for the sun.

Only there was no sun, and the thing that shoved free of the ground had been dead for a very long time.

Cursing to himself, Ngola watched in rising horror as the dead creature clawed up from the lost grave. At first, as he sighted the misshapen head and the uneven shoulders, he believed the thing might be the corpse of a monkey or chimpanzee, then he realized that the shambling figure was that of a dead child.

"God in heaven, protect this wayward servant." Drury's whisper was louder than he'd intended, but his words didn't travel far.

Besides that, the attention of the Portuguese slavers was focused on the bizarre resurrection taking place before them. Some of the slavers crossed themselves in the Catholic fashion. Many of them took steps back and peered fearfully at the surrounding jungle. Captain Salazar, surely the handsome and broad man dressed in finery and a cloak and wearing a fierce mustache and neatly trimmed beard, stood his ground but half-drew the cutlass that hung at his side.

Lukamba lifted his hand and pointed at the Portuguese captain. "Stay your hand if you would live, Captain Salazar." The *bokor's* voice was soft and dry as dust. "If the *ogbanje* senses that you mean it any harm, it will kill you."

The gruesome creature lifted its shattered head and sniffed the air like a hyena. It remained half-crouched, swollen knees bent and desiccated flesh wrapped loosely around the bones. Tattered remnants of a loincloth hung from its waist.

"What is that loathsome abomination?" Salazar demanded. He didn't draw his steel, but neither did he lift his hand from the weapon's hilt.

Beneath the half-skull that masked the upper part of his face, Lukamba smiled genially at the dead thing, like an old grandfather would at a favorite grandchild. He moved slowly, balancing his staff in the crook of his arm and taking a knife from his waist. He drew the blade along a weathered crease in his palm. Blood wept from the small incision. Knotting his hand into a fist, he held it above the creature.

A long, barbed tongue shot from the dead thing's mouth and caught the blood drops as they fell from the *bokor's* fist. Tentatively, the thing reached up for Lukamba's hand with its own. Lukamba allowed the thing to latch onto his fist, and there it nuzzled like a pup to a teat.

"This is an *ogbanje*," Lukamba said. "It is a restless spirit. They are called 'children who come and go' because they are born into a family, then die at a very young age only to be reborn and die again so young. They are creatures of misfortune and bring heartbreak again and again to those to whom they become attached."

The thing suckled noisily, paying no attention to the Portuguese.

"Once an *ogbanje* has been identified in a child," Lukamba went on, "the child's body is broken and mutilated and buried so it cannot come back only to die again." The *bokor* smiled as the creature continued to feed. "Sometimes that breaking and mutilation and burial is not enough. As you can plainly see. Then, if a *bokor* is strong enough, he can raise them and they will be even more fearsome."

Salazar's eyes narrowed and his jaw firmed. "Where is the treasure you said was here?"

Lukamba shook his hand and freed it from the *ogbanje's* grip. The creature dropped to its knees and sniffed the dirt for stray drops that might have fallen. It whined piteously as it searched.

"The treasure is close, Captain. Be a little more patient. I need the *ogbanje* to lead us there." Lukamba held his hand close to the ground again and again, drawing up other *ogbanjes* from different areas within the barren clearing.

Within minutes, three more broken shells of dead children joined the first. Four small craters scarred the clearing. The *ogbanjes* milled around Lukamba like hounds at the *bokor's* heels. Their plaintive keening formed a constant undercurrent of noise that hurt Ngola's ears, as nerve-wracking as a steel blade grating against another. Lukamba allowed each of the new *ogbanje* in turn to feed from his hand for a moment before he shook it away.

"Have you heard of these cursed creatures?" Drury whispered to Ngola.

"I have heard of them, but I have never before seen them." Ngola quelled the primitive fear that threatened to run rampant in him. He had witnessed magic before, good and bad, and had learned to both fear and hate it. *Houngans* and *mambos* had healed wounds and chased away evil spirits from the sick in Haiti, though Ngola had never seen those incorporeal entities and only assumed they truly existed.

"What will Lukamba do with them?"

"I do not know." Ngola pushed that from his mind and concentrated on how he was going to save the prisoners. The people back at the Portuguese ship were safe enough for now, and would be safer still as soon as they sailed. But the women and children – Kangela and Emeka – below remained at risk.

Two of the *ogbanje* stepped away from Lukamba and shambled on their disproportionate legs toward the Portuguese. The slavers drew back fearfully, many of them raising pistols and rifles.

Salazar held up a gloved hand. He spoke in a quiet, deadly voice. "Do not fire. Do not attack them. If you do, I will kill you myself."

The men put their weapons away and stepped back, leaving the prisoners at the mercy of the dead creatures.

The *ogbanje* walked among the women and children. Nearly all of them cried out fearfully, calling on their gods to save them and even beseeching the slavers for help.

Kangela remained quiet and watchful. When one of the *ogbanje* closed in on Emeka, Kangela headbutted it and knocked the undead thing away. The *ogbanje* squalled in pain and rage and set itself to attack.

A sharp command from Lukamba froze the *ogbanje* in its tracks. It protested shrilly, but ducked its dead eyes and returned to the *bokor's* side where it clung to one of the old man's skinny legs.

"All right, Captain Salazar, we may continue." Lukamba gave a command in his native tongue and the four *ogbanjes* scuttled ahead of him, disappearing quickly into the shadows.

Helplessly, Ngola watched as the Portuguese slavers herded the prisoners up and followed the *bokor*.

"Get the men," he whispered to Drury. "Follow the Portuguese."

Drury hesitated only a moment, eyes searching Ngola's face, then he nodded. "Where are you going?"

"To scout ahead for a place that we can set up an ambush."

"Give me a moment to talk to Joao and I'll go with you."

Ngola shook his head. "One man will pass unheard and unseen. If there are two, there are more chances of being found out."

"If you get into trouble –"

Ngola grinned mirthlessly, interrupting his friend. "If I get into trouble, you will know it. Rest assured. Now go. When I need you, the best you can do is be there to lead the men."

"You have my word." Drury clapped Ngola on the shoulder and melted into the darkness that clung to the mountainside.

Ngola looked over the jungle ahead, finding a jagged outcrop of rock towering above the trees to use as a landmark. Lukamba and the Portuguese headed in that direction.

Getting to his feet out of sight of the slavers, Ngola ran along the ridge of the mountain, just short of the crest. Using the skills that Kangela had taught him, he passed through the jungle without leaving branches or brush trembling to mark his passage. He was a ghost among the moon-cast shadows.

4. THE LOST CITY

AT LEAST A THOUSAND yards ahead of Lukamba and the Portuguese slavers, Ngola spotted the rope bridge that spanned a large canyon. The roar of the river racing below reached him before he got close enough to peer down into the swirling depths.

Hidden by trees and brush, Ngola stared down at the rushing river at least two hundred yards below the cliff's edge. Jagged rocks pierced the white-capped water like broken fangs and spray sailed over them.

The bridge was narrow, at least a hundred feet long and only wide enough for one person to cross at a time. That would bottleneck the slavers and force them to cross one at a time. That could be useful, but once the women and children were on the bridge, they would be vulnerable.

Ngola cursed. Staging an ambush there was too problematic. If he and his men crowded the Portuguese, the prisoners could be used as hostages, perhaps dangled over the long drop to the river if things went badly. And there was no time to get around the slavers and return with his men to set up the ambush.

Glancing behind him, Ngola spotted the pale torchlight crowding out the night as the party of slavers approached the bridge. He felt certain they would cross the bridge. There was nothing else that would attract them on this side of the ravine.

Across the bridge, though, the mountain towered another thousand feet or so, spiking toward the dark sky, narrowing to a point like a spear. Trees and shrubs clung to the mountain's exterior. Nothing there gave any indication why Lukamba trekked in that direction. However, the river below was wide enough to have permitted a sailing vessel at some point.

Perhaps the myths about *The Scorpion* were true. If Ngola's family had not been presently at risk, he might have enjoyed thinking about the possibility of riches awaiting the night's efforts. Tonight, though, he planned only bloody revenge.

Deciding he wanted to know more what lay on the other side of the river than to wait on his men and cross later, Ngola sprinted for the bridge with the Baker tight in his fist. Reaching the massive pole driven into the ground at the cliff's edge, he turned without hesitation, but with considerable trepidation, and trotted across the bridge.

The wooden slats clacked and shifted beneath his boots, but they held his weight easily, surprising him greatly. It looked like no one had come this way in years. Moss and small plants had taken root in the braided rope cables and some of the wooden slats.

He reached the other side without being seen, glanced around till he found a game trail off to his left, then followed that for a moment. Inside the brush, the game trail crossed an old stone avenue obscured by the forest.

The jungle had overgrown the stone pathway to a large degree, but there was no doubt that the way had been cut through the brush and trees at one point. And there was no doubt that no one had come this way in years, perhaps generations. The road was eight feet wide and laid with four-foot squares of thick white rock slabs that had been quarried and placed with care.

Stepping onto the nearest stone, Ngola slammed his foot against the surface and found it hard and firm. Grass and roots disturbed the lay of some of the stones, shifting them up at angles and partially covering them, but the direction could be easily discerned.

Ngola stayed off of the pathway, choosing instead to move quickly beside it. Walking on the stones would have left fresh tracks and he didn't want to risk that someone among Salazar's crew might be sharp enough to catch those marks and know them for what they were.

Glancing back the way he'd come, Ngola spotted the Portuguese sailors crossing the bridge in single file. As Kangela and Emeka walked the bridge as it swung, he tried not to think of the long fall that lay below them if the supports gave way. His wife kept one hand on their boy's shoulder, gently guiding him, and he walked with his head high.

The *ogbanje* cavorted around Lukamba, unmindful of the long plunge to the river. They spun and twirled along the ropes, like they were gamboling on a walk.

Ngola said a silent prayer for his wife and son, then focused on seeking out the eventual destination. He started forward again, then paused long enough to make sure the Portuguese and the *bokor* traveled in the direction he'd chosen.

They made the turn and came after him. Their torchlights seared the shadows from the tree canopy as they traveled.

Ngola pressed on.

—ɷ—

THE WHITE STONE PATHWAY came to an end at stone steps that led up into the mountains. A long time ago, walls had stood on either side of the steps. Their crumbled remains lay amid the jungle, almost swallowed up by trees and brush. Occasional moonlight glinted off surfaces, making the straight lines stand out against the riotous form of the jungle.

At the foot of the steps, Ngola gazed up and discerned that the ruins of a small town lay before him. He sifted through the myths and legends he'd heard of lost cities in this part of West Africa, trying to identify which this might have been. There were so many stories, though, so many lost places. Every tribe had its folklore about forgotten civilizations that had fallen through the cracks of time, and all of them might possibly contain a kernel of truth.

So much of Africa's past had been wiped out. Lives had winked out like sparks rising from a cook fire, and histories had gotten lost and scattered. Ngola believed that Africa would remain forever splintered, never again to be made whole, never to be made strong against invaders that preyed upon her shores and took whatever they wished.

He shook those bleak thoughts from his mind and focused on saving his wife and son, and keeping his crew as safe as possible. They would shed more blood tonight, he knew that was unavoidable, but he did not want to lose any more of his people if it could be helped.

With the Baker rifle at the ready and the *bokor* and his inhuman companions at his heels, Ngola entered the forgotten city. Trees and brush grew along the roads that lay half-buried in dirt and grass. Night birds and bats flickered between the branches and through the arches that remained of doorways. Hyenas cackled in the distance. Almost all of the original houses had fallen over the passage of time, but here and there small buildings yet remained.

The town had been built around a natural cistern that formed a deep bowl in the harsh, rocky landscape at the foot of the mountains. Rains had come down the mountain face and pooled in the bowl. A manmade trench three feet wide led back to the chasm where the bridge was. Ngola guessed that the trench had been constructed to keep the cistern from overflowing during the rainy season.

Skeletons of people, donkeys, and other animals lay around the water's edge, enough so that Ngola wondered if the water had been at one time poisoned.

Closer inspection revealed that nearly all of the human skeletons were of full grown men. Many of them had weapons – spears and stone axes and crude swords forged of hammered bronze – close enough to hand that Ngola believed they had died fighting.

Several of the skulls lay cracked and shattered. Smashed ribcages revealed more signs of violence. Some of the newer skeletons, though those were old as well, wore Portuguese breastplates and had more modern weapons, though those too were dated.

Ngola's grip on the Baker tightened as he surveyed the battlefield. Whatever had killed the original inhabitants had risen up and killed again. Fear thrummed through him, a buzzing, insistent force. Every instinct in him clamored for him to quit the place as quickly as he could.

But he would not leave Kangela or Emeka. When he left, he would take them with him. And they would be avenged.

Forcing himself to stand his ground, taking a firmer grip on the Baker and tracing the hilt of one of his cutlasses, Ngola surveyed the cistern's dark water. The bowl was at least seventy yards across. In times past, the water level had been higher. Water stains on the alabaster rock revealed the old capacity. The present level was nearly three feet lower than the highest stain.

Moonlight shimmered across the surface stirred by the whispering wind. The water looked oily and black, and though Ngola would have liked to slake his thirst, he dared not. Nor did he get too close to the water's edge. A cold, instinctive warning trickled through him and he took two steps back before he realized he was moving.

Light flared at the corner of his eye, and he turned toward it, raising the Baker rifle.

Torches burned brightly in the hands of the Portuguese sailors as they tramped toward the ruins. Their gear jingled as they walked, and their whispers sounded tight and frightened.

Ngola melted back into the shadows a short distance from the cistern, staying to the right midway between the front of the cistern and where it butted up against the mountain. Standing behind a stone arch that listed to one side, he made the Baker ready and breathed quietly.

Lukamba walked without hesitation to the cistern's edge. The *ogbanje* paced stolidly at his side, no longer capering like demented children. They were focused and attentive. Their empty eye sockets remained riveted on the dark water.

The Portuguese halted several feet distant and huddled together under the fragile umbrella of light from their combined torches. Fear etched their faces, and Ngola knew they too felt the evil that lurked in the tumbled-down city.

"Lukamba." Hand on his cutlass, Captain Salazar strode toward the *bokor*. "What is this place and why have you brought us here? Where is the treasure?"

Setting his staff on the ground, Lukamba answered the Portuguese captain but kept his attention riveted on the cistern. He stretched forth his empty hand over the dark water. A purple glow emanated from his palm and fingers and the glow reflected on the surface.

"Patience, Captain. Your treasure is at hand." Lukamba closed his eyes as if in prayer. "This place is Abiku, the city of death. Long and long, it has lain here, a corpse of broken rock and shattered power, but within its bones it has held many things of great power."

Salazar kicked at a pile of bones in disgust. "It's a city of corpses, I will grant you that, but I do not see *The Scorpion* or the treasure."

"Abiku holds old secrets here, Captain. Powerful secrets. *The Scorpion* came here, but the ship did not leave."

"Then where is it?"

"Hidden. As many things here are hidden." Lukamba closed his hand and made a fist. The purple glow grew stronger, throwing a cast of light over his withered mouth and the half-skull that he wore. He smiled, and the expression held nothing good in it. "We are here tonight to uncover these things."

New ripples shifted across the cistern.

At the front of the line of hostages, Emeka grew more frightened. He clung to Kangela's hand and stepped back to take shelter behind his mother. Behind the arch, Ngola leveled the Baker rifle and held the sights steady on Lukamba. One of the *ogbanje* slowly turned around and scented the air, then directed its gaze at Ngola's hiding spot.

Ngola cursed quietly, knowing then that the foul little thing was somehow sniffing out his intent. Reluctantly, Ngola shifted his aim and stopped breathing, willing his heart to beat more quietly.

The *ogbanje* shifted a little uncertainly, then uttered a plaintive cry.

Lukamba ignored the dead thing and concentrated on his task. Silently, the other three *ogbanje* turned in Ngola's direction as well, staring at him across the expanse of dark water.

"Abiku is an important place, Captain. A place of power for the man who knows how to wield such power." Lukamba's voice softened yet sounded more powerful as it carried across the cistern.

Ngola knew the change in pitch was affected by the hollow shape of the cistern and the fact that water carried sound better than the land. He watched the *ogbanje*, praying they did not seek him out in that moment.

Shadows flickered behind the Portuguese and Ngola's keen eyes made out the gleam of moonlight on metal. Relief took the edge off the fear that gripped him when he realized Drury and the rest of his away party had joined him there in the ruins. They were still outnumbered, but they had surprise on their side.

For the moment.

"If you were lying to me, old man, I will see you drawn and quartered ere the dawn lights the eastern horizon." Salazar took another step forward.

Instantly, the four *ogbanje* wheeled on the Portuguese captain, no longer searching for Ngola. Salazar drew one of his pistols in a blue of speed that impressed Ngola. Legends insisted on the captain's speed and deadliness. The heavy pistol barrel centered on the back of Lukamba's head.

"Call off your pets, sorcerer." Salazar spoke in Portuguese. "Or I will put a bullet through your brain."

"If you should decide to do that, the *ogbanje* would kill you and feast on your blood." Lukamba continued speaking softly, as if he had no concerns in the matter. "I ask only that you bide your time a moment more. Then all will be revealed."

Salazar held his aim a moment longer, then raised his pistol to point at the heavens. "A moment more is all."

Lukamba gestured to the *ogbanje* and spoke in a language Ngola did not understand. They were guttural words, hard and ringing.

Instantly, the *ogbanje* walked to the water's edge and placed their misshapen hands on the stone. When they lifted them back up, they held tall, conical drums. The *ogbanje* stood the drums before them, then began hammering the tautly stretched skin that covered the instruments.

Taking his spyglass from his pouch, Ngola examined the drums. They'd been constructed of bones woven tightly together. The stretched skins still bore some of the features of men and women that had been sewn together to create the cover. The vibrating skins made it look like the faces were crying out in pain.

The hollow thumping of the drums started off slow but quickly gained speed, filling the dead city with menacing noise.

"What are you doing?" Salazar took a step back in spite of his bravado.

Behind their leader, the Portuguese men huddled more tightly together. Kangela shifted Emeka behind her, placing herself between their son and the *bokor* and the dark cistern.

"I am calling forth that which will not die." Lukamba's voice rose above the thumping of the drums. His closed fist glowed more brightly. "Long and long have I searched for the secret to this place. I did not guess that your search and mine would fall so closely together, but it was meant to be. Perhaps you follow dark gods as well."

"I do not follow heathen gods," Salazar growled.

"You do not follow your chosen god either."

"Do not mock me."

The drums grew louder and louder. Ngola felt the hollow beats burn and leap through his blood. The music reached back into a forgotten part of himself, igniting those memories of Africa and the boy he had been before the slavers had captured him and sold him off to the plantation owners in Haiti. He wanted to weep for all that he had lost, but the fear that slid greasily through him erased all gentle thoughts from his mind.

"The original inhabitants did not know of the god that sleeps at the bottom of this cistern." Lukamba raised his gnarled fist above his head.

"They knew only that this was an easy place to live. Sheltered from their enemies, they built their homes and raised their crops and tended their cattle. They did not know they had trespassed. Not at first.."

The whirling tempo of the drums sped up more as the *ogbanje* beat madly at them. There was not just one beat now. The demonic dead things had woven in two beats that sometimes complemented the original and sometimes fought to be unleashed.

"One day, though, the god awakened and demanded his tribute." Lukamba shivered as though chilled. "Abiku rose up from the water and killed them, leaving only a few to tend his needs. They served him, giving him their children, feeding his dark hunger when he called out to them."

"Why did those people not simply leave?" Salazar asked.

"Because Abiku bound them to him. The people found that when they left this place, they sickened and died. No one could escape. They lived only to be his sacrifices, his amusements and his pleasures and his prey. And their children served in their time. Until they rose up against Abiku and he struck them down."

"Better to die a free man than live in thrall to a demon."

The irony of Salazar's declaration was not lost on Ngola. In many places, the Portuguese slaver himself was cursed as a demonic entity.

"Given the choice, Captain, what would you do?"

"Me?" Salazar forced a laugh, making it loud enough to pierce the drumming. "I would put a ball through your head and end this farce once and for all."

"Would you?" Lukamba smiled, then turned to face the slaver captain. "We will see." The old *bokor* threw his arms skyward, seized his staff in both hands, and barked more guttural words as the *ogbanje* ceased their mad drumming. Something shimmered in the air above the spear, then dove into the water.

The last notes of the drums drifted away, lost in the ruins of the city.

For a moment, fragile silence stretched over the cistern.

Then Salazar laughed. "Perhaps your dark god is not yet ready to rouse from his nap, old man. Or maybe these people killed him and left him to rot in his little pool." He leveled the pistol again. "Now I will have my gold or I will throw your corpse to the fishes and eels that might live in those fetid waters."

The cistern's calm surface erupted in a wave of spray as the monstrous thing that lay beneath lunged up.

5. DARK GOD

THE SERPENTINE SHAPE TOWERED twenty feet above the cistern. A monstrous wedge-shaped head split open to reveal fangs as long as a man's arm, and a forked, black tongue flicked out to taste the air. Two sets of huge ebony eyes were set one above the other, the higher ones spreading out farther to the sides of its face. Great fins flared out on either sides of the thing's head. The moonlight dappled the creature's scales in shimmering blues, greens, and purples. Its belly was lighter in color than its dorsal side.

Captain Salazar swore and shifted his pistol from Lukamba to the behemoth writhing sinuously behind the bokor. The muzzle flash burnt a hole in the darkness and gray powder fogged out, then the crack! reached Ngola's ears.

Abiku loosed an ululating wail, but Ngola knew that the sound was not caused by whatever small wound the Portuguese captain's pistol might have made. The demon-thing was much too massive for a lone pistol ball to have done much damage.

"Kill that thing!" Salazar dropped his first pistol and drew another, stubbornly standing his ground.

Trained to obey their leader in battle, the Portuguese slavers drew forth their weapons and opened fire. The pistol shots sounded brittle and gunsmoke lay thick over the sailors.

"Reload!" Salazar commanded as he drew another of his pistols.

Obeying at once, the Portuguese set their rifles on the ground and reached for powder and shot. They worked mechanically, by instinct, for their fearful gazes were locked on the monster that swayed above them.

The ogbanje beat on their drums again, as quick and threatening as ever.

The thing spoke in a sonorous language. The sounds were too methodical to be incoherent growling. Lukamba turned back to the creature with his staff held high and spoke in the same language. He abased himself in front of it, dropping to his knees, and pointed not at the

Portuguese as Ngola had expected, but at the women and children left huddled in front of the slavers.

Abiku roared and the sound rolled up the mountainside. Quicker than the thing had any right to move, it darted forward and seized two women and a child in its gaping maw. Teeth gnashed together, slicing its victims into pieces, and red blood poured down its chin.

Kangela seized Emeka's hand and propelled the boy backward as the Portuguese sailors fired again. The balls struck the creature, but most of them deflected from the scales and the others only made small wounds that barely trickled green blood.

Ngola raised his rifle and targeted Lukamba. When the sights settled over the bokor's withered mouth, Ngola squeezed the trigger. The rifle jarred his shoulder. At the same moment, Lukamba ducked his head to the fearsome creature gulping its grisly meal before him. The ball struck the skull mask Lukamba wore.

Knocked backward by the ball, Lukamba rolled awkwardly. For a moment Ngola thought he had killed the bokor, but even as Ngola poured more powder down the throat of his weapon, Lukamba stirred and raised himself on hands and knees. The shattered skull mask fell from his face. He shouted at the monstrous thing and the ogbanje beat the drums furiously.

"Reload!" Salazar yelled as he squeezed his pistol's trigger. The crack! pierced the drumming but for a second. Instead of aiming at the creature, Salazar had aimed at Lukamba.

The old bokor lifted his staff and screamed in his foreign tongue. Purple sparks flashed a foot in front of his face and the pistol ball stopped in mid-flight, then dropped to the rocky ground.

Still chomping on his helpless prey, Abiku swept toward the Portuguese. Most of them had started reloading their weapons, but all of them abandoned the long guns and reached for their blades as the monster came for them.

Kangela reached the Portuguese and tried to break through. A swift kick sent one of the men to the ground. Kangela stole the fallen man's knife from his belt and buried it in the throat of another man who reached for Emeka. As the dying man stumbled backwards, the man behind him shoved him aside and leveled his pistol at Kangela.

Shifting his aim from the bokor, Ngola aimed at the Portuguese sailor's face and pulled the trigger. The ball slammed the man's head backward, then he dropped to his knees and fell forward on his face.

Abiku struck the midst of the Portuguese, scattering them at first, then plucking up five of them with long tentacles that suddenly uncoiled from its neck. The screaming men hung like fruit from the monster's appendages, and it ate one of them like taking a grape from a bunch.

"Drury!" Ngola shouted. "Get Kangela and Emeka out of here!"

Lukamba whirled around to face Ngola. Rifle ready again, Ngola took aim at the bokor and fired as the old man lifted his staff and shouted again.

The ball stopped in mid-air amid a shower of purple sparks, then dropped.

Lukamba laughed and preened. "Captain Ngola. I missed you at your village, but I have you now. This is an unexpected pleasure. And your wife and child are here too." He shook his head. "There will be no escape from this place."

Ngola tossed the Baker rifle aside, knowing it would be of no further use. The balls couldn't reach Lukamba and they were ineffective against the creature.

Some of the Portuguese broke and ran, racing back along the way they had come only to be met by Drury and the away party. Drury, Joao, and some of the other men fired their weapons, cutting down the slavers before they reached them. The bodies of the Portuguese toppled to the ground as one of the fleeing women and two of the children raced past.

Abiku loosed another ululating wail that reverberated from the mountain and echoed over the countryside. The air just beyond Drury and the men wavered and Ngola felt the hum of electricity.

The woman and the two children never slowed down, but when they reached the wavering area, eldritch magic stripped the flesh from their bones and they fell to the earth as gleaming ivory skeletons and the demonic drumming from the ogbanje continued around them. Two other children had been at the woman's heels.

Drury caught one of the children and halted her, but the other was past him before he could grab her. She met the same fate as the others, falling to the earth beside them.

Barely controlling the horror that filled him, Ngola stared at the heaps of bones.

Lukamba cackled gleefully. "I told you that none of you may leave this place. You can serve Abiku, or you can die."

Either way, Ngola knew, death was in the cards – if they couldn't find some way to break free of the creature's power. Ripping his cutlasses free of their sheaths as he ran down the incline to the cistern, Ngola thought back to the houngans and mambos he had met while on Haiti and along the West Coast. Vodun was powerful, but it had its weaknesses. Blood, fire, and salt all disrupted spells, curses, hexes, and the evil eye. Even non-practitioners had defenses against the unwanted attentions of the loa.

The hapless Portuguese in the monster's tentacles cried out for help, but their pleas fell on deaf ears. Captain Salazar tried to marshal his men to him, but that task was made harder because Drury and the away team pressed them hard, shooting them and keeping them penned between them and Abiku.

"Father!" Emeka stood within his mother's sheltering arms and stared at Ngola.

"Husband!" Kangela held her position, but Ngola knew she was torn between her son and fear for him.

"Stay, Kangela! Keep Emeka safe!" Ngola sprinted toward Lukamba.

The old bokor raised his staff in defiance and threw out his empty hand. Purple flames lashed out like a whip, narrowly missing Ngola as he slid beneath them. Once the flames passed overhead, Ngola popped back to his feet, still clutching the cutlasses in his fists.

Abiku lashed out at him, dropping its massive head earthward. Ngola leapt, throwing himself high into the air and reversing the cutlass in his left hand. As his boots claimed brief purchase on the monstrous head, he shoved the cutlass deep into the scaly flesh.

Roaring with rage and pain, Abiku lifted its head. Three whiplike tentacles streaked toward Ngola. Swinging his remaining cutlass, Ngola hacked the tentacles off close to the thing's body. Green blood jetted from the stumps. Other tentacles slammed a Portuguese captive into the monster's body close to Ngola.

Holding fast to the embedded cutlass, Ngola reversed his second cutlass and slammed it home into the monster's flesh as well, then yanked free the first. He pulled himself farther up on the thing's head, cutting two more tentacles away as though clearing brush.

Abiku roared again and its pain and anger seemed to shake the mountainside. Writhing, it shifted again, trying desperately to unseat

Ngola. Clinging fiercely to the embedded cutlass, Ngola planted his free blade in one of his opponent's eyes. Bellowing mightily, Abiku crashed its head into the ground.

The impact jarred Ngola loose. Knowing he could no longer manage a hold, Ngola kicked free, angling his fall toward Lukamba. The bokor stood frozen, watching in disbelief as Ngola launched himself. At the last moment, Lukamba realized where Ngola was headed and tried to flee, but it was too late.

Ngola landed boots first on the old man and drove him to the ground. Lukamba's spine snapped like a twig. He lay on his face, huffing and trying to breathe the dirt.

Rolling to the side, Ngola came up with his cutlasses in both fists. His dark gaze raked the monster as it bellowed and wallowed in the cistern. Two Portuguese sailors still lay within its tentacles like bizarre ornaments. They squalled in fear, wide-eyed and crazed.

"Ngola!" Kangela yelled.

Ignoring her, Ngola focused on saving them. Blood, salt, and fire – those were the things used to banish vodun. He hoped that would be enough.

A ragged breath tore through Lukamba's broken mouth. Reversing the cutlass in his left hand again, Ngola slammed the blade through the bokor's back and into the earth. Then, as the monster twisted its gargantuan head to see him again – only one eye on this side now, Ngola knelt to search through the old man's pack. One of the first things Ngola found was the salt sack the bokor kept to create protective circles around himself when he dealt with the dead things.

Ngola claimed the salt as his own and dodged away as Abiku lunged at him. After taking the salt sack in his teeth, Ngola drew one of his pistols and shoved it toward the monstrous thing's remaining eye, then pulled the trigger.

Green ichor sprayed from the ruined orb as a small cavity opened up. Two tentacles snaked along the ground and wrapped Ngola's right ankle. Howling with murderous intent, Abiku lifted its head.

Desperately, Ngola flung the spent pistol away and seized the bokor's staff from nearby. His fingers just grazed over the hardened wood at first, but he got the staff on the second try. He curled the staff into his fist and watched in horror as the thing dangled him over that monstrous maw.

Ngola maneuvered the staff, hoping that the fire-hardened wood and whatever magic it held made it stout enough. The needle-sharp teeth closed around him, then stopped when the staff prevented the massive jaws from closing.

Holding onto the staff to provide leverage, Ngola twisted and thrust the cutlass into the thing's snout, hoping it was sensitive. Undoubtedly the snout was sensitive enough, because Abiku screamed and sent two tentacles slithering for the weapon.

Taking advantage of his momentary respite, Ngola grabbed one of the teeth with his other hand and hauled himself into the creature's mouth. Bracing his back against the roof of the monster's mouth, legs trembling with exertion to keep him locked in place, Ngola opened the salt sack and spilled the contents down the thing's throat.

Abiku's cries came to an abrupt halt as it choked.

Pulling the powder horn from his side, Ngola pried it open and scattered the gunpowder down the thing's throat as well. Taking the mambele from its holster at his back, Ngola sliced a long furrow along his arm. His blood mixed with the salt and gunpowder.

"With my blood, I curse you to hell, to rot and to die, in agony and fire." Ngola pulled his flint from his pouch and struck sparks from it with the mambele.

Flames leapt up as soon as the sparks touched the gunpowder. Some of the powder was wet from the creature's saliva, but enough remained to guarantee a hearty blaze.

Ngola reached up and grabbed the staff as the monster shook its head in a dizzying whirl. Several tentacles snaked into its mouth, rushing over Ngola but not closing on him. He forced himself between the thing's jaws, escaping just before the tentacles pried the staff loose. He landed on the monster's chin as the massive teeth slammed shut.

Smoke blew out the monster's nostrils and gills, and fire lit it up from inside. The head snapped and jerked in agony.

Heaving himself away from the creature, Ngola tumbled to the hard ground and came up on his feet immediately. He lunged to the side, shoved a foot down on Lukamba's corpse, and pulled free his cutlass. He turned to face the cistern again, expecting the monster to come for him.

Instead, Abiku dove into the black water.

For the first time, Ngola realized that the drumming had stopped. He gazed along the shore and saw the four ogbanje lay sprawled in death again. As he stared at them, the corpses withered and turned to ash. Whatever dark magic had animated them had gone. The drums aged and collapsed, falling into pieces as the leathery faces curled up and tattered.

A moment later Abiku's corpse floated to the top of the cistern. The two remaining eyes were glazed over in death.

Remembering there was still a fight to be fought with the Portuguese, Ngola turned around and took a fresh grip on his cutlass and drew one of his remaining pistols.

Captain Salazar lay dead on the ground. His men lay dead around him. None had been spared. Mercy wasn't something Ngola's crew was prepared to give to slavers.

In the next instant, Emeka ran to Ngola. Smiling, Ngola dropped to one knee and wrapped an arm around the boy, lifting him easily as he once more stood.

Tears streaked Emeka's face. "I thought the monster had eaten you."

"No. I crawled inside him and killed him." Ngola grinned. "I only did it to worry your mother."

"She was scared."

"Then it worked." Ngola strode forward and slipped his cutlass into its sheath, then took Kangela under his arm as she came up to embrace him. He leaned down and kissed her, feeling all the warmth and love that a man could ever feel, and those were the things that made the battles a man had to fight worthwhile.

Drury joined them, bloodied and worn.

"How many did we lose, Colin?"

The Irishman grinned and shook his head. "Not a one. The Portuguese were too worried about that thing to pay much attention to us. By the time they decided to attend to us, it was too late."

"Good. Do we have wounded?"

"Not so wounded that we can't leave."

"Then let's leave."

Drury grinned again. "Mayhap you'll want to tarry a little longer, Captain."

Ngola studied his second-in-command silently for a moment. "I have memories enough of this place."

"Aye, and I do as well. However, I wouldn't want to go off and leave all that gold."

Ngola thought about that. "You found The Scorpion?"

"Near enough." Drury jerked a thumb over his shoulder. "While we were scouting the city, Joao discovered one of the collapsed houses covered a tunnel leading down to a cavern at the river's edge. The Scorpion's inside. She's still got her cargo aboard. From what Joao says, it's going to take us a few days to load it all up." He grinned again. "I'm thinking there's enough to give your wife's people a fresh start somewhere else and allow us to take some downtime. God knows we've earned it."

Ngola nodded. "We have, and Kangela's people will need to be relocated. We cannot take any chances that Salazar might have gotten word to the Portuguese that he had found them."

"Want to come down and take a look?"

Ngola started to answer yes, because he was curious about the treasure and the things The Scorpion's crew might have taken all those years ago, but Kangela squeezed his hand and looked up at him defiantly. She understood English well enough to know what Ngola and Drury were discussing.

Ngola shook his head. "Not tonight, Colin. Tonight I am going to take my son to the safety of the ship and open a good flask of wine to share with my wife."

Drury snorted in mock derision. "If I hadn't just seen you kill a god with your bare hands after getting et whole, I'd say marriage was making you soft."

Ngola held onto his wife and son and headed out of the ruins, watching as the sun rose in the east behind them and turned the heavens pink. The Scorpion's riches could wait. He knew that he had all a man could ever hope for.

AGNES VIRIDIAN AND THE SEARCH FOR THE SCALES

BY KIMBERLY RICHARDSON

MEMPHIS. MY HOME EVER since I was born and yet if someone asked me to describe the city, I wouldn't know what to say. Perhaps I would explain that it was a city named after the ancient city in Egypt, both cities lying next to a river like a sleeping goddess, or that it was a city filled with racial strife with undisclosed harmony lurking underneath. Maybe I could tell them that it was a city filled with things that go bump in the night, things that serve their own purpose, master or agenda. In fact, if someone were to ask about Memphis, they would hear the latter description. That was what Memphis was all about in November 1925: ghosts and creatures that would steal your soul just by looking at you while dreams and nightmares come to life right on Beale Street and beyond.

My name is Agnes Viridian.

It was on a cool day when he walked into my office. Normally, I don't like to receive customers, friends or droppers-in on a Friday. Yet when he and a woman walked into my office without any formality, I decided to make this an exception.

The woman wore all white from her feathered hat tilted to the side of her dark haired head right down to her impossibly tall pumps that showed off her bronzed skin as her dress clung to her body, leaving nothing to the imagination. My own outfit for the day was the same as always: all black with my cloche hat on my head and no jewelry. Due to my past, I felt comfort in such a color, plus it contrasted my caramel skin tone. The gentleman, at least that's what I thought he was, was very tall and slender in build. He wore black and red velvet clothing with a smoking jacket, fez and . . . a green satin veil covering his face, save for two oval slits for his very dark eyes. I wanted to look away from those eyes, yet I found myself drawn to them. They spoke of age, mystery and possibly danger. Sounded like a grand time for me.

"Please, sit down," I said just as the two sat in chairs across from my desk. I looked out the window to see people walking up and down Beale

Street and then focused my attention back to the couple.

"You are Agnes Viridian?" asked the man behind the veil. His voice was deep and smoky, as though he had visited one too many opium dens. His accent stumped me for a moment and I glanced to the woman who merely smiled. I would get no answers from her. As far as I could tell, she was there only for support.

"I am," I replied in a steady voice, trying hard not to reveal the quivering inside of me. The masked man leaned forward and I got a whiff of something not unpleasant.

"I was told that you are a... 'resource' for those who have nowhere else to turn. Is this true?"

I nodded yes and I could have sworn that he smiled behind his mini curtain. "Forgive me," I asked in my usual curious way, "but I cannot place your accent. Where are you from?"

"Egypt," said the woman, speaking for the first time. "Please, we have traveled a long way to get here. You are, quite possibly, our last hope." I noticed that her voice was deep and accented as well, yet flowed like honey.

"Tell me of your situation and I'll see if I can help."

The man leaned back in his chair. "I have a set of scales, very old, that have been in my family for many years. Someone has stolen them from me and I intend to get them back." Suddenly, he leaned against the woman and began to cough loudly. I jumped up and got a glass of water for him.

"No, no," said the woman in a calm tone, "this will soon pass. Water will not help him." I slowly walked back to my desk and sat down. After several seconds had passed, he stopped his coughing fit and looked as though he had not coughed in the first place.

"So," I said, trying to resume the conversation, "you've lost-"

The man slammed a gloved hand down on my desk, causing several cracks to appears in the thick wood. I flinched back in confusion while the woman placed a slender hand on his shoulder.

"Please, control yourself," she murmured to him then spoke what sounded like ancient Egyptian to him as she rubbed his shoulder. The man, while his eyes focused on me with burning anger, calmed himself down and leaned back into the chair.

"I apologize if I have offended you," I said in a soft tone.

"The scales were not lost," said the man, ignoring my apology. "They were *stolen*!" He said the last word with a hiss. "I even know the devil who stole them from me."

Thus began my business relationship with Mr. O and his wife Imogene.

They filled me in with the details: a set of small brass scales, stolen from Mr. O's home in the dark of night, by his brother of all people. Apparently, the two had had varying degrees of fights over all sorts of matters, yet his brother decided to "upstage" him by stealing his scales. They were worth a bit of money to the highest bidder in the black market. When the theft was discovered, Mr. O and Imogene traveled all over the world trying to track him; every time they thought they were close to him, he suddenly slipped through their fingers like mist over the Mississippi River. Reliable sources and spies, through months of grueling searching, finally found traces of him in Memphis, Tennessee. If they were going to strike, they had to strike quickly.

"So, why me?" I asked once Mr. O completed his tale. "Why not some other person, preferably a white male who has more access to Memphis?"

"We had heard of you and your 'skills'," said Imogene, "and besides, we prefer working with a Negro woman, especially someone with your abilities. This situation requires it."

Mr. O solemnly nodded. I nodded back.

Thanks to a kindhearted and way-before-his-time French professor named Jean Duvony, I was taken into his world at the tender age of three, away from my family whom I found out later willingly gave me up knowing that I would have a better chance at life with the pale white man than with them. He whisked me away to Paris and there began my training. From then until now and even ongoing, Jean taught me literature, several languages, *l'histoire*, all of the sciences and magick in its many forms. I learned about the Occult, the Left Hand Path, Witchcraft and anything else under the sun that would be deemed as socially unacceptable to the general public, let alone a Negro girl such as myself with caramel skin and eyes the color of a rainy day. We traveled the world and I was able to see and experience things that I thought were only in storybooks.

It was then on my 21st birthday that Jean informed me that the world I thought I knew was not what I had perceived. The real world, he told me over wine and several pipes of opium, was of monsters, myths and legends. Gods and goddesses walked among humans. When he told me this, even after my studies, I refused to believe him . . . . until the woman who had served us wine suddenly arched her back to reveal two long and slender wings. Until I realized that Jean had been alive for over 300 years and did not look a day over 30. I then saw with completely open eyes a very scary and magnificent place.

After that time, Jean became my lover while continuing to be my teacher and guide. I no longer doubted.

When Mr. O and his wife left my office, I set myself to work. They told me that Mr. O's brother had purchased a couple of warehouses along the Mississippi in the hopes of securing a very large deal. I closed up my office and set my sights on Warehouse Row, only a 10-minute walk. The cool air greeted me and I welcomed it. People were hunched down in their coats as if there was a great blizzard swirling around us. I kept walking. At that moment, I "felt" two men suddenly take an interest in me and where I was going. I continued on. I wanted to feel them out first, see if they were friendly or not.

From Beale I went to Second Avenue, then Main Street. The two men still kept up with me. I walked up the hill, then down again to Front Street, then made a left turn. The two men were still following me. Just then, a young white man dressed in ragged clothing coming the opposite way bumped into me.

"Oh Ma'am," he said in a loud Southern drawl, "did I hurt ya?" He brushed off my coat then whispered in French, *"Friend of Jean's. Being followed. Here to help."* I did not ask how Jean knew I needed help. Jean just knows.

I sighed gratefully and said nothing as he reverted back to his Southern drawl. I glanced over his shoulder and saw them: two large and burly white men dressed in nondescript grey clothes walking side by side. My eyes caught theirs and they quickly passed us and scampered down the street. The man stopped dusting me off and watched their retreating backs. When it seemed like the coast was clear, he said in heavily accented English, "Jean figured you would need help. My name is Francois."

My savior was rather tall and lanky with black floppy hair and blue eyes the color of a bright Southern Summer sky. His hawk-like nose pointed down at me as he stared into my certain eyes. I shook his hand with a firm grip and then walked on with Francois in tow.

"Tell Jean I'm grateful," I said as we continued our walk. Francois closed his eyes, smiled then said, "he knows." I had to laugh. Only Jean.

I quickly told Francois of the situation and asked if he had heard anything strange going on around Warehouse Row, which was an understatement. Warehouse Row was the place to obtain anything any time any place. Thanks to Boss Crump and his "furry boys", the city was a major thoroughfare for all activities, both Human and Other. It was rumored that Memphis was worse than New Orleans, but that's another tale for another time.

When we reached Warehouse Row, I motioned Francois to keep quiet and to follow me. He nodded and we began looking around. Thankfully, the workers in the area did not think it too strange to see a white man and a Negro woman walking through the area and did not try to ask us any questions. We walked by several warehouses, all wide open and empty, until we reached one way in the back that smelled bad. Not bad like a rotten egg or sour milk. No, this smell was of pure evil. Darkness enveloped in chaos.

I glanced at my partner and then tried the locked door. After several tries, Francois placed a hand on my shoulder and pushed me to the side. He grabbed the lock with his hands, shook himself once, then quickly turned into a very large and black wolf creature. I merely stared at him as I thought, *Leave it to Jean to send a shapeshifter to assist me.* He yanked the door handles right off the door with a loud groan, then handed them to me like a present. I grinned and placed them in my pockets as we walked in.

The warehouse was semi dark inside and looked to be filled with all sorts of boxes in all sizes. The only light we had came from the windows. I motioned to wolf-Francois to keep an eye out for-

"Well, well, well," said a voice that seemed to be from all around us. "How nice of you to drop in, Miss Viridian and friend." The voice sounded just like Mr. O, yet deeper, darker and reeked of something foul. "I suppose you are here to find his precious scales?"

"That's right." I had nothing to fear from this guy. All I wanted were the scales. I heard movement from all around, soft pattering of feet.

"*Mon Dieu!*" screamed Francois as I felt several somethings crawl up my coat. I grabbed one of the things and realized that it was a rat. A very large black rat. Soon, I felt more and more, their squeaks getting louder and louder while Francois growled and tore at them with his teeth as they desperately tried to grab his fur and skin. I dropped to the floor and discovered it was literally covered in rats. I closed my eyes.

"Shame we couldn't play on an even field, Miss Viridian!" screamed the voice as the rats grew in number. "But, as you can see, I *never* like to play on an even field!" I heard his maniacal laughter all around us as I unbuttoned my coat and flung it away from me. Such a brave act, yet it did nothing to dispel the rats. I looked over to see the hulking form of Francois, biting and tearing rats from his body.

"Stand back, Francois!" I yelled and he did so with rats still clung to him. I stood up and closed my eyes, thinking quickly of a spell that would help.

"*By'ashe quilana whund ich SI!*" I screamed in the Old Tongue as jets of flames flew from my fingers and eyes. Instantly, the warehouse was alight with small burning and screaming bodies. Francois continued his fight to the side while I sprayed the warehouse with flame.

"NO!" yelled the voice. "NOOOOOOOO!" Just then, the boxes were lit with flame. As fire shot from me, I tried to locate the scales with my mind. Scanning, scanning... there! I turned off the spell and raced with unnatural speed toward the small beaten up box with many labels on it.

"OH NO YOU DON'T!"

Just as I placed my hand on the box, I felt a strong force shove me away from my prize. I crossed my arms over my chest and landed on top of several boxes, then got up and raced toward it again.

When I reached the box, I yelled, "Come out, you coward! Come out and face me!" I readied myself with several spells, wondering when and how the voice was going to attack. I heard fluttering behind me and turned. There, in front of the flames, was a figure dressed in a mottled grey robe. His eyes were blacker than the night itself and his long and narrow face wore a smile that could only come from madness.

"So, puny *human*," he said with a tone that dripped evil, "you think you've won against me? ME?! Do you even know what it is you're after?"

"I want the scales," I said in a no nonsense tone, yet hopeful that he would continue talking to possibly show a weakness. I moved closer to the box. The figure lifted his hand toward me and suddenly, I clutched my heart. It felt as though he was trying to crush it.

I dropped to one knee, then mumbled, "Arnae FILIA!" The words pushed him back and I was now free to stand up again. The figure slammed on his heels, then floated toward me and wagged a finger.

"It would appear that our Miss Viridian knows a spell or two," he said with dripping sarcasm. He then snapped his fingers and suddenly the two men dressed in grey from before appeared, only they were no longer human. Both were much larger and had green bumpy skin. They stared at me and showed their drool-covered fangs in a challenge. The figure snapped his fingers again and they rushed at me like lightning. Just then, a furry creature darted in front of them and slammed them both back toward the mound of flaming boxes.

"Francois!" I cried as he turned around to wink at me.

"Go for the scales! I'll handle them!"

I nodded then flipped backwards to land on top of the box just as Francois lunged toward the two creatures and savagely attacked. The robed figure raced toward me with now clawed hands, ready to tear me apart. I grabbed the top with all of my strength and flung the lid toward him. It bounced off his chest and he actually cackled at me just as I grabbed the scales, while he in turn grabbed my neck and slammed me against the wall.

"Nowhere to run, little girl," he sneered with foul breath. He pulled back his free hand, ready to slice me open, when suddenly a mighty wind raged through the warehouse, immediately eliminating all of the fires. Everyone stopped in mid action as footsteps could be heard shuffling carefully toward the fights. I glanced at my enemy to get a good look at his birdlike face...

"RELEASE THEM!" said a booming voice. The two green grunts quickly turned into screaming liquid jelly at Francois' furred feet while my foe continued to hold my neck in a grip. Suddenly, the source of the voice was revealed to be Mr. O as he now walked with a bad limp and a cane made out of ivory with Imogene by his side. He walked closer to where we were and then stopped. Mr. O lifted his cane and said in a calm voice, "Give me back my scales, brother."

"NEVER!"

Mr. O sighed. "Even after you ripped me apart, I still proved to you that I was stronger. I will always be stronger than you." He then raised his hand and I felt my attacker begin to shake. He screamed loudly, then split into pieces before my eyes as his blood splattered across my tattered and burned clothes. I ripped his clawed hand from my neck and threw it on the ground with the rest of him, followed by a well-deserved spit.

Rubbing my neck, I said, "I'm so glad you showed up." I handed him the scales with relief. He clung the scales to his chest like a lover and then began to laugh.

"Set, dear Set," he said as he removed his veil, "you were always so foolish."

I gasped and fell to my knees. There, standing before me, was Osiris, God of the Dead. His green skin and pharaoh's beard glowed in a soft light as he touched Imogene's shoulder and covered her body with the same light. When the light faded, Imogene now wore a white sleeveless tunic that fell to the floor while her hair and eyes still glowed. She was now Isis, his wife.

"I had no idea," I mumbled in a shocked and humbled tone. Osiris raised his hand, lifting me up and then walked over to me and placed a hand on my trembling shoulder.

"I told you," he said in his thick accented voice, "that only *you* could help me on this mission. You are a rare human, one blessed with the gift of old magick. The gods have chosen well with you." I lowered my gaze to the floor in humility and astonishment. Jean had a lot of explaining to do.

"B-but if you knew where Set was, then why didn't you go after him?" asked Francois as he walked over toward me. I had to admit that I wanted to know that as well.

"I was not strong enough to face him on my own," said Osiris. "I needed you and your power to assist me before I tore my brother to bits. I knew where he was, actually; I just needed him to be weakened." Osiris then handed the scales to Isis and gently gathered up his brother's bloody pieces.

"What will you do with him?" I asked.

"He'll receive the same torture he gave to me millennia ago. I will watch his body heal itself and then be ripped apart over and over for all time. Our battles have ended," he said to the bloody mound. Just then it dawned on me; I never asked about payment. Sometimes I get so excited about a case that I forget to ask about important matters like that.

"What about my fee?" I asked. Osiris glanced at Isis and she laughed, a sound not unlike a river filled with diamonds.

"Your fee will be this: there are other deities in this world, as you no doubt know, who are in need of beings like you, Francois and Jean," said Osiris. "If you work for the gods and goddesses of old, we guarantee that you will never need or want for anything again." He extended a bloody hand to me as he cupped the bloody pieces to his chest. "Well?"

I stared at the hand and then shook it firmly. I had nothing to lose. Osiris laughed and quickly disappeared, leaving Isis before us. She walked up to me, stroked my face, and said, "London. Early December," then she too disappeared, leaving me with a bloody and still hairy Francois. I glanced at Francois then opened my mouth, just as a deep French voice spoke in our minds, *"The ship shall be ready tonight."*

I grinned and thanked the gods. All of them.

THE LAWMAN

BY RON FORTIER

FORT SMITH, ARKANSAS 1875

DOOLEY JENKINS STUMBLED OUT of the Lucky Branch saloon and, being somewhat intoxicated, stumbled into his good friend, Conrad Dubois.

"Hey, watch where you going, Dooley," Dubois warned, moving his head back from the whiskey breath pouring from the drunk's mouth.

Jenkins put his hands on Dubois' left arm to steady himself. "Sorry 'bout that, pard." It was then he noticed the large crowd of people marching up the street toward the massive brick building on the corner. "Say, what's going on at the courthouse, Connie?"

Dubois looked at Dooley and frowned. "Where you been the past week, asleep in some alley? Judge Parker is gonna pin a star on a black fellah today; make him an official deputy marshal and all."

"Naw, that cain't be true." Jenkin's pickled brain was having a hard time making sense of what he was hearing. "No one would do somethin' like that…would they?"

"One way to find out, I reckon." Jenkins nodded to the crowd moving past. "Let's go see for ourselves."

Jenkins' eyes crunched and then he smiled. "Now that's a good idea. Let's go!"

—⁓—

THE ASSEMBLY ATTEMPTING TO enter the municipal building's front entrance was made up of mostly Negros with a few Indians and whites amongst them. At the open doors, several deputies, each carrying a shotgun, were herding the visitors into the hall and the main courtroom where the day's historic ceremony would take place.

As they were cautioning people not to shove and to be careful, one of the deputies looked into the crowd and recognized several relatives of the soon-to-be new lawman. He pushed through the throng clearing a path for them. "Make way, folks, let these women through. They're part of the Reeves' family." At that people turned and began moving off to either side to make way for the three women the deputy had announced.

They walked together arm in arm. The woman on the left was of average height, with a hazelnut complexion and long black hair tied in a ponytail behind her head. She had a natural beauty about her with clear eyes bright with vitality. Her name was Jinney and it was her husband being deputized that day. She helped guide the woman in the middle, the one with silver colored hair and chipmunk cheeks made for laughing. She was the candidate's mother, Paralee Stewart up from Texas, and to her left, was her daughter, Jane, of the same height and physique but with a blunt flat nose and black hair. Jane was a gifted seamstress and all three ladies looked resplendent in dresses she had made for them for this august occasion.

Once inside the spacious courtroom, the polite deputy ushered them to the front bench behind the prosecutor's table where space had been reserved for them. As they approached it, all of them finally saw the man each loved in her own way, standing tall and proud beside U.S. Marshal James Fagan.

Bass Reeves stood six feet tall, with a powerful torso, trim waist and long legs. He weighed two hundred pounds; most of it hard muscle. He was a handsome man with piercing eyes, a thin nose a pointed jaw that rarely smiled and skin the color of black coffee fresh out of the pot. Over his upper lip was a thick, brush-like mustache and his hair was an unruly mop on his head. A runaway slave, he had left his mother in Texas at the age of sixteen and fled northwest into the Indian Territories where he'd been readily accepted by the Five Civilized Tribes. When the Civil War erupted, Reeves and his Creek and Seminole brothers had fought with the Union Army in special companies against those tribes allied with the Confederacy.

After the conflict, the big man met Jinney, another freed slave, married and together they had built a decent horse breeding ranch. Eventually Reeves used his earnings to have his mother and sister brought to live with them on the edge of the frontier.

Still the frontier was a wild, unsettled land with all manner of brigands who daily plied their outlaw ways on the hapless citizenry. In March,

President Grant had appointed Judge Isaac C. Parker to the Fort Smith court giving him jurisdiction over an area of 74,000 square miles ranging from Arkansas to Colorado and lying between Kansas and Texas. Upon arriving in Fort Smith, Judge Parker appointed James Fagan as his marshal and together they began the task of recruiting two hundred deputies whose job it would be to enforce the law in this vast Indian Territory.

Isaac Parker was an idealist who believed in the equalizing power of the law. Under its rule, all men and women were afforded the same rights and privileges and held accountable to the same punishments for their transgression. He realized building a police force consisting only of naïve and inexperienced white agents would be a grievous mistake and not achieve his noble goals. No, Judge Parker wanted lawmen who reflected the make up of the land itself. Whereas the Indian tribes had their own courts and Road Agents, there were no blacks to represent his court and he sought to remedy that situation. With the counsel of Fagan and other professional peace officers, the judge was urged to meet and recruit Bass Reeves.

—⁂—

"**H**EAR YE, HEAR YE," the black bailiff, George Winston, called out from his post next to the raised dais, alerting the gallery of the arrival of Judge Parker. "All rise, remove your hats and give listen to this court. The honorable Isaac C. Parker presiding."

The man who entered from the back door was small of stature, but moved with a steady purpose, his head facing straight ahead, a mane of snow white hair falling over the dark blue of his robe. A matching beard of the same pure hue framed his honest face and as he stood behind his massive bench, he solemnly surveyed the gathering before him.

He took hold of his gavel and rapped it once, loudly. "Be seated, all of you and let us begin these proceedings." In one body, the crowd sat and Parker put down his gavel next to the worn King James Bible that always rested on that massive table.

"We are here today to conduct an important civil responsibility by deputizing a member of this community to go forth and enforce the laws of this city, this county, this territory…even this country. The duties of a United States Deputy Marshal are sacred and not to be taken lightly, for once a man takes the oath he becomes a living representative of all that is good and decent in we the people."

Parker wasn't noted for being long-winded when handing down verdicts, but now he was waxing eloquently. He was very aware of the historical precedence of what he was about to do.

Grabbing his bible, he stepped down from behind his bench and called Reeves to step forth. "Put your left hand on this bible and raise your right hand."

Watching her man standing tall, his hand raised, Jinney Reeves was filled with so much pride she thought she would burst.

After the oath had been administered, Judge Parker handed his bible to the bailiff and then reaching deep into his robes he dug out a shiny tin star. He took a step closer to Reeves and, reaching up, carefully pinned the badge to the black man's lapel. Then he stepped back and extended his hand.

"Congratulations, Deputy Marshal Reeves."

The crowd began yelling and whooping as loud as they could, threatening to shake the very rafters overhead. Marshal Fagan slapped Reeves on the back as others rushed forward to add their own well wishes.

Amidst the happy chaos, Reeves looked past the sea of joyful faces to find Jinney. He could see tears running down her cheeks.

—ɯ—

Fall 1875 – The Territories

BASS REEVES PULLED THE ragged cloth cap down tighter over his eyes to shade them from the burning sun as he shambled along through the wide twisting gully. It was midday and that bronze colored sun beat down from a gunmetal blue, cloudless sky.

He wore a pair of heelless old shoes, baggy brown pants held up by a rope belt, a loose cotton shirt and a torn, dirty coat that hadn't been washed in months. Over his left shoulder he braced a thick stick at the end of which was tied a green bindle sack. To complete his disguise as a wandering vagabond, the deputy marshal had smeared his face with river mud.

He looked like a very pathetic soul as he approached the one story sod house that had been constructed against the steep slope that dead-ended the ravine. To the left of the house was a small barn and affixed to it was a large corral in which were a dozen horses.

When he was thirty yards from the abode, the front door opened and a stout, average height woman with gray hair in a faded gingham dress and men's work boots came out to confront him. In her hands was a single-barrel shotgun which she raised and pointed at him calmly, her pudgy face showing absolutely no reluctance to pull the trigger.

"Now you hold it right there, mister," she called out. "Who the hell are yah and what are you doing nosing around my place here?"

Reeves pulled off his cap and, holding it over his chest, bowed at the waist. "Sorry to startle you, Ma'am. I is a lost soul just lookin' for work and some vittles. I mighty hungry."

The woman lowered the rifle. "Well, I don't run no hobo charity. Understand me?"

"Yes, ma'am. I be moving along."

"What's your name?"

"Isaiah, like in da bible. Isaiah Todds."

"Well, I'm Dora Campbell and this is my spread." Now the shotgun was no longer a threat as she held it in the crook of her right arm. "If you are willing to chop some wood there by the of side the barn, I'll feed yah and let you sleep in it tonight."

"Thank you, Ma'am," Reeves smiled broadly, putting his hat back on.

"But tomorrow you have to be on your way. My boys don't like no strangers poking around here."

"Yes, Missus Campbell. Whatever you say. Thank you, Ma'am."

Reeves started walking toward the barn where he saw a chopping block and axe waiting for him. As he passed the woman, she said, "The well is behind the barn. You throw some water on those hands and that face before you come inside the house. Hear me?"

"Yes, Ma'am, I do. Thankee, thankee."

—∞—

REEVES LEFT HIS BINDLE and coat inside the barn, rolled up his sleeves, picked up the heavy axe and started in on the chore the widow Campbell had given him. Never one to shirk good, honest hard labor, he put himself wholly into the task and forty minutes later had split and stacked all the logs.

He went out back and found the well. There was a bucket affixed to a long rope and he dropped it down into the inky dark hole. He heard a splash, waited a few seconds and then hauled it up again. He put it on the lip of the well, put his hands in the cold water, rubbed them thoroughly. Then he cupped his big hands together and splashed water on his sweaty face several times until he felt it was clean. He used his shirt tails to wipe it clean and then tucked them back into his threadbare pants.

The interior of the sod house was built in a basic square design with the major front half being where the fireplace was constructed against the wall. In the middle of the wooden floor was a long table with two rough hewn benches set to either side. Pots, pans and other utensils hung from nails over the rafter by the chimney. It was here Dora Campbell was ladling out heavy portions of hot stew into cheap clay bowls.

"Sit yourself down," she directed when Reeves had knocked and opened the front door. "I've got some spicy rabbit stew here. And help yourself to the hard bread on the table."

"Yes, Ma'am." Reeves had his hat in his hands as he sat down on the bench. He put it down beside him and surveyed his surroundings. The other half of the house was divided into bedrooms of equal size, each entered by a single door which was covered over by a hanging blanket. He assumed one was for Mrs. Campbell and the other for her boys; the reason for his presence there.

With two bowls in hand, the woman sat opposite Reeves, slid one over to him and picking up her own spoon said, "Go on, dig in. Tell me if it's good or not."

Gratefully Bass Reeves grabbed his wooden spoon and carefully tasted the hot soup, careful not to scald his mouth or throat. To his delight, it was delicious.

"Ma'am, this be some of the best rabbit stew I done ever ate."

"There yah go," the widow smiled showing off a few missing teeth. "I told yah it was tasty, didn't I? Now eat up and don't let it go cold on yah."

Having worked up a hardy appetite, the lawman's bowl of stew and several chunks of hard bread disappeared quickly, satisfying his hunger completely.

Just then both of them heard some loud yelling and the sounds of horses approaching the cabin.

"That'd be Danny and Joe," Mrs. Campbell assumed, wiping her hands on her apron and going to the door. "I'll expect they'll be hungry as bears now they is home."

Reeves wiped his mouth on the back of his sleeve and followed her to the porch. Two riders were moving up the ravine herding a dozen horses before them; whooping and hollering and waving their arms in the air to keep them moving.

"Quick," the old woman said to Reeves, pointing to the corral by the barn. "Run over and open that gate for 'em."

"Yes, Ma'am." Reeves ran across the yard and pulled off the horsehair rope that kept the gate in place. The galloping steeds were almost upon him as he took hold of the free-swinging post and swung it out and open. The horses charged past him, their magnificent bodies sweaty from their hard run. Bass Reeves loved horses and knew good mounts when he saw them.

Once in the enclosed area, the animals began pacing and circling, skittish in their sudden imprisonment. He hurriedly pulled the gate back into place and secured it with the rope loop.

"Who da hell are you?"

Reeves turned and looked up at the two riders, both of them pointing handguns on him, their dirt smeared faces looking mean and angry.

"My brother Danny asked you a question," the horseman on the left spat. He was broad across the chest with a long mustache and sideburns under a wide brim Mexican sombrero. "You'd best answer quick, boy!"

"Let up now, Joe," Mrs. Campbell stepped up beside Reeves and gave her sons a welcoming smile. "This here's Isaiah Todds. He's a harmless soul fallen on hard times."

"Where'd he come from, Ma?" Danny Campbell was reluctant to put his pistol away. Like his younger brother, he was a big man with powerful arms, long legs and a dirty, bearded face. He wore an old Union cap over his brown hair. "Might be a lawman come after us."

Dora Campbell looked at the quiet, sad faced Reeves and clapped her hands. "Well if that ain't just the silliest thing you've ever said, Danny." She pointed her hand at Reeves. "Look at 'im. That what a lawdog looks like to you? Sides, if you ain't noticed, he's a negra." Dora and her boys busted out laughing.

Although inwardly Reeves chafed at the insult, he also mentally sighed in relief. For a moment it had looked like Danny Campbell was about to shoot him. The Campbell brothers were known as ruthless horse-thieves, thus a two thousand dollar reward had been offered for their capture; two thousand dollars Reeves was determined to collect.

"Alrightee, then," the outlaw matriarch finally said as her laughter subsided. "Got you boys supper ready in the house." She turned to Reeves. "Isaiah, you rub down their horses here and put them up in the stable."

"Yes, Ma'am. I will."

Holstering their weapons, the men climbed out of their saddles and handed their reins to the disguised deputy marshal. With their mother between them, they walked off to the house and Reeves started for the open barn leading the weary horses behind him. His plan was falling into place perfectly.

—◊—

AFTER THE CAMPBELL BOYS had finished their supper, they joined their mother on the front porch. The sun was almost lost behind the western hills and a chill permeated the air. Reeves came over to join them; the two men were seated on the single step smoking cigarettes and Dora Campbell squeaked back and forth on an old rocker, a heavy shawl around her shoulders and a corncob pipe in her mouth.

"Sit with us a spell," she said indicating the corner of the porch. Reeves nodded and sat back, folding his arms across his chest.

"Where you from, boy?" Danny Campbell asked, blowing out a puff of smoke.

"From Georgia, suh," Reeves replied. "Was a slave 'fore Mistah Lincoln set us all free."

This seemed to placate the burly horse thief and he went back to talking with his brother and mother. They were quite pleased with the horses they'd stolen and hoped to make a fine profit from them in the coming weeks. Reeves had other ideas.

Finally the old woman stood and tapped the bowl of her crude pipe on the door lintel to loosen the cold ash. It spilled to the floor. She shivered slightly. "Gonna be a cold night. Isaiah, you go get your bag and come sleep in the house by the fire."

"Yes, Ma'am." Reeves was delighted. He hurried back to the barn and, feeling with his hands alongside the inside wall, located his bindle sack. He could feel its contents through the cloth and smiled.

By the time he went back to the house, he found the brothers arguing with their mother about his being allowed to stay there. They still did not fully trust him and had both decided to sleep in the big room with him. The lawman knew he would have to be very careful as the next few hours would prove extremely dangerous. Setting his bindle by the left side of the big fireplace, Reeves removed his worn old coat, folded it neatly to be his pillow, then stretched himself out on his back, hands folded comfortably over his chest.

"Night all," he said.

Mrs. Campbell kissed both her sons, then disappeared behind the curtain to her bedroom. Danny and Joe Campbell brought out two ragged pillows from their room, removed their boots and gun belts and stretched out on the floor a few feet in front of the blazing hot fire. Its flame cast a crackling glow around the room and in its shifting, dancing shadows, the brothers fell asleep.

Bass Reeves couldn't afford such a luxury. His eyes half closed, still on his back, he eyed the two still figures and waited. He would wait long into the night until he knew they were both sound asleep and then he would act. Till then, he relaxed and thought of Jinney and home.

—m—

THE FIRE HAD LONG since ebbed to smoldering embers when Bass Reeves thought it safe to make his move. He sat up quietly and reached into his bindle bag, his right hand wrapping around the butt of his Colt .45 hidden beneath folded clothing. Then he cautiously got to his feet and moved around the two slumbering outlaws until he was positioned before them. Each was snoring up a storm and Reeves smiled slightly, part of him regretting having to awaken them so rudely.

He kicked at their feet gently with his shoe and spoke up loudly. "Alright, gents, time to rise up here!"

It took a few seconds and a few more kicks, but Danny and Joe both snapped awake; dazed and confused, each rubbed at their eyes to see clearer in the semi-dark room.

"Watdahell…" Joe started to curse making out the standing figure before him.

"I's Deputy Marshal Bass Reeves," the lawman declared as he reached into his shirt pocket and from it took two folded pieces of paper. "And I's got a writ for both of you signed by Judge Parker in Fort Smith."

Realizing they had been duped, Danny Campbell started for his holstered gun. "Sunovabitch…"

"Move another inch and I'll shoot yah," Reeves warned, cocking his .45. "Don't think I won't. Now you both sit up and keep them hands in the front wheres I can see them."

As his prisoners complied, the curtain behind them parted and Mrs. Campbell appeared holding a lit candle. "What's all this ruckus out here?"

She saw the gun in Reeves' hand and froze.

"I told yah, Ma," Danny Campbell said angrily. "He's a damn lawdog."

Dora Campbell blinked, ran a hand through her unbound hair trying to make sense of the tableau before her.

"Is that true, Isaiah?" she finally asked.

"Yes, Ma'am and my name ain't Isaiah, it's Bass Reeves. If you would be so kind as to fetch my sack over there." He pointed to the bindle by his jacket on the floor.

"What for?"

"Got some leg irons in there. For your boys here. We're going for a long walk."

The widow shook her head in dismay and moved across the room to do as she was told. Under her breath she mumbled a string of swear words.

—ɷ—

POSSE-MAN DOOLEY JENKINS was feeding the horses, all of which were tied to individual trees in a small copse near the creek. Behind him, the jail wagon driver, Stan Ehrlich, was busy getting breakfast going at the campfire with the help of their single prisoner, Hal Lewis; a fat itinerant Deputy Marshal Reeves had arrested for selling alcohol to Indians.

Reeves, like most deputy marshals, hired men to assist him when out on the trail; they were called posse men. That was the role of Jenkins and Ehrlich on this particular hunt.

Hoisting a heavy bag of oats, Jenkins fed the four horses, saving Reeves' big sorrel gelding for last. It was a massive beast a full eighteen hands tall. Being that the deputy marshal was a big man, he required an equally powerful mount even though feeding it meant poor Dooley had to heft the bag almost to shoulder height.

Once that chore was finished, he dropped the feed bag next to the supplies stacked at the back of the wagon and went to get a cup of coffee. The pot had been heating on a flat rock in the center of the campfire. Jenkins grabbed a tin cup and poured himself some of strong black brew, his thick leather gloves just beginning to heat up as he set the pot back down. Ehrlich was cutting strips of bacon from a rack while Lewis rolled out sour dough balls and then flattened them into a greased fry pan.

As he stood to sip his coffee, Jenkins spotted several figures moving down the slope from the other side of the winding creek. When he recognized Bass Reeves, he grinned. The deputy marshal was walking behind two big men wearing leg shackles manacled to their calves. The length of chain between each fetter allowed them to take one normal step, but would make any attempt at flight impossible.

"Lookee here," Jenkins declared. "Looks like you need to make more of them biscuits, Hal. We gonna have company for breakfast."

"Who da hell is that tiny one lagging behind the marshal?" Ehrlick inquired, tilting his hat back and squinting to see through the morning glare. "Damn if that don't look like a ...woman!"

Dooley Jenkins marched down to the creek's edge as the Campbell brothers came across, the water only reaching their ankles. They looked up at him with disinterest and kept moving toward the campsite.

Bass Reeves stood on the other side of the gurgling water as the gray-haired Dora Campbell approached. She had on boots, a dress, a man's leather jacket and a floppy straw head to protect her head from the sun.

"Let me give you a hand," Reeves said offering his arm. The widow grabbed hold of it and together they made their way across the creek.

"Thank you, Marshal," she acknowledged. "I'll go see if I can help your men with the cooking."

Watching her move past, Jenkins shook his head in bewilderment. He turned to his boss. "Jehosophat, Bass. Why'd you bring her along fer?

Ain't no reward on their mother!"

"Got no choice," Reeves explained straight-faced. "Second I started off with the boys, she come running after us. Said she didn't trust no judge and was gonna follow us all the way to Fort Smith."

"So you let her tag along?"

"Don't see what else I could do, Dooley," Reeves smiled slightly. "When a mama bear gets her hair stiff, you'd best let her have her way."

Together both men headed for the campfire, Jenkins laughing all the way.

—ᴍ—

The Texas Border 1878

THUNDER BOOMED LIKE A hundred canons and rolled across the gray heavens. Mighty ripples of lightning followed that brilliantly flashed over the flat terrain being drenched by the early spring downpour.

Deputy Marshal Bass Reeves leaned over his gelding's long neck as it galloped through the heavy rain, doing his best to stay in the saddle. He could barely see twenty yards ahead through the curtain of water, constantly wiping his face with the palm of his right hand as to not lose sight of his prey.

Outlaw Bill Dozier was a vague shape off in the distance, growing larger with each quarter mile they covered. Dozier, a deadly gunfighter wanted for murder, rode an Indian mustang and had led the chase since early that morning when Reeves and his Posse Man, Dell Jackson, had first spotted him. They had soon left their prisoner wagon and its driver, Dave Morgan far behind. The rain had started to fall almost at the same time the race had begun and soon the west Texas dirt underfoot was becoming treacherous as it turned into a slippery mud surface.

Throwing caution to the wind, Reeves had hunkered down over his horse's back determined not to lose Dozier no matter how hard he had to push his big gelding. After the first two miles, Jackson began to fall back, his own horse unable to keep up with the blistering pace.

"Go get'em!" he yelled out, his voice fading in the thundering rainfall.

An hour later Reeves, wearing a floppy serape that did little to keep him dry, thought both he and Dozier had ridden clear off the face of the world into some wet hell. Still he had gained considerably on the outlaw and knew his powerful horse would eventually outlast the smaller pony.

Then suddenly Dozier was gone. One second he'd been there, plowing through the gray fog and then it was as if the earth had swallowed him up completely. Reeves pulled back on his reins, speaking in the horse's ears to gradually slow it down. Thirty yards later his mystery was solved as he came to a rugged box canyon that fell away from the plains via a steep, rock hewn slope. Sitting up in the saddle, Reeves tried to peer into the darkness of the canyon.

A bolt of lightning flashed and the arroyo was painted a dazzling white long enough for him to see a solitary rider disappearing around a bend in the canyon wall. Gripping his reins, Reeves kicked with his heels and sent his horse down the treacherous slope, mentally praying he wouldn't trip on the way down.

The animal whinnied in fear, but somehow managed to maintain its footing and made it to the floor of the gully upright. Now he spurred it forward as continued lightning flashes lit the trail before them.

Still, Bass Reeves knew he simply couldn't charge into the canyon without reservation. Dozier's mount had to be winded and the wily outlaw would be smart enough to realize the massive boulders that dotted the winding path through the narrow gorge afforded him many places to wait in ambush for the lawman.

Thus Reeves kept his horse to a steady, sure gallop and, reaching under his serape, withdrew one of his colt revolvers.

A shot rang out and chips of rock exploded off a boulder to his left. A second shot followed the first and Reeves barely saw the muzzle flash as his horse reared back spooked by the gunfire. He turned it back along the path and jumped off letting the animal find its own safety. He concealed himself behind several giant rocks. More shots tried to find him as they pinged off the tops of his impromptu shield.

"Give it up," Reeves yelled out. "I'm gonna getcha, Bill."

"Like hell, Reeves. But you can die trying," Dozier responded. "I'm waitin' on yah, Marshal."

Bass Reeves raised himself and fired twice in the general direction he guessed Dozier to be hiding. Rather than play out some long waiting game, he decided to move in closer to his target. Taking a breath, he launched himself into the open and sprinted for another boulder on the other side of the gully. Another flash of lightning and bullets rang out.

Reeves crumbled to the muddy ground and was still.

Seconds passed and only the sound of beating rain filled the canyon.

Cautiously a figure stood and emerged from the opposite end of the arroyo and began walking toward the fallen deputy marshal.

"Guess I was the better man after all," Bill Dozier remarked as he neared the body of his hated adversary. Still wary, he stopped within a few feet of the prone Reeves and began to take aim with his pistol.

Suddenly Bass Reeves turned on his side and raised his own gun hand. Both fired simultaneously.

Dozier's shot hit the ground inches from Reeves' right leg. The marshal's bullet struck the outlaw dead center in the chest. He cried out, took a step back and then looking down at his body fell over dead.

Reeves fell back on his side and looking skyward let the cold rain wash the grime and dirt off his face. Each breath he took tasted so sweet.

Somewhere behind him, Reeves heard Dell Jackson calling his name. He hoped his friend had found his horse. He wanted to yell back but was just too tired. Instead he fired a shot into the air and then lay back in the mud exhausted.

—⚒—

The Reeves Farm 1879

THE SKY WAS VELVET red and gold as the day ended spectacularly. Reeves and his brother-in-law, John Brady, saw that all their horses were groomed and fed before leaving the corrals located behind the new barn. The affable Brady was a knowledgeable horse breeder and in the few years since he had moved up from Texas with his wife Janie and their two children, he had helped make the farm a profitable operation. It was also good to have another man around whenever the lawman was off on his manhunting assignments for the law. Leaving Jinney, his mother and sister alone for weeks at a time had worried Reeves constantly. Brady's arrival had eased those concerns and allowed Reeves to keep his focus where it belonged while riding out in the badlands.

This day had been turned out to be anything but routine for the Reeves. Jinney, pregnant with their first child, had gone into labor just after supper and Paralee had chased the men out of the main house immediately. The last glimpse he'd seen of his beloved wife was her being helped by the other women to their bedroom located at the rear of the house.

That had been over two hours ago. Bass Reeves was so anxious, he had all he could do to keep his mind occupied on menial chores.

"Now rest easy there," the robust John Brady advised as they made their way to the second house located a hundred yards from the other. Reeves and some of their neighbors in Van Buren had helped with the construction soon after the Bradys had settled in town. "The first one always takes the longest."

Brady had seen his own two children off to sleep in the single bedroom they shared and then he had come outside to join Reeves on the porch. He brought with him a jug of whiskey he kept hidden in his cool root cellar. He thought it might help the first time father settle his nerves.

After each had taken a healthy gulp of the corn-mash based alcohol, both rubbed their eyes and gave out loud gasps.

"Hooo, doggies," Reeves proclaimed, wiping his mouth with the back of his shirt sleeve. "Where da hell you git that poison?"

"Old man Porter down at the livery stables in town. He and his boy, Willis, made fresh just last week."

"From what, cougar piss?" Bass Reeves joked, still feeling the fire coursing through his belly. "That stuff will curl your toenails, Brady."

"That it will, brotha…that it will." He held out the jug. "Wanna another swig?"

"Aw, naw," Reeves held up his hands palms out. "That stuff gonna burn a hole in me."

Brady set down the jar and sat back in his rocker. Both men's laughter subsided and they were quiet, each relishing the darkling skies now bright with a million stars. Off in the distance beyond the flatland was a natural spring fed pond where they watered their horses daily. Over the crisp, clear night air they could hear a veritable symphony of noises from the croak of green bullfrogs to the constant chirping of crickets.

As if to accentuate the night world melodies, a single coyote cried out from the hills west of the farm.

And then Bass Reeves heard another sound, one he wasn't all that familiar with. It was a baby's cry. Seconds later, the front door to the main house opened and his sister, Jane, emerged wringing her hands on her apron. She peered down to where they were sitting and called out, "Well, don't just sit there, Bass Reeves. You come up here and meet your new son."

He stood transfixed for a second unable to move, his mind trying to wrap itself around Jane's words. Brady slapped him on the back, a huge smile appearing on his brown face. "Get on up there, you is a father!"

Then he was racing for all he was worth across the open yard, his heart pounding in his chest. He leapt onto his porch and stopped long enough for Jane to hug him fiercely and plant a kiss on his cheek. Entering the house, he went through the living room and directly to the door to the master bedroom; it was ajar. He peeked inside and saw his mother, Paralee, leaning over Jinney who was sitting up against several thick pillows. In the old woman's arms was a tiny bundle which she carefully handed to his wife.

"Come on in," Paralee Stewart said, turning her face to him. "Someone here you got to meet, Bass."

He pushed the door wide and walked up to the bed. Candles set on the bureau and end table cast flickering light over the square room. Jinney, her face beaming with joy, nodded up at him and held out her right hand. He moved around the bed, took hold of it and then kneeling, brought it to his lips.

"Are you …well?" He just didn't know what to say.

"As well as can be expected," Paralee chided her son, "for having brought you a fine, strapping boy. Look, see."

Reeves straightened and saw Jinney was cradling the baby against her left shoulder, the little child's face half buried in her neck. Gently she pulled him away so that his round, chubby face was fully exposed. The baby squinted his eyes and made a whimpering noise.

"Ain't he just fine, Bass? Our little boy." Jinney's voice was tired but she couldn't contain her happiness and tears began to swell up in her lively brown eyes, glimmering in the candle light.

"He's ….so small."

"So was you when you came into this world," Paralee smiled. "He'll grow fast enough." She busied herself taking away a dish of water and a few bloody rags. As she exited the room, she looked back and reminded the new parents. "Now you's got to give that child a name."

"A name?" Reeves hadn't given that any thought at all. "I don't know, Jinney. What you thinkin'?"

"I recall my uncle Benjamin from back in Louisiana. He was a fine, upstanding man, he was."

"Benjamin." It rolled over his tongue easily. He looked at his fragile new son and decided it fit perfectly. "That's it, then. He be called Benjamin Reeves."

The new mother looked at her child and agreed. "Yes, it's a fine name. Our little Ben." She looked at her husband and a different look crossed her beautiful face.

"What? You thinkin' on something, Jinney?"

"I am, Bass. I'm thinking how our boy is a free man."

Bass Reeves felt a lump in his throat. His boy was a free man. He clutched Jinney's hand again and bowed his head and prayed. "Thank you, Lord Jesus. Thank you for our boy, Benjamin and his freedom."

Jinney tightened her grip on his hand. "Amen."

—m—

The Chickasaw Nation, 1883

JIM WEBB, A CATTLE trail boss from Brazos, Texas, had shot and killed a Negro preacher during a border dispute. Known for being a deadly shot, Webb had fled into the Nations to elude capture only to have Bass Reeves hunt him down and successfully bring him back to Fort Smith for trial. Much to the lawman's distaste, evidence gathering proved difficult and a full year passed without Judge Parker able to set a court date. In the interim several wealthy white ranchers posted Webb's bail of $17,000 and had him released into their custody.

The second Webb was free, he forfeited the bail and disappeared into the badlands vowing he would never be taken alive, fully aware a hangman's rope awaited him should he be recaptured.

For two years he remained on the loose. One day word reached Marshal Fagan that the wily outlaw had been spotted frequenting Jim Bywaters' general store located in the heart of the Chickasaw Nation. Fagan had a new writ drawn up for Webb's arrest and assigned Bass Reeves to carry it out. Bass in turn recruited his cantankerous saddle companion Dooley Jenkins to accompany him on the hunt.

—⁓—

IT WAS ALMOST NOON on a breezy August day when U.S. Deputy Marshal Bass Reeves and Dooley Jenkins arrived at the long, rectangular adobe trading post owned by Jim Bywaters. Bywaters was an old mountain man who had retired to the plains when age and his rheumatism caught up with him. He was a giant of a man with a thick salt and pepper beard and wore his hair long. He had taken a Chickasaw squaw and together, along with their two boys, they made a decent living selling and trading goods with the local tribes and ranchers.

Reeves was not surprised to find his dwelling was the center of much activity as he and Jenkins rode up nonchalantly. Bywaters', being the only mercantile for hundreds of miles in three directions, was always busy. There were half a dozen wagons, surreys and other buckboards parked in front of the long structure built from dried mud. Several loose dogs were being chased by Indian children while their elders squatted on the wooden porch to either side of the open front door. Horse corrals were situated to the sides and rear of the store.

"You really think Webb's here?" Jenkins asked as he bit off a piece of chewing tobacco from a square he kept in his shirt pocket.

"Dunno," Reeves replied, taking off his hat and lightly scratching his temple over his right ear where traces of gray were beginning to show through his black hair. "Only one way we're gonna find out, Dooley."

"So, what's the plan?" the tall, gangly Jenkins began masticating the plug in his mouth, getting his saliva juiced up.

Reeves studied the store while his mind envisioned several different scenarios, evaluating each for its good and bad points. "I'm thinkin' you need to just go on in there bold like. No pussy-footin', just ride up and walk in the front door like you was coming to buy some goods from old man Bywaters."

Jenkins spit out a black gob of tobacco juices and looked at his friend with a puzzled expression. "And if Webb is in there, you don't think he would shoot me the second I come through the door?"

"Too many witnesses," Reeves countered, his voice filled with conviction. "He won't know if you is alone or with a posse. I'm guessin' he'll bolt like a scared rabbit."

"And you'll be waiting to catch him."

"That's the idea. You got a better one?"

"No, I don't." Jenkins looked back at the store and all the people assembled there, making up his mind to trust Reeves. The man had never let him down before. "Then let's get 'er done. But if I get killed, Bass Reeves, I ain't ever gonna forgive you."

Jenkins spurred his horse and rode on leaving the deputy marshal behind. Reeves took the moment to draw his pistols and check their loads. He wore his two Colt revolvers crosswise on his hips with their butts easy to grasp in a quick draw fashion. Assured both firearms were clean and in passable condition, he tugged the reins of his sorrel and headed toward the open corral to the right of the building.

Reeves had lost sight of Jenkins and nudged his horse to move quicker. It was crucial he be set up behind the store when his friend went barging in. But several Indians on horseback were coming out from the back and he had to move around them in a wide arc until the path was clear for him to proceed.

The area behind the building itself was cluttered with rain barrels, old crates and supply boxes that had just been dumped there. To the right was the major horse corral where the trader kept his animals and several of the top fence posts were adorned with saddles.

Reeves had visited Bywaters' many times and was familiar with the adobe's construction. The only exit on the back wall was a window three feet high. Now it was wide open and someone was jumping out of it, a Henry repeating rifle in his hands.

"Webb!"

The Texan landed on his feet in a crouch, looked up and spotted Reeves. He came erect, raised the rifle to his shoulder and fired at the lawman.

The bullet tore at Reeves' left sleeve, ripping it at the wrist. His horse stood up on its rear legs. Reeves couldn't hold onto the reins. Webb fired a second shot and the horse continued to paw the air. Reeves was a sitting duck unless he could arm himself and retaliate.

Giving up on the sorrel, he pulled his feet out of the stirrups and fell back into the dirt behind the animal just as a third shot smacked into the saddle horn. The horse dropped to all fours. Reeves hit the ground on his side and scrambled to get on his feet.

Webb had cocked the Henry and was aiming carefully, angry his first three shots had missed their target. Reeves slapped the gelding on the butt and he moved away just as Webb's fourth round tore his hat off his head, the sound of the blast ringing in his ears.

With nothing between them now, Bass Reeves whipped his guns from their holsters and fired them together. Webb was hit in the chest and spun around, his rifle falling from his grasp. Hastily he turned clawing for his own handgun strapped to his hip.

Reeves fired again and again, hitting him twice. But the gunfighter didn't fall. Instead he took two small steps forward and then collapsed to his knees, the six-gun still clutched in his right hand, barrel pointing down. A red stain bloomed from under his cotton shirt and his head hung down beneath his battered Stetson.

From around the corner behind Reeves, people began gathering. Dooley Jenkins appeared, gun in hand, followed by storeowner Jim Bywaters. They stopped behind Reeves, everyone eyeing the wounded outlaw.

Cautiously Bass Reeves began walking toward his fallen foe. Webb raised his head with difficulty and looked up at him.

"Drop your gun," Reeves ordered.

Webb lifted his hands and examined the pistol as if not knowing how it got there. Then he tossed it aside, sighed and fell over on to his back.

Bass Reeves moved closer, kicked Webb's pistol away before holstering his own Colts. Webb raised his right hand to him, blood painted his lips.

"Give me your hand, Bass," he said weakly. "You are a brave, brave man."

Reeves dropped to one knee and took hold of the dying man's hand. "I gotcha, Webb."

"I want you to accept my revolver and scabbard as a present," Webb forced himself to continue. "And you must accept them. Take it, for with them I have killed eleven men, four of them in Indian territory, and I expected you to make the twelfth."

Reeves merely nodded, acknowledging the badman's final declaration. With that Jim Webb breathed his last.

Before leaving the station, Bass and Dooley Jenkins helped bury Webb on a small hill behind the store. Then Reeves collected the man's boots and gun belt to present them to Marshal Fagan later as proof the warrant had been served.

In the years to come, when talking about his career as a lawman, Bass Reeves would say Jim Webb was the bravest man he ever knew.

—⁂—

Epilogue

ALTHOUGH THIS STORY IS A fictional dramatization, the events depicted actually occurred. In his thirty-two years as a U.S. Deputy Marshal, Bass Reeves brought in over three thousand felons, was involved in fourteen major gun battles and only wounded once. He died on Jan. 12, 1910 in Muskogee, Oklahoma at the age of 72. He was the greatest western lawman of them all.

JAGUAR AND THE JUNGLELAND BOOGIE

BY MICHAEL A. GONZALES

Chapter One

WITH THE EXCEPTION OF Coltrane Jones' employee Moses blasting a Juice Crew mix-tape on the other side of the closed office door, his cool nightclub the Bassment was peaceful. Sitting in the cluttered space, he silently stared at the striking photograph of legendary jazz singer Myrna Ashley on the cover of the afternoon paper. TORCH SONG TRAGEDY, the headline screamed. Kidnapped from her home the night before, the village of Harlem was on high alert to locate the middle-aged diva.

Coltrane softly stroked his black cat Winnie, whom he named after the dignified Mrs. Mandela. Studying the alluring image of the missing singer gracing the front of Harlem's only black daily newspaper *The Lenox Observer*, he thought the Bert Andrews photograph of her was beautiful.

Although it was 1988 and rap music ruled the airwaves, Myrna Ashley's regal appearance transported Coltrane back to those forgotten days when saloon singers shimmered in sequined gowns, exuding glamour from their perfectly powdered skin.

To Coltrane, she still looked as majestic as he remembered her from his youth, when the vocalist was his mother's best friend and regular visitor to their Riverside Drive apartment.

Finally focusing on the article written by journalist Nelson Tate (Mr. 1-4-5), one of the few newspapermen who still cared about the citizens of America's premier chocolate city, the story was heartbreaking. Reading aloud from the tabloid text, Coltrane muttered, "The intruders broke into the spacious St. Nicholas Avenue apartment of the sixty-year old Harlem diva between 10 pm and midnight. Her beloved poodle Tiffany was found, hanging from a leash, dangling from the living room chandelier. Stapled to the dog's broken neck was a note that read, 'Kill That Noise!'"

"The perpetrators shattered mirrors, broke furniture and disgustingly soiled an elegant Persian rug. Of course, at press time, the police had no suspects. However, anybody who has their ear to the Sugar Hill streets knows that this must be the latest dirty work of the musical maunder Jazzmatazz. More than likely a bugged-out bopper who still resents when Miles went electric, he is now determined to 'Kill the Noise' of rappers rocking the mic and DJs scratching records until the break of dawn."

Disgusted, Coltrane threw down the newspaper.

Six-months ago, Jazzmatazz's crusade against rap music began with the firebombing of popular uptown hip-hop spots Harlem World and Broadway International. As the owner of a popular hip-hop spot located on the corner of 145th and Convent, he was understandably concerned.

Yet where he came from nobody volunteered to stick out his neck for nothing. The following week, the villain stepped up his wrath a week later when he bombed the recording studio Primo's, where the Fearless Four were recording their new single.

Contacting the *Lenox Observer* reporter via recording over the phone after snatching Myrna Ashley last night, the lunatic ranted, *"Though I know it's too late to get rid of this hip-hop trash on a national level, I would like to rid it from the streets of Harlem. No more boom boxes, no more freestyling on the corner or in back staircases, no more hip-hop studios, no record playing DJs performing in bars and no more jazz/rap collaborations. Bring back real music or suffer the consequences. If this order isn't met by midnight tomorrow, Myrna Ashley will die in the name of jazz purity."*

What the paper didn't say was *why* Jazzmatazz had targeted Myrna to send his anti hip-hop message, although Coltrane had already figured out that it had to do with a series of jazz meets rap showcases his homeboy Fab Five Freddy was planning. A few years before, Fab had done a similar event with Max Roach at the Mudd Club, and this latest jazz/hip-hop throwdown was going to be dope.

In his excited voice, Fab explained, "I'm getting Miles Davis, Ornette Coleman, Max Roach and Myrna Ashley on the microphone, team them up with some fly b-boys and let their genius just flow."

Coltrane thought about the last time he saw the missing jazz angel. On stage a few years ago, from the moment she sauntered to the microphone, the chatty crowd completely hushed. With cigarette smoke stinging her eyes, she purely internalized the misery of the world and made Cole

Porter's elegant ode of unrequited love "Down in the Depths" into a depressing suicide soliloquy that she sang beautifully.

Standing under the harsh lights, her lush playing quartet scattered perfect musical gems at her high-heeled feet as she crooned bittersweet standards. There was rarely a dry eye in the room when she finished.

Hailing from the hallowed sidewalks of Harlem, she was fond of telling friends and strangers, "That's where my black ass was born, and that's where my black ass is gonna die." Like Holy Scripture rolling from the tongue of a preacher, that prediction might come true if she wasn't located before midnight.

Coltrane's family were upstanding citizens who became social climbers and church folks. As a bridge-playing member of The Sugar Hill Society Club his mother chaired, he recalled Myrna's boisterous bragging, constant cursing, Jack Daniels jugging and chain-smoking ways.

On the sneak tip, she allowed Coltrane to sip from her lipstick stained glass whenever his mom went to the bathroom. "It'll put hair on your chest," Myrna swore. But to then as now, his chest remained smoother than Kojak's head.

Back in the day, when Myrna Ashley had been his first older woman crush. The fact she was as old as his mama meant nothing to Coltrane. All his horny twelve-year-old mind registered at the time was that she would one day be his woman, hanging off his arm as she sang sweet secrets into his ear.

"Why must you have that crass woman around?" his daddy inquired.

"Myrna's an artist, Gerald," Mrs. Jones answered. "She doesn't live by the same rules that we do." Blinded by the glimmer of minor celebrity, his mother excused Myrna's bad behavior. "Plus the fact, I think your baby boy is in love with her."

The clamor of the telephone shattered Coltrane's deep concentration, pulling him back to the present. He snatched up the handset of the heavy rotary phone. Knowing instinctively that it was his now widowed mother calling, he stared at the Jessie Jackson for President poster that hung on the wall across the room and prayed for strength.

"Have you seen *The Observer* this morning?" Connie Jones asked, her voice slurred. Although it was only two o'clock in the afternoon, it was obvious she was already sipping sauce. "I can't believe I just went to see her perform two weeks ago, and now she's been kidnapped. Between the crazy jungle music you kids listen to and everybody smoking that stuff, Harlem feels like it's about to explode."

Connie Jones droned on about the bleakness of the world, her paranoid theories linking the kidnapping of her friend to the slow death of the community itself. In her mind, as well as in the thoughts of Jazzmatazz, the bombastic spread of rap music, with its brutal bass and anti-social stance, was the end of civilization, as they knew it. While listening to his mother, Coltrane got a White Owl cigar from his desk drawer, a bag of weed from his pocket and rolled a blunt.

"It's a terrible thing, Mom, but I seriously doubt it was a rapper that kidnapped Myrna. Jazzmatazz is the only one behind this and he ain't hardly no b-boy."

Immediately, he regretted his sarcastic tone and bad grammar. Still, he had grown weary of being the defender of the musical revolution that his mother and other proper Blacks equated with cultural Armageddon.

"I want you to do me a favor," Connie said. "Find out what you can about Myrna's kidnapping. You need to find her, I know you can." Coltrane pictured his red-bone mama, with her grim expression, sitting in the plush living room that overlooked Riverside Park, looking out of her sixth-floor window.

"I might be dark, Mom, but I ain't no knight. Just how do you expect me to do that?"

"She is a friend, you know. We belonged to the same society clubs, went to the same church. To think that somebody could just break into her apartment and drag her away is crazy. Suppose somebody did that to me?"

"But, what am I supposed to do? I run a hip-hop club, I ain't Starsky or Hutch." Taking another hit from the blunt, he exhaled white clouds of smoke from his nostrils.

"You know those streets as well as your father did. You know them from the good side and the bad side." Arrested on a minor drug charge when he was a teenager--toking trees on the stoop of his homeboy Shep's crib, he now had a family rep for being streetwise.

"Unlike Pop, I'm not a cop. What do you want me to do?"

"I don't know," she slurred. "You were in the Persian Gulf War, you were in the Marines, you have what it takes to make a difference. You're a fighter and that's what the streets of Harlem needs right now, somebody who isn't afraid to fight and do what's right."

"All right, Ma," he said, stabbing the blunt in a glass ashtray.

"Maybe you should talk to Gus," she suggested. The older man, one of his father's jazz club cronies, had become his friend over the years. Additionally, Coltrane and Gus' son Aaron had been classmates in grammar school. "If anybody knows what's going on in those streets, it's him."

"I think you need to stop watching those midnight mysteries and get some sleep at night," Coltrane joked, then added, "But I'll see what I hear around."

Although raised on jazz, rap music and hip-hop culture had taken artistic control of Coltrane's soul in 1978 and never let go. Hanging out with his best friend Shep smoking sess on Riverside Drive eleven years before, the two accidentally stumbled onto a rocking block party where DJ Hollywood and Lovebug Starski were throwing down a new brand of funk that didn't even have an official name. As Starski cut and mixed funk and soul jams, playing the "get down parts" continuously, Hollywood rapped into the mic and commanded the listeners to throw their hands in the air and wave 'em like they just didn't care.

From that moment, he was hooked; from that moment, there was something about that style of music that he just couldn't shake. The following year, when the Sugar Hill Gang released "Rappers Delight," it was over, Rover; the levee broke in New York City and the world drowned in hip-hop.

With Black comic book super hero names like Grandmaster Flash and the Furious Five, Pebblee Poo Jazzy Jay, Kool D.J. A.J., Busy Bee, Afrika Bambaataa, Sheri Sher, Kurtis Blow, Run-DMC, KRS-One, Roxanne Shante, Ice-T, Public Enemy, Ice Cube and Gangstarr, they and thousands of others began contributing their own version of musical genius to the raw aural landscape.

After getting out of the service in 1985, with a few thousand he had gotten from the government, Coltrane hosted parties for a year at various downtown venues. Later, he decided to open his own spot and the Bassment was born.

Rising from the comfortable chair, he cradled the phone. Over the rowdy gangster beat of Big Daddy Kane's superb single "Raw," Coltrane stared at his collection of illustrated two-color posters and graffiti-lettered flyers advertising past Bassment Jams.

Admiring his clothes in the mirror behind the office door, Coltrane's starched black t-shirt and black leather pants were perfect. Custom made by an aged Haitian dude who had once been Nicky Barnes' tailor, the pants had a feline quality that reminded him of a skin of a giant cat. Soft to the touch, but durable.

Although he loved hip-hop culture, Coltrane could never dress exactly like the kids and did not have much patience for the so-called "fresh" fashions of the day; the gaudy gold chains, crass Cazels, Troop jackets and straight-legged Lee jeans just weren't conducive to the aura of cool he wished to project. Even his footwear was different, preferring stylish Italian lace-ups to anything made by Nike.

Reaching into the closet for the one ghetto couture item that was a favorite, Coltrane grabbed his lightweight black and red Dapper Dan leather coat. Known for making clothes with high-end logos, like Gucci and Louie Vuitton all over them, he was famous for the pieces he made for rappers Eric B. & Rakim, Salt 'n' Pepa and others.

Coltrane's coat was a black maxi joint covered with the Jaguar car logo. Picking up the coat from Dapper Dan's spot a few weeks before, he had fallen in love with the fit instantly. It was sleek, as though the jungle cat logo gave the coat an animalistic quality and a cool power.

The instructional fumes of Pine-Sol hovered in the air as Moses mopped the drink-stained floors.

"I'm stepping out for the rest of the day. Remember, its ten bones at the door. No guest list."

"No guest list?" Moses asked, surprised.

"Of course there's a guest list, just tell riff raff you don't know nothing about it. If they're not Garry Harris, Fab Five Freddy, Russell Simmons, Grandmaster Flash or Red Alert, they pay." The main problem Coltrane faced with opening the Bassment in his own hood was homies trying to act as though their friendship befitted them free admission and drinks.

"Devin and Shelia are bartending tonight, but I should be back before it gets too late."

CHAPTER TWO

FRAGRANT WITH FRIED FISH and uptown funk, the air outside was warm as Coltrane crossed the quiet street. A trio of blue jean and suede Puma clad kids leaned against his recently acquired Jaguar.

Arguing over who would win if The Terminator fought Robo-Cop in a machine dream duel to the death, the kids nervously jumped up and stood stiffly as he approached. "We was just watching your car Mr. Coltrane, that's all," David, the underage gang's ringleader, yelped. "We wasn't doin' nothing bad."

Last year he had caught the same brats trying to jimmy open the trunk of his old Cadillac, but their life of crime was short lived. "You little snots staying out trouble?" he asked, dramatically grimacing for effect. The dusty ragamuffins nodded their nappy heads. Coltrane reached into his pants pocket and gave each boy a crisp five-dollar bill. "Go to the movies or something. Hanging out on these streets don't bring nothing but trouble." Again, the boys nodded in frightened agreement.

While Jaguars were closely associated with Jamaican drug gangs, Coltrane nonetheless preferred the brand. As much as he'd adored his old yellow mack-daddy Caddie, he felt the sudden need for sleekness and simplicity in his life. Having bought the smoky gray ride fresh off the lot with cash, Coltrane swore he heard the pretty Jag whispering his name whenever he turned the ignition.

Coolly driving toward Broadway, he turned on Harlem's favorite radio station WBLX, where Frankie Harper was the ghetto superstar jock. Unlike some older jocks, Frankie Harper didn't discriminate against any kind of music. As long as it sounded good, he spun it, playing a '70s Aretha Franklin track produced by Curtis Mayfield next to a new-jack swing Teddy Riley jam constructed in St. Nicholas Projects.

None of the new jack swingers Coltrane knew was suave as Gus Axlrod. A neighborhood father figure, Gus was an older cat who sold jazz records from the back of a dusty Ford station wagon, his trusty Doberman bitch Brandi laying lazily next to the vehicle.

Wearing his trademarked weathered raincoat, khakis and crisp collared white shirt, Gus stood beneath the decaying marquee in front of the hip-hop club Broadway International. "Where you been hiding, giant steps," Gus croaked, his voice raspy from years of smoking. "Ain't seen you around here in a Charles Mingus minute."

"Been taking care of the Bassment, not a lot of free time anymore." As oblivious pedestrians paraded down the bustling block, Myrna Ashley's cover of "Trouble in Mind" blared from the battered speakers.

"How's your boy Aaron, doing?"

"You know, he's doin'. Still playing his trumpet, horn blowin' mofo trying to get gigs. Bitter as usual. Boy too young to be so angry."

"It's hard out there for a Black jazz musician."

"It's hard out there for a Black anything. You hear this mess about Myrna. It's tearing out my heart."

"Sad thing, huh," Coltrane said.

"Yeah, man. I was just talking to Fab Five the other day and he was telling me he was going to get Myrna in his new show, some jazz meets rap something or another."

"I didn't know you were friends with Fab."

"Friends with 'im? I done known that boy longer than I known you. His daddy used to be my accountant. Fab comes by here sometime, buys records and chats. You know that boy like to talk." They both laughed.

Coltrane leaned over and picked up one of the album jackets that featured Myrna's striking smile. "She was such a beautiful woman in her time."

"She's still beautiful. Like Lena Horne, some broads just get finer as they get older." Coltrane had to admit that Gus was right.

Gus continued, "But, Myrna is a beautiful woman with a lot of problems. Sometimes I wonder if ugly folks really know how lucky they are?"

"What you mean? What kind of problems?"

"Messing with that slick nigga who calls himself Deacon Blue, used to be a jazz producer, but drinking and gambling ain't never been good for anybody, so he became a pimp instead."

"I've heard Deacon Blue stories since I was a kid. Used to hear Dad and his cop friends talking about him."

"Well, he was supposed to be her new manager. You know the type, walks around with a pocket full of quarters for the bar pay phone that doubles as an office."

"I've seen a couple of guys like that around the club," Coltrane laughed. "Every time the phone rings they think it's either a club booking or their parole officer."

"Yeah, Blue been on the scene for years, but he ain't half as fly as he used to be. I guess Myrna was his latest hustle to try and get back in the music game. Anyway, two weeks ago Myrna did a show at Cafe Mojo. Sold out crowd and the whole nine."

"I heard about it. My mother went the first night."

"Yeah, I saw her then." There was always a blissful gleam in his voice whenever Gus spoke of Connie. "Anyway, I'm talking to Tony Fontaine, the manager at Mojo's and that fool Blue runs up making demands, acting like a big shot with his entourage, making demands like he some big shot.

"And?"

"And, I know that nigga knows something, that's all I'm saying."

"You know where he hangs?"

"Try the Devil's Nest over on St. Nick. I heard that outhouse was the brother's second home."

CHAPTER THREE

LEANING HIS ARM OUT of the car window, Coltrane admired the dazzling Dominican dames strutting down Broadway. Spring was in the air, and big-booty delicate flowers bloomed in the sun. Turning on the radio, he listened to the iceberg coolness of Frankie Harper playing Soul II Soul's 'Keep On Moving.' The smooth bass line served as the perfect soundtrack to Coltrane's afternoon as he went to find his old friend Shep.

Like a psychotic Falcon to Coltrane's calm Captain America, like Robin in need of Ritalin, like a crazy brother from another mother, Shep was always by his side when they were teenagers,. With his wild-styled reddish brown 'fro, Shep became his numero uno homeboy when they were students at George Washington High School.

Having an older blood brother who once worked for the notorious gangster Guy Fisher in the seventies, Shep was a scrapper who protected his friends and demolished his enemies.

Coltrane made a left on 151st Street, and sped down the hill. In front of a battered building, he stopped and laughed as an oblivious Shep rolled a thick spliff on the stoop, constructing the joint with the skill of a reefer engineer. If he wasn't in jail, then the stoop was Shep's spot. Turning down the radio, Coltrane yelled, "Can a brother get a hit off that?"

Shep glanced up angrily. "Boy, I was fixin' to put your ass on the missing persons list," Shep replied, slowly rising to his Adidas clad feet. His soft hair was cornrowed over his greasy scalp. "Never even visited a nigga in the joint or nothing." Although he was only twenty-five, hard times had made him look older.

Dressed in burgundy from head to feet, Shep adjusted a cool Kagol cap with the precision of a player. At five-feet-six inches tall, Shep might not be the tallest brother in the world, but he was one of the baddest.

"I been trying to stay away from wild boys," Coltrane laughed, unlocking the passenger door. "Get in."

Shep slapped Coltrane five. "I've been out about a week now. I been meaning to make it over to the club, but you know how it is." Looking at Coltrane's sharp threads, Shep whistled. "Hey, you got a court date today or something?"

"More than likely a funeral. Let's go get some grub and talk about the weather."

Roaring over to 8th Avenue and 145th, he parked outside the literal shack that was Willie's Burgers. They ate the best fried cow for miles. Between bites of his burger, Coltrane explained to Shep his mother's insistent request to find the missing torch singer and bring down Jazzmatazz. The recently released convict laughed.

"So, what you saying? You saying we become superheroes or some shit?"

"Superheroes have super powers," Coltrane corrected. "We'll be just regular heroes, like Dick Tracy or Shaft. But, we can wear masks if you want. Like Batman."

"Masks? Shaft didn't wear no mask. Superman don't wear no mask and most dummies still can't tell he's Clark Kent."

"Maybe just something that covers our eyes, like The Spirit."

"Fuck that, if I'm going to be a hero, I want people to see my face. So, what's our names. Every hero needs a name."

"Well, since I already drive one, I was going to call myself Jaguar."

"Jaguar, that's cool. But, you know they're usually solitary animals. Jaguars don't hang around others for long."

"How you know so much about Jaguars?"

"Man, when you been to prison as much as me, you do three things:

work out, read and watch television. Sometimes, we watch these nature shows where they show animals getting down; it's like porn for us. Anyway, they claim Jaguars mate and then they break out."

"Sounds good to me."

"What about me? What's my cool crime fighting name."

"You've already got a cool name, Shep," Coltrane said, cruising away from the burger shack and merging into traffic. "For now, we'll just think of ourselves as the Jaguar and Shep." As usual, Shep was down for whatever.

Chapter Four

MINUTES LATER, JAGUAR PARKED in front of the Devil's Nest.

"Talk about your freak shows," Shep mumbled, as they walked through the door. While outsiders usually remained outside, the intoxicating enthusiasm exuding from the bar was enough to convince the neighborhood hoods that this noisy nook was their personal hide-away.

Jaguar and Shep stood silently in the doorway of the chaotic bar, before moving over to one of the red patent leather stools. Suspended from the ceiling were two dusty fans that merely circulated the hot air. In the corner was a neon lit jukebox stacked with ancient soul hits, a battered payphone that hardly ever worked and a Fireball pinball machine.

With a demon on the decorative back glass hurling fireballs, Coltrane hadn't seen an old Bally game in years. On the walls, there were a few black velvet posters of brawny African brothers petting the head of a lion, beautiful nude black sisters riding the back of a panther and a freaky-deke astrology chart featuring twelve impossible sexual positions. The Nest's owner, a fat Jamaican named Ed Rose, stepped to the bar.

"Can I get you boys something?" His voice was a cheerful lilt he reserved for new customers who paid cash. "We got a two for one special until eight o'clock, mate."

"In that case, bring us two Black Labels, neat," Jaguar answered.

"And don't forget to wash the glasses first," Shep added.

Ed gave him a nasty stare. A minute later, he slammed the glasses down without spilling a drop and walked away in a huff. Jaguar and Shep downed their scotch in a single swallow.

The bar was filled with the usual seedy suspects. "You suckers lookin' for somebody or just passing through," a voice behind them hissed. They both looked in the mirror behind the bar and saw a cock-diesel dude lingering in its reflection.

The regulars called him Scar Jah, a blood crazed rasta with a slashed cheek. With the build of a Mack truck, he towered over the two men. Although the outside temperature had soared to almost seventy, Scar Jah was clad in a heavy black turtleneck and heavy jeans. Battered work boots covered his feet. When Jah spoke, his scaly scar twitched.

"You motherfuckers deaf or something?"

Jaguar felt a surge of adrenaline rush to his brain, while Shep merely laughed. Pretending to be oblivious to the threatening presence lurking behind his shoulder, Shep ordered his other scotch. He turned around and stared the giant straight in the eyes.

"Nah. We was looking for your mother. Wanted to tell her that the dog that impregnated her had rabies." Before Scar Jah completely digested the insult, Jaguar sprang up into an Ali stance, ducked his head and crashed his iron fists into the monster's tight stomach.

Now it was Jah's turn to laugh. "You're a funny, bloodclot." He snatched Jaguar by the collar of his duster and flipped him onto the floor. For the first time Coltrane noticed the strange design of multicolored Christmas lights strung across the ceiling.

Furiously, Ed Rose rushed from behind the bar screaming like a mad man as glasses were broken. From the floor, Coltrane slammed his fist into Jah's face, shattering the giant's jaw with one punch. From behind, Shep slapped Scar Jah with one of the rustic barstools and the crazy Rasta went down. Jaguar got on his feet.

Sticking his hand in his pocket, Jaguar planted his size 13 foot onto the chest of the beat down fool.

"Get out, get out, get out!" Ed screamed. "I have enough problems with the regulars, I don't need strangers smashing up my shit too."

"Relax, big man," Jaguar said. "We ain't going nowhere until we talk to Deacon Blue."

"There ain't no deacons in this hell hole. The church is up the block." Shep spit blood on the floor and chuckled. Even the jukebox was quiet.

"Drag that animal out of here before he wakes up," a strong voice ordered from the rear of the bar. A couple of young cats rushed from their stools; they eyed Jaguar and Shep closely as they pulled their friend through the barroom door as Deacon Blue emerged from the shadows.

CHAPTER FIVE

DEACON BLUE ALWAYS SAT in the rear of the riotous bar. A few feet away from the now quiet balls on the Dynamo pool table, the old school hustler had once been a pimping legend on those sweet streets of Harlem. "Bring these boys a drink," Blue croaked. "Bring them whatever they want."

Nodding his thanks, Coltrane remembered those old stories about the pimp sitting in front of him.

Ever since he was a young boy, Deacon Blue had been determined not to be just another pretty face caught up in the nickel 'n' dime rat race that controlled the losers of the world. Moving to Harlem from Georgia in the late fifties, Blue transformed from a country bumpkin into king of the alley cats who also had a knack for music. Though he could have been the next Duke Ellington, some say the streets had a stronger pull.

While in his late teens and early twenties, Deacon Blue was a wunderkind music producer, making hits for Riverside Records, but when the bottom fell out of the jazz game, he had slid easily into the pimp game, with twenty fine ass Stellas working those corners like it was some kind of ho factory.

Standing inside the Devil's Nest with his ornate walking stick, Blue fiercely evil-eyed those bitches all night. It didn't matter if it were twenty below or humid as Hades, those birds knew better than to flock back to the roost without Blue's loot. Once his mean green was dropped off, he flashed enough cash to strangle an African elephant and steal its ivory tusks.

For although he'd lived larger than most of the cats in the sporting life, between buying drinks for his friends and tooting the devil's dandruff, Blue didn't have much left in his piggy bank. Blue had once belonged to a higher echelon of Harlem street legends, yet, as the brothers on the boulevard liked to say, "That was then, but this is now."

Dressed in one of his trademarked blue suits, blue silk tie, handmade blue gators and classic blue brim, Deacon reflected a funky flamboyance. "You're Detective Jones' boy, Coltrane ain't it?" the old man asked, wiping spittle from his mouth with an aqua colored silk handkerchief. The big-boned waitress flashed her brown sugar thighs as she put down three neat scotches. Shep stared at the old man suspiciously.

"You can call me Jaguar and this is my partner, Shep." Uptown, dudes had so many strange monikers, nobody ever questioned a name, no matter how odd. "My father used to talk about you."

"Bad guys and cops have a way of telling each other's stories," Blue laughed. "Hell, used to be many a soul on these streets who bumped heads with your pops. In the days when pimping was pimping, he made many a sporting man find another way of life."

"When pimping was pimping," Shep mocked sarcastically. He was sitting in the chair backwards tapping his foot. He stared at the old man with a hatred usually reserved for roaches. "What is pimpin' now, Grandpa?"

"You wanna know what pimpin' is now, youngblood, just look on those streets. Hell, a pimp these days ain't nothing but one crack head and his crack head girlfriend." Jaguar and Shep both laughed. "That's the truth. The game ain't what it used to be when I first got into it. These new jacks ain't got the same style or grace that we possessed. All they got is their crack and their guns, killing niggas just for fun."

"So are we to assume you wasn't pimping Myrna Ashley," Jaguar accused. He watched carefully as the remainder of the blood drained from the ancient pimp's grill. He watched just as carefully as the man picked up his glass and drained the remainder of the copper colored liquor.

"You got a lot of nerve steppin' to me with that bullshit, youngblood. You realize if this was twenty years ago I'd have you slit like a pig for steppin' to me that way? I had another life before my pimp days, a respectful life, you know. Worked with Max Roach, Thelonious Monk, all the big boys. Produced brilliant sides with geniuses before them free avant-garde freaks started recording noise and chased away the little bit of Black fans we had."

"So what you saying?" Shep erupted. "You want us to respect our history, is that it? You want us to bow down and worship the ground you walked on because you made a fortune selling musical music, dreams and pussy? Shit, look at us, me and Jag part of that new jack generation -- you know, killin' fools just for fun.'" Shep had a hysterical gleam in his eyes that scared even his best friend.

"Chill, man," Jaguar whispered, gently touching Shep's shoulder.

"Fuck chilling," Shep muttered. "I'm ready to get heated." Nervously, Deacon Blue tapped his lead lined walking stick on the scarred floor.

"Do you know when a pimp stops being a pimp?" Blue mumbled. "When he falls in love. A pimp stops being a pimp when he falls in love."

CHAPTER SIX

DOWNING ANOTHER SHOT OF scotch, Deacon Blue told them the story of meeting Myrna Ashley in a bar called the Oasis two years before. Having just finished her set, Blue invited her to join his table.

"Of course, being rather notorious given my chosen profession, Myrna recognized me by reputation alone. She knew my work, my real work, but she fell for me anyway. After a while, Myrna's love filled me in ways I no longer thought possible.

"I gave up on the pimping game and began concentrating on getting Myrna higher paid gigs in a better grade of clubs. I knew cats who ran clubs downtown, in Atlantic City, guys who owed me favors. Some of those dudes didn't even know Myrna was still alive until I started booking her gigs."

"But, who would want to kidnap her?" Coltrane asked.

"I wish I could help you, but Harlem is different now; it's is not the Harlem I moved to in 1958; this is a place for ruthless pricks, like your friend here."

"Again with the history lesson," mumbled Shep. "Again with the teaching."

"I'm just saying, I love that woman more than I love myself. I know people think I was pimping her too, but that is a lie. I was planning big things for her career."

Deacon Blue held his hands in front of Jaguar's eyes. "Do these look like the hands capable of snatching a woman, the woman I loved, from her home?" Staring at Blue, he felt sorry for him. Since the threat of violence between the men had lessened, Shep had lost interest in the conversation and wandered away.

Like old plaster, Blue's voice cracked. "You know, talk of this Jazzmatazz fellow got me thinking. There's this guy, older cat who used to come to Myrna's shows. Very intense dude, always ranting about the purity of jazz music, shit like that. He was a weird kind of cat."

"What is his name?"

"Stanley Crouch Freeman. He used to be the music teacher over at P.S. 168 over on 116th Street, around the corner from Graham Courts."

"I know the joint and I know Freeman. Ain't seen him in years. You know where he lays his head?"

"Wish I did, but that dude can walk through walls. Sometimes he disappears from the club and I don't even notice he left the room. He's a sneaky bastard."

As though Jaguar had just won the jackpot on a casino slot machine, bells rang and memories of his strange music teacher popped into his mind.

Freeman, as Jaguar remembered him, was a lanky man who wore round spectacles, sharp suits and a black cape as though he was the Phantom of the Opera. Having been in P.S. 168's last graduating class in 1975, Jaguar recalled the eccentric instructor playing old school jazz standards to a room of bored students.

Every year he had his jazz club students do tributes to Charlie Mingus, Billy Strayhorn, Louis Jordan and Dizzy Gillespie. "He was musically arrogant, but kind enough to the kids." The year Coltrane entered the school, Freeman recruited him to play soprano sax with the band, but he never really got better than novice level.

"You'll never live up to your namesake," Mr. Freeman said, shaking his head. Although he allowed Coltrane to play in the final concert, a tribute to Cab Calloway's jazzy jive, you could tell it pained him. "Of course," Jaguar blared, "our band was called Jazzmatazz."

CHAPTER SEVEN

A FTER DEACON BLUE HOOKED up his new friends with some artillery that he stored in the cellar of the Devil's Nest, it was almost nine o'clock when Jaguar and Shep got back on their grind.

Cruising the nighttime streets, Jaguar and Shep peeked at random faces from behind the car's tinted windows. Listening to the radio, cool Frankie Harper gave them a shout-out.

"We've been getting reports by way of the electronic drum that a brother calling himself Jaguar is on a mission to rid the streets of Jazzmatazz. Along with his partner Shep, that nocturnal creature Jaguar is walking tall in the jungle tonight, brothers and sisters. They're ready to bring this menace to his knees. Here's a track they should find inspiring." Harper played Kool & the Gang's "Jungle Boogie."

Coltrane drove pass Myrna's ancient apartment building across the street from the Harlem School of the Arts. Once a grand building, in the years since the white tornado of crack began blowing through their hood, the once stunning structure was a sagging eyesore. Ten minutes later, they finally reached the school on 116th Street.

Constructed during the Harlem Renaissance, P.S. 168 was once the premier shining jewel of the community, but time and decay had faded it from its former splendor. Sold to a local church in 1979 with hopes of making it into a Boys and Girls Club, the conversion was never completed and the school was left to rot.

In front of the school was a dumpster filled with old throw cushions from the Acme Pillow Factory next door. The front door was unlocked. "This goddamn building smells like death," Shep choked.

The worst part, Jaguar thought, was there were people living inside that filth. There were a few bonfires roaring, as the crack zombies slithered past them.

"Freeman's class was on the fifth floor," Jaguar whispered as they stood in front of the disgusting steps. "There is another staircase at the other end of the hall. Maybe we should split up and circle around." Shep nodded and drifted off.

Moving with swiftness of a stalk and ambush predator on a mission, Jaguar crept up the stairs with his back against the graffiti scrawled walls and didn't stop creeping until he reached the last landing. Stopping on the top floor, he heard the jazz of Duke Ellington's "Echoes of the Jungle" playing frantically. It was one of Ellington's masterworks from his Cotton Club period that Freeman used to play in class often.

"So its jungle night," Jaguar thought. Concentrating on the tune, he didn't hear the two henchmen sneaking up behind him. Wearing black jeans, white sneakers and a white t-shirt illustrated with a picture of a metronome, one of the badmen slammed Jaguar across his back. Fluttering slightly, Jaguar regained his balance and swung around swiftly with his iron fist swinging and contacting the punk's solar plexus.

Soon, there were two more Metronome men trying to kill him. Mixing martial arts with some breakdance moves he copped from Crazy Legs in Rock Steady Park, he went wildstyle on them -- tossing in crazy b-boy moves that included everything from windmilling to top rocking. As one attempted to slice Jaguar with a wood-handled 007 knife, Jaguar twisted his opponent's hand, kicked him roughly in the shin and bent his arm far enough back for the loser to stab himself in the eye.

The other pawn rushed him from the side and tried to push him down the stairs. Jaguar, sweating profusely, slammed his right fist into the man's throat. Coughing and spitting blood, dude wasn't dead, but he wished he were.

"Never send a metronome to do a man's job," Coltrane grumbled, looking around. Like the rest of the wasteland building, the lights on the fifth floor had been broken long ago, but a bonfire in an oil drum filled with wood at the end of the hallway provided enough glare.

Part of the roof had collapsed and, gazing upwards, Jaguar could see a shooting star soaring across the sky. When he could go no further, he stood silently outside where Freeman's classroom used to be and he kicked open the door. Littered with broken records, sheet music and busted instruments, there were candles of various sizes and shapes scattered about, flickering.

In the center of the room, Myrna Ashley was bound to the top of a battered player piano. Dressed in one of her sequined glamour girl gowns, Myrna's head hung limply over the edge. Playing nothing but Ellington cuts, the song "Black Beauty" ended as Jaguar stared at Myrna's frightened face. Her beautiful eyes were vacant.

Obviously too shocked to utter a word, inside her head Myrna was screaming as her lower lip trembled uncontrollably. Jaguar touched her pretty face: it was chilly, but not cold. Underneath the piano was a ticking time bomb set to go off at midnight.

"I didn't mean to hurt her, but she was screaming so atonally, it was driving me crazy," a strange voice said. At first, Jaguar didn't recognize the speaker, but he knew that it wasn't Freeman. But, he thought, if Mr. Freeman isn't Jazzmatazz, then who was behind this musical mayhem. "How poetic that the worse student Mr. Freeman ever had would become my nemesis," the voice mocked.

Turning around, it took Jaguar a minute but he finally figured out that the jive cat in the porkpie hat, red zoot suit and a deep voice was no other than his old classmate Aaron Axlrod, his friend Gus' jazz musician son.

"You look like Kid Creole without the Coconuts," Jaguar laughed. In mid chuckle, a throwing dart shaped like a musical notation whizzed pass his left ear and stuck into the wall. Jag stopped laughing.

"For the record, I missed on purpose," Jazzmatazz said as Jaguar slowly spread open his Dapper Dan jacket as though they were angel wings and revealed two nine-millimeters tucked into the waistband of his leather pants.

"You've gone too far with this mess, Aaron." Jaguar was again surprised when another throwing dart zoomed past his right ear.

"Kill that noise, because Aaron is dead. This is all about Jazzmatazz and saving the music that was once so vital to the streets of Harlem. Jazz is pure, rap is trash and, as long as Jazzmatazz rules, there will be no mixing of the music.

"How could somebody whose daddy named him Coltrane be part of the conspiracy to destroy jazz? Your pops must be turning in his grave right now. He names you after one of the greatest musicians in the world and you open a damn hip-hop club."

Pulling out his guns, Jaguar aimed both barrels at Jazzmatazz. "I'll call you whatever you want me to, but you keep my daddy out of this. You're crazy if you think you can get away with this shit. Even if you did kill Myrna, you can't kill the musical tastes of the community. Hip-hop is the new jazz, and it's the music we choose."

"Enough!" Jazzmatazz screamed and clapped his hands together twice. Out of nowhere, one of those metronome freaks popped up and handed his master a trumpet case and a pair of earplugs. Quickly, each of the thugs plugged their ears.

Opening the box, Jazzmatazz pulled out a shiny horn and began to blow a screeching that was deafening. The ultrasonic sound caused Coltrane to fall to his knees; he felt as though his eardrums might pop. Seconds felt like hours, then the burning oil drum from the hallway rolled through the door, upsetting Jazzmatazz and causing him to drop the trumpet.

At the same time running into the room, Shep screamed, "Throw me the guns." As though they had been a team for years, Jaguar threw the pieces in an underhand movement, watched as they twirled in the air three times and cheered silently when Shep caught them gracefully. Without hesitation, he aimed both barrels at Jazzmatazz's dome.

"Shep, behind you!" Jaguar yelled, getting up from the floor as two more Metronomes ran into the room. One the size of Fat Albert jumped on Shep's back, forcing him to the ground as one of the guns slid across the floor. The second dude tried to dive for the piece and landed flat on his chest. Jaguar picked up the gun and kicked the clumsy cat in the mouth; blood and teeth splattered to the ground.

Running over to Shep, where the fat man had him pinned to the floor, Jaguar slapped the sucker across the skull with his nine. The bastard's head shot up as though mounted on a wall and he rolled off Shep. Shaking himself off, Shep picked up the gun from the floor and without a word emptied the nine into Fat Boy as Jazzmatazz made a mad dash to the far end of the classroom.

Jaguar watched the blood spatter on the wall as Shep dropped the gun. "Come on, we got to get out of here," Jaguar said. Seconds later, he and Shep gazed at the clock connected to the bomb beneath the player piano, which was playing "Air-Conditioned Jungle." It was quarter to twelve; fifteen minutes before the bomb went boom.

Suddenly, overhead was a whirling helicopter with a painted picture of Charlie Parker on the side; on the other side was written BIRD LIVES. A henchman threw down a rescue ladder through the opening in the partially collapsed roof and Jazzmatazz grabbed it. "This isn't my coda, boys," he screamed as the helicopter lifted him higher. "You haven't heard the last of me."

"Let him go for now, there's always tomorrow," Jaguar said to Shep as he quickly untied Myrna Ashley, who was now fully conscious. The three of them ran over to the window. Looking down below, they saw the dumpster filled with pillows. Jaguar and Shep looked at one another and grabbed Myrna. Placing her in the middle, they each held an arm and dropped to safety.

Quickly climbing out of the dumpster, the trio piled into the car and sped away as the song "Jungle Nights in Harlem" played on the player piano. Seconds later, as Jaguar raced toward Harlem Hospital, the school building was blown to smithereens.

CHAPTER EIGHT

AFTER LEAVING MYRNA IN the caring hands of his doctor friend at Harlem Hospital, he and Shep cruised back to The Bassment. Shep stared out the window of the car, watching the numerous sights on Lenox Avenue. Genuinely relaxed for the first time in hours, he pushed the butter smooth seat back and stretched his legs as Coltrane turned onto 145th Street.

Pulling up in front of the club, stepping out of the stilled car, Coltrane said, "You know, if you want to make a few legal dollars you can always put in some hours down here."

"Plus, we need to track down Jazzmatazz," Shep added. Coltrane lit a cigarette, stared for a moment at the teenagers standing in line as Rob Base and DJ E-Z Rock "It Takes Two" flowed from the speakers.

"Let's go have a few nightcaps in my office and figure out what other diabolical criminals are on the list for Jaguar and Shep to send straight to hell."

"You don't have to ask me twice." Shep replied.

A SEAT AT THE TABLE

BY GAR ANTHONY HAYWOOD

I.

Eddie Sharpton blinked once, twice. Stared up at the ceiling lamp glaring down upon him with all the force of the sun and thought, "Like a ghost."

That's how fast the guy had moved, how hard he'd been to see in the blur of all the shooting. Every man at the poker table save for one, peppered with lead before they could drop so much as a single card from their hand. Eddie wondered now if there'd been something they should have seen, some hint that there was a killer in their midst...and he seemed to recall that there had been. But what? The more he thought about it, the less he could put his finger on what it was.

Overall, the game had appeared to be as it always was: same hotel, same room, same eats and booze at the table. Two of the faces were new, but they'd been vouched for by guys in the know, guys who could be trusted. So there'd been no reason to suspect either man had come to do more than play a few high-stakes games of poker.

Eddie coughed violently, felt something warm and liquid bubble in his throat, trickle down the side of his neck to the carpet below. Blood. Jesus Christ. Sure as shit, he was dying.

He tried to turn his head left and failed. Tried to turn it right and got the same result. It didn't matter; he didn't have to turn his head to know there were bodies all around him. Al Pellini. Lew Baxter. Big Harry Pike. Saunders, Stan, one of the two new faces; bad mustache, pockmarked face. Lew had brought him in, described him as a player from Chicago in the skin racket. The other stranger was the Judas, the goddamn thief who'd called Al's C-note raise with a gat spitting fire.

The lanky blond with the milky blue eyes and the flashy gold tiepin had given his name as "Tom Wilson." But that was probably bunk, just like everything else about him. It had been Jack's recommendation that said the supposed "Wilson" was on the square, had bought the so-called "Philly numbers man" entry to the game, and it would be Jack's head that would soon be ordered served up on a silver platter -- in a mob-controlled deli somewhere out on Gratiot Avenue -- as a result.

Eddie tried to find some comfort in the thought, Jack getting what was coming to him for having turned one of the richest and most exclusive private card games in Detroit into a goddamn shooting gallery, but he was too busy dying -- and hurting -- to give a damn. His mind was fast taking a powder on him, memories piling up on each other like junkers in a wrecking yard, and coherent thought was halfway out the window. He continued to have the feeling that he'd missed something important, something or someone in the room should have tipped him off that trouble was around the corner, but he still couldn't figure out what it was.

Water. Dirty water. It had something to do with dirty water.

Eddie knew he had to remember what it was, and quick, because Eddie Sharpton was nothing if not loyal to his friends and employers and he owed them all the dope on what had happened. All he had to do was hold on until help arrived. Where the hell was Krupp, the Book-Cadillac's hotel dick? How many gunshots did the boozehound need to hear before he got off his keister and came up to the room to investigate?

Eddie fought to concentrate, forced his clouded mind to travel back in time four hours, to his arrival at Room 618, before it all vanished in the haze forever.

—∞—

Harry Pike had greeted him at the door. He patted him down with the professional efficiency of somebody who didn't know Eddie from Adam. They'd known each other for years. They'd gotten their starts in the rackets at the same time, under the same boss, but tonight, that didn't seem to matter to Pike. Tonight he was off the bottle and actually doing what he was being paid to do.

Only when Eddie turned up clean did the big gorilla finally offer him a proper "How goes it?" and wave him into the room.

The other four there for the game were already at the table, ice chattering in their drink glasses, faces veiled behind a thick wall of tobacco smoke. From the open seat they'd saved for Eddie, Lew Baxter sat at his left elbow, followed in order by Al Pellini, Lew Baxter's pal from Chicago Stan Saunders, Pike, and finally Wilson, who was seated on Eddie's immediate right. Lew did the introductions for Saunders but Wilson introduced himself, shaking Eddie's hand with a grip that belied the affable, toothy grin of a shoe salesman.

Eddie didn't immediately trust the guy, but then, he never trusted anyone immediately, Stan Saunders from Chicago included.

The game was the usual five-card draw. Baxter dealt the first hand. Eddie got nothing but rags and his luck took a nosedive from there. Lew went on an extended rush that eventually flamed out with a string of flops; everyone else took turns sliding the pot around the felt. The two new faces, Saunders and Wilson, maintained a streak of bad luck that Eddie couldn't help but find reassuring.

Then, somewhere around 2 A.M., Al Pellini went to the john and came out screaming.

—∞—

Eddie coughed up more blood and the memory went to pieces, his focus gone. He tried to get it back but the pain in his chest had his full attention now. The only thing he could recall with any clarity was Wilson making like the Great Blackstone and producing a heater out of nowhere.

He shot Harry Pike first, then Saunders and Baxter in succession, no doubt figuring Eddie could wait because his hands were busy feeding his face. It was a solid bet because Eddie was just lurching to his feet, ham and rye bread flying, when Wilson put a slug in his chest at close range, leaving him free to clear the table and lift every wallet in the room at his leisure. Eddie figured the mug must have gotten away with something in the rarified neighborhood of twenty-five big ones.

Eddie could remember other things, too; fleeting fragments of the whole that had preceded the gunplay but now ran through his mind in no particular order:

Lew Baxter, cackling like a hag as he laid down an unlikely winning hand of Huey, Dewey and Louie.

Pike screaming curses into the phone.

Brown, rancid water.

Al Pellini's hundred-dollar Florsheim shoes.

Wilson's ostentatious, diamond-studded tie pin.
A deep, disembodied voice saying, "Very much obliged to you, sir."
Stan Saunders spilling his drink straight into Wilson's lap.

None of it made any sense, or maybe it all did. Eddie couldn't say. He could feel something slowly drifting away from him, realized it was the pain. He was going numb. He'd seen enough guys croak, in the war and here at home, to know what it meant when the pain went away. He figured he had a minute left, three at the most, to go on breathing. Then it would be time to find out if all those stories about Jesus and sin and eternal damnation had been true. He sure as hell hoped they weren't.

His sense of light and color was going the way of his pain when he thought he heard something, a sound it seemed to take him forever to identify: voices. Then, a knock on the door. Hard, loud, no politeness in it:

"Open up! Hotel security!"

Krupp, finally. So fat and out of shape, Eddie could practically <u>hear</u> the man sweating from the exertion of climbing the stairs. He tried to get his thoughts together, already resigned to having little time to speak, if he'd be able to speak at all. What should he say and how should he say it? Wilson's name, of course, for what it was worth, but after that...

His thoughts drifted back to the beanshooter Wilson had used in the room, a blue steel revolver with a long barrel that Pike should have lifted off him before he ever reached the poker table---and something finally clicked. Suddenly, all at once, Eddie knew what it was he had to tell Krupp. It was the itch he'd been longing to scratch, the missing piece to the puzzle Eddie's pals would need to have in order to find Wilson and their dough. Realization had dawned too late for Eddie; he'd had his chance to put two-and-two together before all that lead started flying, and he missed it. Now there was nothing to do but pass the info on with his last breath, go out with at least the faint hope that his death, and that of the four other stiffs in the room, would soon be avenged.

He heard a key in the door before it was thrown open and Krupp exclaimed, "Jesus!" It seemed to take the hotel dick an hour to notice that Eddie was still alive, the dumb cluck apparently choosing to check every other body on the floor first. Then his moon-like face was hovering over Eddie, just as Eddie's vision was doing a final fade-to-black.

"What happened, Eddie? Who did this?" Krupp asked.

Two words. That was all Eddie could manage before his ticker did its last tock:

Wilson.
Yellow.

II.

"Tom Wilson," whose name was really something altogether different, couldn't stop laughing.

"Like taking candy from a baby," he said.

He was talking to the man who'd set the heist up, the old army pal who'd known about the card game in detail and had figured out how to take it down. To look at him, one would never have guessed he had the smarts, and that, Wilson marveled, was part of what made him so dangerous.

They were divvying up the score in a parking garage down the street from the Book-Cadillac, twenty-five Gs split 70-30, "Wilson's" end being the shorter one. As the partner who had to do all the shooting, he'd always thought thirty percent was working on the cheap, but he wasn't going to argue about it now. They were unlikely friends, two joes who had formed a solid bond while in the service overseas, and he wasn't going to let a little thing like greed louse things up between them. Besides, his partner had disarmed him the moment he'd arrived for their rendezvous, lifting the gat out of his pocket with one hand while showing him a heater of his own with the other, so complaining was not exactly an option.

"You're sure they were all dead?" his partner asked for at least the third time.

"I'm sure. I checked. We're in the clear, I swear it."

Wilson's friend looked like he might ask how closely Wilson had checked, but then he just nodded his head, satisfied, and shoved the .45 into his waistband. "Let's get on with it," he said.

Wilson counted the money out quickly, the other man watching his hands with the vigilance of a hawk. When the counting was done and each man had his cut, he said, "Okay. Time to get lost. Permanently."

He held out his hand to shake, offering all the goodbye he intended to say. It was what they'd agreed to from the beginning. If they wanted to pull tonight's job and get away with it, this would have to be the last time they ever saw each other.

"Sure, sure," Wilson said, only slightly offended by the brush off. He shook the offered hand. "But how about you giving me my rod back first?"

His partner took a long time deciding how to answer the question. He hadn't double-crossed Wilson yet, but he still had time. At least, he had until he drew Wilson's revolver---the one the blond had used to kill four men less than an hour ago---out of his jacket pocket and handed it over.

A moment of silence passed between them. The trust each man had developed for the other in the heat of war was put to the ultimate test. If it didn't break down now, it never would.

"Be seein' ya," Wilson said at last.

He straightened the knot of his tie, dashed over to the gray Plymouth he'd parked in the building earlier, and drove off.

—⁂—

Jimmy Niles watched the Plymouth go and immediately felt a twinge of regret. Both the cops and the mob would be looking for "Tom Wilson" now and their lives depended on him never being found. It would have been so easy to make sure he never was---alive and conversant, anyway---by putting a slug or two between his watery blue eyes.

Trouble was, killing didn't come half as easy to Jimmy as it did his old army buddy. Thinking was more in Jimmy's line. He could bump an egg off if there was no other choice, sure, but the way he planned things, there was always another choice. You worked with the right people, people you could trust to show damn near as much smarts as you had yourself, you didn't have to sweat somebody squealing.

Jimmy's instincts told him the pal who'd just filled every man at the Rotelli family card game with daylight was that kind of guy, a man whose brains in a pinch, and sense of loyalty to a friend who'd saved his bacon on the battlefield more than once, outweighed his sometimes reckless potential for violence. And Jimmy's instincts were rarely wrong.

Still, making his own escape from the parking garage behind the wheel of his old green Packard, he wished there were some way he could know for certain that "Tom Wilson" would never rat him out.

III.

"So what happened?"

"We're still trying to put it together. Everybody in the room except for the shooter came out wearing a sheet, so witnesses have been kind of scarce."

"They killed everybody?"

"Wouldn't you?"

"How'd they get a gun in the room? We didn't have a man at the door?"

"Sure we did. Harry Pike."

"Pike? I thought---"

"We gave him one more shot. He'd been on the wagon for months and he was a good joe. He must've picked that night of all nights to nibble a few."

A heavy sigh. What in the hell was the world coming to? "So how much'd they get?"

"We figure between twenty and thirty Gs."

"Christ. Tell me we know how many mugs we're looking for, at least. One? Two? A hundred?"

"No way to know. Like I said, nobody who was there is still breathing. But..."

"Yeah?"

"Eddie Sharpton was still alive when they found him, and apparently, he stuck around just long enough to give us a lead. It ain't much, but it's better than nothing."

"Eddie? They got Eddie?"

The other man had forgotten that Eddie and this guy went way back. They were regular visitors to this joint who were often seen together, chumming it up. Eddie was a nephew of the guy's brother-in-law, or something along those lines.

"Yeah. Sorry, I thought you knew."

"Well, you thought wrong." Things had just gone from deeply

annoying to personal. A big leap. "He gave us a lead, you said. Spill it."

"It was just two words: Wilson and yellow."

"Yellow? What the hell is that, 'yellow'?"

Something hit the linoleum floor at their feet and rattled around. They looked down to see the shoe shine boy at the club picking up the lid to his can of polish. They'd both forgotten he was there. Some niggers, silent and dumb as a stick, could behave so much like a mouse, you had to look three times just to notice them in the room.

This one looked up at the two white men looming above him, about to apologize, when the older, larger of the two said, "Beat it. When I want you to finish, I'll call you."

He knew the young boy's name but saw no need to use it. The negro bowed his head with a barely audible "Yessuh," and slunk off.

"You were saying?"

"We ain't figured out what 'yellow' means yet. But 'Wilson' was the shooter. He was there under the name of 'Tom Wilson,' by the invitation of Jack Geddis. Geddis says he's an up-and-coming numbers man from Philly, but that don't check out, much to Jack's regret."

"Don't worry about Geddis. We can deal with him later. Wilson's the one we want."

"Don't worry. We'll find him. These guys always make a mistake."

IV.

Several hours later that same day, the phone in Izzy Scapone's barber shop rang. Izzy left the head he was working on to answer it himself.

"Yeah?"

The man on the other end of the line said, "You wanna know what 'yellow' means?"

Izzy bunched his nose up in a frown. Kids were constantly calling his shop cracking wise, and always at his busiest hours. "Say that again?"

"Word's out you people are trying to find out what the word 'yellow' means. Is that so, or not?"

Izzy snapped to attention, catching on now. "Yeah, yeah. That's right. Who's this?"

"My name's not important. All you need to know is that my info's good."

"So what's your info?"

"'Yellow's' short for 'high yellow.' It's what they call a fair-skinned nigger. In this case, from what I hear, a really fair-skinned one. You catching my drift?"

For a moment, Izzy wasn't. But then he got smart, fast. "You mean Wilson---"

"His name isn't 'Wilson.' It's Anderson. Levon Anderson. He blows a horn at the Graystone every Monday night. You know the Graystone, or have I gotta spell that out for you, too?"

Izzy ignored the sarcasm, said, "Levon Anderson. Got it. Many thanks, pal. You know, if this dope pans out---"

He was going to offer the caller a few berries to show his appreciation, but he never got the chance. The guy hung up without another word.

V.

Levon Anderson had a room up on the fourth floor of the Hotel Fairbairn on Columbia, and the two goons who broke in on him just before 2 AM went through the door like it was made out of old matchsticks.

They yanked him out of bed, didn't wait for him to open both eyes to start working him over. They could see right away they'd come to the right place: Anderson had to be colored, as that was the Fairbairn's only stock in trade these days, but they'd never have known it just to look at him. His skin was as pink as a newborn babe's and his blond hair, brushed to the rear of his scalp, was as straight as the edge of a razor.

When the questions came, short and all at once, Levon had no answers for any of them. They were all about money and a card game, and four dead white men, and Levon had no idea what any of it could possibly do with him. Of course, his denials and empty responses only angered his visitors all the more. They hadn't come here to establish his guilt, because that was a given; they'd only come to recover the dough he'd stolen and make him pay for stealing it. The longer he made them wait before coming clean, the harder they were going to make these last few minutes of his life.

Eventually, one of the two jammed the barrel of a heater in his mouth while the other started ransacking his room, shredding his clothes and turning the Fairbairn's furniture into kindling. There was nothing he could think but that someone had made a terrible mistake---until the flat-faced mug destroying his room knelt down to look under his bed and pulled out an envelope that had been taped to the underside of the box spring. Then Levon knew he'd been set up. He'd only been afraid before; now he was furious, too.

"Tha' ain' mi'm!" he screamed despite the gun barrel jammed between his teeth.

That ain't mine!

The torpedo with the envelope fingered through its contents, looked up to show his smaller partner a sneer. "There's only eight hundred here."

"Tha' ain' mi'm!" Levon cried again.

His mind began to race. Who could hate him bad enough to do this to him? The trumpet player had no shortage of enemies---even his friends knew him as a liar and a cheat, and what his charm couldn't weasel out of people, he liked to steal outright---but a fix like this had to have something to do with a woman. Between his white boy good looks and alacrity with a horn, Levon went through skirts like a knife through butter, they came at him in droves and he boffed them the same way; wives, girlfriends, even a few mothers. The line of men his conquests had bent out of shape would have run around the block three times. But this...what lousy backstabbing punk could have done this?

When the answer finally came to him, too far into the beating that would ultimately take his life to actually say it out loud, all he could do was hope he and the crazy nigger would meet again in another life:

Jimmy Niles.

VI.

Frank Kennedy had made up his mind to keep his lips zipped. It was a calculated risk, because spilling the beans could earn him some cabbage and not spilling them could get him fitted for a pine box, but after much deliberation, he'd decided that he liked his chances of avoiding the latter better if he just kept what he knew---or what he thought he knew---to himself.

What Frank thought he knew was how the guy who'd shot up all those gangsters at his hotel two nights ago had gotten a gat into the room.

Frank was the night clerk at the Book-Cadillac, so it had been he who had answered the phone when Harry Pike had called the front desk all in a lather, complaining about a toilet that had overflowed and flooded 316's bathroom floor. Frank immediately offered to give Pike a new room but the offer was declined, for reasons that would have been obvious to anyone who knew---or merely suspected, as in Frank's case---what Pike and his pals were doing up there. They wouldn't want to disrupt the game, upset money down and cards already dealt. And anyway, Pike wanted the toilet fixed instead, and he wasn't in the mood to take "no" for an answer.

Ordinarily, Frank would have roused Woody Dembek, the hotel's regular handyman, from a deep sleep to deal with the toilet, but Woody was bedridden with a concussion, the result of being mugged by an unknown assailant only the afternoon before. Frank was about to thumb through the book in search of an outside plumber to call, already cursing his luck over what the guy was no doubt going to charge, when a kitchen boy who'd overheard his house phone conversation with Pike volunteered to help. The shine had only been working at the Book-Cadillac a week, Frank barely remembered his name, and he figured mopping up the mess in 316 was the negro's idea of getting in good with his bosses. Frank almost said no, but then he asked himself what kind of fool would pay a white man big money to do something a jig was all but begging him to do for free.

He sent the boy up to 316.

Less than an hour later, what seemed like the guests in every other third floor room, and a few on the floors above and below, were calling down to the front desk, complaining about fireworks going off in 316. Frank found the hotel's worthless dick, Cecil Krupp, in the lounge, polishing off a bottle of rye as discreetly as he was able, and ordered him up to the third floor to investigate. All hell broke loose soon thereafter.

It didn't occur to Frank that the boy he'd sent up to 316 to mop piss water off the bathroom floor could have had anything to do with the robbery and killing that took place there until the cops---and some of Pike's friends---started pouring into the Book-Cadillac like the Allies storming Normandy. He overheard Krupp jawing with one of the mob guys, both of them trying to figure how the shooter, whose name was apparently "Wilson," could have gotten a gun past Pike, and suddenly it dawned on him why a negro who washed dishes in the kitchen would be so anxious to take up a mop.

He should have spoken up right then, laid his suspicions out for Krupp and his friends and let the chips fall where they may. But he didn't. Instead, he went looking for the colored boy they called "Ray" himself, scouring every inch of the hotel until it was obvious he was gone, no doubt for good. Now it was too late to come clean, because now Frank had lost his nerve. If they found out Wilson and the snowball had been partners, and that Frank had been the one to send a kitchen boy up to 316 instead of Woody Dembek, why shouldn't they think Frank was in on the heist, too? With Ray on the lam, possibly forever, who was there to say otherwise?

Frank thought it over for two days, and decided he was damned if he did and damned if he didn't. The people looking for Wilson would cut his heart out if they found out he'd been holding out on them, but they'd do the same thing only <u>slower</u> if they suspected he and Wilson---and that little nigger Ray---had all been working together to kill everybody up in 316 and take over twenty Gs of their dough.

So Frank had made up his mind: He was going to keep his lips zipped.

VII.

"I got good news and bad news."

"In that case, the good news had better be <u>real</u> good."

"We found Wilson. Real name Levon Anderson, he's a trumpet player and grifter, spent a few years in Jackson on a manslaughter beef."

"And our money?"

"That would be the bad news I mentioned."

"You'd better explain that."

"All our boys found when they rousted him was a little less than a grand. What he did with the rest of it, we don't know."

"Why the hell <u>don't</u> you know?"

"Well, that's where the bad news gets worse. Anderson kicked off before we could grill him in full. Seems one of the bumpers we sent to pick him up has a real beef with the coloreds and leaned on him just a little too hard."

"The coloreds?"

"Did I forget to mention? 'Yellow' was short for 'high yellow.' Anderson was a fair-skinned spade."

"Christ."

"Yeah. Man can't trust his own eyes to know when he's talking to a nigger anymore."

"Are we sure he pulled the hotel job alone? There ain't a partner out there somewhere holding onto the rest of our spinach?"

"We're still looking into that possibility, of course. But it seems doubtful. The dick at the Book-Cadillac said all the doors and windows in the room were intact, meaning nobody broke in from the outside. And if Anderson did all the shooting himself, what would he need with a partner?"

"You're telling me he blew almost thirty grand in two days, all by his lonesome?"

"Actually, what we figure is, he stashed the dough somewhere, or with somebody, except for the eight hundred and change we found under his bed. And now that the dinge is dead..."

"Okay. I get it." The older man took the cigar out of his mouth just long enough to let out a heavy sigh. "We take this one in the keister. Swell."

"Hey, don't get me wrong. My people won't stop looking for the dough, but---"

"It's most likely history. I follow, already. No need to paint me a picture." The fat man jammed the cigar back between his teeth. "If it were more than thirty large, I wouldn't be so fast to forgive. But these things happen."

"I appreciate your understanding."

"Never mind my understanding. Just take my advice: Don't let anything like this happen again. For both our sakes." He let the other man take that in, then said, angrily, "Now, <u>blow</u>."

And blow the other man did.

The fat man with the cigar remained in the club dining room to finish his meal, using the time to think things over at his leisure. His friends upstate were not going to be happy, learning that a clever colored boy passing for white had bumped off four of their own and taken thirty grand of their hard-earned moolah to his grave. They would feel insulted and humiliated, and would bump their gums to no end about the Book-Cadillac heist being proof that negroes were the real threat to society, not them. Some would probably find it necessary to make an example of some poor porter or stock boy somewhere, just to let off steam.

The man with the cigar was not so uncivil. He was no friend of the negro, to be sure, but he recognized them as a necessary evil, a tool to be used by white men and women like any other. They couldn't help being ignorant and lazy; such traits were as much in their nature as barking was in a dog's. And if they stepped out of line to commit a crime now and then, like this horn player Levon Anderson, that was only a matter of mimicry, them doing what they saw white people doing the way monkeys did at the zoo.

The man with the cigar was considering all this, congratulating himself on his utter lack of prejudice, when he started past the shoeshine stand on his way out of the club. The boy he'd talked to so harshly the other day was standing there, waiting for his next customer. The two caught each other's eye and the boy in the smart white uniform smiled good-naturedly.

The white man with the cigar went over to talk to him, and this time he used his name.

"How's business, Jimmy?"

The smile got bigger. "Mighty fine, sir."

"Glad to hear it." The white man plucked the cigar out of his mouth, used the other hand to draw two bits from his trousers pocket. "Keep up the good work."

He dropped the coins in the negro's open palm and walked away.

"Very much obliged to you, sir!" Jimmy Niles called after him.

When he was sure the fat bastard was gone, he left, dropping the two quarters in his hand into a trash can as he rounded the corner. He wanted to laugh, but didn't; laughing at a private joke in public could be perceived by some white folk as insolence, and an insolent colored man was not an invisible one. And Jimmy liked being invisible, especially here at the gentleman's club where a negro could learn some things he wasn't supposed to know, if he smiled like a fool and kept his eyes and ears open.

His girl Lita, the one Levon Anderson had once made the mistake of moving in on despite Jimmy's warnings against such, was waiting in the car in the alley when he got there. He slipped behind the wheel and Lita smiled, greeting him by the name she always used for him, the one he'd earned in the war for exhibiting a lady-like fear of rats, but only rarely used at the club.

"Hey, Yellow, baby." She kissed him full on the mouth.

Lita was the only one who could make the name sound good.

THE HAMMER OF NORGILL

BY TOMMY HANCOCK

DIRT.

Stirred up from the bowels of a mountain itself, clods of earth flung hard, slices of ground pounded into dust finer than any lady's powder from Paris. Men of all sizes, stripes, and colors stood around that day, white and black and a handful of colors in between. Yet they all wore the same shade that afternoon. Dirt gray.

Some displayed it as if they'd bathed in it. They might as well have since their work was in the bowels of Big Bend Mountain just outside Talcott, West Virginia. Most though, from the rag clothed water boy to the finely dressed C & O Railroad Company Representative wore an ever-thickening layer of dust as clouds of dirt belched from the growing hole burrowing ever deeper into the mountain. Even the one woman, standing along the partially completed railroad track, her rich caramel skin covered in its own veil of dirt and grime, stood waiting with the pensive, silent throng of men. Only when she wiped her worried brow with her left hand, her right clutched to the blouse of the hand sewn calico dress she wore, did her skin shine through, hidden almost instantly by another fine sheen of falling dirt. But she kept wiping so dirt would not cloud her eyes. She'd barely blinked since late morning and wasn't about to miss what was unfolding before her.

"Listen to that devil," a husky usually red faced Irishman with hair to match barked, standing to her left. "It's unnatural, it is. The whinin' and groanin' of steam 'n' steel doin' work meant for 'onest men.'"

"T'ain't right," sneered another man standing behind the Irishman. His overalls hung down about his waist, the straps undone, leaving his broad coffee colored chest as bare as his bald head. "Sounds like Scratch hisself is diggin' through that mountain."

"No, boy," guffawed an uproarious voice from the other side of the track from where most of the men and the woman stood, "Nothing devilish about my little beauty. Just progress is all." A pear shaped man in a bowler hat and sporting a diamond pin on the paisley vest barely containing his bulk shoved his way through the rather unforgiving crowd of rail workers to the front of the gathering. He stumbled to a halt just at the woman's left shoulder. Inhaling a gallon of air with each breath, he said, "Just pure and plain progress."

Shouts of protest riddled the mass of humanity, some yelling out just what the sharply dressed man could do with his progress. "Yer' tetched," drawled a skinny tow headed lad on the other side of the woman, his bony finger jabbing his temple as he talked. "Our man's in that hole with yer tinplated toy and hammerin' right alongside it!"

Before the man in the bowler hat could debate the thin railroad worker, a horrendous clanging suddenly echoed from the mountain. Something coughed deep inside the tunnel, a terrible strangling noise accompanied by shrill whistles, like a fifteen tea kettles near to boiling.

The gathering of nearly a hundred men surged forward, carrying the one woman almost off her feet at its head. Their approach was halted by a burst of heat and the rumble of an explosion in the tunnel. Billows of black roiled out from the mountain, the stench of burnt air and burning metal tainting the air.

"No!" the woman screamed, bolting for the now partially hidden tunnel opening. Six men, including the brawny Irishman and the equally strapping black man beside him, grabbed hold of her, all of them shouting that it was too late, to stay back. She still surged ahead, restrained, but not stopped. Behind her the man who'd spoken of progress swore savagely, flinging his bowler hat to the ground and stomping it.

Men peeled off from the crowd and made for the tunnel. Shouts of 'We gotta get 'im out!' and 'We're comin'!' rang in every ear. Some grabbed hammers that had lain silent since the beginning of this audacious afternoon, others snatched up axes in case the tunnel frame had collapsed. Two more men latched onto the woman, still dragging her first six saviors along the ground. The dandily clothed Railroad man ripped the tailor made long coat and vest from his body, rolling up sleeves like he hadn't done in twenty years and snatched up a hammer himself. Moments ago, everyone working with the C & O Railroad had watched in awe, witnesses to history they thought. Now they were getting ready to retrieve and bury another railroad worker.

"Wait!" shouted one of the first men to charge headlong into the shroud of dust and smoke pouring from the tunnel. "There's somethin'… someone movin' in there!"

Murmurs and whispers rippled from man to man as the advancing rescuers halted. The eight men, failing to hold back the woman, let go. With tears of anger and grief already plowing tracks down her dirty face, she ran madly, her arms outstretched.

Men watched helplessly as she scrambled across open ground toward the mountain. Most didn't know her name, although they'd enjoyed her cooking while she'd been following the C & O workers along the line. The few she'd gotten to know started after her, unsure of what good it would do, but unwilling to let her face what she'd find alone. Regardless, all of them knew why she was running. They knew who she would find bloody and dead.

Ten feet from the tunnel's maw, she screamed his name and dropped to her knees. Those who had followed rushed to her, thinking she'd been overcome with grief. As they huddled over her, she continued shouting, her hands pointing forward. "Thank you, Lord Jesus!" she yelled, almost singing as she shook pointed fingers at the tunnel.

She saw a shift in the curtain of gray steam and filth hanging like thick gossamer in the hole. A figure appeared, the outline of a person. A near giant.

A figure parted the shroud of dust and filth stirring from the manmade crevice in Big Bend Mountain. Eyes widened and mouths gaped as a giant of a man walked into the sunlight. Even covered in sweat soaked mud, he cut an impressive figure in front of the tunnel opening. Standing over six feet tall, his obsidian skin rippled with muscles like iron chains wrapped around his bare arms and broad chest.

Taking in a lungful of the freshest air he'd breathed in hours, he marched forward. His nearly two hundred pounds moved slowly, but with a confident, yet precise grace most men his size could not manage. His arms hung at his side. In each hand he gripped a fourteen pound hammer, tendrils of smoke curling from both hammer heads, the ends fading from molten orange to steel gray.

No one spoke as he crossed ground toward them. Three or four men ran past him headlong into the tunnel. Later they would boast about how they'd been the first into that shaft, all fourteen feet of it hewn out by a man and his two hammers. For now, they were just like everyone who watched him: stricken silent with awe.

He came to a stop just a few feet from the woman. He looked down at her, his cocoa colored eyes sparkling, but his face absent the wide grin he usually wore. She stood up, taking tentative steps forward, but smiling. He'd come back to her.

"Polly," he said, his voice a gentle rumble of thunder, "Work's done. I'm plum tired."

She nodded, her mouth opening to speak, to tell him that they'd go right down to their tent in the rail camp and she'd whip him up every bit of bacon and grits she could lay hands on. Before she could, though, he wavered, a great tree threatening to fall. His hands opened, each hammer dropping to the ground on its head, standing upright beside him as he pitched forward, a painful groan breaking free from his lips.

She yelled, lurching forward to catch him. Four men jumped with her, taking hold of his massive arms and lowering his now limp body gently to the ground. She dropped down beside him as the audience of rail men closed in.

"He done it!" someone shouted from the tunnel. "Fourteen feet! And that ol' steam drill blew its innards at nine! John Henry done it!"

Whoops and cheers rocketed skyward from the outer edges of the crowd like fireworks on Independence Day. At its center, no one spoke as Polly Ann Henry cradled her husband's head in her lap.

"Don't go, John," Polly pleaded, her fingers caressing his close shaven black hair. "Don't you go away from me now."

The corners of his mouth turned up into a weak grin as John rasped, "I ain't never going to be away from you, Polly. No matter where-" his voice failed and his eyes fluttered.

"John!" she yelled. "Don't go, John!"

He opened his mouth again to speak, but no words came. Instead he struggled to raise his arms, his fingers clenching into fists, then opening. Polly, tears burning her almond colored eyes, saw him strain, reaching out. She nodded, lowering his head to the ground. She then gestured at the men standing around her, waving toward the hammers.

Two men grasped a hammer each and laid it in John Henry's open hands. As the handles touched his skin, his fingers wrapped like iron snakes around them. His eyes opened and tension and agony lining his face faded away as his mouth finally turned up into the broad white toothed grin everyone knew him for.

"John," Polly said, her voice soft like a Virginia breeze, a storm of grief boiling behind it. "Don't you go away from me."

"It's all right, now, Polly," John Henry said between staggered breaths. "I won't ever be too far from you." He turned his head toward her, his eyes finding hers. "Never."

Polly pressed her hand to his face as one last breath escaped his body and his eyes closed.

—⚒—

"BON*YIL HAM-UR. FET^HAN BON*YIL. Bon*yil Ham-Ur."
Music flowed through him thickly, like molasses filling his

veins. High notes crying for the night sky, even higher than those he remembered his momma hitting in the cotton fields when she sang to get him through the day and past the foreman's whip. A song gently twisting and turning into unfamiliar words, a lyrical voice like nothing that had ever fell on his ears. Passionate, like Polly's when she sang from the side of the tracks as he drove spikes and shattered mountains into so much dust. But different, as if the throat which birthed the melodious voice belonged to something other than a woman.

John Henry was dead. He was sure of that. His beautiful Polly Ann staring down at him with tears in her wise eyes was freshly seared in his memory. The feeling as if his heart had burst, his chest collapsing like a tunnel caving in. Breath and life leaving him. Yet, his chest still heaved, air struggled down his throat and back out again. And his heart thundered in his present darkness, the low rumble of a locomotive, growing more and more powerful with each shovel of steam. He had died. Hadn't he?

John Henry tried to raise his head up as his eyes fluttered open, a storm of colored haze assaulting him, forcing him back down flat. Dark reds, brilliant yellows, heavy blues. And gold. Gold like woven sunlight. The golden skin of a woman.

"Bon*yil Ham-Ur."

John squeezed his eyes shut hard, trying to make sense of what he'd seen and fighting the rising creep of nausea in his stomach. "Thought," his normally powerful voice whispered through lips as dry as hardtack, "wasn't s'posed to be no sickness in Heaven." Taking in a haggard breath, he opened his eyes again.

The visage of a woman hovered over him, but not one like he'd ever seen. She knelt beside him, her skin almost shimmering gold and without blemish. Her face cradled almond shaped eyes, pupils the color of peaches floating on a sea of black. Hair the color of midnight skies rolled off her head, tying off in a complicated braid trailing down the left side of her body. Her lips moved, her voice rich and smooth pouring out from between them. Words like music. A voice like no other.

Her eyes widened when she realized he was awake when he spoke. She dropped back, almost out of his vision, a golden hand palm out lifted to her face. John Henry tried to speak again but only one word came out as he watched a pair of golden wings open behind her, large, exquisite feathers seemingly sprouting from her statuesque shoulders.

"Angel."

He lifted his right arm up, reaching out to her. Leaning on his left arm, his elbow bent against a hard ground floor, he pushed, trying to at least sit up straight. The woman bleated something sharp and staccato that he did not understand as she moved close to him, her wings pulling in against her back, her hands out. Halfway up, John Henry's entire body convulsed, a seizure of queasy agony bolting through him. He collapsed back to the floor, his head caught in her hands, her long, tapered fingers caressing his clammy black skin.

"Mebbe," John managed after a few moments of her touch, a hint of a smile on his face, "I's dug so much that I's gone the other way. But then," he added, his eyes locked on the figure at his side, "Preacher never said nothin' about a creature like you down there."

The expression on the exotic female's face might have passed for amusement. She lowered his head to the ground, her hands searching for something on the ground beside her he could not see. She leaned forward, her full lips pulling close to his face.

"Bon*yil."

A stench like flop sweat and swamp water burned John Henry's nose. His eyes followed as her hands came back into view, both wrapped around a crudely crafted gray bowl, almost resembling a turtle's shell. A viscous orange fluid sloshed over the edges of the vessel. Plumes of smoke spiraled up from the liquid, tentacles of steam at first, swirling and spinning around one another. As the winged woman moved the bowl closer, John watched in awe as the tendrils of smoke tangled together, thickening, tying themselves into a serpentlike cloud. One that was now just under his nose, rearing back like a rattlesnake ready to strike.

John opened his mouth to protest whatever was about to happen. Before words could come, the serpentine smoke shot forward, diving between his lips. John Henry groaned as his body arched viciously, his back raising up off the ground. His eyelids snapped open, his eyes rolling back in his head. His jaw hung open as every wisp of ethereal steam disappeared through it. The golden skinned woman placed her hands on his body, massaging his bare chest with strong, tender strokes of her fingers. A tremor rumbled through his muscular frame, his arms and legs stiffening out to his side as the smoke vanished from sight and filled his body.

Sweat beaded on his ebony skin, pouring off of him in rivulets after what seemed like four forevers, but was only a matter of seconds. Closing his mouth, John Henry rolled his head over, still unable to rise, but no longer nauseous. His eyes narrowed at the woman who'd just worked some sort of magic on him, he was sure. Both anger and confusion warped his face as he demanded, "What in the-"

The woman's face contorted in gold hued terror before John finished. The red dirt walls lined with tangles of canary yellow vines running like seams every few feet quaked as if struck. Several arms appeared behind her, thick like tree trunks heavy with long fur the color of pine needles. Furred sausage-like fingers grappled her by the arms and shoulders. She screamed, a shrill sound, like a falcon's cry, and slapped behind her, trying to tear free. She jumped from the ground, her wings suddenly snapping wide, but one of the arms slapped her hard in the back, knocking her face first to the dirt beside John. As more arms appeared and mangled her feathers by savagely grabbing her wings, she lifted her face and looked into John Henry's eyes.

"Bon*yil, Ham-ur. Fet^han Bon*yil!"

A warbling growl from far away echoed in John Henry's ears. Other grunts and howls haunted him, these only a few feet from him. The golden woman's body jerked, her hands suddenly clawing at the ground, trying to dig in, to hold on as she was being dragged away. Her peach colored eyes stayed locked on the man she'd been caring for until a few moments ago and she kept screaming.

"Bon*yil! Fet^han Bon- wake! Awake! Rise and Protect! Awake!"

As if a fog had lifted from his mind, John Henry heard her musical voice lilting in terror in his ears. He understood her.

"Hey!" John Henry roared, wrestling his way from the ground. Rolling to his left, he got both hands underneath him and pushed upward. Before he could pull his legs under him to stand, something large and green crossed his vision, a leg like a plantation house column. A clawed fur covered paw slammed into the side of the rail worker's head, shoving John Henry hard back into the caked dirt.

—m—

CHAINS. EVEN IN THE miasmic darkness of near consciousness he swam in, John Henry knew he was bound. Scarred memories ricocheted in his mind. The obscene cadence of heavy iron links clinking together, hobbling skinny black legs as they marched across the dais, hungry eyed white men watching, studying. Hungry for profit, for the next sale, for just how much money working a young five year old boy's body near to death would put in their pockets. The crushing weight of newly forged chain crossing the chest of a sixteen year old boy that the foremen in the fields had grown afraid of, so much so they'd lied about him stealing and swore he would kill them all in their sleep, smash their lily pure heads between his brawny arms like melons. Chains yanked, tugged harshly, dragging him away from his family and to four stone walls where they meant for him to die.

The stinging odor of burnt ozone ravaged his nose suddenly, his ears riddled with the crackling of far off lightning and echoing tortured screams. He jerked his head up, yelling, "Polly!" at the top of his lungs. His chest heaved as if his heart would explode out of it as he struggled, fought the chains and shackles suspending his arms above his head. Oddly colored hard dried green mud creaked under the large man's attack, but the chains held.

John gasped, taking bellows full of air into his lungs with each try. Pain rippled through his chest and arms, clearing the fog of unconsciousness and memory. He opened his eyes and looked around, not sure if he'd see the rolling hills of Virginia or the golden winged angel who'd ministered to him before. He saw neither, but what he saw was familiar.

Four walls, green like horse apples, surrounded him, a ceiling above the same color and of the same material. His feet stood flat on the dirt floor, this a rich burgundy color. A brown skirt or sheet of some kind hung from his waist, tied on with a thin yellow rope. Swinging himself around to take it all in, he saw it was a small room, large enough to hold one man his size bound as he was. Cylindrical bars the shade of jaundice made up the wall in front of him, thick bars—bars of a jail cell.

John Henry tugged on his chains once more, reveling in the slightest hint of give. He narrowed his eyes to look outside of his dimly lit cell through the bars. Another room like his was across a narrow hall from him and, although he could not make out features, John Henry saw it too contained a figure. Hanging from its ceiling.

"Wake up to an angel," John Henry said aloud, "then wake up in jail." He shook his head, a wry grin crossing his ebony, glistening features, "And the Preacher always said Heaven'd be different."

A peal of laughter rumbled up out of the big man's chest, roiling out of his cell and down the hallway like thunder. John Henry had learned a long time ago the Lord had given him many gifts, like two arms that could outrun a steam drill, muscles of the like Samson only dreamed of, and the love of a good woman. And laughter, being able to find the lighter side of any dark cloud. That gift, not the others, was the one that had gotten him through life. Through his time as a slave. Through his time of being unlawfully imprisoned. And through whatever in Providence was happening now.

A shrill cry of anguish cut off his laughter suddenly. It riddled down the hallway from some distance away, above him, John Henry realized. As it faded, a gruff, ragged voice shouted, "Polly! Polly!"

Stunned by the exclamation, John jerked forward, his chains screaming as metal scraped together. "Who said that?" He demanded, desperate in the hope that maybe, even in this oddly hellish afterlife, maybe she was here.

"You did, Ham Ur," croaked the voice from moments ago. "When Galena sang her song of torment before, you exclaimed, "Polly' in return. I am but a humble subject and could only do the same."

"Galena?" Henry asked, confused. "I...was asleep, I reckon. Heard a woman being hurt, thought it was Polly. My wife." His head dropped, his chin slamming his chest in despair. "Thought she was here."

"Wife?" the throaty voice murmured, unsure of the word. "I know of no family of Vedan on Norgill called 'wife', Ham Ur. Is she special to You?"

Lost in despair, Henry replied, "All that matters. God and her. All that matters."

"Then Vedan will provide for her," the unseen speaker soothed, "Vedan will provide for this 'wife' and 'god'. For Ham Ur he will provide."

"Name's Henry," John said, "John Henry."

"Indeed, Ham Ur. It is said in The Teachings, The One of No Color will breathe under many names. So written, so it is."

"No color?" John's coffee colored eyes looked at down at his own chest, at the rich darkness of it. "What does that mean?"

"Vedan," the voice intoned, much like a well practiced preacher, Henry realized, "set up houses for all families and cast upon them the myriad colors of his own hair. Families carry many shades, all of which Vedan wears about his head. And even with that blessing, families fight. Vedan's children became lost. And Vedan promised one of no family, one of No Color, but solely of him, would come. Would save us from ourselves."

"You're talkin' foolish, makin' no sense," John Henry rumbled, "Nothin's right in my head." He looked up, his eyes open, toward the roof of his cell. "I was dyin'. I know I was. Layin' in Polly's lovin' arms, all the dirty faces of railroad men around me, my hammers on the ground. I'd won the race, but I was dyin'. Then," the image of a winged golden skinned woman flamed to life in his mind, "she was there. And I thought the Lord had brought me home. To Heaven."

"Norgill."

"What?" John Henry snapped.

"I know not of this Heaven, Ham Ur," the voice belched. "We are all of families of Norgill, the world which Vedan granted us. It is said Vedan gave life and to life gave three gifts- Vedan for our home, Rystag the Pale for our understanding, and Ham Ur of No Color for our salvation."

"Salvation?" John Henry snorted, tugging at his chains. "Friend, I ain't savin' nobody. Can't even save myself."

"Then," the voice lowered sadly, "Galena will die. All the families of Norgill will die."

"Galena?" Henry asked again.

"Yes, Ham Ur. The Priestess of Vedan. The Talori have her above, punishing her for blasphemy against the Talori Gods. Torturing her for saying she had found Ham Ur born grown full as prophesied in the Dry Lands."

"Galena." This time he said it firmly, knowing the name belonged to his golden nurse. The woman with the wings. "They are killin' her... because of me?"

"Because of her belief. Vedan is outlawed in the family of Talori. Those who have been indentured into the family are forbidden to believe. But..."The voice coughed, struggled, "many of us still believe."

"No." John Henry said, the word cracking in the air around him like a gunshot. Another crackle of energy and accompanying shriek of agony reverberated from above down the hall, ricocheting off the walls of his cell.

The voice across from John Henry said only more thing. "Vedan, take her."

John Henry gritted his teeth. He planted his feet firmly on the burgundy ground and rolled his spike thick fingers into massive fists above his head. "Hey!" he roared. "Somebody best come get me 'fore I bring the whole house tumblin' down like Jericho! Hey!"

Two husky green furred creatures bounded down the hall, their footfalls thudding off the walls. They stopped abruptly in front of John Henry's cell, both turning nearly in unison to face their prisoner.

Each stood about six feet tall and a coat of rich green fur covered their entire bodies from head to toe. Armor encased their muscular almost catlike forms, each wearing a brown leather like toga and what John Henry took to be matching chaps on their legs. A helmet encased their heads, rounded at the top, shaped much like a brown leather egg. Each one wore a long scabbard on its right hip and held an orange shaft, about four feet tall and with no markings or attachments, in their left claw.

"It speaks," one of the guards warbled, his voice sounding as if it were speaking underwater. "It speaks Talori."

"Sin!" the guard on John's right, his partner's near twin, mewled. "Some trickery of the winged heretic!" Stepping close to the bars, the Talori warrior spat, "What do you want, pretender?"

"Her," John Henry said quietly, rage seething under every word, "to Galena. I want to go to where she is."

The Talori looked at each other curiously, then began laughing, an odd noise trapped somewhere between a purr and a bark. "You will," the one on the left explained, "have your brief moment in The Presence soon enough, when the yellow blasphemer is dead. Do not rush your demise, pretender!"

"Tired of talkin'," John Henry rumbled, "and not bein' heard!" Emotions long capped stormed through the imprisoned man. Anger at first being enslaved and being reduced to property. Fury from being jailed for a crime manufactured by fearful men. And finally righteous rage, held in chains once again for the shade of his skin, albeit for other reasons. No more, John Henry determined silently. He did not live and die simply to be handed over to someone to die again, this time because he sounded like someone from some story and was black. No more.

Spreading his feet apart, John Henry lunged forward suddenly at the bars, scaring his Talori guards into springing back against the bars behind them. He pulled at his chains, the shackles cutting deep into his obsidian wrists. He howled like a caged bear, his head lowered, his eyes clenched shut. His broad shoulders bunched up around his thick neck like bending railroad ties. The chains screeched as they rubbed one another, sparks flying as the large man took one step, then another forward. The hooks holding the chains into the green bricked ceiling whined as they begin to uncurl.

Regaining their composure, both Talori guards leaped forward, shoving their orange shafts between the bars of John's cell and into his abdomen. Air crackled and burned as tendrils of white energy first encircled each baton and then ran along them and struck John Henry like miniature lightning bolts.

John Henry threw his head back as his body spasmed and a scream ripped itself from his throat. Still he moved. One foot, then the other, until his face was nearly pressed into the bars. The orange shafts pressed hard into his skin as he walked into them, energy encircling his abdomen and crawling up his arms and down his legs like electric vines. Links in the chains over his head popped like corn, one after the other, and the ceiling hooks wailed one last time before snapping. John Henry's arms dropped to his side, bloody shackles and remnants of chain hanging from his wrists.

Dumbfounded, both Talori stumbled back again, their batons going with them. No one could withstand the power of Talori Stingers without collapsing in misery, much less advance on the valiant Talori. They looked, yellow eyes wide, as John Henry stood on the other side of the bars from them, his body covered in sweat and dust, his face a mask of violence, yet his voice somehow eerily calm.

"I want to go to her."

John Henry took two steps back, his arms crossed behind him. Stunned, one of the Talori wrapped its claws around the middle of the top bar, turned it, and unhinged it. Repeating this with all the others, the Talori swung a panel of bars out, his fellow guard stepping in, orange Stinger raised and ready. Once the door was open, the other Talori lifted its baton and both watched as John Henry, his still manacled hands clasped behind his back, calmly walked out of the cell and turned himself the direction they had come from.

As the Talori started to prod him along with lifeless stingers, John Henry glanced into the cell across from his. There hanging as he had from the ceiling moments ago was a diminutive nearly round form. Tiny spindly arms wore shackles and chains half the size of Henry's and the hay straw thin legs of the gray colored bulbous eyed frog like thing dangled nearly three feet of the ground. The peat colored eyes turned slowly and looked reverently and intently at John Henry.

"Vedan take you, Ham-Ur."

"Yeah," John Henry said solemnly. "God Bless You, too, friend."

The corridor was nearly a hundred feet long and arched upward progressively. The walls were of the odd hardened mudlike mixture of his cell and contained other walls of bars, each empty. Orange light filtered in from the opening at the end, orange like a ripe pumpkin. As he reached the end, John Henry squinted to see, not accustomed to the strange hue or raw brightness of what passed for sunlight wherever he was. Even through clenched eyes, what the railroad worker saw staggered him, his breath catching in his throat.

He stood at the back of a grand arena, a massive horse apple green structure gilded with a glittering purple metal of some kind, decoratively arranged around balconies, ledges, and precipices. Archways, all without doors, lined the walls of the arena at ground level. Each one of them had a Talori guard and a rack beside them. A rack holding a variety of weapons, some John Henry recognized as swords or spears, others that he couldn't identify. Somewhere from a child's memory, huddled around a fire near slave quarters, hugging a woman every child in the camp who didn't have one called 'Mama', he realized this is what the coliseums where the Romans fed Christians to the lions must have been like.

Looking up, John Henry saw people—not people the way he figured them, he realized, but people nonetheless, the people of Norgill. They sat in seats that went on into the sky for at least twenty rows, packed in like slaves on a train, except they seemed happy to be hear. Cheering fur filled faces, squawking tweets from long birdlike beaks, guttural toots from short trunks, and so many other sounds all pouring out of this cavalcade of creatures. Applauding. Ranting. Demanding.

His eyes followed the trail of their gazes, the path of their screams into the wide open space at the base of the arena. Hard packed blood red dirt spread from where he stood all the way to a dais at the opposite end, probably a hundred yards or more. On the platform, nearly ten feet off the ground, stood several other Talori, all resembling the guards that stood at his back. All but one, the only one sitting.

In physical form, he was most definitely Talori, but he was not adorned in a leather tunic or helmet. What sat upon his head John Henry fancied was their version of a crown, but it looked more to him like a tangle of leafy twigs and bushes, mangled together in a mound. This particular was bare chested, the only clothing on his body a skirt of black held on his waist by a green leathery belt. His belly hid the belt, climbing up and over the skirt's hem.

Under his breath, John Henry seethed. "Just a fat cat feedin' on the misery of mice."

Aware of his surroundings now, John Henry turned his eyes to the only occupants of the massive killing field between he and the royal Talori. Three Talori guards stood in a circle in front of the dais. Each one had a stinger raised and sparking with blue death. They held them high, unmoving, an odd triangle of torture. Movement wasn't required as their prisoner hung by her hands from a gray six foot tall post driven into the ground.

A bar extended out from the post and she dangled from it, rivulets of burgundy blood running from her manacled wrists. She swung back and forth, her wings hanging limp against her back, either from the slight wind whipping occasionally through the arena or just the involuntary impulses of her own broken body. Regardless, she drifted back and forth, into the end of one stinger, then another. And each time her tarnished golden hued skin tapped a stinger, tentacles of blue energy snatched her, embraced her violently, ripping into her skin, forcing her eyes to bulge like a bullfrog's, her mouth jerking open involuntarily, offering nothing except spittle and screams.

John Henry closed his eyes and took a breath. His mind was awash, a flood of memory and emotion, confusion and sudden clarity. Only a few things were certain, but they were important. Although he was not sure where he was, he knew he was not where he had been born. He remembered dying, but yet he stood now, breathing and feeling. And still the color of his skin mattered almost more than the man himself did. Before it made him property, here it made him, as near as he could reckon, some sort of figure some worshipped and others feared.

Two more things counted sure and certain as John Henry opened his eyes, the scene before him cast with a different sheen. Polly was not here and if possible, he had to find a way back to her. And he hated seeing people hurt and in chains. Any people.

Neither guard at the back of the muscular dark skinned man stood prepared for what happened. John Henry brought his hands up hard from behind his back, throwing his forearms up sharply, his hands now fists that smashed into the Taloris' muzzles. Growls and curses tumbled from bleeding lips as both guards, still holding their stingers, raised them to attack. John Henry now faced them, his hands unrolling, his fingers wrapping around their necks, iron nails squeezing life from their furry bodies. Both guards struggled, trying to make noise, to raise alarm, but they had no chance. John Henry smashed their heads together like ripe melons and dropped them to the ground, unconscious.

Splintering bone and pained mewling reverberated off the walls of the arena, catching the attention of Talori standing at the other archways. As they saw their fellow warriors in a pile at the prisoner's feet and his arms unchained, they reacted. Some shouted orders, bidding more Talori to appear from the archways, others took up the fight on their own and began running across the field, ready to take on this strangely colored beast.

Watching more guards charging toward him, John Henry looked at the racks on either side of the archway he'd been brought from. Sundry weapons populated the stands, probably there for gladiators to use in their last moments. Long blades, curved clubs, thick pudgy spears…and then there it was. At the end of the rack on the left. And on the right weapons stand, in the middle, there was another one. John Henry smiled.

Two long handled square headed hammers, the black heads' corners beveled. Heads like great steel fists.

"Time," John Henry rumbled, "to lay some track."

He dipped his shoulders low, scooping the hammer on the left into his strong hand first, then snatching its twin on the right. As he raised back up to full height, a Talori armed with a slender metallic blade roared and leaped into the air, the sword raised high. John Henry hollered back and swung one of his hammers with every ounce of force his railroad tie thick arms could muster. The head collided with the Talori's chest, crushing it like an orange. As the body flew and crashed in a heap to the ground, John Henry charged forward in a mad run. His eyes locked on the hanging winged woman, her trio of torturers still at their job. And his gaze never wavered.

Like a whirling dervish of obsidian, John Henry fought his way across the arena. One Talori warrior, standing nearly eight feet tall, bolted from the right, a large club in its claws. Swinging hard, the Talori snapped a mouth of jagged teeth at John Henry, nipping his shoulder. John went to one knee as the cat like creature rose up its club to smash him into the ground. As drops of his blood disappeared on the red dirt, John Henry jumped up, the hammer in his right hand flying up head first. The hammer collided with the giant Talori's open jaw, shattering bone into slivers, coloring its fur with its own blood.

Lowering his head, John Henry ran into his latest attacker, knocking the Talori down and out of his way. From the left attacked three more, each with stingers. Swiveling around on his left foot, John Henry swung both hammers, extended horizontally out in front of him. The leather armored guards folded like wet sheets as the hammers cut them down like scythes.

From atop the dais, the crowned Talori watched, at first with amusement at the stupidity of the odd being trying to escape. When his largest warrior, Grenat, fell at the cyclonic attack of the black man, he stood, ordering those attending to his knees into the fray below. As the three collapsed as one, he leaned over the platform, shouting curses and orders.

"Destroy the Pretender! Kill the False God!"

As his words echoed off the arena walls, they landed in open, curious ears. The enslaved peoples of the Talori, all forced into the family of their conquerors, filled the arena. They were forced to watch when traitors or prisoners, people of their own kind, were sentenced to the Presence's games. The last few moments, they'd stood bewildered, even stricken with terror at what they saw. Someone trying to escape. Someone standing up against the feared Talori warriors. How could he? Didn't he know that the Presence would simply take it out on all of them? That there was no hope?

Some heard what The Presence screamed, saw the anger and fear in his fur lined features. Pretender. False God. They looked again at the two legged thing tearing its way through Talori after Talori. Large, muscular, and ebony. The forbidden color. The color that only one would ever wear on his skin. Then the murmuring began.

"Ham-Ur."

Nearly halfway to Galena, John Henry faltered, taking a much needed breath. As he lowered his hammers only slightly, two cracks ricocheted in his ears as strands of leather suddenly coiled around him, one about his neck, the other about his right arm. His skin stung with the bite of whips as the straps dug into it, bloodying his arm, choking his throat. John Henry hunched his shoulders forward and, when the whip on his arm drew taut, raised his right arm and swung out broadly, then yanked hard. The strap slackened as the Talori at the other end of it stumbled and fell. John Henry then turned, glared through pained eyes at the other Talori, and flung the hammer in his right hand.

The hammer landed with a resounding thud in the Talori's abdomen. Bone cracked as the warrior doubled over like a folded piece of paper. Reaching up and yanking the strap from his neck, John Henry dashed for his hammer. Two Talori took advantage, each from different positions and sprang at him. John Henry grasped the hammer's handle and pivoted about face, both hammers hitting their marks, knocking the two guards out of the sky like fallen sparrows.

As the bodies hit the ground, the other Talori closing in on the fugitive all thought better of it. Some simply grew terrified as they watched this stranger injure or kill their comrades and they ran, deciding to hide in the bowels of the arena than die out in the open. Others, at first intoxicated by fury and honor, hesitated long enough that they heard things. Words, mumblings that grew louder. Nearly a chant buzzing around the arena like the buzz of insects. And as they watched this force of nature smash his way through their ranks, they began to wonder.

And some even to believe.

John Henry did not notice that his enemies were less the farther he ran. It didn't matter, one or a hundred. Just like the mountain, just like the steam drill, it didn't matter. John Henry had a purpose, a mission, and some place to be. Wasn't nothing going to stop him.

He yelled thunder as he halted before Galena, her head hanging, her eyes half lidded. The three torturers had broken ranks, now standing in a straight line in front of their prisoner, their stingers primed and ready.

John Henry glared at them from about ten feet away, his chest heaving, his entire body glistening with a sheen of sweat, making him look like burnished, polished black steel. The hammers rested head down toward the ground in his hands.

As John Henry leaned left to swing from the right, the middle Talori screeched, pressed the trigger panel on its stinger, and flung the blue flickering orange staff at its foe. The stinger turned spear hit John Henry dead in the center of his chest, energy arcing along the wet surface of his skin.

Roaring in agony, John Henry lifted his hammers and swung wildly as he forged forward. The three guards separated, the two with stingers flanking him and jamming their rods into his sides. He screamed this time, the pain setting his bones nearly afire, but still he stomped ahead. As the Talori, now all three armed again, readied to attack in unison, John Henry raised the hammer in his left hand above his head and brought it down on the bar Galena hung from. The bar snapped like a twig and Galena dropped to the ground, her eyes snapping open and her hands still extended above her head. A swing from John Henry's other hammer shattered the chains holding the winged priestess hostage.

Three stingers sang in horrific harmony as the Talori pressed them hard, one nearly breaking skin, into John Henry. He tried to turn, to work his hammers one more time, but blue lightning riddled his body, arcing off his sweat laden skin. He dropped to his knees, his hands still not surrendering the hammers as they splayed out to either side and his would be killers moved in closer.

Raising his head with great effort, John Henry looked skyward, as he had many times before. As he did, he saw a golden angel rise up, her wings spread wide, her skin nearly aglow as she hovered over him.

Galena held her arms wide and turned to face The Presence, now cringing back against his throne. "Do you hear, Talori?" She shouted, her voice unnaturally loud, like the beautiful tolling of a bell. "Listen to what the people you oppress declare."

From his throne, the Talori monarch had been doing just that for the last few minutes. Nearly every being in the arena, for he and his three soldiers below were the only remaining Talori, stood, their mouths open, their voices loud. And they all said the same name.

"Ham-Ur. Ham-Ur."

The three Talori pressed even harder, closer together, forming a shell of green leather bound fur around their captive. Ducking his head, John Henry tensed every muscle in his body, his arms rippling like black water.

The hammers quivered, then snapped to his side, the one on the right unsettling a Talori from its feet. With a shout of triumph mingled with a roar of agony, John Henry erupted, his arms outstretched, hammers brandished. The other two guards yelped as they were thrown back. The first one to fall had already made his get away, but his two companions thought themselves better. Each went for his stinger to show this pretender who was superior. And each regretted that choice as their skulls caved in simultaneously, John Henry's hammers leaving their mark.

The crowded arena exploded with chants and cheers. Creatures ran, flew, slithered from the audience seats, all trying to get close to their sudden savior. Some, though, had other things in mind, as a myriad of beings filled the dais where the Talori Presence unsuccessfully tried to climb down from its perch. The green furred tyrant squealed, begging for Ham-Ur to save him, but the pleas were drowned out as he vanished within a throng of frenzied former subjects.

Galena lighted in front of John Henry, his hammers on the ground at his side now, handles up. She bowed on one knee, her wings laid wide in supplication. "Ham-Ur," she reverently said, "Vedan, Take us all on this day. I am yours in all ways, Ham-Ur."

"No, Ma'am." He looked around at the suddenly chaotic arena. So many strange things, so much to learn, to know, to discover. And yet, only one thing entered his mind. "I already got a woman. You don't belong to me, you don't belong to no one. And," he said, framed by the two hammers at his side, "my name is John Henry."

LIFTING EVERY VOICE

ABOUT THE AUTHORS

WALTER MOSLEY is one of America's most celebrated and beloved writers. His books have won numerous awards and have been translated into more than twenty languages.

Mosley is the author of the acclaimed Easy Rawlins series of mysteries, including national bestsellers Cinnamon Kiss, Little Scarlet, and Bad Boy Brawly Brown; the Fearless Jones series, including Fearless Jones, Fear Itself, and Fear of the Dark; the novels Blue Light and RL's Dream; and two collections of stories featuring Socrates Fortlow, Always Outnumbered, Always Outgunned, for which he received the Anisfield-Wolf Award, and Walkin' the Dog. He lives in New York City. Check out more at: **http://www.waltermosley.com**

—∿—

JOE R. LANSDALE is the author of over thirty novels and numerous short stories. His work has appeared in national anthologies, magazines, and collections, as well as numerous foreign publications. He has written for comics, television, film, newspapers, and Internet sites. His work has been collected in eighteen short-story collections, and he has edited or co-edited over a dozen anthologies. He has received the Edgar Award, eight Bram Stoker Awards, the Horror Writers Association Lifetime Achievement Award, the British Fantasy Award, the Grinzani Cavour Prize for Literature, the Herodotus Historical Fiction Award, the Inkpot Award for Contributions to Science Fiction and Fantasy, and many others. His novella Bubba Hotep was adapted to film by Don Coscarelli, starring Bruce Campbell and Ossie Davis. His story "Incident On and Off a Mountain Road" was adapted to film for Showtime's "Masters of Horror." He is currently co-producing several films, among them The Bottoms, based on his Edgar Award-winning novel, with Bill Paxton and Brad Wyman, and The Drive-In, with Greg Nicotero. He is Writer In Residence at Stephen F. Austin State University, and is the founder of the martial arts system Shen Chuan: Martial Science and its affiliate, Shen Chuan Family System. He is a member of both the United States and International Martial Arts Halls of Fame. He lives in Nacogdoches, Texas with his wife, dog, and two cats. His latest book, THE THICKET, debuts from Mullholland this fall. More about Joe and his works can be found here: **http://www.joerlansdale.com**

—∞—

GARY PHILLIPS, Mystery and New Pulp writer, has penned short stories for Moonstone's Kolchak: The Night Stalker Casebook, the Avenger Chronicles, the Green Hornet Casefiles and the upcoming Spider: Extreme Prejudice anthologies. His most current novel is Warlord of Willow Ridge which Booklist said of the work, "Phillips is a veteran crime novelist who creates a plausible post-apocalyptic scenario in which the safety of middle-class America can dissolve in a moment. Exciting, violent, and entertaining." He also has out the ebook novella, The Essex Man: 10 Seconds to Death, a homage to '70s era paperback vigilantes. Please visit his website at: **www.gdphillips.com**

—∞—

CHARLES SAUNDERS was born in 1946 in English, Pennsylvania, a small town located near Pittsburgh. He also lived in a bigger town, Norristown, near Philadelphia before going to Lincoln University, where he graduated with a degree in psychology and curiosity in 1968. Since 1985, Charles has lived in Nova Scotia. Charles has worked as a community college teacher and research assistant. Journalism found him in 1989, when he began writing an opinion column. He later became a copy editor, and his last day job - which was really a night job - was editorial writer and editorial page editor for the Halifax Daily News. The first spark of Imaro, his most celebrated work, came to Saunders in 1970 and the flame has risen and fallen ever since. He has also written non-fiction books, two screenplays for direct-to-video movies, and two radio plays. These days, he is concentrating on the revival of Imaro, as well as other African-oriented fantasy ideas. Charles keeps up a blog about his work here: **http://www.charlessaunderswriter.com**

—∞—

DERRICK FERGUSON is from Brooklyn, New York where he has lived most of his life. He has been married for 27 years to the wonderful Patricia Cabbagestalk-Ferguson who lets him get away with far more than is good for him.

Derrick's interests include old radio shows, classic pulps from the

30's/40's, comic books, fan fiction, Star Trek, pop culture, science fiction, animation, television and movies. His primary love is reading and writing and he's written several books to date: Dillon And The Voice of Odin, his love letter to classic pulp action/adventure with a modern flavor and the sequel, Dillon And The Legend of The Golden Bell as well as Four Bullets for Dillon; Derrick Ferguson's Movie Review Notebook and it's sequel The Return of Derrick Ferguson's Movie Review Notebook; Diamondback Vol I: It Seemed Like A Good Idea At The Time, a spaghetti western disgused as a modern day gangster/crime thriller.

Anything else you'd like to know about Derrick, check out more here: **http://dlferguson-bloodandink.blogspot.com**

—m—

D. ALAN LEWIS is a native of Chattanooga, Tennessee who now resides in Nashville with his children. He has been writing and illustrating technical guides and manuals for various employers for over twenty years but only in recent years has branched out in to writing fiction. In 2006, Alan took the reins of a Novelists Group where he has been working to teach and aid aspiring writers. Alan's debut novel, The Blood in Snowflake Garden was a Top Ten finalist for the 2010 Claymore Award. He also has a number of short stories published as well as other projects in the works. Find out more at: **http://www.snowflakegarden.com**

—m—

PROFESSOR CHRISTOPHER CHAMBERS, a Washington, D.C. native and Georgetown University professor, is author of the best-selling of the Angela Bivens series for Random House, and is co-editor of Darker Mask: Heroes from the Shadows. He was a PEN/Malamud finalist for short fiction. He is also commentator for The Root, RT America, MSNBC and Huffington Post Live. His novel Yella Patsy's Boys will drop in 2014. Keep up with Professor Chambers at here: **http://dangerfieldnewby. tumblr.com**

—m—

MEL ODOM writes in a number of fields, but always with the hope of telling an interesting tale that will incite a reader to think for himself or herself, to examine his or her own place in the world, and offer a little nudge in the direction of dreams, faith, and personal growth in spite of whatever odds a person has to face. Mel also believes we were all put here for a purpose. Hopefully, several purposes. Mel is a father, a little league coach, a teacher, a friend, and a writer. He holds tightly to the belief that he is doing all he can be doing, and doing what he should be doing. Follow Mel here: **http://www.melodom.blogspot.com or http://melodom.com**

—∞—

KIMBERLY RICHARDSON After being found as an infant crawling among books in an abandoned library, Kimberly Richardson grew up to become an eccentric woman with a taste for jazz, drinking tea, reading books, speaking rusty French and Japanese, playing her violin and writing stories that cause people to make the strangest faces. Her first book, Tales From a Goth Librarian, was published through Dark Oak Press and named a Finalist in both the USA Book News Awards for Fiction: Short Story for 2009 and the International Book Awards for Fiction: Short Story in 2010. Ms. Richardson is also the author of The Decembrists (Dark Oak Press) and Mabon/Pomegranate (Dark Oak Press); both were enlisted for the 2013 Pulitzer Prize. Ms. Richardson is also the Editor of the award winning Steampunk anthology Dreams of Steam, the award winning sequel, Dreams of Steam II: Of Brass and Bolts, and Dreams of Steam III: Gadgets and Dreams of Steam IV: Gizmos, all published through Dark Oak Press. Other short stories and poetry by Ms. Richardson have been published through Sam's Dot Publishing, Pro Se Press, Midnight Screaming and FootHills Publishing.   See more about Kimberly here: **http://nocaesthetic.blogspot.com**

—∞—

RON FORTIER has been a professional writer for over thirty-five years. He has worked on comic book projects such as The Hulk, Popeye, Rambo and Peter Pan. With Ardath Mayhar Ron penned two TSR fantasy novels, and in 2001 he had my first play, a World War II romantic comedy, produced.

Ron is currently writing and producing pulp novels and short stories for various publishers and has several movie scripts floating around

Hollywood looking for a home, and if that isn't enough, he also has a review column at the www.pulpfictionreviews.blogspot.com website. Ron is Cap'n over at Airship 27: **http://www.airship27.com**

—∿—

MICHAEL A. GONZALES Spinetingler Nominee Michael A. Gonzales has written fiction for Crime Factory, Needle and Bronx Biannual. A former NY Press columnist, his essays have appeared in NY magazine, The Village Voice, Spin and XXL. Gonzales blogs @ **Blackadelicpop. blogspot.com**, Twitters @ **gonzomike** and lives in Brooklyn.

—∿—

GAR ANTHONY HAYWOOD, born in 1954, is the Shamus award-winning author of the Aaron Gunner mysteries. Born in Los Angeles, he spent over a decade as a computer technician before first publishing fiction in the 1980s. Influenced by a love for the Los Angeles mysteries of Ross Macdonald, he wrote Fear of the Dark (1987), winning the Shamus award for best first novel and introducing the tough-nosed L.A. detective Aaron Gunner.

Haywood continued the Gunner series through the bestselling All the Lucky Ones Are Dead (2000), and in between Gunner novels produced the two-book Loudermilk pair of serio-comic mysteries. In an effort to broaden his fan base, Haywood wrote two standalone thrillers, Man Eater (2003) and Firecracker (2004), under the pen-name Ray Johnson, finding critical acclaim for both. He has also written for newspapers and television, including an adaptation of the Dennis Rodman autobiography, Bad As I Wanna Be. His most recent novels are Cemetery Road (2010) and Assume Nothing (2011). You can find his website here: **http://www. garanthonyhaywood.com**

—∿—

TOMMY HANCOCK Steeped in pulp magazines, old radio shows, and all things of that era's pop culture, Tommy Hancock lives in Arkansas with his wonderful wife and three children and obviously not enough to do. He is Editor in Chief for Pro Se Productions, is an organizer of the New Pulp Movement, was a founding member and original Editor-in-

Chief of ALL PULP, works as an editor for Seven Realms, Dark Oak, and Moonstone. He is also a writer published by Airship 2 works as Promotions and Marketing Coordinator for Moonstone Entertainment, is the Editor in Chief of ALL PULP, a full news site devoted to Pulp and the Coordinator for PULP ARK, the premiere Pulp Culture Convention in the South.

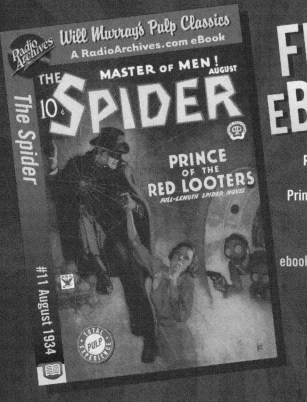

Made in the USA
Columbia, SC
25 July 2019